Praise for Randy Henderson's *Finn Fancy Necromancy*

"*Finn Fancy Necromancy* is a magic-politics story . . . and much more of a romp. . . . Someone is trying to restart the Fey-Arcana wars, using Finn as a pivot. In the final showdown he has to rely on gnome mercenaries and bloodwitches too, though the real dangers lie in his own family—just as if he was a 'mundane,' or 'mundy,' like the rest of us."     —*The Wall Street Journal*

"Even though it deals with sinister magic and family tragedy, it counterbalances that darkness with something that's become increasingly rare in fantasy fiction: laughs, laughs, and more laughs."
—NPR

"If you want something that will grab you by the scruff of the neck and keep you going, this is a book for you. And there is a little more to it than that. Henderson has his pulse on how many millenials seem to feel: Finn has literally been exiled for twenty-five years and has no idea how to fit into the new society that's grown up in his absence. . . . This is a difficult theme to examine; Henderson does it well, in the background, while producing a fun, exciting read. This is the first of a three-volume series, and I'm eager to read the next one."     —*Locus*

"A delightfully fun fantasy full of magic, wit, colorfully drawn characters, and a ton of 1980s pop-culture references."
—*Shelf Awareness*

"Both author Henderson's clever yet unassuming voice and the shenanigans of his bumbling, half-grown protagonist—accidental wielder of spells basically indistinguishable from huge, silent farts—are certifiably humorous. And obviously, this is a fantasy: gnomes, unicorns, and fairies fill its pages."
—*The Seattle Times*

## TOR BOOKS BY RANDY HENDERSON

*Finn Fancy Necromancy*
*Bigfootloose and Finn Fancy Free*
*Smells Like Finn Spirit*

# BIGFOOTLOOSE AND FINN FANCY FREE

## RANDY HENDERSON

**TOR**

A TOM DOHERTY ASSOCIATES BOOK
NEW YORK

This is a work of fiction. All of the characters, organizations, and events portrayed in this novel are either products of the author's imagination or are used fictitiously.

BIGFOOTLOOSE AND FINN FANCY FREE

A Tor Book
Published by Tom Doherty Associates
175 Fifth Avenue
New York, NY 10010

www.tor-forge.com

Tor® is a registered trademark of Macmillan Publishing Group, LLC.

The Library of Congress has cataloged the hardcover edition as follows:

Henderson, Randy, author.
    Bigfootloose and Finn Fancy Free / Randy Henderson.—1st ed.
        p. cm.
    "A Tom Doherty Associates Book."
    ISBN 978-0-7653-7810-1 (hardcover)
    ISBN 978-1-4668-5914-2 (e-book)
    1. Magic—Fiction.   2. FICTION / Fantasy / Urban Life.   I. Title.
    PS3608.E52735 B54 2016
    813'.6—dc23

                                                                2015032370

ISBN 978-0-7653-8608-3 (trade paperback)

Our books may be purchased in bulk for promotional, educational, or business use. Please contact your local bookseller or the Macmillan Corporate and Premium Sales Department at 1-800-221-7945, extension 5442, or by e-mail at MacmillanSpecialMarkets@macmillan.com.

First Edition: February 2016
First Trade Paperback Edition: January 2017

Printed in the United States of America

0   9   8   7   6   5   4   3   2   1

*To the lovers and the dreamers,*
*keep making the world a better place.*

# ACKNOWLEDGMENTS

Book two! I guess I have to admit at this point this isn't a dream. At least, I haven't shown up at any readings in my underwear. Yet.

I'm writing these acknowledgments in July 2015. I wrote *Bigfootloose* during 2014, which was hands down one of the busiest, insaniest, most emotional-rollercoastery years of my life, between serious Life Changes and the craziness of Writers of the Future and *Finn Fancy*. It was also a year of tragedies, controversies, and difficult conversations for many (and not just because of the *How I Met Your Mother* finale).

As such, my thanks go out to all those who tempered my angst and supported my dream.

To the readers and fans of *Finn Fancy* who came to my readings, wrote reviews, had me on your blog, invited me to your book club, got a *FFN* tattoo, built a small shrine to *FFN,* invented new ice cream flavors like Fudge Fancy Nutomancy, or named all your children after my characters: this adventure continues thanks to you, and for you, and I hope you enjoy the results. And if you read this and think *Wow, I really missed some opportunities there to prove my love of Finn Fancy,* well, now there's *Bigfootloose.* Sasquatches and knitting=so much potential! Just remember, pictures or it didn't happen.

To all the librarians and booksellers who recommended *Finn Fancy Necromancy,* and those who invited me or hosted me for readings, you all seriously rock (and, though I would never say it for fear of appearing immodest, *people* say you have excellent taste).

To my parents, Frank, Mary, and Elaine; my biggest fan, Dave Henderson; and the rest of my family: thank goodness you share blood ties with me, otherwise your level of support would be kind of creepy.

To my family most deeply affected during this time, who have offered me love and understanding and continued support: Shelly, Lucas, and Kylie, may every day bring you magic.

To Christy Varonfakis, without whom I really might have shown up at a reading in my underwear—and then realized it wasn't even my reading. Or my underwear. I'm grateful for every bench and every nudge, and look forward to many more.

To everyone who critiqued *Bigfootloose,* or provided reassurances through the inevitable dark period of Imposter Syndrome, thank you. To name a few (alphabetically): Curtis Chen, Isis D'Shaun, Lauren Dixon, Spencer Ellsworth, Neile Graham, Lucas Johnson, Tod McCoy, Kat Richardson, Vicki Saunders, and Emily Skaftun. If your name should be here but isn't, due to my terrible memory, I blame Infomancers for altering reality; but now you can make me feel bad every time I see you and I'll buy you a drink out of guilt, so, you know, that's not bad, right?

To everyone at Tor, especially my editor and *Finn Fancy* champion, Beth Meacham, without whom, again, *Finn Fancy* would not exist; the tireless Amy Stapp, who keeps the process moving along; my awesome publicist, Desirae Friesen, and the queen of publicity, Patty Garcia, for all their help in spreading the *Finn Fancy* love; the copyediting (and geek savvy) skills of Edwin Chapman; and everyone else who has contributed to the life of the Finn Fancy books—thank you, truly.

To Peter Lutjen, Irene Gallo, Tomislav, and the rest of the Tor art and design department, thank you for the look of the Finn Fancy series. The covers certainly stand out, and I've grown quite fond of them.

And, last but not least, to my agent, Cameron McClure, who has provided all the support and agentiness I could have hoped for, and to Katie Shea Boutillier and everyone else at Donald Maass Literary Agency, who have far more than earned that 15 percent: I hope I make a million dollars someday. You know, just for you.

# CONTENTS

# BIGFOOTLOOSE
## AND
# FINN FANCY FREE

## Once Bitten Twice Shy

Imagine the sweetest-smelling perfume, something candy-like, perhaps worn by tweenaged girls. Now, pour a bottle of that into your eyes. Welcome to the joys of fairy embalming.

I stood beside a stainless-steel worktable on which a fairy's parakeet-sized body rested, in the familiar chill and antiseptic smell of our family's basement necrotorium—a mortuary for the magical.

And by fairy, I don't mean a true Fey. Actually, I'm not even sure what a Fey smell might be. During the twenty-five years I spent exiled in the Fey Other Realm, I don't think I smelled anything that didn't come from my own imagination. No, by fairy I mean the little flitting Tinkerbells you see in gardens, especially in a charming little waterfront town like our own Port Townsend. Well, that you'd be able to see if you were a human arcana gifted with magic, or a feyblood creature like the fairies themselves.

The fun part of this job, or at least the creative part that I actually enjoyed sometimes, was hours away. I would reconstruct the fairy's features using putty and cosmetics so that you'd never know she'd enjoyed a brief and shocking birdbrained attraction to the brightly colored insulators on an electric fence—and then been hit by a weed whacker before waking. I had, however, carefully glued the plastic wings on after the Department of Alchemical Administration came and collected the real ones, a donation for which the fairy's family would receive generous payment.

My younger brother Pete stood opposite me, his huge body hunched over the table as he monitored the embalming tubes that ran into the fairy's body. Petey had always been a big guy—not fat, or all muscle, just big like a grizzly. His round baby face scrunched up in a frown of concentration that better belonged on a child trying to eat Cream of Wheat with chopsticks, and fit his nature much more than his considerable size did.

My girlfriend, Dawn, sat on a stool in the corner strumming her guitar, the incandescent lighting glinting off the silver rings that covered her every finger. Her hair, a springy cloud of fading turquoise with black roots, masked her eyes as she leaned over her guitar, but she occasionally paused to lift up the decapitated head of my old *Six Million Dollar Man* doll that hung from a cord around her neck and look through his bionic eye at the fairy. The toy head had a crystal jutting out of the neck and a crown of rune-covered metal, an artifact my father created in one of his (more) lucid moments, that enabled mundanes to see the normally hidden world of magical energies and creatures. But Dawn's mundy senses still made her impervious to the fairy odor.

For me, even the smells of embalming fluids and bleach couldn't mask the cloying smell.

Pete removed the customized embalming tubes with the kind of delicateness one might expect from a Jedi manscaping his nethers with a lightsaber. Despite his size, Pete was one of the gentlest people I knew. Or at least, he used to be. Since being bitten by waerwolves three months ago, he'd cycled between reclusive and rabid as he struggled to control the Fey wolf spirit that now shared his body.

*I envy your brother,* a voice sounded in my head. *If a body must needs be shared, then a wolf seems a most desirable companion. At least a wolf spirit knows how to have fun.*

Alynon Infedriel, Fey knight of the Silver Court, former changeling for yours truly, and pain in my spiritual buttocks, gave a martyred sigh only I could hear, and fell silent. I wasn't sure how a Fey spirit trapped inside my brain could sigh when he didn't have actual lungs or breath of his own, but he did. A lot.

When I'd returned from exile in the Other Realm, I was supposed to inherit twenty-five years of catch-up memories from Alynon as he departed back to his own Fey body. Instead, an accident had caused me to be stuck with him in my head.

That had been a real lose-lose kind of day.

"Shut it," I muttered at Alynon.

"I'm getting to it!" Pete said, the hint of a growl creeping into his voice.

"What? Oh, no, I didn't mean shut the incisions," I said. "I was talking to the royal Feyn in my Butt."

"Oh." Pete hunched in on himself a bit more and began stapling the incisions closed. Now it was my turn to sigh.

*Sincerely,* Alynon continued, *your nature could benefit from a touch of bestiality. I am certain Dawn would enjoy it.*

Dawn stopped her strumming. "What'd Aly say?"

"Nothing worth repeating," I replied.

*Liar,* Alynon said. *You know I am right. Bright, but that I still had control of your body. Pax laws or no, I'd tear me off a piece of that.*

*Really?* I thought, focusing the thought on him so that he could hear it. *"Tear me off a piece of that"? What does that even mean? I think you wasted your time in our world if that's the kind of thing you filled your head with.*

Dawn's eyes narrowed slightly as she leaned toward me, exposing her cleavage.

*Mayhap,* Alynon said. *But speaking of my head, I know where I'd like to—*

*Seriously?!*

Dawn leaned back. "I can tell you're still arguing with him about something."

*Indeed, seriously!* Alynon responded. *I spent twenty-five years in this hormone factory you call a body, being bombarded with sexual images left and right, and I was forbidden by Pax Law to act on any—*

*Wow, I really feel for you. That sounds so much worse than being without a real body and having your memories fed on by Fey.*

*That's not my point. I am merely saying, it *may* have made me a little sex-obsessed.*

*Gee, you think?*

*What I *think* is you're crazy for not ripping her clothes off and—*

"There," Dawn said. "Only Aly can make your eye twitch like that."

I replied in a level tone, "We were just arguing about how the Fey keep pushing into areas where they don't belong."

"Uh huh." Dawn resumed strumming. "You'll tell me what he said when you're ready." She stated it as a matter of fact.

"I wish you wouldn't do that," I said. "Declare what I will or won't do."

Dawn arched an eyebrow. "You can pretend you don't like how I'm always right, but I know it just makes you like me more."

"No. Mostly, I like you for your modesty."

"Yeah, I am pretty perfect." Dawn winked.

But she was right about always being right, damn it. If I didn't know better, I'd think she had a touch of clairvoyance. But really, she just knew me.

Or at least, she knew who I'd been before being exiled at age fifteen. I didn't even know who I was now. Not in the sense that I had amnesia or anything—well, I *had* lost my previous memories of Dawn in exchange for knowledge from beyond the grave, but my memories were otherwise intact. It was more that I didn't know who I was in the same sense that made people seek direction and identity through religion, or pyramid schemes, or by taking a passionate side in the cola wars. It was dangerous. It was the kind of path that led to Tammy Faye Bakker, secret societies, and New Coke.

*You're not moping again, are you?* Alynon asked. *I can practically taste the ennui in your brain chemistry.*

*I'm not moping! I'm trying to figure things out. I don't want to just fall into—*

*Bright, save me. If you're going to play the sad philosopher again, can you at least pretend to be Kant? *He* knew how to party. I remember once—*

*Remind me later to double my efforts on figuring out how to exorcise you.*

*You already worked out how to exorcise me.*

*You know what I mean. Without it lobotomizing me.*

*Ah, fine.* Alynon was quiet a second. *Say, don't forget to double your efforts—*

*Hilarious,* I replied.

I really did need to focus more on getting him out of my head. Not just for my own sake, but his. It was not his fault that my grandfather's minions had attacked and disrupted the process that would have returned Alynon to the Other Realm. And it wasn't until I'd died briefly, drowned while escaping my grandfather's underwater lair, that I'd even been able to hear Alynon. But now that I knew he was in my head, able to experience everything I did but unable to exert any physical control, I could only imagine how difficult and frustrating that must be.

Well, I didn't have to *only* imagine. He reminded me of it pretty regularly.

Someone knocked on the glass door behind me.

Our necrotorium filled the basement of my family's old Victorian house. A wall with frosted glass windows divided it in half, with the traditional mundane mortuary equipment on this side, and the altars, protective circles, and other accoutrements of our family's necromancy trade on the other. Through the frosted glass of the door, I could make out the blurry shape of a waifish sixteen-year-old girl a second before the door swung open and Mattie said, "Uncle Finn?"

"Yeah?" I replied, and coughed when I sucked in fairy stench.

"There's a, uh, client here."

"Where's Mort?" I asked around my coughs. My older brother seemed to be easing up a bit on his paranoia that I was plotting against him to take charge of the family business. I wasn't going to ruin that progress by greeting new clients without his permission.

"No, not for us. A client for you, for your dating service."

Dawn stopped strumming and sat up straight, an excited smile on her face. I blinked.

I'd started a dating service for magicals three months ago, inspired by how good it felt to help Pete and his girlfriend, Vee, find happiness together. It certainly felt better than the thought of spending my life around death, trading bits of my own life energy to Talk with spirits. But not a single arcana or feyblood had come seeking my help in those three months. My sister Sammy had even made me a website, and still not a bite.

I'd pretty much given up on the idea, which really depressed me since I had few other immediate career options besides necromancy. My skills coding video games in BASIC were, I'd learned, a bit outdated.

"I'll be right up!" I said. "Show . . . him? Her?"

"Him."

"Show him to the parlor. Please."

"I did. But your client? He's . . . a sasquatch."

Pete growled softly.

A sasquatch. Oh, shazbot.

Sweat sprung up along my arms. I didn't have a great history with sasquatches. In fact, my only real history was with a sibling pair of sasquatch mercenaries who'd been hired by my grandfather in his bid to be voted Arch-Villain of the Year. They'd attacked pretty much everyone around me, and the female sasquatch had died at the hands of blood witches while defending my grandfather—blood witches I'd sent against him.

If my grandfather's extremist Arcanite buddies ever hired that sasquatch for another job, it would probably be to kill me for upsetting their plans to start a race war. Either way, I hoped never to see that sasquatch, or any of his relatives, again.

"And Uncle Finn?" Mattie said.

"Yeah?"

"This sasquatch? He says he knows you."

Double shazbot.

"You said you showed him to the parlor?"

"Yes."

Which meant she'd already let him inside the house's protective wards. An understandable mistake, given the types of customers we'd had lately.

Dawn slid off her stool. "Awesome! I've always wanted to see Bigfoot."

I shook my head. "Not awesome. Dangerous. I think he's here to hurt me."

Pete pulled off his apron and gloves, and strode toward the door. "Nobody hurts my brother."

I grabbed his shoulder and pulled him to a stop—or more accurately, he stopped, preventing me from being dragged along behind him. "Hang on. Let's play this smart and safe. We can't afford to have the parlor rebuilt again after that troll incident." And Pete couldn't afford to give the Arcana Ruling Council any excuse to lock him up as a rogue waer. "Let's gear up first, and then I'll try to lure him outside."

I turned to Dawn. "It might be best—"

"If I go home?" she said. "Let's see, who has saved the lives of every man in this room, raise your hand." Dawn raised her hand. She *had* helped to save Pete after both a witch curse and a waerwolf attack. And she'd given me CPR after I drowned while escaping Grandfather's lair.

Dawn lowered her hand. "So, you can give me a weapon, or a healing potion, or both, but I'm sticking around."

Alynon chuckled.

Frak.

"Okay. Fine. You keep Mattie safe down here," I suggested. Dawn might do something crazy on her own, but she wouldn't do anything too risky with Mattie's safety on the line.

"I don't—" Mattie began, but Dawn put a hand on her shoulder.

"Really?" Dawn said to me. "And what if Bigfoot comes down those stairs? We'd be trapped down here. Shouldn't we at least come upstairs where there's all kinds of ways to escape?"

*No one puts Baby in a corner!*

*Stick it.* "Fine. Come on, let's not keep our guest waiting."

I threw a cover over the fairy, and we all crossed to the small basement area set aside for Father's thaumaturgy experiments. Most of the stuff in his lab was harmless—being possessed by Mother's ghost had left Father mentally unstable, so it was best not to give him objects that might cut, burn, explode, or, as we had learned too late to prevent a reverse mohawk, could be used to animate an electric razor—but I grabbed a can of spray adhesive, which could be used like pepper spray in a pinch, and handed it to Mattie.

Then I opened the small safe, pulled out an extendible steel baton, and handed it to Dawn. A wizard's weapon, the baton had once belonged to Zeke, an arcana enforcer, and would inflict at least some pain even to a sasquatch.

"And a healing potion?" she asked.

"Still out," I replied. Unfortunately they were crazy expensive, and nobody in my family had an alchemist's ability to activate the magical properties of potion ingredients. In fact, of the five human branches of magic—alchemy, wizardry, thaumaturgy, sorcery, and necromancy—alchemy was the only one that hadn't manifested somewhere in our family bloodlines.

"What about you?" Dawn asked, eyeing the revolver that still sat in the open safe.

"Bullets tend to bounce off sasquatch fur," I replied, and closed the safe. "Worst case, I'll threaten to rip out his spirit." And hope he wouldn't call my bluff.

Soul destruction was the ultimate necromancer threat, but I felt neither powerful nor skilled enough to actually do it—one of the drawbacks of having missed twenty-five years of necromancy training and practice. But I could at least give him one hell of a headache by trying.

Dawn tapped the small silver artifact hanging by a chain around my neck. A spirit trap. It looked like one of those metal puzzles where you have to figure out how to twist the pieces apart, except these were forged together. From its center peeked a tiny mouse skull covered in runes. "What about this thing," she asked. "You've been 'charging it up' for weeks. Isn't it supposed to trap souls?"

"Disembodied spirits," I said. "I can't use it as a weapon against someone living."

*Not true,* Alynon said.

*True enough,* I replied.

Actually, it could be used to tear the soul out of a living being, but to do so would require the destruction of a spirit already trapped inside it, creating a kind of spiritual vacuum, and that would be one of the darkest forms of dark necromancy—the destruction of another being's spirit to fuel my magic.

I led the group up the stairs: myself, Pete, and Dawn, with Mattie trailing last. We emerged into the mud room without incident. Gray Washington daylight glowed through the back-door window. On cloudy Pacific Northwest mornings like today's, the sun was more a pale fluorescent apology than a glowing engine of warmth and life. Never mind that it was June.

"Okay," I whispered to Dawn and Mattie. "You stay here, please."

Dawn crossed her arms, the baton dangling at her side, but didn't argue.

Pete and I tiptoed our way to the library, where I grabbed the silver-coated sword from the wall above the fireplace. At least the sword made for good show without the danger of accidentally hitting my brother with a ricochet; and better the sasquatch grabbed for the sword than my throat.

We continued to the front entryway, and the closed double doors for the viewing parlor. The sasquatch would most likely be just inside, near the ring of folding chairs where Mort liked to sit and do his business with prospective customers. Those chairs would make handy projectiles for the sasquatch.

I opened our home's front entry door quietly, the better to flee through, and took a deep calming breath of the chill morning air before returning to the parlor doors.

"Ready?" I whispered to Pete, worried at the look on his face. Pete began to pant, and held his hands to his chest in shaking fists. His eyes went from dark brown to pale blue.

"Don't wolf out on me, Brother," I whispered. "Let's deal with one problem at a time, okay?"

"I—I'm trying," Pete whispered back, his voice harsh. "But I can smell the sasquatch, and—" His nails began to elongate. "No no no!" He shook his head. Tears sprang to his eyes. "I don't want to change. I don't want to go wolf, I don't want to hurt people."

Crap. "Breathe, Petey, just breathe," I said.

He closed his eyes, causing twin tears of frustration to run down his cheeks, and he took several deep breaths through his mouth. The nails receded.

"Maybe you should sit this one out," I whispered.

*You really are no fun,* Alynon said.

I ignored him as Pete replied, "No. I'm not going to let that sasquatch hurt you."

"I'm just going to lure him outside, and I'll run around to the side door and come back in before he can lay a finger on me. The house wards will keep him out until enforcers arrive."

Pete looked dubious.

"Look," I said. "You go back down the hallway a bit, keep him from heading toward the girls, okay? Keep *them* safe."

My heart broke at the puppy dog look of hurt and frustration on Petey's face as he nodded and shuffled off down the hallway.

Damn.

I really would have felt better with Pete watching my back. I eyed the front door. I could do this.

I counted to three, then threw open the parlor doors and gave a challenging shout, sword raised.

The sasquatch leaped up from a folding chair—nine feet of red-brown hairy muscle wearing combat boots and wielding what looked like bodkins or some other thin blades carved from wood. He let out a horrible . . . yelp?

"Is youself crazy?" the sasquatch shouted.

## Looking for a New Love

As I stared at the sasquatch, I realized that a bit of cloth dangled from one of his thin blades and a tail of yarn ran down into a satchel propped up by the chair.

They weren't blades. They were knitting needles.

"You're, uh, not here to attack me?" I asked.

The sasquatch sighed, and sank back down on the chair. "Arcana be crazy. But Iself even craziest." His head hung down, and he blushed. "Iself came here heart-hoping for love."

I lowered my sword slowly. "Oh. Sorry. Let's . . . talk." I moved cautiously into the parlor, but remained standing.

The parlor contained rows of cushioned pews facing a slightly raised stage, which held the casket platform, speaking podium, and projection screen. During a viewing, the open area in the back where we stood held tables with pictures, artifacts, clan banners, or other meaningful items, but right now it held a half-dozen folding chairs and one sasquatch.

This was definitely the same sasquatch who'd worked for my grandfather. Not only was his coloring and face familiar, with that stripe of black that crossed the tiny black pearl of his right eye, but he was the only sasquatch I'd ever seen or heard of who wore boots. I'd nicknamed him Harry, but didn't know his real name.

The sasquatch stuffed the knitting needles and yarn back into his satchel as I said, "What shall I call you?"

"Iself be named K'u-k'a Schken'ah Saljchuh," he said, or as close as I could tell, making clicking noises as he pronounced his first name. He looked at me as though he expected me to make some comment. When I didn't, he said, "Youself not talking words of Klallam firstmen?"

"No. What does it mean?"

He looked down at his booted feet, and his ears turned bright red. "Not important. Youself can call me Sal if youself want. Everyself call I Sal. Except youself's clan-kin, Grayson, always calling I 'Squatch' and 'boy.'" He growled. "Iself no like Grayson-mage."

"Uh, yeah, I had my problems with him, too, as you know. That isn't going to be a problem here, though, for us, is it? What happened before, I mean? I am very sorry about your . . . loss."

"Sistermine was drinking Grayson's badbright juice; made her crazy."

I winced. My grandfather had apparently used some kind of mana-based drug to secure the loyalty of his feyblood mercenaries, both before and after stealing the body and identity of his apprentice (and bastard son), Grayson. Another black mark on the Gramaraye family name.

"Again, I'm very sorry."

Sal shook his head. "Sistermine always trouble-looking." The sasquatch's voice thickened as he continued, "All of lifelong, Iself trying to keep her happy-safe. But herself in Great Forest now, beyond-beyond. Herenow, Iself can start making the happylife for I."

"So . . . you really want me to help you find your true love, then?"

"Yes." His ears turned red again.

"Okay. I can do that! If you want to wait right here, I'll just need to gather some things. My brother Pete can grab you some water or something while you wait. Hey Pete!" I called. "It's okay. Can you give me a hand?"

Pete peered through the doorway, then stepped into the room.

Sal sniffed. "Yonman is brightblood changer." He seemed to expand in size as his fur fluffed up. "Shadow-sworn."

"Yes, he is waer, and he does have a wolf spirit," I said. "But he hasn't aligned with the Forest of Shadows or any Fey demesne."

"Wolf changers always go shadow-sworn," Sal said. "Theyself

always want a pack, and wolf-changer packs always go shadow-sworn."

Pete shook his head. "My family is my pack," he said. "And my girlfriend, she's got a squirrel spirit." Squirrel spirits tended to align with the Islands of the Blessed, not the Shadows.

As if on cue, Vee walked in through the open front door.

Violet Wodenson looked like a Viking warrior woman: not the Barbie-in-horned-hat variety, but a tall, broad-shouldered woman who could row a boat and pillage a village with the best of them. Or at least, she did in those rare moments when she wasn't hunched in on herself, giving off an air of vulnerability, like now.

Vee took in the scene in the parlor with red-rimmed eyes. She blinked at Sal, but didn't react to him beyond that. We'd had plenty of other feybloods come through here seeking our necromancy services, some more frightening looking than Sal. Particularly with the damage to our family's reputation, first with my being accused of dark necromancy, then with Grayson/grandfather's plot, we'd had to take some of the riskier clients just to make ends meet. But Vee did frown at my sword, and when she looked at Pete her face filled with worry. "Dear heart, are you okay?"

Pete nodded. "Fine."

"You look . . . worked up. Perhaps we should take you out to your room and have some tea?"

Pete frowned. "I should be taking care of *you* right now."

Vee waved a hand. "I'm okay. It was good, helping to finalize Zekiel's display for the wake, especially after all of the ARC's stupid delays to 'debrief' his spirit." She sighed. "And as for 'should,' we take care of each other, kjære, that's what partners do."

Sal sighed. "Youself good mate," he said to Vee. "I heart-wish I had mate like you."

Pete growled, and the hair at the base of his skull actually stood up. "She's taken," he said.

Vee grabbed his arm. "Come on. You need to calm down." She looked past him at Sal. "I'm sorry, he's still adjusting to his wolf.

Please excuse us." She dragged Pete away as he ducked his head like a puppy caught misbehaving.

A throat cleared from the hallway. "Finn?" Dawn called. "Okay if I come in?"

I glanced at Sal. He did not seem to be in a dangerous mood, for the moment anyway. And Dawn's enthusiasm for all things magical rang clear in her voice. "Yes, come in."

Dawn poked her head around the corner, peeking through the plastic *Six Million Dollar Man* head. She opened her other eye, then let the toy head drop when it was obvious she could see Sal without it.

"Sal," I said, "this is Dawn. She's an Acolyte."

"Greetings," Dawn said. She waved, grinning like a six-year-old who'd just said hello to Mickey at Disneyland. One of the silver rings on her right hand held a ladybug suspended in amber. The ring was courtesy of Lila Drake Jewelry, the traces of spiritual and magical energy that charged it were courtesy of me, and together the amber and energy marked her as an Acolyte, a mundy with accepted knowledge of the magical world. But most feybloods would go to extremes not to be seen by mundies, Acolyte or not.

I watched Sal warily. He hesitated, sniffing at the air, then bowed his head. "Greetings, Dawn."

Dawn stepped fully into the room. She held a plate with a slice of banana cream pie in one hand, the other hand behind her back—holding the baton, I assumed. "I took a peek in your catering book," she said to me. "We didn't have much that a sasquatch would like, but I had this."

Sal sniffed at the air like a dog picking up a scent, and his fur fluffed up again, though this time he also made a kind of purring sound.

Our family's catering book covered the diets of most common feyblood species that lived in the area, in case we needed to throw a wake or reception for any of them. I knew from memory that sasquatches enjoyed salmon, and pinecones, and mushrooms, and apparently could digest bark pretty well. But if you wanted to make a sasquatch happy, nothing worked better than banana cream pie.

It was like catnip to cats, or brownies to brownies, a sure way to put them in a happy trancelike state.

Sal dropped his satchel and crossed the distance to Dawn in two steps. She didn't even flinch, but just handed him the plate. "Enjoy." Sal ate the pie in three fast bites, and began licking his hands and the plate.

"Big heart-thanks to youself, Dawn," Sal said between licks.

"You're most welcome, Sal!" Dawn said in a tone that said she was totally psyched to be talking to a sasquatch. "Killer boots. Do you have to wear them because of all the broken bottles and crap people leave in the forests? Or are they so you don't leave those foot-prints everyone's always making casts of?"

Sal's ears glowed red yet again. I winced, and stepped between him and Dawn. She had a habit of talking to everyone like they'd been lifetime friends, no topic off limits. Most times, I was amazed at how she instantly bonded with them. But sometimes, it got her in trouble. In this case, trouble could flatten us with his fists. "Dawn, can you do me a favor and ask Mattie to bring the Kin Finder?"

Dawn arched one pierced eyebrow at me, and a second later Mattie wheeled in the Kin Finder 2000. At least, that's what I called Father's invention. About the size of a microwave, it looked like half clockwork slot machine, half distillery, and half of a Transformer's innards, three halves that somehow made a single whole.

"Uh, thanks," I said to Mattie. Even at sixteen she was far more organized than I.

"No prob, Uncle Finn. I'm going to check on Dad and Grandpa G. Shout if you need anything."

"Right. Good. Will do." Way more organized.

"So," I said to Sal as Mattie left. "Let's find your true love, shall we?"

Sal picked up his satchel. "Iself am not having much for paying, but—"

I shook my head. "This one's free, Sal. I owe you for what hap-pened with my grand—with Grayson."

And one thing I had learned from our family business was that word of mouth made the best advertisement. If I could find true love for Sal, him being a sasquatch mercenary and former enemy, then hopefully word would spread that I could find love for anyone.

Before Sal could argue, I went to work setting up the Kin Finder 2000. I moved the cart to a spot on the floor marked by a small piece of electrical tape, a set home-point from which the results could be accurately measured, and aligned the machine to true north using the compass on its top.

"What does itself do?" Sal asked as I next extended a mechanical arm and adjusted it to the right extension and height.

"It uses the spiritual resonance between two living beings to locate one using the other," I said. "Normally, we use it to locate next of kin. But I can also use it to locate a person's soul mate."

"Soul mate? Iself have heard speak of this. Itself is being human brightstory."

"Brightstory?" Dawn asked.

"Myth," I translated, and slid a pen into a small ring at the end of the mechanical arm.

Dawn smiled at Sal. "Well, they say you're a myth, too, right, Sal?"

Sal shrugged. "Some say Iself are myth. Some say gods are real-real. Some not always be true-right. Dawn, has Finn found youself's soul mate?"

"Yep," Dawn said. "Though sometimes I think he wished he hadn't."

I looked up from the machine. She'd said it in a joking manner, but a note of something more serious had crept in. "Hey, that's not true," I replied.

Dawn gave a quick shake of her head, as if admonishing herself, before her mischievous smile returned. "Well, maybe you should explain to Sal here just what it means to find your soul mate . . . ?"

I raised my eyebrows at her. She raised a single pierced brow back. I sighed.

"Well, for one, it doesn't guarantee instant love," I said. "You'll still have to get to know your soul mate, Sal, and fall in love. But it should be easier with the . . . being who is your soul mate than anyone else, and once you find love it should last forever. Well, as long as you don't take it for granted."

"Should, huh?" Dawn asked, and crossed her arms.

Sal appeared to waver for a second, as if a heat wave passed in front of him. Like many feyblood creatures, sasquatches had a natural glamour that shielded them from mundy view, and could even mask them from casual arcana sight. To the unaware, they might appear as bears, or heavily bearded woodsmen, or death metal band members.

"Dawn," I said, "I think we're making Sal uncomfortable." He probably wasn't even aware the glamour was activating, he'd just picked up on some subtle threat.

I wouldn't mind knowing why it had activated, either.

"Well," Dawn said. "*We* wouldn't want to do that. I think *we'll* go fix *us* second breakfasts." She looked to Sal. "Sorry if I really did make you uncomfortable, Sal. With Finn and me, joking's just how we show our love. Which is one of the many reasons we're perfect for each other: nobody else could stand us—right, oh love of mine?"

"Uh, right," I said.

"Iself understand," Sal said. "Iself hope to find a mate who is perfect also."

"Good." Dawn smiled. "Well, I'll leave you boys to it. Have fun." She swept from the room.

"Uh," I said, turning back to Sal. "Okay. I'll need a small bit of your fur."

Sal plucked a tiny tuft of fur from his arm and handed it to me. It felt like steel wool. I put it into a metal bowl with some water and inserted it into the machine's interior, then lit the Sterno beneath the bowl.

I pointed to a small crystal ball at the back of the machine. "Place your hand here, on this ball, and think of your desire to find love."

Sal put one huge finger on the crystal, covering it.

"Good. May I place my hand on yours to work the magic?" I asked. Sal nodded. I placed my hand over his finger and the crystal ball, and focused on the bright locus of magical energy within me. I called up a portion of the energy and formed a summoning. But instead of summoning the spirit once attached to a body, I summoned the spiritual match to Sal. The machine began to hum lightly.

It didn't take long for the water to begin boiling, sending steam through a complex series of tubes within the machine. It began to ping and clank and sproing. The mechanical arm lowered and drew out a straight line, then lifted. The machine quieted, and I blew out the Sterno.

I took the sheet of paper, and said, "Please wait here. I need to consult my maps to determine the exact location of your true love."

"That be all and done?" Sal asked.

"That's it," I said. "I'll be right back."

Sal looked skeptical, but sat back down and picked up his knitting.

I closed the sliding doors on the parlor, and with a slight exertion of will backed by another trickle of magical energy from my core, I activated the ward that had been built into the doors for just these types of occasions. Not that I expected trouble, but I'd learned the hard way not to trust my assumptions about people, or beings. The ward wouldn't stop Sal if he decided to smash his way out of the room for some reason, but it would give him a shock and, more importantly, would set off an alarm. It used to also release a powerful sleep gas, but a key ingredient in sleep gas is nightmare urine, as in the pee of an actual Fey equine-of-the-night. Worse even than cat urine, the smell was as difficult to get rid of as a preconception wrapped in a rabid skunk.

I went to find Mattie. She was in Father's room, at my mother's old desk, wearing headphones and typing on her laptop computer. I still had a hard time believing the incredible power of modern computers compared to my trusty old Commodore 64. I had tried to get up to speed on the Internet and everything that had changed while I was away, but it was just overwhelming. I'd felt like a kid transferred from the fourth grade into an advanced high school class mid-semester and told there was a quiz on Everything next week.

Father sat at his own desk, beneath a window overlooking Mother's garden, or at least the wild tangle it had become now that nobody tended it. Bits and scraps covered his desk, including pieces of broken watches, a variety of crystals and stones, a small collection of polished bones from creatures both mundane and magical (purchased legally, not taken from our customers, of course), and the pieces of an old Robotix set. I'd donated or purchased a lot of the materials, and borrowed the rest from the piles of junk left in Dawn's yard by her artist ex-boyfriend.

Once upon a time, Father had been a skilled thaumaturge, an inventor and creator of magical artifacts. Married into a family of necromancers, he'd used that skill to create many artifacts that allowed our family to compete with other necromancer families who had more money or influence, artifacts like the Kin Finder 2000; or like the Podium of Politeness, which enhanced a speaker's ability to say nice things about even the most wretched or boring deceased with full (if temporary) sincerity and belief, making the speaker feel rather good about themselves. He'd also made a number of smaller, non-magical objects he would sell to tourists in the shops on Water Street.

Once upon a time. Before Grandfather used Mother's ghost to forcefully possess my father and make him do horrible things, driving him mad in the process.

Three months since Mother's ghost had been exorcised, and no signs that it had helped Father's madness. But he still had his ability to imbue artifacts with magic, and occasionally the inventor or artist in him peeked through the madness. I was doing everything I could to bring him out fully.

"Finn!" Father said, looking up from his desk. "Finn Fancy, learn to dancey."

At Father's loud greeting, Mattie quickly shut her laptop and looked at me as if caught looking at pornography—something her father apparently did on a regular basis according to our sister, Sammy, who refused to fix Mort's computer any longer.

"Everything okay?" I asked.

"Okeemonkey," Father said.

"Yeah," Mattie replied. "All good. I was just checking Tumblr."

"Tumbler. Right. That's not, uh, something inappropriate for a young lady, is it?" I asked.

Mattie rolled her eyes. "No."

I'd have to ask Sammy about it. "Okay. Well, I was hoping you could help me with this?" I held up the sheet from the Kin Finder with the line drawn across it. I could use the line in conjunction with Thomas Guide maps to identify where the line pointed to, but I'd never been good at it. "You said you found a better way to do it?"

"Sure!" She took the sheet from me and scanned it using the printer on the desk. "Uncle Finn?"

"Yeah?"

"Could you talk to Dad? I'm worried about him."

"About what? His fashion choices? Because they worry me, too."

"No, for reals. He's been seriously moody lately. And sick a lot."

"He's not always like that?" I asked, surprised. In the three months I'd been back, I'd never seen Mort look particularly happy or healthy. The one time I'd tried to ask him about it, he'd told me to mind my own business.

"No. Well, he used to be better, anyway. But it's been getting worse lately. And he didn't used to stay in his room all the time. I tried to get him to tell me why, but he won't." Mattie finished scanning the document and then began doing something on her laptop.

I could think of a number of possible reasons why Mort would hide in his room. He probably still resented my being back. Or maybe he was afraid Pete would bite him again now that Pete really was a waerwolf, in retaliation for all the years Mort *pretended* Pete was a waerwolf as a prank.

Or perhaps Mort was just busy breaking his computer again.

Whatever the case, I couldn't simply ignore Mattie's request. And if something really was wrong, I couldn't ignore that, either. Damn it.

"I'll talk to him."

"Thank you. Here you go." Mattie pointed at her screen. A little red dot showed on a map. Thankfully, it wasn't on the other side of the world—a possibility I'd dreaded. Rather, it was right here in Washington State, and even on the Olympic Peninsula.

"Elwha River. Great! Can you print that for me?"

As Mattie fussed with the printer, I went over to Father. I knelt down beside him and put one hand on his shoulder. "Hi, Father," I said.

"Look at that!" he said, his tone irritated, and pointed out the window at the wild remains of Mother's garden. "Where are the flowers? All the flowers have died."

"We had to prune, remember? So that Mother's ghost couldn't be used against you anymore?"

"Your Mother's going to be mad when she sees what happened to her garden."

"Mother is—here, look at me, please." I leaned over to catch his eyes. "What is my name?"

"Phinaeus Gramaraye," he said with a touch of his old humor, and I saw recognition in his eyes, like I'd suddenly come into focus. "Why, did you want to change it again?"

"Again?"

"Yes, you wanted to change it to Door at one point, remember?"

Oh. That. I'd read several Xanth novels when I was around eleven, and for some crazy reason I'd briefly wanted to change my name to Dor. I'd also wanted a tattoo of Pee-wee Herman when I was fifteen. Thank the gods my parents had forbidden both. "Yeah, I remember that. I had my nose stuck in those books that whole summer. Remember when we went camping out by Forks that year, and I tried Talking to the spirit of all the inanimate objects—"

Father thrust my old pocket-sized Simon electronic game into my hand. A plastic circle with four different colored push pads, it had been MacGyvered, or as I liked to call it, MacFathered. A small spirit trap sat secured in the center—another twisted metal puzzle that had no solution, with what looked like a bird's skull in the center, all covered in runes—and crystals protruded from the push pads with copper wire attaching them to the spirit trap.

Father's eyes found mine, and I could see him making the effort to truly focus on me. "A gift."

"What does it do?" I asked as I took it.

The left side of Father's face twitched, and he said, "Over there, other there, criss-cross spirit sauce."

I sighed. I couldn't make sense of his words, but Father had a small touch of prophecy, and when I'd returned from exile he'd gifted me the ring that made the Kin Finder locate true love. That gift, and a few seemingly mad words, had helped me to put an end to Grandfather's plotting. So I held on to a growing collection of Father's gifted objects for fear that the one I chose to dismiss as just a product of his madness would be the object that could save my life somehow.

"Thanks, Father."

Father blinked one eye spastically several times. "Edwin?" he said. "Where's Father?"

It was like a steel shutter slamming down over the window, cutting off the light. For a brief moment, my father had been back. And now, he was lost to me. Again.

"I'm not your brother," I said, my voice thick with sudden emotion. I cleared my throat. "I'm your son, Finn. Father, concentrate. Please."

Father waggled his finger at me. "Please and thanks, or you'll upset the ranks."

He turned back to his desk and began picking up random objects, turning them over and pressing them together as if trying to fit puzzle pieces.

I patted him on the back. "I'll bring you some food." I took the map printout from Mattie with a quick nod of thanks and left the room.

I gently closed the door behind me and stood for a second, my hand resting on the doorknob.

"You okay?" Dawn asked behind me.

I turned, and put on my best smile. "Do bears bare? Do bees be?"

Dawn's eyes narrowed. "Uh huh. Want to try that again?"

"Weren't you making second breakfasts?"

"Weren't you about to tell me what's wrong?"

"Really, I'm fine—" I said.

"Sure. Get your stubborn man butt over here." Before I could protest, Dawn pulled me into a hug.

I gave a resigned sigh, and returned the hug as much to humor her as anything. But as I stood there holding her, being held, tears leaked out.

"I understand, you know," Dawn said. "Well, kind of. It wasn't easy, watching Dad fade away." Her own voice took on the edge of tears. "But at least your father is healthy. And you have Vee to help read his memories. And potions, and all kinds of real magic I don't even know about yet. I'm sure you'll find a way to help him."

I kneaded my fingers into her shoulder in acknowledgment, then took a deep breath of her candy and coconut scent, exhaled slowly, and stepped back.

"About our date today—" I began.

"Oh no," Dawn said. "Don't go trying to sneak your way out of our plans now, it was hard enough agreeing on a time to begin with."

"That's because you have twenty-seven jobs."

"I only have one job, sir," Dawn said. "And I'm well on my way to being named café queen in charge of making *all* the granola, thank you very much. Who needs more than that?"

"Well, you have the animal shelter, and reading Tarot, I consider those jobs. And—"

"Yeah, yeah." Dawn put her hands on her hips in a dramatic manner. "And don't forget that I keep the streets safe at night as Awesome Girl, too."

"Hey!" I said. "You're not supposed to tell me that! You're

supposed to protect me by keeping me ignorant of your identity. Well, until I'm kidnapped to use against you that is."

"Damn. You're right. And you *would* look adorable in a short skirt and wet T-shirt, tied up and oh-so-helpless, waiting for rescue." Dawn got a mischievous grin. "Hmmm. If you don't have something better planned, I think I have an idea of what we could do later." She waggled her eyebrows at me.

"I'm not sure I have a skirt that would work," I replied.

"Are you sure? Don't lie on my account, I'm totally fine if you do. I seem to remember you wearing eyeliner and dangling earrings in high school."

"That was the eighties, and it was cool," I said, crossing my arms.

"Uh huh," Dawn replied. "Well, I have plenty of skirts for you."

"And a superhero costume for yourself?"

"Are you kidding?" Dawn said, thrusting out her chest and lifting her chin. "I have three."

I laughed. "Of course you do. Okay. The date is still on. But I'm not sure how long this thing with Sal will take."

"That's fine. I have an appointment with Dewanda anyway."

Dawn's hair appointments were never a quick thing. There were no places close to home that knew how to deal with her natural hair *and* passion for colors, and the process itself was time consuming.

"I forgot," I said. "And you have the gig tonight. Are you sure—"

"It'll be fine," she said, and I caught that momentary flash of sadness I'd seen all week whenever the topic of her gig came up. Then she punched me in the shoulder. "Jesus, make a girl feel wanted why don't you?"

"What? No! Sorry. I'll try to be back here and ready to go no later than, say . . ." I glanced at my Pac-Man watch: Almost nine A.M. "Two o'clock?"

Dawn scrunched her hair between her fingers. "That should work."

"I think you're going to like what I have planned."

"Is it gonna be frickin' classy?" Dawn asked. " 'Cause I'm a girl with refined tastes, you know."

"Oh, it's going to be classy like you won't believe," I said. "You're with me, baby, and I only fart through silk."

"Wow," Dawn said in a most unimpressed tone. "I am a lucky lady. I can already tell this date's going to be hotter than Jake Gyllenhaal nude sunbathing on the Sands of Time while drinking a double-hot spicy chai."

"You know it," I replied. I wasn't sure who Jake whats-his-name was, but I waggled my eyebrows anyway.

Sadness drifted briefly across Dawn's face like the shadow of a swift-moving cloud.

Damn it.

I knew what that meant—there was some response she'd expected from the old days, or some word game we used to play, perhaps, that I'd forgotten when I lost my memories of us.

Another reminder that maybe I wasn't really the guy she thought she was in love with.

"Dawn, I—"

She waved a hand dismissively. "It's cool. I'll get some food for your dad, you go back to your matchmaking, Emma."

Her *Emma* reference caused my own pang of sadness as I remembered a similar joke Zeke had made. I didn't want to end the conversation on a down note, but I didn't know what more to say. And I did have a sasquatch sitting in my parlor.

I gave Dawn a quick kiss on her cheek, and headed back to the viewing parlor.

Sal looked up when I opened the doors; he was still sitting awkwardly on the folding chair and knitting away.

"Youself know who is my heart-love?" he asked.

"Not yet. But I know where they're at. On the Elwha River."

Sal's eyebrows rose. "Iself grow up near Elwha. And a Silver Court steading is yon-there."

"Well, there you go. Maybe your love's the, uh, sasquatch next door." Like Dawn. Being the girl next door, not a sasquatch. "So I can meet you at the river in, say, about two hours?"

"Iself can fastwalk there much sooner," he said, with the tone of a child asking if he can open a present on Christmas Eve.

"Unfortunately, I can't," I replied. Humans couldn't walk the fairy paths without going mad. "It will take me some time to get there. But I'll bring the Kin Finder so we can confirm—"

The doorbell rang.

"Now what?" I muttered. "Sal, I'll be right back." I closed the parlor doors, and crossed to the front door. I swung it open, and froze.

A man stood on the porch, easily identified as an enforcer by the black suit and tie also popular with the FBI, missionaries, and hip movie stars, and by the handlebar moustache that held a silver bead braided into either side. He held a small white television dangling from one hand, and a piece of parchment in the other, with a suitcase leaning against his leg. A silver ring glinted on his right hand—a persona ring, the arcana world's equivalent of government-issued ID—and its red stone identified him as a wizard, but that was unsurprising as most enforcers were wizards. I noted, however, that his suit stretched to accommodate his ample belly, his face appeared lined more with weariness than wisdom, and he had that aura about him seen on police officers forced to choose between inventory duty in the basement or midnight guard duty at a downtown grocery store.

The two women who flanked him were another matter. The one on the left stood a head taller than me and wore a leather jacket that was more biker gang than New York fashion, and with her short-cropped red hair she looked like Red Sonja gone punk. The Hispanic woman on the right wore a fitted suit and looked like a district attorney ready to put away the city's major crime boss for life, even if she had to go vigilante to do so, damn it.

I did not see persona rings on the women's hands, which meant they were likely feybloods.

Frak.

"Uh, hello," I said. "What can I do for you?"

"We're here to speak with Paeteri Gramaraye and Violet Wodenson," the enforcer said.

I glanced back in the direction of the parlor. The doors were open, but Sal was nowhere in sight. Just as well.

"Can you come back later?" I asked. Pete wasn't exactly in top form for stressful company. "We—"

"This cannot be put off any longer," the enforcer said, and held out the piece of parchment. "They've ignored three summons from the Arcana Ruling Council already."

I gave a whatcha-gonna-do shrug. "Those must have been lost in the mail. I'm sure if you call later—"

"Hilarious," the enforcer said without the slightest trace of humor. "But *I'm* sure if they do not speak with us now I *will* put out a warrant for their arrest and they'll be handled as rogue feybloods."

Double frak.

## Don't You Want Me, Baby

Pete and Vee sat on one side of our long dining room table, holding hands on top of the polished oak surface, and the three visitors sat on the other facing them. I sat at the end, ready to intervene as best I could. I wished our sister, Sammy, were here. She was more used to dealing with legal issues, since her job often brought her into conflict with the Arcana Ruling Council. But I could at least stand witness, prevent any abuse or coercion. And Alynon, as a full Fey, might give me some unique insight or edge—

*I warned you this day would come,* Alynon said. *But you would not heed.*

Or not.

"Paeteri Gramaraye and Violet Wodenson," the ARC enforcer said. "I'm enforcer Vincent, knight lieutenant for the Department for Feyblood Management. This is Minerva, representing the Forest of Shadows"—he nodded to the Red Sonja wannabe on his left—"and this is Zenith, representing the Silver Court." He waved at the lawyerish-looking woman on his right. "And we are here today because neither of you have declared your loyalty."

I laid my hands flat on the table, my persona ring with its black stone clicking against the wood. "That's because their loyalty hasn't changed. They are arcana, and Pete is a member of this—"

"They are not arcana," Vincent said. "Not anymore. With respect, they are feybloods—"

"Brightbloods," Minerva, the Forest of Shadows rep, growled.

Brightblood was apparently the name the feybloods called themselves now, just like they called magic 'the bright.' Having been stuck with a Fey in my head for only a few months, if I were fused with a Fey spirit for life I could easily see the attraction of trying to put as shiny a spin on it as possible.

Enforcer Vincent grunted and continued in a passionless tone that suggested this was a discussion he'd had countless times. "While I sympathize with the fact that this is not by choice or birth, that doesn't change the fact that you each now have a Fey spirit bonded with your human spirit. So I'm afraid you *are* feybloods under the rules of the Pax Arcana treaty last established with the Fey, and by definition of ARC Law."

I waved at Vee. "She's been a waersquirrel for a couple of decades and nobody's complained before about her loyalty."

Vincent shrugged. "Miss Wodenson avoided declaring her loyalty until now because she was under care at the Haven House facility—"

"The Hole," Pete said with an angry edge to his voice, and squeezed Vee's hand. "And she's not going back."

"That's entirely her choice," Vincent said. "For now. But make no mistake. If you do not declare a loyalty, then you *will* be classified as rogue feybloods."

"Fine," I said. "They'll be rogues, and continue living here, not in a feyblood steading subject to feyblood restrictions. No offense," I said to the two women. "But this is their home."

Vincent didn't even look at me, but just sighed and recited, "As rogues, you wouldn't be protected or supported by the ARC or any Fey Demesne. Should you find yourselves in danger, with a magical illness, or in need of mana, you will be on your own. Should you expose your nature to the mundane world, we may cover it up but you will be held fully accountable for the costs. If you should lose control of your Fey spirit, or present any danger to yourselves or others, you will be put into an ARC holding facility. And you will be magically inhibited from having offspring."

Pete and Vee looked at each other on that last, as if both trying to read the other's thoughts, and I could tell they both were thinking the same thing—they did want to have children, together.

*Holy Aal, a Pete and Vee baby,* Alynon said. *Could the world survive that level of cute?*

*I don't know, but I'd like to find out,* I thought back.

Minerva leaned forward. "I'm sure you'd father strong children." She smiled at Pete like it was five minutes to closing in a singles bar and he'd just strolled in looking like a naked Robert Downey Jr. covered in chocolate.

"I'm confused," I said. "What's the Forest of Shadows even doing here? It was a Shadows waer that infected my brother against his will. By Pax law they can't recruit Pete, right?"

Enforcer Vincent frowned at Minerva, and said, "The waerwolves involved in infecting your brother were all declared rogue before the attack, having left the service of the Fey to work for Grayson." He didn't sound any happier about it than I was.

"In fact," Minerva replied. "I'd argue that your brother shouldn't be allowed to stay under the influence of *your* family, given that his attackers were loyal to Grayson. Magus Grayson was practically your brother, too, wasn't he?"

"Grayson studied with us, but he was *not* part of this family," I replied in a sharp tone. "And I nearly died fighting to end his plot. As did Pete, and Vee." I looked back to Vincent. "They've earned the right to live free, as arcana."

Zenith, the Silver Court representative, tugged on the jacket of her suit and said, "I object to the implication that our brightbloods are not free."

*Our* brightbloods? She must be a changeling, a true Fey spirit temporarily inhabiting a human body under some arrangement between the ARC and the Other Realm. Alynon had been a changeling once, granted use of my body during my exile, before becoming stuck in my head.

"I meant no offense," I said with a nearly sincere tone.

*Do you know her?* I asked Alynon.

*Right, because all of us Fey know each other.*

*That's not what I meant. But she is another changeling from your own Demesne. And I know the ARC thinks you were communicating with other changelings during my exile.*

*Oh, absolutely. We plotted to replace George Lucas with one of our changelings and have him create movies so terrible they would destroy all hope. We called it Operation Pandora's Jar Jar. And it almost worked.*

I gave an exasperated exhale through my nose. *You're deflecting, avoiding the question.*

*I'm deflecting? What of you? Grayson did turn out to be your uncle. And possessed by your grandfather's spirit.*

*Minerva doesn't know about that, though.*

*Doesn't make it less true.*

*Fine. If you don't have something useful to say—*

"Maybe you did try to stop Grayson," Minerva said, and I realized I'd completely missed Zenith's response. "But the way I heard it, he was just trying to complete the work of your grandfather, to start a war for arcana supremacy, so either way it *was* your own family responsible for Pete receiving the bright blessing. If—"

"Blessing?" Pete burst out. Vincent's hand jerked to the silver-plated baton holstered at his side, while Pete's hands curled into fists on the tabletop. "You call this a blessing? I feel like I have this big mean monster inside of me always trying to burst out and hurt the people I love. I have these feelings, these . . . urges—" He stopped, his round face red and eyes brimming with tears. Vee put her arm around him, pulled him close.

"I understand, cousin," Minerva said. "I didn't mean to upset you. I'm just surprised you would remain loyal to a family that has caused you so much pain." Her hands reached toward Pete on the tabletop. "I can help you, like no other here can. Join my pack, and I will teach you what it means to be free, to embrace—"

Vee's eyes narrowed. "You try to embrace any part of Pete, wolf girl, and I'll spay you with a plastic spoon."

So Minerva was a waerwolf.

"Enforcer," Zenith said, "the Shadows representative is speaking out of turn, trying to influence—"

"Yes yes," Vincent replied. "Everyone, enough arguing and posturing. Minerva, you know the procedure. I have to finish giving them the Department's official line, then you'll get to make your case."

He picked up the remote and turned on the small television. As he did, I asked, "Where are the other Demesnes? Shouldn't there be at least a dozen representatives here?"

"They chose not to come," Vincent said, pushing play on the remote. "They did send brochures and written offers, which meets their obligations."

"Why wouldn't they come?" I asked.

Vincent shrugged. "If you wanted to meet them all, you should have attended the Feyblood Job Fair at the high school gym last night."

The static on the screen ended and the video began, with the title So, You're a Feyblood Now in neon letters cued to a song that was a bad synth knockoff of the *Beverly Hills Cop* theme.

"Hello," an enforcer said, wearing a *Miami Vice*–style uniform, feathered hair, and extremely bushy moustache. "So, you're a feyblood now. I imagine you have a lot of questions and concerns. And I'm here to give you some answers."

*What would you do?* I asked Alynon with some reluctance.

*If I had that hair? I'd kill myself.*

*Hilarious. Which Demesne would you choose if you were Pete or Vee?*

*I am no brightblood in need of patronage,* Alynon said. *I am an Aalbright of the Silver Court. You were in the Other Realm more recently than I. What do you think?*

*I wasn't exactly on a world tour,* I replied.

My twenty-five years exiled in the Other Realm had been spent in the wildlands outside of the shaped Demesnes, confined to a pocket of space not unlike a holodeck where I could re-experience any memory but not create anything new, not control my own appearance or apply my imagination. Fey would come from all of the Demesnes to experience my memories directly, to incorporate them into their own being and feed on the emotional energy, but they rarely offered anything in return. So while I learned a lot, matured a bit, and gained sympathy for most of my teachers by reliving every school lesson and significant experience of my first fifteen years over and over again, I learned very little about the Fey while there.

The enforcer on the video didn't offer much help either, going over the same basics I'd learned in Arcana Summer School before exile.

"The Other Realm is the place from which all raw magic flows," he said, "and to which some shamans, dreamwalkers, and early arcana found their way, spiritually or physically, in the long ago. The first true Fey took their shape and identity from the memories, dreams, and fears of such visitors. Those Fey became sentient individuals over time and gravitated toward others like themselves in nature, grouping together into clans, and shaping areas of the Other Realm into the Demesnes that reflected those natures."

Alynon snorted in my head. I wondered if that ever left spiritual snot on my brain. *'Tis a damn shame that Hugh Hefner or Bugsy Siegel weren't shamans in the way back. Then mayhap I'd be a knight of the Feyboy Mansion, or the Las Feygas Strip, and those self-righteous bastards in the Court would not have—*

He fell abruptly silent.

My eyebrows raised. *Weren't you just bragging about being an Aalbright of the Silver Court? Is there something I should know about them, a reason for Pete to avoid them?*

*There are many things you should know. But I'm not here to instruct you.*

I sighed as the video continued. "And when the early Fey spirits began following human visitors back into our world, many joined with people, animals, even plants, forming the feyblood races of myth."

*And that is just embarrassing,* Alynon said. *I mean, how

would you like it if I kept bringing up that your cousin slept with a horse or married a tree?*

*You clearly haven't met my cousins,* I replied. *That would be the least embarrassing thing you could say.*

"Then the Fey demanded recognition as true beings," the narrator said, "and fair compensation for the magic drawn from their realm."

*Damn straight.*

"The arcana refused for generations to acknowledge them as more than manifest memories parroting real thought and emotion. There remains debate as to whether they may be considered true living beings even today."

*How rude!*

*I don't know,* I thought at Alynon. *I still question if you have any thoughts or emotions of substance.*

"The resulting wars eventually led to barriers being erected between the worlds, cutting off the free passage of spirits or magical energy, and finally the Pax Arcana was established to formalize the rules of interaction and exchange. The Arcana Ruling Council took on some of the responsibility of protecting and managing feybloods in exchange for magical energy from the Fey. And the feybloods in return each swore loyalty to a specific Fey Demesne in order to enjoy the benefits of that arrangement, as well as further the interests of their Fey patrons in our world."

*Why wouldn't the other Demesnes send representatives then?* I asked Alynon. *I'd think they'd jump at the chance for two arcana recruits.*

*Arcana who are given the bright blessing against their will, especially so late in life, often have the hardest time accepting the rules and restrictions of brightblood life, and continue to treat their cousins as of a different class from themselves,* Alynon said.

*Still, to not even show up, how can they know if Pete or Vee would be cool or not?*

*La, 'tis also true your family has not garnered much love among our kind, between your grandfather's actions, your own battles against the brightbloods, and the Fey wardens who died in your transfer from exile.*

*That wasn't—*

*Your fault. Mayhap. But not all Fey believe that. And the truth, that it was the actions of your grandfather and Grayson, does little to recommend your family regardless. I'm afraid Pete and Vee may have very few options indeed.*

"And so," the narrator concluded, "in order to maintain the careful order and balance of the Pax and ensure the safety and happiness of yourself and others, you are now about to embark on a thrilling new phase of your life by declaring loyalty to one of the Fey Demesnes. Choose wisely, and enjoy the exciting adventure that awaits you."

Adventure. Heh. Excitement. Heh. More like being pressured to become indentured servants to the Fey.

Pete looked at me with worried, pleading eyes as the video ended. I could tell he was hoping I'd find a way out of this for him as his big brother. I gave him a reassuring smile. We'd figure it out. Somehow.

Vincent clicked off the television. "Now, Zenith, you may make your offer on behalf of the Silver Court."

Zenith gave him a nod, and said, "Simply put, there is no better Demesne for a brightblood to pledge than the Silver Court. Our brightbloods enjoy the most freedom of movement, the greatest number of options for working among the mundanes, and more offspring allowed than any other brightblood clan."

Not surprising, since the Silver Court had remained neutral on the Fey side of the last Fey-Arcana war, while their feybloods had actually fought beside the arcana. They had benefitted from the ARC's favor ever since.

Zenith smiled at Vee. "A waersquirrel would feel right at home in our local brightblood community, as long as she was able to control her compulsion to take others' possessions. Our local brightbloods roam the Olympic National Forest with great freedom, and are great stewards of the land." She cleared her throat, and looked much less happy as she regarded Pete. "While your strength would also be most welcome, I am certain, waerwolves most often go with the Shadows. The Silver Court rarely seeks out your kind. If you wished to pledge to the Silver, we are prepared to hear your argument for why we should accept you, of course. We do not seek to separate you one from the other, but neither do we suggest that pledging the Silver is best for both of you."

*Of course not,* Alynon said in a bitter tone.

*Do you think she's lying?* I asked.

*No. Your enforcer would detect it. I'm just being cynical, pay me no heed.*

"Is that all you wish to say?" Vincent asked.

Zenith gave another tilted nod of her head. "The advantages of pledging to the Silver Court are well known, I am sure."

"Very well," Vincent said, and looked at Minerva. "The Forest of Shadows may now make its offer."

"If I might be so bold," Minerva said, "I believe the Silver's making my case for me. Not just here, but for months now." She looked at Vincent. "It's true, ain't it, you enforcers been having all kinds of trouble from Silver brightbloods, all over the place lately?"

"Whether we have or haven't isn't a matter for discussion here," Vincent said.

"Yeah, okay," Minerva said. "Suffice it to say, the Silver Court may not be teacher's pet much longer, and—"

"I hardly think—" Zenith began sharply.

"Got no doubt about that," Minerva replied.

Zenith's eyes nearly flashed lightning as she glared at Minerva. "You would insult an Aalbright, you childish half-bright?"

"Enough," Vincent said. "Keep the peace, or suffer the consequences."

"Crap, yeah, okay," Minerva replied, then shook her head. "Apologies, Bright Lady, I'm more used to putting down challenges from my pack than being all polite and political, or in the presence of such exalted company."

Zenith gave a curt nod, though her expression was anything but forgiving.

"So let's get right down to it," Minerva continued. "The Silver'd bond you both to unhappiness just to swell their ranks."

"Ware, brightblood," Zenith said, her tone dangerous.

"I'm just speaking truth here," Minerva replied, and looked at Petey. "Dig. She told you right out you wouldn't be welcome among the Silver. Yet she dangles your woman there like a fat bloody steak over a trap, trying to tempt you to throw away real happiness and freedom for a mongrel's life of bitterness and regret, and makes you actually beg for the privilege."

Vee's face grew red. "What the hell is that supposed to mean?"

"It means if Pete goes with you to the Silver he'd be treated with suspicion if he's lucky, or like some feral dog if he ain't, and he'd never truly feel part of that clan anyways. With the Shadows, he'd be free to follow his wolf nature, be among his own kind, know the joys of running and hunting and . . . bonding with the pack."

Pete shook his head. "I don't *want* to let the wolf out."

Vee nodded, putting her hand on his arm. "And I wouldn't be any more welcome with the Shadows than you say Pete would be with the Silver. Or safe."

"Maybe," Minerva said. "And that's why you should each go your own ways now."

"*Excuse* me?" Vee said.

"No!" Pete said at the same time.

"That's your offer?" I asked. "You're not exactly making it tempting."

Minerva shrugged. "I'm just speaking the truth, even when it ain't pretty, which is what you'll always get from the Shadows. You both say you want the other to be happy. Well, you'd each be happier with different patrons. If you pledge together, then one of you will be placing your own happiness over the other's, while one of you will be sacrificing their happiness. You really think that'll lead to a long and happy relationship?"

"I'll be happy so long as I am with Petey, period," Vee replied.

"Seriously?" Minerva asked. "How long would you really be happy seeing Pete all miserable if you both go Silver? Or how long you think before you get all bitter and resentful about sacrificing your happiness if you both pledge the Shadows? Better to end it now. You have no children, no bond of marriage or even of years between you." She shrugged. "But should you be determined to stay together, the Shadows will of course welcome you both. Pete, you would be honored for your strength. And I'm sure we could find some arrangement for the squirrel-bright to keep her . . . safe."

Pete and Vee looked at each other, their expressions troubled.

*She's right. They're both right,* Alynon said, and his voice sounded strange. *Most waerwolves declare for the Forest of Shadows. Pete is not likely to be welcomed with open arms by the Silver.*

So what does that mean? I asked.

Alynon was silent for several seconds, then said, *It means I will help you as I may, where their fate is concerned at the least.*

I blinked in surprise. I refrained from asking what made him suddenly willing to help. I didn't want to jinx it.

How? I asked instead.

*I will put in a good word for Pete with the Silver Court,* Alynon said. *For whatever that is worth. And help as I may otherwise.*

I don't suppose you'll tell me what swearing loyalty to a Demesne actually means? What do the Fey really get out of it? How do you enforce loyalty?

*That I may not do, no,* Alynon responded.

I sighed. As much as we were stuck together, Alynon remained a Fey in the end, with Fey interests first and foremost in whatever passed for his heart.

"Well," enforcer Vincent said when it became clear Minerva had finished. "There you have it. And now, Mr. Gramaraye and Miss Wodenson, you may make your case to either of the representatives here as to why you feel they should accept you, or you may ask questions of any of us."

Pete and Vee both glanced at me. Vee cleared her throat. "I think we just need some time to think about it all. We—" She paused, and looked at the empty seat beside her for a second. She was, I knew, listening to Sarah, her Fey squirrel spirit. Or an imaginary projection of Sarah, nobody really knew for sure. She said in a low voice, "Why? We don't need—" She shook her head. "Fine." She looked across the table again with an embarrassed expression, and said, "I'm sorry, Sarah really wants to know if we would have easy access to peanut brittle?"

A frown passed across Zenith's face, and a smirk across Minerva's.

Enforcer Vincent sighed. "I'll answer this to save time. Every Demesne has feybloods who live as wild, or as close to civilization, as their desire and nature allows. As you clearly have no problem blending in and dealing with the human world, and the ARC would not consider *you* an exposure or safety threat, I'm sure you would be allowed to live in whatever housing they maintain within town limits, and would have access to all of the amenities you are used to."

Sure, and prisoners have free food and television and recreation yards. Doesn't make prison a resort spa or mean the prisoners had freedom. And I noticed he didn't look at Pete when he said that, regardless.

Both Zenith and Minerva nodded agreement with Vincent's assurance.

"Okay," I said, standing up. "Well, thank you all for coming, it's been lovely. Now if you'll excuse us, Pete and Vee have a lot to think about."

Enforcer Vincent ignored me again and looked between Pete and Vee. "Do you have any further questions or arguments for the representatives?"

"No," Pete said, and Vee shook her head.

"Very well." Vincent stood, and everyone joined him with the sound of several chairs scooting back across the wood floor. "It is just short of ten a.m. now. You have until Tuesday at ten a.m., three days from now, to make your decision. Should you fail to declare loyalty to a Fey Demesne at that time, you will be classified as rogue feybloods by the ARC."

Nobody said anything in response. Vincent pulled a stack of envelopes out of his briefcase, which I assumed were the offers from the other Demesnes, and tossed them onto the table. Then I led him and the representatives back to the front door, leaving Pete and Vee holding each other, their heads leaning together.

Vincent exited last, and as he stepped out onto the porch he paused and turned back to me. "Look, arcana to arcana, of course this sucks for all involved, but in the end the Laws exist for good reasons. Do what you can to encourage them to declare loyalty to a Demesne. I've seen what happens to most rogue feybloods, and trust me, whatever they think of feyblood clan life, it's better than the alternative."

"They're doing just fine here," I said. "Maybe you're just not used to feybloods having supportive families."

Vincent shook his head. "Whether pledged or rogue, their arcana gifts will be blocked, and their memories of training in those gifts removed. If they stay here, what purpose will they have? What kind of life? They will not be arcana, and they will be feybloods unable to express their feyblood natures. Let them go, Gramaraye, for everyone's sake."

*He has a point.*

*Not now.* "I'll keep that in mind. Thanks."

"Uh huh. And one more thing. I agree that they should think about splitting up, declaring for separate Demesnes. It will be better for them in the end. Especially her."

"What the frak does—"

Vincent turned and followed after the feybloods to a minivan parked on the road.

*I don't think he likes waerwolves.*

*You think?* I responded. I shut the door, and returned to the dining room.

Pete and Vee still sat holding each other, his round baby face pressed into her white-blond hair. Mattie stood behind them now, a worried look on her face.

"Hey guys," I said. "We'll figure this out. I'll talk to Reggie, and—"

"Thanks, brother," Pete said, looking up. "But I think we need some time to think about stuff. And aren't you supposed to be helping that sasquatch?"

"You two are more important than finding Sal a girlfriend," I replied.

"Pete's right," Vee said. "There's nothing you can do here right now. You shouldn't pass up this chance to finally get your business going. We'll be okay."

I sighed, and glanced at my watch. Ten minutes to ten. "Okay. I can call Reggie on the way to Elwha, see what he can do. In fact, do you guys want to come along? Sal said there was a Silver Court steading in the area. It might help you make a decision one way or the other."

"No, thanks," Vee said. "We've visited several steadings already."

"Really?" I asked, surprised. "Oh. Well, uh, if you guys need anything—"

"Thank you," Pete and Vee both replied.

I nodded, then headed upstairs to where most of the bedrooms were. I needed to change into my Woodland Adventure Finn outfit.

The hairs on my arm stood up, and I felt a familiar tingling between my eyes, resonating from down the hall.

A spirit was being summoned in Mort's bedroom.

# Wanted Dead or Alive

I tried the doorknob to Mort's bedroom, but it was locked.

"Mort!" I pounded on his door. "What's going on?"

I heard a muffled curse, and then Mort replied, "I'm busy. What do you want?"

"I wanted to talk for a minute. Did you—are you summoning in there?"

Silence.

Then, "No. What do you need?" His voice sounded scratchy, and he began coughing.

I knew what I'd felt. There had been a disembodied spirit in Mort's room, and given recent events, I didn't trust it was a random haunting or visitation. Either Mort had summoned the spirit, or someone had summoned it and sent it to Mort, possibly to possess him.

I tried the knob again. "This is stupid. Open the door so we can talk."

"Piss off. Go play with your girlfriend or something."

Well, that sounded like Mort. Which meant he probably wasn't possessed, at least. Just a dickhead.

"Mort, open this door or I'm going to break it in."

"Who died and made you Merlin of the world?"

"Who died and made you a douche? Gods, dude, I'm just trying to help."

"Well, if I need help, I wouldn't ask the guy who doesn't even know what Wi-Fi is," he replied.

"You know what? Screw it. You're clearly not possessed, or being attacked, so have fun playing necromancer with yourself. And don't come to me if you need someone to shave your palms."

I strode off. Mattie would be disappointed, but there was only so much I could do when it came to Mort. If anything strange started happening outside of his room, I'd do something about it. But I didn't have time right now to deal with Mort being stupid on his own time and energy.

I changed into the steel-toed boots, Carhartt pants, and leather jacket I'd bought before our assault on the EMP sanctum a few months ago—the closest thing I had to armor—then stopped down in the basement. I retrieved a couple of items from the padlocked case near the stairs: a hex amulet to protect against witch curses, a pair of specially coated women's sunglasses to protect against stone gazes, and then grabbed Zeke's silver-coated steel baton, which Dawn had returned to the safe.

I reluctantly left the revolver behind again. The Pax forbade civilian arcana to use guns outside of home defense. There were exceptions, of course, especially for enforcers or their assistants, but one of those exceptions was not, unfortunately, simply going into feyblood territory. In fact, guns were doubly restricted there to protect feybloods against poaching or hunting. But those same rules forbade feybloods from having firearms at all, so it was to everyone's benefit they not be given the excuse for an arms escalation.

Besides, sasquatches could smell gun oil a mile away, and I didn't want to spook Sal's love before we got close enough for them to meet.

I loaded the Kin Finder into the back of the hearse and headed out.

I turned onto Washington Street and stopped to let a family of deer cross the road. The waterfront of Port Townsend spread out below me and to the left, where a steady stream of people moved along the row of brick and stone buildings. Tourist season was in full swing, people attracted by the artsy small-town charm, countless Victorian buildings, and wooden boat culture. I still wasn't used to how much the town had become focused on the tourists. Gone were the days of community barter and families gathering at the tavern every evening.

Even the arcana families seemed more worried about their property taxes or running small businesses than improving the world through magic; they ordered their magic supplies online and interacted more through cell phones and the Internet than meeting in local moots or forming circles. They barely celebrated the Wheel of the Year, where once we could count on large house or beach parties at least four times a year.

I'd certainly wanted to get out of necromancy and chase my own mundy dream once, and so I found my own reaction to all the changes even more confusing.

Maybe it was just that I didn't really have anyplace else to call home. And if Pete and Vee were taken away, it would feel even less like home.

As if reading my private thoughts, Alynon said, *You must face that your brother is no longer arcana. Sooner or later, he shall need help related to his waer spirit, the kind of help you cannot give.*

I turned on the radio rather than respond. It was set to the "oldies" station. Before my exile, the oldies station played classics from the '50s and '60s. Now, it played the music of the 70s, 80s, and even 90s, music I'd grown up with, the music that defined my teen years and music that would have defined my early adulthood if I'd been around to hear it. I tried not to think about that too deeply, and changed to an empty station. I pushed play on the iPod that Dawn had given me.

"Love Shack" by the B-52's started playing over the radio.

"Seriously," I said. "How amazing is this thing? There's, like, hundreds of albums worth of music in here!"

*Yeah, amazing,* Alynon replied in a less-than-amazed tone. *A few clever thaumaturges have begun moving human experience from physical objects into a virtual cloud, where experiences are only given form when manifested through choice and action and a bit of power. Hmmm, I wonder where they got that idea from?

I mean, it's not like there's an entire Other Realm that works something like that?*

"Whatever," I said. "At least I don't have to keep a pencil around to rewind the cassette every time it tangles." Our hearse's cassette player had eaten tapes with the enthusiasm of Slimer in a hot dog factory.

*Indeed. And soon, your infomancers will have control over everything you own and are.*

"Paranoid much?" I asked.

*Clueless, much?* Alynon responded.

"At least I have an excuse," I replied, and turned up the music.

I had twenty-five years of history and pop culture to catch up on, everything that happened between my exile in 1986 and 2011 when I returned. At Dawn's suggestion, and with her help, I was doing it chronologically. We'd started at 1987, the year after my exile, and each month we moved to the next year. We watched movies and television shows of the time, and highlights of the year on YouTube. And she made me playlists of all the best, or at least most popular, music from that year.

Dawn promised it would get better around 1991, but that was a whole two months away.

Not that I wasn't already exposed to stuff from later years here and there of course. And wild horses couldn't have kept me from watching *Lord of the Rings*. But despite wonders like hand-held computers and the Internet, the world itself hadn't really changed much. The Russians had never invaded or started World War III, no doubt daunted by the prospect of facing Rambo and the insurgent Wolverines. We weren't driving fusion-powered hover cars or teleporting, thanks, in Dawn's opinion, to oil corporations; and we weren't able to transport into virtual computer worlds, or create computer-generated lovers by wearing bras on our heads and hacking NORAD Satcom (which was actually a good thing, probably).

So taking time to truly grok each year seemed like a decent plan, especially if I wanted to be able to talk as if I'd been there, and really understand pop-cultural jokes. Which, when hanging around people like Dawn's friends, seemed an important skill to have.

It took an hour and a half to drive from Port Townsend to Port Angeles along the northeastern edge of the Olympic National Forest, and from there up into the Elwha River campground. Early summer sunshine glistened off the melting snowpack of the Olympic mountains, and a light breeze caused the spruce and cedar trees to sway gently.

I parked and made my way along a hiking trail to the viewpoint for the Elwha Dam, a small hydroelectric structure of concrete and great steel tunnels that spanned a choke point in the narrow river ravine and filled the air with a deafening whirring sound.

I left the main hiking trail, and made my way up to a hidden path that paralleled the river.

Sal stepped out from behind a giant cedar tree, his red-brown fur matching the color of the tree's bark, his head brushing against branches I would have to stretch to touch. "Youself late, Finn-mage."

"Sorry, Sal. I had a bit of ARC trouble. Ready to go find your soul mate?"

"Iself ready to try."

"Cowabunga!" I held up the map and compared it against what I could see of the river's path. "It looks like we should find your true love about two bends up the river."

Sal nodded. "That is near Silver steading."

"Okay then. Shall we?"

I put on the saucer-sized women's sunglasses of Protection Against Stonegaze, despite the −5 hit to my Charisma, and we hiked upriver, leaving the man-made trails and the whirring of the dam behind. I followed Sal, who better knew how to find those fey-blood trails invisible to the untrained or, in some cases, unmagical eye. Whenever our path brought us close to the river's edge, my stomach began to churn, my knees felt a little wobbly, and I walked as far from the water's edge as possible. Ever since I'd drowned while escaping my grandfather's underwater super-villain lair, I'd had difficulty with large bodies of water, or the thought of being submerged.

"Stop!"

A faun stepped out from behind a tree. He looked like a tan little man with goat legs, and wore a camo vest, a Utilikilt that hung down to his furry goat knees, and a Budweiser baseball cap that didn't quite cover the nubby little horns on either side of his forehead. He held a crossbow loosely in his hands, and he spit to the side of the trail.

"Where do you two think you're going?" he asked.

"Uh, hi," I said. "Do you know where they keep the nuclear wessels?"

He frowned, and raised his crossbow. "Nuclear what?"

I raised my hands. "Sorry. We're just heading up the river a bit. We think my friend here might have a, ah, connection with someone there."

"Good connection or bad?" the faun asked, lowering the crossbow again, and looked at Sal. "You're not on a job, are ya?"

Sal shook his head. "Iself not on a job. Iself looking for a truefriend."

"Uh huh. Well all right then. I'd best lead you in so you don't hurt yourselves. Go ahead and just continue down that path there, I'll follow right behind ya."

Sal began striding down the path, and I hurried to catch up.

The faun trailed behind us, giving occasional directions to walk around a spot in the trail, or to take a side path marked only by a cluster of mushrooms or other subtle marker.

"Had a couple of amateur hunters get so drunk that the glamours and our will o'-the-wisp didn't even work on them, they just stumbled right into our steading," the faun explained as we walked. "So we started putting traps on the paths."

"Is that where you got the gear?" I asked.

"Naw. Garl, this waerbear friend of mine, he sometimes likes to scare campers and hunters for fun. They leave all kinds of stuff behind."

"And the DFM doesn't mind Garl's games, or these traps?" I asked.

"The Department of Feyblood Mismanagement don't care what we do long as we ain't collecting guns or causing them any paperwork."

Sounded about right. "My name's Finn, by the way, and this is Sal."

"Don," the faun said. "Don Faun. And yes, my sires hated me."

We emerged from the thick patch of forest into a clearing at the river's edge—a clearing filled with feybloods.

They stood in a crowd with their backs to us, facing a young woman. Behind her stood a single cedar tree on the riverbank, its branches covered in drooping bunches of needlelike fronds doing a slow dance in the breeze.

In the crowd of feybloods I spotted a bear, a frog-faced fellow, a jackalope, a wolf, and a fox, a moving pile of dirt and rocks that must be a dwarf, several fauns who didn't share Don Faun's clothing appreciation, a couple of river nymphs—and a single sasquatch female. Now, I just had to convince her to return with us to the car, and I could verify with—

"Got some visitors!" Don Faun called out, then tipped his hat at us and disappeared back into the forest.

All heads turned toward us.

Great.

I saw no feyblood likely to have a stone gaze, so I removed the sunglasses and smiled as friendly as I could.

"Greetings, newcomers," the young woman near the cedar tree called out. Her expression wasn't nearly as welcoming as her words.

"Uh, hi," I said, and waved, showing my persona ring in the process.

The bear growled. The dwarf shifted his face of dirt-covered-stone and spat dust in my direction. "Arcana," he said in a gravelly voice. "Send him swimming in fastwater!"

Sal put his hand on my shoulder. "This arcana is Iself's guest, come here for I."

"Thanks," I said in a low voice.

Sal grunted, and said, "Do any bad-bright tricks and Iself will be first to tear off youself's arms."

The young woman walked to us as Sal spoke, the crowd parting to let her through. Five-foot-nothing, she looked and moved like a Jazzercise instructor on her day off, her simple movements hinting at a greater strength and grace, her auburn hair chopped short and streaked with traces of green. She was beautiful in a way that wasn't quite human, as though Boris Vallejo had airbrushed her into reality. She wore a green dress I thought at first was sequined, then realized was made of woven grass, leaves, and pine needles that covered her from neck to knees. The tip of a pale scar could be seen where her neck met her shoulders before it disappeared under her dress.

"I'm called Silene," she said. "What brings you to my tree?"

Her tree? Of course. Silene was a dryad, a tree nymph.

Interesting fact: for the longest time, it was a rite of passage for male arcana to be taken to a nymph by their father or grandfather on their fifteenth birthday, and it was not unheard of for bachelor parties (or parties in general) to end up in nymph groves. In fact, if you look, you'll see that the stage area of Woodstock abutted a grove of trees—this was not accidental. But then the ARC declared that it was exploitive (and quite possibly a risk to public health) to have sex with feybloods. Interestingly, this change occurred shortly after the first unicorn ranches were opened, tailored toward female customers, though the ARC maintains the timing was pure coincidence. Of course, while the unicorn ranches were closed down, nobody was cruel enough to suggest cutting down the nymph groves. And the number of unicorns working as personal trainers and riding instructors increased considerably.

Seeing Silene's beauty, I understood the allure of nymphs. And looking past her to the tree, I saw that a pale scar split the reddish-brown bark of the cedar for several feet, lined with char. A lightning strike, which explained the scar on Silene's neck. A dryad was connected to her tree, caring for it and the life of the surrounding forest while gaining strength and life from it in return. Except their caring usually took the form of celebrating the beauty of nature and encouraging the whole rebirth part of the cycle of life. I'd never heard of a dryad leading a crowd of feybloods to do anything except dance and feel good.

But these feybloods did not look like they were in the mood to dance or . . . dance. At all.

"Hi," I said. "I'm Finn, necromancer under the local ARC. I just came here to help Sal find someone." I looked at the female sasquatch. "Miss, may we have a word with you?"

"I told you!" the fox said, rising up onto its rear legs. The fox transformed, her rust-colored fur flowing into a dress, the white into gloves and shoes, the black into long flowing hair. Her face settled into the features of a young woman of indeterminate race as she turned to the dwarf and pitched her words to address the crowd. "I told you they would come for us, blame us. And they even hired a squatch merc!"

The dwarf spat dust again, this time in the direction of Sal. "Clan before mana!"

"Uh, what?" I said.

"Iself not on job!" Sal declared.

Silene's eyes narrowed, and she said over her shoulder, "The ARC would send a group of enforcers, not a necromancer. And they wouldn't trust a fellow brightblood, not for this."

I raised my hands. "I honestly didn't come here to do anything but help the big guy here. I don't want any trouble."

Silene glanced from Sal to the female sasquatch, then said, "Many of us have not been treated well at the hands of arcana. Some even have reason to fear our sasquatch cousins. What *is* your purpose here?"

I looked up at Sal. I didn't want to embarrass him. "Well, Sal here recently lost his sister, and is seeking someone to . . . spend time with. I was able to use a bit of magic that indicated he might find such a friend here."

"I see." Silene crossed her arms, and looked at Sal. "You are welcome, of course, if you can earn the trust of those here. We are all pledged to the Silver, as I sense are you. And . . . I'm sure Challa would speak to you, in time." She looked at me. "I think it best, however, if you leave. There is much anger here, and I would not want it to ignite."

"I don't want to put myself at risk, obviously, but if we could—"

"You mistake me," Silene replied. "My concern is not for you. I worry that if one of my brethren were to harm or kill you, then your ARC would punish all of us. Now please, go, and—"

"DFM!" A voice projected from the tree line as if from a loudspeaker. "Everyone stay where you are, and nobody will be harmed."

Three men and one woman stepped into the clearing and spread out to form a half circle between the feybloods and the forest. Enforcers from the Department of Feyblood Management. They wore padded tactical gear and heavy boots that shifted color to camouflage them, and protective helmets with shaded visors no doubt enchanted to protect against psychic attacks, stone gazes, and more. One man wore a Fu Manchu–style moustache with silver beads woven into the dangling ends. The woman and, I was surprised to see, two of the men had instead two small braids with the same style beads dangling from behind their ears, visible beneath the edge of their helmets. And they all held telescoping batons that glowed blue like lightsabers.

The dwarf's obsidian eyes flashed at me. "You lie. You come for us."

"I didn't, I swear." I raised my empty hands to show both the dwarf and the enforcers I wasn't a threat. Beside me, Sal fluffed up, and I saw Challa do the same. The water nymphs slipped quietly into the river and were gone.

The dwarf shouted, "Dunngo do nothing wrong!"

Silene raised her own hands. "Everyone, just stay rooted. We have our rights. They cannot take us away without good cause."

The woman enforcer said, "Actually, we have good cause, and I think you know it." To the crowd, she shouted, "I'm Knight-Captain Reyes, here to bring in four suspects for questioning. If those involved in the attack on the alchemist will just step forward, we can make this quick and easy." She looked at me. "Gramaraye, please step away from the feybloods."

"Gramaraye?" Challa demanded, and a ripple of unhappy sounds passed through the crowd.

The waerfox looked to her fellow feybloods and said, "He wants to make us his slave!"

"Romey, don't—" Silene began.

"Dunngo not be slave!" the dwarf said, and surged toward me on a wave of dirt, stony fists raised.

Oh crap. It was clobberin' time! And I was the one about to be clobberin'ed.

"Stop!" Silene shouted.

I turned and ran. I had nothing that could stop a charging dwarf.

I corrected my direction for the space between two of the enforcers so they didn't think I charged at them.

I could hear the rumble and grinding of earth and rocks growing close behind me. Sweat sprang up cool and sudden on my arms and forehead.

The nearest enforcer closed the distance to me, dropped to his knee and slammed the butt end of his glowing baton against the ground as if spiking a football. The grass and moss rippled out from his strike like water from a dropped stone.

I was thrown forward to the wet earth, and as I tumbled I saw Dunngo's waist crumble out from beneath him, sending his upper body rolling across the grass.

"Enough!" Knight-Captain Reyes shouted.

The dwarf righted himself, and earth mounded up beneath him to form a new waist.

"Dunngo, stop!" Silene said. "Think of our clan, our cause."

Dunngo raised his fists again, and leaned in my direction.

"Please," Silene pleaded. "You won't avenge your son by dying."

The dwarf turned his obsidian eyes from me to Silene and back, and lowered his fists. "Dunngo say all arcana badbright mud-hearts."

"Duly noted," Reyes said drily. She raised her voice again. "For those four feybloods involved in the attack on the alchemist, this is your last chance to submit yourself for voluntary questioning as subjects of the Silver Court. Otherwise, we will identify and arrest you as enemy combatants."

Romey, the waerfox, shouted, "Did you arrest the alchemist for questioning, too?"

"That isn't your concern," Reyes responded.

"Of course not," Romey said.

A wave of grumbling and restless stirring swept over the feybloods, like news spreading through a prison cafeteria that the meatloaf really *is* horse meat. The four enforcers shifted their booted feet and raised their glowing batons, prepared to swing or cast their magics.

Silene stepped forward, facing Knight-Captain Reyes. "There was no attack except against us. We only went there to protest, as is within our right. The alchemist, and arcana like him, they exploit brightbloods for—"

"I'm not here to discuss the reasons," Reyes said. "I'm here to take custody of those involved. And I'm losing patience. You've got until the count of ten to comply. One. Two—"

"Stop!" Silene said. "We'll comply, of course. But I will be reporting this to our Archon."

"Report away, as long as it's not on my time."

Silene turned back to the crowd. "Step forward and go with the enforcers. We have nothing to hide and no reason to fear them. Each injustice just makes our cause stronger, and the Silver Court will not abandon us."

*She assumes much,* Alynon said, and I detected a tone of bitterness.

After a few seconds of uncomfortable silence, three feybloods moved forward. Frog face. A faun. And surprise surprise, Dunngo.

And lastly, Challa pushed through the crowd with her long sasquatch strides.

Bat's breath.

Each enforcer approached a feyblood and placed a silver collar around their feyblood's neck.

Reyes secured Challa, and said so all could hear, "You will be taken to the Sequim DFM facility, and given all considerations accorded you under the Pax. The regional Silver Archon will be notified, and a changeling ambassador will be present for all questioning." Then she looked at me. "Gramaraye, your presence here has been noted. Don't leave the domain of the North American ARCs. We might want to question you as well."

Great. "I won't. But—"

"Let's go," Reyes said, and the enforcers guided their feyblood prisoners back into the forest, in the direction of the roads.

"Friendly bunch," I muttered.

You'd think, after being falsely sent into exile and then helping to stop a major conspiracy by an ARC magus, I'd get a bit more respect from the enforcers. But they still treated me more like Rodney Dangerfield than Aretha Franklin.

*Welcome to my world,* Alynon said.

Right, speaking of which—

I turned around to find the feybloods all glaring at me. Silene stood watching me with her arms crossed and eyes cold.

I raised my hands again. "Really, I had nothing to do with this. In fact, I'd, uh, like to help if I can."

"We don't want arcana help!" the bear grumbled.

"Don't be foolish," a faun said. "We can use all the allies we can get."

Romey crossed her arms over her fox-colored dress. "We don't need an arcana coming in and playing hero. Especially not a Gramaraye. We brightbloods can do for ourselves."

Especially not a Gramaraye? Great.

"Look—" I began, when the sound of snapping branches and someone or something crashing through the underbrush came from the forest behind me, from the opposite direction of the enforcers.

A centaur burst out from the trees, carrying an unconscious girl in a gauzy dress slung across his back.

"Strange things are afoot at the Circle K," I muttered.

## Sign O the Times

"I found another," the centaur bellowed as he landed in the clearing and skidded to a stop, his hooves plowing furrows in the mossy soil.

"Quick," Silene said to the centaur, "lay her down beneath my tree." She looked to me. "If you truly wish to help us, then help her."

"I don't understand," I replied. "Help how? What's wrong?"

Silene scowled. "She suffers Grayson's Curse."

"Grayson's what-now?"

"You should know, *Gramaraye*," Romey said.

*Ooo,* Alynon projected. *That doesn't sound good.*

I blinked, and looked to the centaur as he laid the girl out beneath Silene's cedar tree.

Silene strode swift and graceful toward the moaning girl, her delicate feet leaving no trace in the blue-gray mud and emerald moss. "It is what we call the drug your fellow arcana give our brightblood cousins to make us their slaves," she said.

"Oh." Of course. The mana drug my grandfather had created with the help of Heather, once high-school crush of yours truly. Not many knew Grayson had been possessed by my grandfather's spirit during his brief reign of evil evilness, but since grandfather had practically adopted Grayson in life, it made little difference. It still came back to tarnish the Gramaraye name regardless, as Minerva had demonstrated at the house, and as evidenced all too clearly now by the hateful glares I received from all directions.

I glanced up at Sal to gauge his reaction. Thankfully, he seemed more concerned at the unconscious girl's state than caught up in the crowd's anger toward me.

My feet squelched and slipped in the damp earth as I followed after Silene.

I saw that the girl actually appeared to be nineteen or twenty, but waifish, a faint glow around her visible now in the tree's shade, pulsing to her heartbeat. A will-o'-the-wisp. A hint of her normally compelling beauty could still be seen, but shadowed by the effects of withdrawal from the mana drug, her delicate features now too thin, her shimmering hair clumped by sweaty knots, her lips no longer whispering half-heard promises but instead dry and cracked and twitching around moans. And she had nasty scratches around her throat and chest that I guessed were self-inflicted, which explained why her wrists were bound.

I didn't remember any will-o'-the-wisps in my grandfather's little army. Not that wisps were fighters anyway. Sammy said a lot of them had found success creating websites of easily shared web content, full of videos and articles with titles like "Most Embarassing Celebrity Stripteases Involving Sauces—With Recipes!" or "9 Mistakes Every Man Makes on Dates—Number 6 is Illegal in Kansas!" meant to lure people and lead them down a never-ending trail of hyperlinks through forests of advertising and off the cliff of distraction. But I doubted my grandfather had been hip enough to organize any kind of online campaign, either.

"I thought Grayson only gave the drug to a handful of feybloods."

"Your brethren continue giving it to many brightbloods," Silene responded.

Damn it. The Arcanites, grandfather's little extremist group of Fey haters, it had to be. He must have given the formula to them. "They are not my brethren, the ones doing this."

"Then you will help?" Silene asked.

"I . . . I don't know how. I would need to talk to an alchemist, and—"

"We tried that," Silene said, and knelt beside the wisp. "It did not go well. Do you not have a healing potion?"

"No. Sorry." Heather had been willing to brew them for my family cheap, but was unfortunately no longer around to help us out. Even more unfortunate was the reason—she'd tried to freeze me on behalf of my power-mad grandfather, and then went fugitive. Too bad, too, because if anyone could help these feybloods, it would be her.

Silene sighed. "I shall have to do what I may, then." She placed her hand on the wisp's forehead, and closed her eyes. Her tree began to sway back and forth gently, each sway greater and longer than the last. The sunlight glistened off the swooping cedar fronds, and a green light rose up around the moaning woman. Silene started to sway back and forth in time with her tree. The wisp arched her back, and the green light rushed up through Silene's hand and along her arm, until it surrounded her. It faded, and Silene slumped back to sit on the mossy earth, her legs folded to one side. The tree slowed in its swaying, and the wisp lay still, breathing slow and steady.

"You healed her?" I asked.

"No," Silene said, and her voice sounded strained, tired. "I drained the poisons from her body, filtered them through my tree. She will rest a while. But the craving will rise in her again, and she will require more of the drug or she will die. I have only bought her a brief rest."

I frowned. "I'm sorry, but . . . I've never learned what the drug does, exactly. Why would your cousins use it, knowing this might happen?"

Silene looked up at me, her eyebrows raised. "I find your ignorance surprising indeed." Her mouth pouted to the side, as if she were uncertain whether to tell me more or not. Then she said, "Not all brightbloods take it willingly. But for those who do, it offers many temptations. Pleasure, of course. Escape from unhappy memories. For Elene, I believe she took it to heal the Fettering. She desired offspring, but none was approved."

The Fettering was a kind of spiritual birth control, on par with having a vasectomy or your tubes tied, that prevented brightbloods from having true offspring without ARC intervention. It was used to enforce the population controls approved in the Pax. Even waer couldn't infect others if they were fettered. Which explained how Pete was infected, if the drug had unfettered the waer who attacked him.

"Oh." I felt awkward. "So, does this have something to do with why the enforcers were here?"

"In a way, yes." She tried to stand, but fell back to the ground. Sal stepped forward and offered his catcher's mitt-sized hand to help her up. She frowned at his boots. "You are the one who has been wrapping trees in yarn for the humans to see."

"Iself just trying to make humans stop and see the trees, realize the beauty," Sal said.

"The yarn allows rot and insects to grow beneath," Silene replied. "And you're covering up their true beauty, not displaying it."

"Iself take the yarn down before rot begins," Sal said. "Why youself be so badger-angry? Youself dryad, use beauty to protect trees, too."

"Not anymore." Silene's hand moved to her chest, but stopped just short, and closed into a fist. "I have a new purpose now."

"We all do," Romey said behind me. "And you're not part of it."

*And here we go,* Alynon said.

"What?" I turned to find the feybloods had closed around me, looking like I'd just been caught eating filet of faun. I glanced at Sal, but he just stared back, giving no indication of helping.

*Clan before mana,* Alynon said.

Great.

"Uh, hey guys," I said. "Crazy day, huh?"

Romey stepped forth from the crowd, her narrow fox-like features scrunched even narrower by her scowl. "Maybe we should take you prisoner, the way your enforcers took our cousins."

"You could try," I said. "But then, the ARC would come back with a small army."

"They would have to find us," the wolf, a shunka warakin, said. "And we would have you while they did." He padded forward, his hackles rising.

Crap.

I whipped the spirit trap out from beneath my shirt, though it was useless as a weapon, and held the twisted metal amulet up as I shouted, "Anall nathrach, oothfas bethad, dochiel dienvay!"

The feybloods flinched back, some covering their eyes or heads.

"Touch me, and suffer!" I said, then lowered the amulet. "Or, we can talk. You can tell me what's going on and maybe I can help."

Romey growled a little fox-like growl, and looked to either side. "He cannot stop us all."

"Nope, but I can rip the soul out of most of you," I lied. "So, you know, there's pros and cons I guess."

Sal grunted. "Finn-mage is not problem."

"Romey," Silene said. "Stand down!" She struggled to her feet. "All of you, we agreed that we would not use violence to achieve our goals."

The waerfox scowled, and she glanced at her fellow feybloods. "Maybe it is time for a new agreement."

"How will that prove that we are more than beasts?" Silene asked, stepping up beside me. "That we are worthy of being treated as equals? Why would they ever allow us to move freely among the humans, or give us representation in their council?"

I looked at her, surprised. Feybloods on the Arcana Ruling Council? She really was dreaming. The council had only recently allowed women arcana in their highest positions.

*Fa,* Alynon said in a dismissive tone as the feybloods grumbled and mumbled between themselves. *Always there is talk among these children that they should separate from their patrons, form their own nation, and make of themselves partners equal to the arcana, la la la. But soon enough the arcana reject them, they feel the lack of our protection and magic, and need prevails over foolish wanting.*

Sal stepped up on the other side of me, casting me in his shadow.

He looked over my head at Silene. "Brightbloods are not having to prove anything to arcana. Brightbloods can stay in forests, do what weself want."

Romey snorted. "Bold words from a brightblood who sells his services to the arcana."

Sal blushed. "Seeahtik tribe need mana sometimes, too, like any brightblood. Even fox spirits. Even dryads."

Silene crossed her arms. "We should not have to be their slaves to get what we need."

Sal looked angry now, and leaned over me toward Silene, making me feel like I was between a rock and, well, an angry sasquatch. "Iself nobody's slave. Grayson made sister-mine a true slave, and if heself were not dead, Iself would end him."

*Awkward!* Alynon said. *What say we tell him your grandfather—or "Grayson"—may be alive in truth?*

*Anyone ever tell you that you suck?*

*Many indeed, starting with my parents. Which just goes to prove how few beings have any taste.*

Silene said, "Running and hiding is no more an answer than violence." She looked at me. "If you cannot cure the curse, then how could you help us?"

Romey spat on the ground. "If you are going to deal with arcana, especially a Gramaraye, I will take those willing to fight and we shall start our own movement."

Silene raised one eyebrow to Romey for a second, then without taking her eyes from the waerfox, she said loudly, "We will get our cousins back, and we will continue the fight. Just as the Klallam firstmen have won the freedom of our river from its concrete shackles, so, too, we shall win our freedom from the shackles of the Pax. Our lives and our cause burn with the fire of the bright in our blood, and both shall endure long after those arcana who came here today are naught but bones and dust. We shall not give them an excuse to end our light, but we shall instead let our light shine upon their injustices for all to see, and, our cause being just and right and true, we shall prevail!"

A ripple passed through the feyblood crowd, of heads nodding and murmurs of agreement. Romey looked around her, and scowled like Archie Bunker at a Pride Parade down Martin Luther King Way, but didn't agitate any further.

"Come, speak with me," Silene said, and Sal and I followed her around to the far side of her tree. Romey joined us. Because, of course. As I neared the river, my knees felt unsteady and my hands shook. I turned away from it.

Silene sat and leaned back against the cedar's trunk, facing the river. She let out a long sigh, resting her hands on the roots that cradled her to either side. "This all will change soon," she said.

"The feyblood's role in the Pax?"

"The river." She motioned to it. I risked a quick glance. The water ran clear and green, cutting through a gray, clay-like ravine beneath forested hills. In the cool breeze coming off of the river, I could smell the cooling sweat on myself. It held the sharp tang of fear as though I'd just run through a fine mist of Christian Dior's Holy Crap I'm Going to Die.

I took a step back as Silene continued, "Soon, the mundanes will take away their dams to let the river flow free and the salmon spawn. The Klallam firstmen did this, won the freedom of the river. Many trees may be lost along the riverbank when the river finds its new way. But many more will grow again where now there is a lake. All of this I learned the day after my tree was struck by lightning, when I lost my—beauty."

Sal harrumphed. "Iself not seeing how youself lost beauty," he said.

Silene looked away from us.

"So . . ." I asked. "Is that a good thing, with the river? Will your tree be safe?"

Silene shrugged. "The future is uncertain. But it awakened me. The lightning. The victory of the Klallam firstmen. I realized that if I had but a short time left, I might spend it winning a victory for my own clan, to ensure their roots were strong enough to weather coming storms and their ambitions great enough to touch the skies.

So I began organizing a movement among those of us pledged to the Silver Court."

"And that is why the enforcers were here? Because of your movement?"

"Because they fear it, yes. And . . . because one of my sister brightbloods was killed by an alchemist, and they cover for him."

I frowned. Romey cocked her head, and said, "You do not believe your fellow arcana capable of such behavior? Or did you not believe us brightbloods capable of recognizing it, because we are just stupid beasts?"

"Neither," I said. "Don't get me wrong, enforcers can be total tools, and they're a tad overzealous in the same way the Hulk is a tad unhappy, but one thing I've learned is they truly believe in truth and justice and the arcana way. They wouldn't knowingly arrest the wrong person—or feyblood for that matter—and certainly not to cover up a crime."

"Of course you would defend them," Romey said.

"Finn-mage may be wrong," Sal said. "But heself is not responsible for enforcers. Heself is just spirit talker. And Iself see other arcana try to kill Finn-mage."

"It is not our way to blame a falling leaf for the winter winds," Silene replied, I assumed in agreement.

"Sal's right," I said. "I can't control what the enforcers do. But do you know if the ARC necromancers have questioned the spirit of your dead cousin, the one killed by the alchemist?"

"If they had," Silene said, "and they are as honest as you say, then they would not have had cause to come here and arrest us."

"Then allow me to leave and speak to the spirit of your fallen cousin, to learn the truth of what happened."

Romey scowled. "And how are we to trust you will do so, and not just try to blame her death on us somehow?"

"I won't lie," I said, my arms crossed. "I give you my word as a necromancer that I will Talk to your dead cousin and convey the truth of what I find to both the ARC and yourselves." I looked at Silene. "I will want to be quick, though. There's a cost to Talking.

So if you can tell me what happened, and why, that will help me know what to ask."

"We do not know what happened, exactly," Silene said. "Only that the alchemist is to blame."

"Okay, why do you think that?"

"What other explanation could there be? That we killed our own, or attacked an arcana openly? For what gain?"

I frowned. "Maybe we should back up a bit. Why was your cousin even with the alchemist in the first place?"

Silene sighed. "She and those arrested today were protesting outside his shop. Our campaign against alchemists was to be the first seed sown in our growth toward freedom. Alchemists exploit us. They need us for so many of their potions—our blood, bone, and flesh, our hair, horns, and venom, everything. Even the ink that the wizards use to make their tattoos requires some part of brightbloods."

Sal gave a low growl. "Theyself use Seeahtik feet for sexstrong potion. Weself feet, and skin of unicorn . . . horn."

Thank the gods I'd never drunk that particular potion. I wondered if Mort had. Seemed likely. I'd have to mention the ingredients to him, maybe over breakfast.

"This has always been true, though," I said. "The alchemists get those ingredients from the licensed necrotoriums, and in exchange the feyblood's family gets mana."

"And how much mana would you feel is fair in exchange for your mother's eyes? Or your father's feet?" Romey challenged.

"No amount," I admitted. And I had a sudden, terrible thought— would someone try to harvest something of Pete or Vee after their death for an alchemist's potion? "But . . . I thought most feybloods didn't care about the physical body once the spirit had left?"

"Some," Silene said, looking at the wisp. "And some are just desperate to leave their family a little mana. Even so, the mana we get for the bodies of our fallen is never enough to meet our need, yet just enough that many cannot refuse it."

It was like rabbit's feet, I realized. I'd won them as colorful little trinkets at the arcade when I was young, and knew what they were called at the time, yet somehow hadn't connected them as having once *actually* been on a cute little living rabbit, not until I was a teen. How many familiar artifacts and potions had I also never thought to question the origins of?

Silene continued, her voice becoming more passionate, "We have more to offer of value than our bodies, yet most are denied permission to perform such work—they say to keep humans safe and our natures hidden, but we know it is also to keep us dependent."

Romey snorted. "And because they fear we shall prove their betters."

Silene gave a slight shrug. "We hoped our peaceful protests would remind the arcana that the potions and powders they buy come from our dead, to demand fair return for our sacrifice."

*How like a brightblood to blame everyone else for their lowly state,* Alynon said. *But if brightbloods had the ability to care for themselves, they would have done so by now.*

*Isn't that what Silene is trying to do?*

*A child's rebellion against those who care for her, that is all. It shall prove short lived and symbolic only, as all such brightblood movements are.*

*Don't be a jerk,* I thought.

*You may call me the jerk, but if you arcana wished to reduce your dependence upon these brightbloods, it would be but a matter of small effort to do so.*

The ARC had, I knew, found artificial replacements for some of the more rare feyblood ingredients. In fact, several popular medicines, two artificial sweetners, and a rather hostile and short-lived breed of Sea Monkeys were also discovered by accident during the ARC's experiments. But such work was expensive in resources and mana. Easier to just pay feybloods for their donations, and maintain the Pax Arcana's status quo.

"No response, I see," Romey said bitingly.

I shook my head. "Just thinking. So what went wrong with your protests?"

"We do not know," Silene said, "except Veirai was killed."

Romey growled. "She was murdered by the alchemist."

Silene shrugged. "They said it was self-defense, that he acted out of fear for his life. I do not think that likely."

I frowned. "Are you sure Veirai didn't attack this alchemist, maybe try to force him to make a cure for Grayson's Curse?"

"I'm sure. We do not speak of the curse except to those we trust, to prevent spreading awareness of its existence. We've already lost too many to its trap—Dunngo's son among them—and too many out there already see us as little better than animals, to be used as pets and slaves."

"Ah." I wasn't sure what to say to that. "Okay. I'll do what I can to find out why this alchemist killed Veirai, and what the ARC is doing about it." I turned to Sal. "And we'll verify that Challa is the right . . . friend for you once she's free. I promise." I gave him a pat on the arm, and winced as my hand found a sharp burr caught in his fur. I plucked it off my palm and tossed it away with the difficulty of tossing away a bad dream made of sap and static cling.

Silene ordered the other feybloods to let me leave in peace rather than pieces, and I wasted no time in getting back to my car. I arranged to meet Sal the next day at Fort Worden, when I'd hopefully have the sasquatch Challa, or at least some good news.

*You are a fool to get involved in their troubles,* Alynon said as Don Faun led me back toward my car.

*I'm not—what do you care anyway?*

*I care if it puts us in danger.*

*Offering to help got us out of danger. And it's the right thing to do. I promised Sal I'd find him love. And Grayson's Curse—*

*Ah, you hope to improve your family name? Perhaps so Pete may pledge here to the Silver?*

*Pete won't have to pledge anywhere. He's arcana,* I said.

*Of course.*

*It will not come to that,* I said, and knew I was trying to convince myself as much as him. *I'll find a way to keep them free.*

*Free like you? Chained to your family business, your guilt, your—*

*Drop it.*

*Dee Niall isn't just a lass in Scotland.*

"Whatever," I muttered.

"What?" Don Faun asked.

"Nothing. Sorry. Just talking to the annoying voice in my head."

"Oh," Don said, "you got one of them too?" He looked around us, then cleared his throat and said in a low voice, "Mind if I ask you a question?"

"Uh, sure."

"Does your voice ever ask you to, ya know, dress up special when you get amorous-like? You know, like maybe a, uh, coyote?"

"Nooo," I said slowly. "But I don't think he'd complain if I did."

*Hell, I'd be fine if you dressed up like a Smurf, long as you got to the amorous part.*

"Oh, yeah, well, mine either," Don said quickly. "But I've heard rumors of others. You know."

"Of course."

I reached the car without further incident. On the drive home, I called Reggie, Zeke's old enforcer partner, and explained the situation to him. His manner of speaking, like his appearance, always reminded me of Louis Gossett Jr.

"Shoot, son, I don't know what to say. I've been trying to find a way to help Pete and Vee since Zeke's death, and still don't know how to keep them free. I'll keep trying, though. As for this feyblood death, I can probably get you a chance to Talk with her spirit. And get you in to speak with those feybloods they just brought in. But that won't happen until tomorrow morning at the soonest."

"Can you tell me anything about what happened at the alchemist shop?" I asked.

"It's an open investigation, so no, I can't. Officially. But I'll look into it for you, and give what help I can."

"Okay. Thanks." I hesitated. "You doing okay, about Jo, and Zeke and all?"

"It's getting better, man," Reggie said. "Thanks for asking. It helps that we are rooting out and tearing down the Arcanites one mad magus at a time."

"Any sign that Grayson is still alive?"

"You know if there was, you'd be the first person I'd tell. After I beat his ass to a pulp."

"Yeah. Okay, thanks."

I pulled into the driveway of my family's home, the gravel crunching beneath the tires of the old hearse. The early afternoon sun shone bright but weak, having barely begun its descent toward the madrona and pine trees that screened our yard from the street and our neighbors. I climbed out of the driver's seat and stood for a minute, looking up at the black and white Ansel Adams clouds of a distant storm.

What mess had I gotten into now?

Maybe I should have run away from magic when I had the chance, instead of sticking around and trying to start a magical dating service. But my family needed me. And even after being home for months, I still had no clue what else I could do.

That worried me more than a little to think that, without magic, I had nothing. Nothing to do. Nothing interesting about me. No—

"Don't freak out," a woman's voice said behind me.

I turned to find Heather, fugitive alchemist and one-time crush, standing in the shadow of the hedges. She wore a long black jacket, and she'd chopped her normally blond hair short and dyed it black, which only served to accentuate the dark circles under her eyes and the shadows of her sunken cheeks. She held a water pistol pointed at me, and I felt pretty sure it wasn't filled with water.

I freaked out.

## Every Rose Has Its Thorn

I spun away from Heather to run for the house—and banged my shin against the bumper of the hearse. "Ow!" I hopped and grasped at my shin.

"Way to Harding yourself," Heather said. "Didn't I just say don't freak out?"

I flinched, but no potion splashed over me. I turned back to face her. "You're an alchemist pointing a water pistol at me. And the last time I saw you, you tried to freeze me."

"And you shot me. I'd say we're even."

"That was an accident. And—never mind. What are you doing here?"

She sighed. "I need your help."

"You're kidding, right?"

Heather lowered the pistol. "Look, I understand why you wouldn't exactly trust me—"

"Did I mention you tried to freeze me?"

"We were also friends. And lovers, if only briefly. Do you remember that?"

*I certainly do,* Alynon said. *Think she'd be keen for another round?*

*Don't be a smeghead.* "Are you still working for the Arcanites?" I asked.

"I never worked for the Arcanites. I did things for Grayson because he was my boy's father, and I needed to protect Orion from him. I couldn't do that from the outside. I had to play along, do what he asked."

"Is Grayson still alive?" I asked.

"I don't know," Heather said. "If he is, he hasn't found me. And I haven't looked for him. Finn, I was trying to protect you, too, you know that, right? Grayson had feybloods he would have sent after you if I hadn't promised I could keep you . . . distracted while he did what he needed. And I only tried to freeze you so you wouldn't get hurt in the fighting."

"That wouldn't have saved Sammy, or Mattie." Anger swelled in my chest. "It didn't save Zeke."

"I know. That's why I'm here. I want to try and make up for my mistakes."

"Then tell the ARC everything you know."

Heather shook her head. "Orion knew more than me. I'm sure he's already told them everything I could and more. I would just be sent into exile. And I can't do any good in exile. Surely you can understand that?"

Ah, bat's breath.

"What do you want then?"

"I—I don't know. There's got to be something I can do to make amends."

"The mana drug that Grayson was using. You created that, right?"

Heather blushed. "Yes. I did a lot of terrible things. I know."

"Well, that is what you can do for starters. The Arcanites are still using the drug. The feybloods need a cure for the addiction. Do you have one?"

"No," Heather said.

"Just no? Can't you create one?"

Heather looked away. "I—something else. Name something else for me to do."

"What? Why?"

"Too many people in power want to use that drug now. If I provided the cure to it, if I took that weapon away from them, they would make sure I was exiled or worse, no matter what other good I did. Please, just ask me to do something else."

"Merlin's beard, Heather! Seriously? This is exactly the kind of thinking that got you in trouble in the first place. You need to just stand up and do the right thing."

Heather's face flushed. "Says the overgrown boy who wanted to run away from his responsibilities and make video games."

"But I didn't," I said, feeling my own neck and face heating up. "I stayed."

"Because you didn't have much choice."

"There's always a choice," I said, feeling like a hypocrite indeed. "Just like you have a choice now."

"Gee, thanks, Afterschool Special, now I realize I should have Just Said No."

"What the hell, Heather? You came to me. Do you want my help or not?"

Heather's eyes suddenly overflowed with tears. "I'm sorry. I've been running, hiding, I don't know what to do, I just don't want it to end like this."

"Then make the cure for the drug, Heather. Please." I stepped toward her, reached out to hold her arm, to reassure her.

Her hand jerked up with the water gun, and she shot me in the chest.

"Wha—!"

Numbness spread out from my chest, and I fell limp to the ground. I wasn't frozen, it just felt like every muscle in my arms, legs, and face had gone to sleep.

"I'm sorry!" Heather said. "I didn't mean to—I'm sorry." She looked around her as if afraid enforcers, or worse, would pounce on her any second. "I can't make the cure to the feyblood drug. I'm not even sure it's possible. But if you think of anything else I can do to make amends, to earn your forgiveness, then just . . . hang some shoes on that silly rope thing of yours." She waved up at the rope pulley that ran from my bedroom window over the hedge to Dawn's house, a way to exchange objects and messages when we were teens.

The pins and needles of waking limbs began in every muscle at once. Oh man, recovering was going to suck worse than a Scrappy Doo movie.

"Mmffmumff," I said as Heather turned away, a bit of drool running down my cheek. Heather faded into the shadows.

Somehow, I doubted she would heed my eloquent final words.

It took several minutes of painful writhing for the effects of the potion to wear off, as I made hopeless attempts to find just the right position where my muscles could wake up with minimal pain. When I could at last move without wincing, I climbed to my feet and stumbled into the safety of the house and its protective wards.

Pete poked his head out of the kitchen, lowering a half-eaten chicken drumstick from his mouth. "Hi Finn!" he said, then gave a guilty look down at the drumstick. Our family had been raised vegetarians, as most necromancer families were—one of the side effects of being able to sense the residual spiritual energy in anything that once had a nervous system. But Pete's new wolf nature was less discerning.

"Hey Petey, how're you doing?"

Pete glanced back into the kitchen a second, then crossed through the dining room to join me in the entry hall as the kitchen door swung back and forth behind him. "I—hey, are you okay? You don't look so good."

"I'm fine, Petey, thanks. What's up?"

Pete blushed. "Oh. Can I talk to you for a minute?"

I sighed. All I wanted to do was clean up, drink something with lots of caffeine and sugar, and meet Dawn for our date.

"Sure. What's up?"

Pete looked down and shifted from foot to foot in that golly gawrsh way he had. "I just—I was thinking about asking Vee to marry me."

"Holy—wow! That's awesome, dude. And quick. Does this have something to do with what happened this morning?"

"A little, maybe," Pete said. "But I was thinking about it even before that."

"Okay. But are you, well, do you know if she's ready for that?"

I asked not just because they'd only been together for three months, but because Vee had spent a good part of her adult life in the Hole, a special facility where noncriminal arcana and feybloods were "cared for" if they were unable to care for themselves, or might be a danger.

"I think she's ready. She keeps saying she spent too much time waiting for her life to start, she doesn't want to wait no more."

They'd been together three months and were ready to marry. I'd known Dawn the same amount of time, at least from my perspective. So why couldn't I even say "I love you"?

The Kin Finder had confirmed Dawn to be my soul mate, the same as it had confirmed the connection between Pete and Vee. But what did that mean? I had been eager for some clients in my dating service, not only to have some alternative to being a necromancer, but also so I could better see just how the Kin Finder worked. The fact that it had found Sal's soul mate close by, and near his own stomping grounds, made me wonder if it didn't so much find your one and only soul mate as just the best match closest by. And how much of the love seeker's expectation played into that?

When I'd used the artifact, it had been after I'd lost my memories of Dawn, but I had been *told* that I loved her. Pete already knew he loved Vee when he used it. And Sal, well, why wouldn't some part of him equate love with the comfort and familiarity of his home territory?

But Pete and Vee truly were a perfect match. And now Pete was ready to propose. This was exactly the kind of thing that made me worried I'd lost more than just memories of Dawn, that I'd lost some important part of me, maybe part of what had made her love me, maybe even my fundamental ability to love her back, to truly love in the way Dawn deserved.

I knew that I had fun with Dawn, and loved to spend time with her. And she certainly knew me, perhaps even better than I knew myself. But—

Pete slumped. "You think it's a bad idea," he said, sadly.

"What? Oh, no, sorry Pete. I was having a pity party in my head.

Look, I—marriage is a pretty big deal, you know. Are you sure *you're* ready for that?"

Pete nodded. "Our counselor says we're good for each other, even though, you know, I sometimes want to eat her." He blushed again.

"Counselor?"

"Brightblood relationship counselor. We've been seeing one for a few weeks now."

"Oh! You didn't say anything."

Pete shrunk in on himself, and said in a soft voice, "Everybody is already scared of me. I don't like to remind you of what I am now."

"Petey, we're not—" I stopped. I wanted to say we weren't afraid of him, or at least that I wasn't afraid of him. But that wasn't true. I realized then how far from him I was standing, that when he'd entered the entry hall I'd actually taken a step back to maintain that space.

"Nobody lets me cook anymore," Pete said. "Like I'm going to spit in the food or something. And you haven't come to my house to play games with me and Vee, or watch movies, even though I keep asking you."

"Oh man, Petey. Come here." I pulled him into a tight hug, and slapped him on the back as we stepped apart. "I'm sorry. How about tomorrow morning you make us breakfast, and we can watch Saturday-morning cartoons?"

"They don't have Saturday-morning cartoons anymore," Pete said.

"I know. But I'll bet Mattie can help us find some on her computer, or something we can watch, some of the good ones. *Bugs Bunny. Thundarr the Barbarian. Superfriends.* Whatever you want."

Pete's mouth squished to the side as he considered it.

"Tomorrow's Sunday," Pete said at last.

"Fine. We'll make up our own tradition. Sundurday Morning Cartoons."

Pete's last reservations collapsed beneath the wave of a huge smile sweeping across his face. "That sounds fun."

"Okay. It's a plan. And as for Vee, I agree with your counselor.

You two make a great pair. If you think you're both ready, I say go for it." And if they were married, maybe it would be harder for any-one to split them up. Of course, it might also make it easier for any Demesne to reject them both.

"Thanks, Brother," Pete said. He gave me another hug, then re-turned to the kitchen, gnawing enthusiastically on the drumstick as he went. I was tempted to check for chicken stains on my back, but I was going to clean up anyway, so it didn't really matter.

I checked in on Father, who was happily distracted assembling knickknacks and working his way through a bag of saltwater taffies from Elevated. Mattie had left a note on her desk asking if I'd pick her up after Arcana School that evening.

I checked the time. Nearly one. Just over an hour until I was sup-posed to meet Dawn for our date. Our first real date, at that. We'd hung out plenty, usually around her shows or at each other's jobs, or at hurried meals at home; but all the catch-up since my return and our crazy schedules had made it difficult to do an actual planned activity together.

I hurried upstairs to get ready. In lieu of a shower, I used one of the magical stones we used to sanitize bodies for the major clean-ing work, and a damp washcloth to refresh.

Dawn stood waiting for me when I stepped out of the bathroom in my threadbare blue bathrobe, her hair now a vibrant purple cloud of finger twists.

"You look amazing," I said.

"Aw, you're going to make me blush. So, how'd things go with Sal the sasquatch? Did you find his true love?"

"I think so," I replied. "But there were some . . . complications. I'll figure it out, though."

"I want to hear all about it. You ready for this friggin' classy date you promised me?"

"Almost," I said. "But you're not. You're going to want to get dressed up, I think."

The Port Gamble renaissance fair was not the largest in the area, but it lacked nothing in enthusiasm, and had at least a sampling of anything you might expect from such a fair put on by The Society for Creative Anachronism. I noted with particular interest a pay-to-play arena where groups of visitors beat each other with padded weapons, each group competing to win a stuffed dragon that looked suspiciously like someone had stitched wings onto an Eeyore knockoff.

Plenty of people wore costumes that spanned several centuries of medieval and renaissance history—sometimes all at once. I hadn't gone for accuracy myself, wearing my old *Dragon's Lair* T-shirt, plus a gray plastic conical helmet and white canvas backpack.

Dawn had outdone me. She wore a blue long-sleeved shirt, a brown leather vest, and brown leather pants. A mandolin lay slung across her back, she had clipped a small white feather on either side of her lavender hair, and a plastic sword swung at her side.

Around us, white canvas tents and booths offered everything from swords and leather armor to elephant ears and potion bottles full of dragon ale. It was pretty easy to tell the area residents come to shop or entertain their children versus the folks who would happily live in a renaissance fair if given the choice.

Less easy was telling the difference between mundies, arcana, and feybloods.

Dawn and I stopped beside a fairy sitting in the shade of a tree. Not a real fairy, at least not that I could detect, but a woman wearing costume wings, with glitter paint on her face and flowers in her hair. She sat on a blanket where she displayed handmade bracelets, and languidly wove a new one.

"Excuse me," I said. "Do you know where the musical instruments are being sold?"

She made a chirping kind of sound, and pointed past the roped-off area, where a man in fencing gear and a white sash demonstrated basic moves to a young boy. She chirped again, and held out her hand, offering something. I extended my own palm, and she dumped several Skittles onto it.

"Oh! Uh, thanks," I said. She gave a regal nod, and I led Dawn in the direction indicated.

Dawn took my free hand. "You don't have to buy me an instrument," she said. "I doubt there'll be anything I need here."

"Okay," I replied.

"I'm just saying, I think a renaissance fair is an inspired choice for a date, but—"

"You sure?" I asked, suddenly uncertain. "You're not disappointed? I was a little worried it wasn't very, I don't know, date-ish? I mean, for my one real date as a teenager, my mother drove us to the movies. So I don't have a lot of experience. And adult dates involve things like dinners and walks on the beach as far as I can tell, but we already eat and walk together all the time, so—"

"Relax!" Dawn said, and laughed. "I love this. And just so you know, I've been on plenty of dates, and basically what I've learned is a good date is just about having chances for conversation and a bit of fun. With plenty of escape routes in case it sucks, of course. So, you know, if I'm not enjoying myself, you'll know by the fact that I distractify you with something shiny then disappear all ninja-like, Poof!"

I breathed a little easier, and said, "The only thing distracting me is your smile."

"Aw, how sweet. And cheesy. Maybe I'll start calling you my little cheesecake. But seriously, about the instruments, you do know I was joking about being a material girl living in a material world? You don't have to go trying to buy my heart with gifts."

"I know. I thought I already won your heart anyway," I said.

"Well, you certainly had a running start, before you gave up your memories of me."

I sighed. "I didn't give them up, I was tricked out of them."

"Still, 'I dwell in darkness without you,' and it went away?!"

"Egads, woman! Do I need to fight a dragon as penance?"

"Wouldn't hurt," Dawn replied. She took my hand. "So if you're not going to buy me an instrument, why go to the instrument booth?"

"You'll see," I said. "Just trust me."

"Okay, fine," Dawn said, and her expression became serious. "Actually . . . I've been debating whether to say anything, but I might need some major boyfriend support tonight, just to warn you. I've been thinking about making tonight my last gig for a bit."

I sighed. "I kind of thought you might, the way you've been talking, but why?"

Dawn shrugged. "I need to get serious about making money for a while. I've still got a mountain of debt from when Dad was sick, and, well, it's been years and I'm still playing the same places for the same faces. Not that I don't appreciate all the local love, I just think, short term—" She shrugged.

"But you love your music. And you're really good," I said. "I'd hate to see you give it up."

"Great!" she said. "Don't suppose one of your wizard friends runs Capitol Records and owes you a favor?"

"Uh, no," I replied.

"Didn't think so. And I didn't mean to be a bummer on our date. It might even be a good thing. The ladies at the massage school are still trying to get me to do their program. And—Blah, enough about me. Tell me about your morning."

I groaned, and explained how I'd rapidly gone from one problem—finding Sal's soul mate—to also finding a way to protect Pete and Vee from being declared rogue feybloods, and helping Silene's feybloods to clear their name.

"Not to sound uncaring, but you know these aren't all your problems to solve, right?" Dawn asked.

*See?*

"I *know*," I said a little more sharply than I'd intended. "I'm just doing what I can. And in a way it's all tied together, anyway."

"How's that?"

"Well, I have to help the feybloods free Challa so I can keep my promise to Sal. And doing a good deed might improve the Gramaraye reputation a bit, which can't hurt."

\*And the Silver Court is the best choice for Pete and Vee if they must needs choose a Demesne—\*

*We've been over that. Drop it.*

"Well, you know what you're doing," Dawn said. "Probably."

"Thanks."

"Uh huh." Then after a second, she said, "Does this place we're going have magical instruments? Is that why you're taking me there?"

"No," I said.

"You're no fun," Dawn said when it was obvious I wasn't going to give her any clues. But the bounce in her step and her tone said otherwise.

We got more than one odd glance as we walked through the crowds.

The best glances were clearly due to our outfits. Well, okay, due to Dawn's. It was easy to spot those very few who recognized her as the bard from *Bard's Tale* by their enthusiastically geeked-out reactions.

The worst, by contrast, were the obvious "why is he with her?" glances, as if there needed to be some reason to explain why I would be holding *her* hand—something in my background or character that made me like them black girls, or "settle" for a woman with some extra padding, or such a quirky sense of style.

A few glances may have just been due to the rarity of a black woman at a fantasy event, which I'm sure was one of the reasons it was rare. If people kept looking at me like I was out of place, I'd have a hard time feeling like I belonged.

Dawn noticed the looks as well, and waved jovially in response to them all. The more negative or sidelong the glance, the more animated her reaction.

There were a number of words Dawn insisted were made up, and "subtlety" was one of them. Literally. When I tried to point out "subtlety" in the dictionary, she pointed out that no real word would be that misspelled. "There's no such thing as a silent 'b'," she'd said. "So it's a completely messed-up word, and since it was designed to make life easier for completely messed-up people, obviously they're the ones who made it up."

I knew that *she* obviously knew that subtlety was, in fact, a real word in our world. But one of the things I'd quickly learned was that there were actually three worlds, not two: the Other Realm, our world, and Dawn's World; and in Dawn's World, she defined her own reality.

I completely envied and admired that about her.

We stopped at several jewelry, leather, and clothing booths, and finally reached the booth with the musical instruments, an open-sided tent with mandolins, ukuleles, pan flutes, and regular flutes hanging around the perimeter. Tables were arranged beneath its shade, covered with hand drums, harps, lyres, and other heavier instruments.

A woman sat in a camp chair near the back of the booth, leaning forward over a low folding table as she strung a lute. She wore a layered dress of white and blue cloth, and her hair rested like a braided crown atop her head, woven through with white flowers.

"Elowyn?" I asked.

She looked up and smiled at Dawn and me. Her eyes flicked to my persona ring, and she raised an eyebrow. "I am she. Do you have a question?"

"Actually," I said, "I wondered if you could listen to Dawn sing a little bit, and maybe give her some advice?" I pulled a small silver mana vial out of my pocket and held it up.

"Wow." Dawn said. "Uh, excuse us please." She grabbed my arm. "Can I talk to you for a minute?"

She pulled me back to the front of the booth. "What the hell? First of all, what makes you think I want her advice on my singing? And second of all, what makes you think I need it? Not exactly a great date move, insulting my singing."

I raised my hands. "I'm not trying to insult you. Elowyn, she's—" I looked around, and lowered my voice. "She's a muse."

Dawn blinked. "Wait, you mean, literally a muse?"

"Yeah. Well, not one of the actual muses from the myths, but she's a euterpe, a feyblood who has an affinity for music."

Dawn looked back at Elowyn, who smiled serenely. "Is this because I'm thinking about giving up my gigs?"

"Maybe a bit. I love your music, but, well, I know my opinion doesn't mean much since I'm not a musician or anything. I thought maybe Elowyn's would."

"And if she says my music sucks?"

"Then she's a muse with lousy taste, and I'll summon up the spirit of any musician you want to tell you so."

"Any musician?" Dawn arched an eyebrow. "Hmmm. That could make one hell of a reality show. Get Sid Vicious up there insulting the singers—"

"So does that mean you'll give it a try?" I asked.

Dawn looked at Elowyn, her lips pursing to the side, then shrugged. "Sure. How often do you get to play music for a muse?"

Elowyn had Dawn set up just outside her booth, and loaned her a guitar since Dawn's best songs were better suited to it than her mandolin.

Dawn stepped away for a few minutes to do her secret pre-show ritual, then returned to sing "Order Up Your La La La" and "Sticky Sad Saturday" and "Godzilla Shops for Swimsuits Too," her songs that typically got the best reactions from her regular followers. As she did, a crowd gathered to hear her play. Her music was folksy and playful enough that it fit well with the mood of the fair, enough to be forgiven lines like "I look for your number between my thighs, but you only left teeth marks and sticky lies," or "So if you see Godzilla in the changing room mirror, remember she has fire and no monsters to fear."

When she finished and the crowd had offered its applause and moved on, Elowyn led Dawn behind the tent, away from the moving crowds of people.

"So," Dawn said. "Is this where you tell me I should stick to playing for my friends?"

"No," Elowyn replied. "I'm not going to tell you anything. You are." She touched Dawn's forehead, and Dawn's eyes widened, then a smile settled on her face.

Dawn experienced what Elowyn had experienced when watching her sing. More than just listening to a recording of herself, Dawn got to experience firsthand what it was like to hear her own songs for the first time.

Fifteen minutes later, Elowyn removed her hand, and Dawn blinked.

Dawn looked at me, a beautiful smile lighting up her face.

"Best date ever," she said.

"The date's not over yet," I said. "Not until you win me a stuffed dragon by beating the crap out of some kids, oh great bard."

"Ooo, classy."

"Frakking classy," I said. "All the way."

I gave Elowyn the mana vial as payment, and led Dawn by the hand toward the dragon pit.

Dawn grinned as we strode through the crowds. As we cut between two vendor tents, she said, "You know, for someone who doesn't remember me, you know me pretty damn well."

"Well, I—"

Dawn stopped, and pulled me into a kiss.

We had kissed before. The first time—the first time I remembered anyway—was a quick, passionate kiss in her car that had helped convince me to not give up or return to exile, to stay and fight my grandfather. That had been like a brief shock to my system.

And we'd kissed since then, but there had always been a kind of uncertainty or self-consciousness about it because of my fears and doubts about myself, or about us.

But this kiss was like rebirth.

I felt in that moment as though Dawn drew my life energy into her, and poured hers back into me. I became acutely aware of the feel of her, the smell of her, the warm enveloping presence of her. Hunger filled me for more of her kiss. I pressed myself into her and pulled her into me.

The kiss ebbed and surged from deep to playfully light and back again, like the swell and crash of ocean waves, or the rise and fall of the voices at the fair. I soon lost all sense of the outside world, focused only on the warm world of Dawn's lips, the rhythm of her tongue.

Someone blew a screeching note on a horn, returning me abruptly to the fair, to the world of up and down, left and right, inside and out, the world where I existed separate from Dawn. We eased our way out of the kiss, blinked at each other for a second.

I still wasn't sure what she saw in me. I still had my fears and doubts. But none of that seemed to matter just then.

We both grinned like idiots.

"Hey," Dawn said, her voice going Jessica Rabbit low. "What say we skip the dragon and go back to my house?"

I grabbed her hand, and pulled her toward her car at a sprint as she laughed.

## 7

## Didn't We Almost Have It All

Dawn's house was a simple two-story home built sometime around the seventies, with none of the Victorian stylings of my family home but solidly constructed with heavy wood and plaster throughout. As we stepped inside, she closed the front door and slid up close to me.

"Come into the bedroom in, say, five minutes? And then I'll make you *really* comfortable." She waggled her eyebrows. "If you know what I mean."

"I think I know what you mean," I said.

"Are you sure?" she asked, and headed down the hall toward her bedroom. "Sometimes you can be a bit slow."

"Yeah, I got it." I smiled.

"Because I mean sexy time," she said over her shoulder. "Me and you. All naked and stuff."

I laughed. "Oh, that! I thought you meant you were going to let me use your zebra snuggie."

"Nobody touches ZeeZee but me!" Dawn called from the bedroom.

I stood in the entryway, by the stairs leading to the second floor and the opening to the "office" area. Art covered every wall in Dawn's home, a lot of it pieces she'd accepted from local artists as partial payment for a tarot reading or pet sitting or other service. And between the art pieces were pictures of Dawn, her father and her mother all from before her mother's death: some from Georgia, some in front of their old house in Seattle's Central District. Several framed certificates covered the office wall as well, including

Dawn's Jack and Jill community service certificate, and her father's engineering degree.

I tried not to think of his spirit watching us from the beyond.

When five minutes had passed, I went down the hall to Dawn's room. The space looked like a clothing bomb had gone off, spraying skirts and shirts across every surface. Beneath were stacked books, a set of bongo drums, an ancient television, and more items whose nature and identity were mysteries to be uncovered by some future archeologist.

I kicked off my shoes, socks, and pants, and crawled into her bed, wearing my boxers and T-shirt.

I shifted nervously beneath the comforter.

Dawn and I hadn't exactly jumped into the physical side of things, taking it slow as we got to know each other again. I'd had plenty to adjust to, twenty-five years of changes in the world and the people I knew, and the betrayals and troubles of my family, which had slowed our reintroduction process.

There was also the fact that I'd been a virgin until Heather seduced me three months ago, and as wild as that experience had been, it had not left me feeling suddenly a confident and knowledgeable lover. Dawn seemed to have the libido of Captain Kirk in a room full of Orion dancers, and while she made no secret of her ability to please herself, I knew she'd want her boyfriend to be able to do so as well.

And I wanted to do so. Hell, I'd even snuck in and stolen the copy of *The Joy of Sex* that had still been hidden in the back of my parent's closet, despite the fact that I wanted so much to remain in denial that my parents had ever been naked in their lives, let alone tried different positions. I'd studied, and rehearsed this moment in my head countless times.

But while there was no question that I wanted to sleep with Dawn—hell, sometimes I wanted to just rip off her clothes—the question was whether I *should* before we were both certain of our love. Soul mates or not, how many perfect couples had ended up awkward friends because of poor timing and poor decisions—or a terrible first time in bed?

Dawn entered the room, a towel wrapped around her, her smile hungry as she pulled a shower cap off her hair, unleashing the springy curls. "Prepare to have your mind blown. For starters."

She let the towel fall to the floor, then slid into the bed next to me, naked.

"What's this?" she asked, snapping the elastic on my boxers.

"I, uh—" I blushed.

Dawn helped me pull off my remaining clothes. Then we entwined, and devoured each other.

I followed her lead, brushing my lips and tongue across her neck, her throat, her nipples, the soft indented curve that ran from the top of her leg to inside her thigh, and breathed in the scent of her. An animalistic hunger rose in me as I kissed my way upward, and I bit into the ample flesh and smooth skin of her stomach as if to tear off a piece of her, until she squealed and slapped my head to stop. I laughed, and we shifted and turned until I lay behind her, teased my way up her spine with soft and unpredictable kisses, wrapped my hand around her throat, kissed the back of her neck, reached around with my other hand to—

*Take her already!* Alynon shouted in my head.

I pulled back.

"That's good," Dawn said, her voice husky, and reached back for me. "Don't stop."

"I—Alynon's spoiling it," I said, as my . . . excitement slowly fell. *Damn it. Why couldn't you have stayed quiet!*

"I don't fucking care," Dawn said. "He can watch all he wants."

"That's because he's not in your head," I replied.

*I'll be quiet, truly,* Alynon said. *I shan't even watch. Scout's honor. Go for it.*

*Too late.* I flopped onto the bed and sighed out my frustration.

Dawn let out a long, slow breath of her own, then snuggled down next to me, holding me close. "It's okay. We'll figure this out."

"Yeah," I said. One more thing we had to work out.

How long before Dawn decided maybe I wasn't worth all the work?

I turned toward her, and she followed my movement, turning so that I spooned her.

"This feels right," I finally said.

"You have no idea," Dawn murmured with humor clear in her voice. She wriggled back into me, closer.

"I'm sorry," I said.

She punched me in the leg. "Knock it off, idiot."

We enjoyed the warmth of each other and the shared sound of our breathing for several minutes. Then Dawn said, "I think tonight's show is going to be pretty amazing. I feel . . . inspired."

"They're always amazing," I replied, giving her a loving squeeze.

"Sweet talker. By the way, Amber and Barry and the rest want to have a little after party."

"Oh."

Dawn shifted, looked back at me. "What, oh? Why don't you ever want to hang out with my friends?"

"What? I didn't say anything like that." Frak. Why was it so hard to hold on to the good moments?

"You said enough for me to know how you're feeling. And this isn't the first time." She rested her head on the pillow and snuggled back against me again. "I wish you'd just talk to me. I can tell something's going on with you, with us, beyond Alynon. It isn't going to go away by ignoring it."

I shook my head. "No, it's just been a long day, with Sal, and Pete and Vee, and the feybloods, and—I'm sorry. I know your friends are important to you. I'll try."

But I wasn't looking forward to it. Especially not with Barry, mister "life of the party." And though Dawn's other friends were nice enough, they were all mundies as well, so I couldn't exactly share my day with them. I'd have to come up with some lies about what I'd been up to, and I was a lousy liar.

And given my complete lack of pop-cultural knowledge of the past twenty-five years, small talk inevitably led to me staring blankly. I'd finally had to give the lame cover story that I lost my memories of the past twenty-five years due to a tragic head injury. Which made them look at me sometimes like I was Sheriff Rosco P. Coltrane applying to the FBI, with a mix of pity and condescending amusement at my ignorance. And the cover story still didn't help when they asked about how Dawn and I met, or how we fell in love.

*I could help, you know,* Alynon said.

*You've already helped enough, thanks.*

*No, in truth, I could help with her friends. We could Roxanne it.*

*Roxanne it?*

*La! I could feed you words, like Steve Martin doing his Cyrano De'whats-his-name homage?*

*Oh, right, and I'm sure you'd resist the urge to embarrass me on purpose.*

*Fine. But I'd kill for a bit of fun.*

*More like you kill fun.*

*You do know why you really don't wish to revel with her friends tonight, yes?*

I kissed Dawn's neck, then began sliding out of bed. As if I could escape a spirit trapped inside my own head.

"Hey," Dawn asked sleepily. "Where you going?"

"Sorry, I should pick up Mattie from Arcana School, and you probably need to prepare for your gig."

"Well, I guess I could send out reminders." She slid out to sit on the edge of the bed. Her back was beautiful as she bent over to retrieve her clothes, her spine a sinuous line of light and shadow that ran down to—

I looked away, acutely aware that Alynon saw everything I did.

*Ignoring wisdom is the height of arrogance,* Alynon said.

*I'm not ignoring wisdom, I'm ignoring you,* I replied as I slid on my jeans.

*Of course you are. Because you do not wish to hear that going to a party with her friends would be a fast track to Dawn realizing just how boring you truly are, how lacking in anything of interest outside your work. The novelty of the magical world distracts her for now, but once the shine of that wears off, you fear she'll see the truth of you.*

*Unless you want me to play "Kokomo" on repeat every chance I get, I suggest you shut it.*

*You wouldn't.*

*Try me,* I thought as I pulled on my shoes.

Alynon did not respond.

Dawn and I finished dressing, and I gave her a long, lingering kiss.

"Maybe you should sleep here tonight," Dawn said. "You know how a gig gets me worked up."

"What about the after party?"

"You're all the party I need," Dawn said.

*For now,* Alynon said.

I started humming the tune to "Kokomo."

Dawn arched her pierced eyebrow at me. "Aly giving you crap?" she asked.

"Yeah," I said.

"Hey, you in there," she said, knocking gently on my head. "You be nice to my man here, or you'll never see any of this again." She waved at her body.

Alynon remained silent.

Somehow, that wasn't comforting.

## Notorious

I pulled into Fort Worden just past 5:00 P.M. to pick up Mattie from Arcana School.

Fort Worden State Park used to be a U.S. Army base protecting access to the Puget Sound from the Pacific, with enormous cannons mounted in concrete bunkers. The bunkers remained, ghostly gray structures with mossy walls and rusting steel doors and labyrinthine tunnels beneath.

The bunkers were spaced out along bluffs and hillsides covered in thick forests of pine, cedar and madrona, huckleberry, holly and ferns, with a maze of trails connecting the various points of interest. And it all overlooked a stretch of rocky coastline that featured a lighthouse, Marine Science Center, and campground. Altogether, it was a fantasy playground.

To mundies it was perhaps best known as the film location of *An Officer and a Gentleman.* But for arcana and feybloods, Fort Worden had been a critical site in the last Fey-Arcana War. The Fey breached the barriers between our world and the Other Realm and established a beachhead on, well, the beach. It had taken a desperate move by one of the most powerful Arcana, Arch-Magus Katherine Verona, to close the breach and end the war—an attack into the Other Realm equivalent to the bombing of Hiroshima.

With the breach closed, the Fort was converted into a processing facility for all of the new Fey spirits and their allies trapped on our side of the barriers. As cover for these activities, the ARC had influenced mundy policy and had the base converted into a juvenile detention facility for nearly fifteen years.

And now, it was a state park open to the public, most of whom had no clue as to the true history and significance of the land they hiked and played upon. Not that this was surprising. Most mundies didn't even know the rich Native history of the lands they lived upon, and unlike Native Americans, arcana had an entire organization devoted to hiding our history and activities from the world.

Mattie stood waiting on the steps of the white barn-like woodworking building, along with an old man wearing jeans and a faded Blue Öyster Cult T-shirt, his thinning gray hair pulled back into a ponytail.

"Finn!" he said as I walked up. "Good to see you, my boy."

It took me a second to recognize him as Magus Kagan. When I'd attended Arcana School during the summers of my youth, learning about arcana history, the five branches of arcana magic, the Pax laws, and every other boring academic aspect of the magical world, Magus Kagan had been the necromancy instructor. At the time, he'd been a strict but patient instructor with dark hair and an undertaker's fashion sense.

"Hello, Magus Kagan."

"Just Rick, please," he replied with a dismissive wave. "Well, you've certainly changed since I last saw you. You look good."

"Uh, yeah, you, too. So you're still teaching?"

"Indeed. And I was just telling Mattie here that you were one of my better students."

"Yeah, well, Grandfather tutored us constantly."

"Ah, yes, Gavriel. A shame what happened with him, he truly lost his way. But you know, despite all of that, I never did believe what they said about you performing dark necromancy. I even said so to the ARC before your trial."

I blinked. "Uh, thanks! I always thought you found me, well, irritating."

*I know I do.*

*Well* that's *the pot calling the kettle marijuana.*

Magus Kagan—Rick—laughed. "I was a little more focused on my ambitions back then, and frankly resented teaching. But I've made peace with my place in the order of things, and quite enjoy my role now." He placed a hand on Mattie's shoulder. "I think this one here may well exceed every student I've had, you included."

"Aw, thanks, Teach," Mattie said, and grinned.

"Of course," Rick said. "But Finn, what are you doing to further your own education, young man?"

I frowned. "Well, I was looking into some programming classes—"

"I mean your necromancy, obviously."

"Oh." I raised my eyebrows. "I guess I hadn't really thought about it. I've been a little busy just adjusting to life."

"Well, you left a year before Basics graduation, and never officially apprenticed. While I have no doubt you learned quite a bit from your grandfather and the family business, there are entire areas of necromancy, whole levels of ability, I'll wager you haven't even explored yet."

"I know." True masters of necromancy could use their control of spirit to sustain life in the dying, slow aging, charm people, detect lies, and even to kill without resorting to dark necromancy. "But to be honest, I'm trying to move away from necromancy, not get deeper into it." And I certainly had no desire to be officially eligible for ARC employment.

"Hmmph," Rick said. "You can't move away from what you are, young man. And expanding your skills will only expand your options, not to mention remove the temptations to use . . . shortcuts. I'd be willing to tutor you."

"Oh, well, that's—I appreciate that. I'll think about it," I lied, hoping to move off the subject.

"Sure, sure," Rick said, and slapped me on the back. "Well, it was good to see you again, lad. Stay out of trouble, now."

"Yeah," I said. "I'll try." I waved to Mattie. "Come on. Let's get you home."

And then, it was off to Dawn's gig and hanging with her friends, which promised a whole other kind of trouble.

I walked down from our house to The Street. The shops and galleries were closed for the day, so most of the tourists had gone home, or returned to their hotels, boats, or Fort Worden campground. I was beginning to recognize the locals again, though nothing like in the old days.

Accessed by a subway-style covered stairwell, the Undertown was tucked safely down at basement level off one of the passages once used to shanghai sailors and smuggle goods.

My sister Sammy stood beside the stairs, smoking a clove cigarette. She had short-cut black hair and thick black glasses, and wore a Rat City Rollergirls T-shirt.

"Hey Sis," I said. "Come for the show?"

"No, I heard that if you stand in this exact spot, you'll attract really dumb questions. So far, the rumors seem true."

"Good to see you, too. Fatima come with you?"

"Yeah, she's inside. Cutting it close, aren't you?"

"I had a busy day. In fact, maybe you can lend me a hand." Sammy was allergic to magic, which had created some tension and resentment growing up, but had also led her to become a truly skilled hacker of not just mundy tech, but a lot of magical systems as well.

Sammy snorted. "I'm not running interference with Dawn if you screwed up with her. She's my friend, too, you know. And probably still will be long after you've screwed things up with her so bad the ARC comes in and wipes all her memories of you, you idiot."

I rolled my eyes. "You look like a normal person, but actually you are the angel of death."

"Where do I know—ah, yes. Wow, quoting *When Harry Met Sally*." She patted me on the head. "Look at you learning new things! Next thing you know, you'll only be twenty years out of date!"

"And you'll still be a brat. I don't need help with Dawn. But I could use some info on an alchemist, and a few other folks, some of them feybloods."

Sammy dropped her clove butt and ground it out, then headed down the stairs.

"Did you check if this alchemist has Twitter or Facebook?" Sammy asked as we descended.

"No. But I don't think the kind of info I need would be on the Web."

"You'd be surprised. People love to post all kinds of personal stuff online. Because obviously we're all dying to know what amazing thing they mixed with quinoa today. But sure, give me the names, and I'll see what I can dig up."

"Thanks."

We entered the Undertown. It was split into two large areas, the nearer side with a wraparound bar, the other mostly tables and the small stage. The walls were uneven brick and stone, the woodwork looked antique, but they'd slapped up some shiny new decorations over it all, and there was space-age-looking equipment for making fancy coffee and serving local brews.

The place was packed tonight; unsurprising, given Dawn's popularity and the lack of local hangout options. Fatima waved at us from the bar. An Iranian woman somewhere in her late twenties, Fatima had been with Sammy for a couple of years, and she was the only person I'd ever seen who could make Sammy show her sappy and vulnerable side.

"Cutting it close," Fatima said as we drew close. She set down her ever-present sketch pad and pulled Sammy into her arms.

"Yeah yeah," I said. "Have you seen Dawn?"

"Beautiful woman with the curves of Aphrodite and the voice of an angel? Never heard of her. Why?"

"Ha. Let me guess, she's doing her ritual?" I asked.

"Yeah. She said her friends are saving you a seat up front."

"Great. Thanks."

Dawn's friends. I smiled and waved as I approached the table where a half dozen unmistakably artistic-looking men and women sat. Some of them I even liked. Georgie and Amber in particular were a great pair, a couple of street performers that Mattie called "hipsters." Doris, Tom, and Shawna were okay.

And then there was Barry. He had only moved to town a couple months ago, shortly after my own return, but had quickly charmed his way into being Mister Popular. He had an accent that was hard to place but might be Peruvian, his tan face maintained *Miami Vice* stubble, and his sandy-colored hair always looked artfully messy. He gave off the vibe of an adorable puppy, the kind you'd find on the street and want to take home, and was constantly surrounded by a cloud of patchouli smell. Dawn certainly liked him.

I didn't trust him for a minute. He wasn't wearing an ID ring or a glamour I could detect, and he'd never attacked me or given me another excuse to violate his spiritual privacy, so if he was anything but an obnoxious mundy, I couldn't tell. But there was something about him that just instantly set my teeth on edge.

I did my best to make small talk with Georgie and Amber and Dawn's other friends as we all sat around the table waiting for her to perform. Thankfully, we didn't have long to wait, and once her music started I had the perfect excuse to focus only on her.

How to describe Dawn's music? It was like happy folk music written for a child, with lyrics that never failed to amaze me in the way they laid bare dreams, fears, anxieties, daily struggles, and nightly passions, punctuated with dirty jokes and biting observations as might be worded by an old drunken truck driver.

It was honest, raw, and yet always left you feeling happy somehow when it was done.

After the show, she came down off the stage, her smile radiant.

"You were awesome," I said, and gave her a kiss.

"Thanks," she said. "I totally messed up the bridge on 'Slappy Dance,' though."

I chuckled. "Nobody noticed, I'm sure."

Her friends all gave her praise and congratulations, and ordered another round of beers. The next hour passed slowly as they drank and joked and talked about things of which I still had only a passing knowledge.

Sammy and Fatima came over and joined us for a bit, then said their farewells. I stood to give them hugs.

"I'll drop by tomorrow," Sammy said as she gave me her patented pat-pat hug. "We're house-sitting for a friend in Poulsbo for a couple days, so I'll be around."

She and Fatima left. I turned back around to find Barry with his hands on Dawn's ears, rubbing the sides of them gently.

"Right there, you feel that?" he said. "It's supposed to totally free up the creative energies."

I knew every energy pathway in the body, and right then I knew Barry was channeling his bullshit energies.

"Actually, Barry," I said sharply, feeling on solid ground for the first time all evening, "creative energy is focused in the throat."

"May be," Barry replied, still smiling at Dawn. "But let me ask you, brah, weren't you moved by Dawn's music?"

"Of course," I said. "What does that—"

"So are your emotions, like, in your ears?"

"What? No. But—"

"So, just because creativity doesn't rest in the ears, that don't mean that massaging them can't bring out creative energy, brah. Just like Dawn's awesome voice massaging your ears brings out emotion, dig?"

"No offense, Barry, but that's the dumbest thing I've heard in a while."

Dawn sighed, and placed her hands on Barry's wrists, stopping him from continuing. "Thanks, Barry. That felt nice, but the only thing it inspired in me was the desire for a real massage."

"I feel you," Barry said to her in a meaningful way, and glanced between me and Dawn, as if sharing some inside joke. Heat rose up from my chest as Barry leaned back in his chair and said, "Finn, brah, we're going over to Sarah's house for a little after-party, play some drunk *Rock Band*. You down?"

I managed not to roll my eyes. Barry loved *Rock Band* because he got to show off his drumming skills. Apparently, however, it was difficult for him to stay in a real band for long.

Dawn looked at me a second, then shook her head. "Actually, I think we're going to head home. We've both had a long day."

"Ah, come on," Barry said. "It won't be an after-party without you. And it's always groovier playing *Rock Band* with a real rock star."

"Well, if you meet one then you should ask them," Dawn said. "No, really, we both need to get to bed before the sun rises this time."

"So be it," Barry said. "Guess I'll see you tomorrow at the shelter."

"Oh, right," Dawn replied. "See you there."

Barry and the others stood and left. Once they were gone, I asked, "Barry volunteers at the animal shelter now?"

"Yeah," Dawn said, gathering up her things. "Started last week. The dogs love him, the cats not so much."

"Smart cats," I muttered.

"What?"

"Nothing. So, you guys sure seem to have a lot in common."

Dawn arched an eyebrow at me. "You have no reason to be jealous of Barry."

"Of course not."

"You know I'd love for you to work at the shelter with me. I've asked you before."

"I know. Okay. How about tomorrow?"

"Wow." Dawn grinned. "If jealousy gets you this competitive, maybe I should have Barry take me on a weekend cruise, really up the stakes."

"Hilarious. And I'm not jealous. I really do want to volunteer with you."

"Uh huh." We headed for the door. "Okay," Dawn said. "But not tomorrow, they aren't interviewing until the day after. And if you flake out on me again—"

"I won't flake. I promise to go with you on Monday."

"Come on, Romeo," Dawn said, holding the door open for me. "Let's go home and you can rub my ears if you want. For starters."

We left the Undertown and climbed the uphill slope of Washington Street, holding hands in silence. The storefronts fell behind us, replaced by houses and ivy-covered walls.

Dawn smiled. "Remember Mister Gibson?"

"Algebra teacher who completely abused his power in class?"

"That's the one." She pointed at the small white church that sat on the bluff. "You don't remember, probably, but you and I, we crashed his wedding there, and hinted to the guests that we were his secret illegitimate children."

I burst out laughing. "No! Really?"

"Yup. It was all your idea."

"I find that hard to believe."

"Oh, fine, maybe it was mine. But you were always willing to get into trouble with me."

"Well, if you were anything then like you are now, I don't know if I had much choice. You're like a force of nature. Like, you know, a really beautiful hurricane. A tsexami?"

"Aw, you say the sweetest things." Dawn grabbed my arm, bringing us both to a stop, and stepped in close. "I think even back then, I wanted to do this."

She leaned in for a kiss.

I caught the flicker of movement from the corner of my eye.

I shoved Dawn back just as a charging black bear crashed into me, slamming me to the ground. The impact knocked the wind out of me, and concrete and gravel scraped painfully into my elbows and palms.

The bear pinned me to the sidewalk with its paws on my shoulders. It had a white V of fur on its chest, and eyes that looked too human.

"Good-bye, meddling magus," it said with a roughened female voice. Her mouth gaped wide, and she leaned in for my neck with fangs that would give a vampire compensation issues.

## Bad

I dug my hands into the waerbear's fur, and tried to focus my will enough to summon her spirit.

I was not going to be fast enough.

A rock the size of my fist hit the bear in the cheek, jerking her head to the side, but not knocking her off of me.

"Hey, Sexual Harassment Panda!" Dawn shouted. "Nobody eats him but me."

The distraction, and the surge of fear for Dawn, gave me the time and push I needed. My will snapped into focus, I pulled from the locus of magical energy just below my chest, and summoned the bear's spirit.

Summoning the spirit of someone still alive would not actually rip out the person's "soul"—not unless the necromancer was insanely powerful, or used dark necromancy—but it hurt like hell for both the victim and the summoner. It's like placing your ear against the speaker at a Spinal Tap concert during the guitar feedback. Even knowing what was coming, I hadn't fully prepared myself. The explosion of sharp pain in my head, like I'd shotgunned a dozen milkshakes and then stabbed myself between the eyes with a screaming baby, caused the summoning to disintegrate. But it was enough. The bear roared in pain, and fell to the side.

The bear shimmered, and shifted into the form of a beautiful Japanese woman with eight spider legs growing out of her back.

A jorōgumo, a shapeshifting spider feyblood. Not good.

Creepy as hell, yes, but definitely not good.

"Run," I shouted at Dawn as I struggled to my feet. "The post office."

Dawn instead helped me to my feet, then we made a run for it together.

I glanced back. The jorōgumo still lay on her back, twitching. It would take longer for her to recover as the victim of the spirit yanking, but not long enough for us to reach any warded home in the neighborhood I knew of.

The post office loomed above the street like a four-story Romanesque castle made of carved sandstone bricks, complete with tower and arched windows. It hadn't changed much, on the outside at least, since it had been built as a U.S. Customs office over a hundred years earlier.

"It's closed," Dawn said between panting breaths.

"Lucky for us," I replied, and led her around to the back entrance by the loading dock. I turned my persona ring around on my finger and placed the black stone into a small indent in the archway.

A click, and the metal door swung open. "Come on," I said, and pushed my way inside. I heard a skittering sound behind me that caused the hairs on my arms to stand up. I slammed the door shut behind us.

The jorōgumo, or perhaps a small rhinoceros, crashed into the door, causing a hellish squealing noise as brick dust sifted down from the wall above.

"Ah crap, follow me."

I led Dawn up the stairs to the main hall. We ran down the worn marble floor past a row of teller windows held in an ornate wooden structure. It looked like the kind of place where Bonnie and Clyde might have tried to rob George Bailey, and smelled of damp wood and paper. Another loud crash boomed from the back door as we rounded the corner into the room of post office boxes.

Hand-sized rectangles of tarnished brass with multi-hued number plates covered one entire wall, matching the honey-colored wood surrounding them. I hurried over to the wall, searching for the correct two boxes.

Dawn raised her eyebrows. "I assume you have something magical up your sleeve and aren't just checking your mail?"

"Actually," I said, "I forgot I'd ordered an Oingo Boingo tape before exile and want to see if it's still here."

"So, let you concentrate, then?"

"Wouldn't hurt." I found the numbers I needed—the dates of two major Fey-Arcana wars. I touched the two plates, summoned up more magical energy, and said, *"Aperire Ostium!"*

A series of soft clanks and clicks vibrated the floor beneath me, and several rows of floor tiles began sinking at the floor's center, slowly forming a staircase.

Too slowly.

A loud crash echoed through the post office, followed by the clanging of the door bouncing across the floor, and a screech of triumph. I pointed to the stairs. "As soon as those stop moving, run down them and touch the metal plate on the wall at the bottom."

"But—"

"Dawn, just do it! Please!"

I ran back into the main hall. The jorōgumo skittered toward me, her spider legs carrying her human form suspended above the floor.

Dawn wouldn't escape if we fled together. I had to stop the creature so she had time to get away.

I placed my hand on the nearby wall, and summoned the building's spirit.

This was going to leave me with a Tetsuo-sized headache.

Not every building has a spirit, at least not one strong or cohesive enough to be summoned. And spirit might not be the best word. It isn't really the same as with a living being, whose spirit grows and changes with them based on their choices and experiences. The spirit of an old building like this was more a built-up residue of often-repeated emotions and strong thoughts, which after enough time formed a kind of patchwork ghost.

The building's presence manifested, rolling over me like the heat wave from an opened oven, if what was being baked in that oven was a triple-layer emotion cake. Impatience, anticipation, dread, hope, frustration—I nearly staggered beneath the weight of it all.

"Spirit!" I said, Talking to the post office. Life and magic both drained from me, a sensation like spiritual peeing, except it was not very relieving to have my life trickling away bit by bit. Such was the cost of Talking to spirits.

There was no response. I'd feared as much. It was too much to hope that the building would understand human speech.

I took my fear for Dawn and myself and projected it at the spirit. And I focused that fear around the jorōgumo, and then imagined fire, and earthquake, and rats, and wild children with hammers, and real estate developers—anything I thought a building might fear.

The spirit rolled over me, past me, and I could sense it descending on the jorōgumo, concentrating its overwhelming presence on that creature.

The jorōgumo stumbled and fell, its eight legs entangling and curling inward. She put her hands to her head, and screamed.

"Come on!" Dawn said behind me.

I spun around. "Dawn! Damn it! Run!"

Dawn held a brass pole normally used to support a rope barrier, wielding it like a club. "We leave together."

"Fine! Go, I'm—"

The weight of the building's fear slammed back into me, knocking me to the ground. It was not just Dawn's distraction. I realized I'd been a fool to think I could control it. I was no master necromancer, just a half-trained idiot, and the building's spirit lashed out wildly now.

I released the summoning, and the ghost dissipated.

The jorōgumo rose and skittered toward me drunkenly, her woman's body swaying back and forth as her spider legs held it suspended in air. Dawn grabbed my arm, pulled up. I struggled to my feet and tried to push her back toward the escape.

Too late. The jorōgumo reached us. Dawn swung hard at the nearest spider leg, a black shell-like scythe thick as my thigh and covered in a scattering of wiry hairs. The jorōgumo moved swifter still, jerking the leg back.

And then the jorōgumo plunged her spear-like foot through Dawn's shoulder, slamming Dawn back to the ground.

"NO!"

I lunged for the jorōgumo's nearest leg. The hairs felt like steel wire as my hand pressed against them, and I could feel them cutting into my palm and fingers as I pressed past them to the hard shell of the leg.

A huge surge of anger and fear poured through me and mixed with my magic and will, like napalm mixing with a pissed-off biker gang.

I ripped the bitch's soul out. Or at least, I tried.

The jorōgumo screamed, and the scream cut off like someone had pulled her plug. She fell back, her foot ripping free of Dawn's body. I could feel her spirit, stretched, still screaming, like steel cord being pulled past its endurance.

But I was not strong enough. Not even close. The spirit rebounded, nearly pulled my spirit free in return.

I released the summoning and collapsed to my knees, fighting the urge to vomit as the jorōgumo twitched.

Dawn moaned.

"Dawn!" I scrambled over to her. Blood pooled on the floor behind her.

I pressed my hand to the wound, but there was nothing I could do to stop the blood seeping between my fingers. I had no skill with magical healing.

"Ow." She winced, then said in a dreamy, detached voice, "Help, I've fallen, and I can't get up."

The jorōgumo jerked, and sucked in air with a hiss.

"Dawn, come on, I'm sorry, we have to move."

I lifted her, as she had lifted me just a moment ago. She cried out in pain, but struggled to her feet, and together we stumbled over to the hidden stairwell and down it. When we reached the tunnel at its bottom I slammed my hand against the metal plate on the wall, and the stairs rose on pillars of stone. I saw the jorōgumo's furious face just before the entrance to the stairwell sealed closed, and her scream of frustration could be heard over the grinding of stone settling back into place.

"Damn you and your stubbornness," I said to Dawn, and pulled off my shirt, pressing it to her wound.

Dawn began to shiver, and said with chattering teeth, "If I w-weren't stubborn, I w-wouldn't still b-be with you."

*That's certain true.*

"Ha ha. How about you use it for something good and don't die on me then," I said, and helped her as we marched down the tunnel. "Because if you do, you know I'll summon you up and chew you out."

We hurried as well as Dawn could manage. The feybloods used the tunnels heavily, but I doubted the jorōgumo could open the wizard door we'd used. Still, best not to linger, especially with Dawn leaking blood. Her steps grew increasingly heavy and sluggish, her eyes drooping.

I shook her. "Hey. Talk to me."

"What was that thing?" Dawn asked finally, her words slurred.

"A jorōgumo. A true shapeshifter, able to take any shape she wishes whenever she wishes. Rare, and very dangerous."

"Gee, really? I'll be careful then." After several steps, she asked, "Why the hell was a jorōgumby thingy attacking you?"

"Good question."

*She called you a meddler,* Alynon said.

*Yeah, I caught that.* I thought about it a minute. "Maybe . . . it's because I agreed to help Silene and her feybloods, and somebody doesn't want that. The Arcanites maybe, if they're behind the addictions. Or the alchemist, if he's got something to hide. Or maybe some group in the ARC or Fey who wants to keep the feybloods from getting ideas of equality. Or—crap, I don't know."

"Don't sound so unhappy," Dawn said. "Looks like you're finally popular!"

"Oh, yeah, it's awesome. I love the 'who's trying to kill Finn' game."

"Oh, that's easy," Dawn replied in a sleepy voice. "Clowns. Trust me, you dig deep enough, you're going to find out it's clowns."

"I'll keep that in mind."

"You do tha—" Her voice faded out, and she slumped against me.

"Hey!" I said, panic rising in my chest. "Stay with me!" I summoned up my magic, and gave her a slight jolt of my own life energy.

Her head jerked back up, and she blinked. "Did you just ask me to live with you?" she asked, and we continued to stumble forward together.

"Sure. You can share my twin bed."

"I'm the luckiest," Dawn mumbled.

There was no way we were going to make it to the hospital. I took the next exit from the tunnel, a sloping ramp that ended at a wall behind the old theater, and half-carried Dawn to the nearby house of a local thaumaturge.

Jared had a questionable reputation among the arcana community, and looked like Christopher Walken's creepier brother, but I didn't care about the rumors of how he'd learned his skills just then, only that he had them and was close by. After a quick negotiation, he worked on a little wax "voodoo" doll, forming a wound to match Dawn's then closing it again. Dawn's flesh knit together, like a reversed film of taffy being pulled apart, and she screamed so loud and so long I worried about her voice. But in the end she slumped down on Jared's couch, covered in sweat, her wound and eyes both closed, and her breathing steady.

We reached Dawn's home two hours later. She'd slept over an hour on Jared's couch, then drunk a pint of orange juice before leaving. Exhaustion showed clear and heavy in her face and movements, but she was able to walk. I called home on the way to warn my family that, once again, they might be in danger because of me. I also reported the attack to the ARC, who said they'd send people to the post office to clean up and investigate.

I helped Dawn get her pants and shirt off, and she crawled into bed.

"My hero," she murmured, her eyes closed, her breathing already growing slow and heavy.

"Hardly," I said. "You're the hero."

"Fine. My princess. You'd so better put out after—" Her voice trailed off, and within a minute she was snoring.

I ran my fingers lightly over the scar where the jorōgumo's wound had closed, a line of pale pink knotwork across her smooth brown skin.

I was a fool. Despite all I'd learned in those years of reliving memories, despite the lessons of battling my grandfather, I was still acting like a stupid teenager, running off and getting involved in feyblood troubles like it was some adventure. I was no wizard knight. I was a half-trained necromancer with one foot out the door of the magical world.

And Dawn had nearly died for it. She'd carry that scar for life.

"I'm sorry," I whispered, and kissed the scar.

I needed to grow the hell up.

And I would find whoever was behind the jorōgumo's attack, and make certain they never came after me, or anyone I loved, again.

Um, in a totally mature and safe way, of course.

# New Sensation

I woke to Dawn looking down at me, smiling.

"So what are we doing today?" she asked. "Riding the Loch Ness Monster?"

"You're resting," I replied, wiping sleep from my eyes. I turned away slightly so I didn't hit her straight on with my morning breath. "I'm going to go question a dead feyblood."

"Sounds fun. I'll drive," Dawn said, and slid out of bed. She moved gingerly, but seemed otherwise okay. "You might need me to save you again."

I sat up. "Uh, I think you have that backwards."

"Really? If I hadn't let you carry me out of the post office, you'd be dead now."

I stared at her a second. "Dawn, this isn't a joke. You almost died last night."

Dawn froze, her back to me. After a second, she said in a more subdued tone, "I've done plenty of crazy and reckless things in my life. And people close to me have died. And, I don't know, I guess I got through most of that because I thought I had a pretty good handle on the way the world works, and didn't stress too much about what happened after this whole life thing was over. I mean, it wasn't something anyone could actually know for sure, and certainly not control, right?" She turned and looked at me. "But you've kind of flipped that upside down. These past few months, I've been learning how little I actually know about the world all around me, and that there definitely is some kind of life after death, and people like you can control or even destroy my soul."

"I wouldn't—"

Dawn raised her hand, and winced, rotating her shoulder. "My point isn't to make you feel bad. It's just, the way I deal with it, the way I always deal with crap, is to keep moving forward and try to make today a good day. Because if I stop and just start thinking about it all or worrying about it too much, I'm going to end up a crazy hoarding cat lady who never leaves her house. And I don't think either of us want that."

I slid out of bed and gave Dawn a long, tight hug. "Okay then," I said, leaning back and smiling at her. "You're coming. I'm just going to an ARC facility today anyway, that should be safe enough. And whatever I find, I'm letting the ARC handle it."

"Perfect," Dawn said, walking into her bathroom. "Now, you can go home to clean up, or—" She turned and gave me a come-hither look only slightly dulled by ghosts of exhaustion and pain, and waggled her eyebrows. "You can join me in the shower."

Her mention of a shower was like a splash of cold, salty water, and my stomach clenched. "How about you take a shower, I'll go clean up, and you can pick me up after."

Dawn sighed. "I love you, and I can't imagine how fucked up it must have been to drown. But it's a little weird you can deal with sasquatches, and ghosts, and a creepy spider lady, yet a simple shower freaks you out."

"It doesn't freak me out, I just . . . need some time to get comfortable with it again is all."

"Okay, well, go do your thing, and I'll be ready. And if you dare sneak off without me, I'll tell Alynon your childhood nickname."

I didn't bother questioning her willingness to do so. I got dressed and headed quickly for home.

The morning sun crested the madrona trees surrounding our yards, lighting my path across our yard to the back door in a carpet of glistening morning dew. I stepped through the door into our mud room, and the protective wards around our house tingled over my skin, a feeling like placing your tongue on a nine-volt battery powered by hugs.

I went down the hall and through the kitchen's back entrance. Pete, Vee, and Sammy stood around the kitchen island, each chopping or cutting different vegetables. Sammy arched an eyebrow at me. "Well, look who's doing the Sunday morning walk of shame."

"Shame is about right," I replied.

All three stopped their chopping. Vee asked, "Is everything okay between you two?"

"Yes, we're fine," I said. "I think. But I nearly got her killed."

"I warned you," Sammy said, scowling now as she resumed chopping, perhaps a little more emphatically than before. She was still not thrilled by the fact that Dawn and I were dating. Her day job involved counseling mundy women (and sometimes men) who'd been seduced or courted and then dumped by an arcana or feyblood, helping them deal with the aftermath. She continued without looking up, "I assume the danger you called about last night is somehow tied to the alchemist you asked me to look into?"

"I think so. Did you learn anything?"

Sammy shrugged. "Not much. Except he's a black marketer."

Bat's breath. That wasn't good.

If he was a black market alchemist, that meant he was getting feyblood ingredients via unofficial channels—possibly including poachers and grave robbers. And that meant the feybloods had even greater motive to attack him, and for the ARC to want to cover it up. The ARC didn't want to give the Fey any justification to claim grievance, and more importantly, didn't like anything related to magic being outside their control—or to be cut out of any profits.

Was this black market alchemist working for someone? Perhaps even the Arcanites? If so, he might not fear killing a feyblood if he knew his friends in power could make the problem go away. And a black market alchemist might also know something about the mana drug, perhaps even a cure. Silene had surely known that.

"And she didn't tell me," I muttered.

*Silene? Of course not,* Alynon said. *They may let you do them a favor, but you are not one of them, nor do they trust you.*

"Well, I don't see how they expect me to help if they're withhold-ing such important info."

"You're doing that talking to yourself thing again," Sammy said. "It's creepy, even if you do have an actual voice in your head."

"I don't think it's creepy," Vee said as she hunched in on herself and added in a softer voice, "and neither does Sarah."

Gods, Vee would not do well living among the wilder Shadows feybloods.

And if Silene and the Silver really were getting mixed up in some kind of magical gang war, the Silver Court might not be a good option, either.

Not that they were going to have to choose.

"How are you guys doing?" I asked, looking between her and Petey. "Have you come to any decisions?" One day down already, only two left to decide.

"No," Pete said. "But Sammy is working on something."

Sammy shrugged. "I have a couple of contacts among the fey-bloods, a few friends, but I don't know if there's anything they can do yet."

"That's okay," Pete said to me. "If we can't figure something out, I know you will."

Right. Me, the guy who almost got his girlfriend killed just hours ago. "I'm doing my best," I said. "Speaking of which, I need to go Talk with a dead feyblood and deal with that situation before it makes this situation any worse. If you'll excuse me . . ."

Pete said in a small voice, "I guess we're not watching cartoons?"

I turned back. "What? Cartoons?" And then I remembered, I'd promised to watch Sundurday Morning cartoons with him. "Crap. I'm sorry Petey. This whole feyblood thing came up, and then with the attack and—"

"I understand," Pete said, looking down at the vegetables like a puppy rejected by his favorite boy. "It's okay."

Vee put a hand on his back and rubbed gently.

Oh gods.

"Really, I'm sorry Petey. How about we do it tomorrow? Assuming I get this thing resolved by then."

"Tomorrow's Monday," he said in a quiet voice. "And then—" He fell silent.

And then, they might have to go live in some feyblood steading, or else declare themselves rogues.

"Don't worry, Petey. We can still watch Sundurday morning cartoons on Monday. We're grown-ups, we can make our own rules now, right?"

Pete shrugged, but a small smile emerged on his face. "Okay."

"Awesome. Okay, the sooner I get this over with, the better and safer I'll feel."

I went up to my room, grabbed a change of clothes, and cleaned up in the upstairs bathroom. As I exited to the hall, I sensed a spiritual presence once again coming from the direction of Mort's room.

I really didn't have time to deal with whatever Mort's issue was. But if the Arcanites were involved with the jorōgumo attack, what if they were also influencing Mort, like they'd influenced my father before?

I dropped off my stuff in my room, then went to his door and raised my hand to knock.

I stopped.

Given my recent experience, I was done giving Mort the benefit of the doubt.

I pulled out my skeleton key, hanging on a cord around my neck. An ancient necromantic artifact made from the fingerbone of a thief, it too had once been Zeke's, but Vee had gifted it to me. It was creepy, but handy (or at least fingery). I touched it to the doorknob, and the door unlocked with a soft click. I focused my will, called up and readied the well of magic from the locus of my being, and threw open Mort's door.

Mort's bedroom had the warmth and softness of a Cylon base star, decorated entirely in black and shiny silver, dominated by a television the size of a starship view screen. Mort lay on his back, entangled in his black sheets and comforter, writhing with his eyes closed, and—thank every god and goddess that ever existed— wearing his black satin pajamas.

And mounted on top of him, a woman's spirit undulated in sinuous rhythm to Mort's writhing, her eyes closed and her head thrown back as her red hair floated out in a wavy cloud behind her. With each thrusting undulation, I could see with my arcana senses a trickle of Mort's life energy being drawn up into her.

By Crom!

*Holy—can we get in on this?* Alynon pleaded.

"Mort!" I shouted.

Both Mort and the spirit opened their eyes with a start, and stared at me. Mort looked dazed and confused, like he'd just tumbled all the way down the stairway to heaven and hit his head on every step. The spirit looked more "Black Dog." Her eyes practically glowed red, and her face was distorted, the soft beauty replaced with a look both demonic and ravenous.

She flew at me, hands grasping, mouth stretching impossibly wide.

I threw my will against her like a shield. She slammed into it and fell back, and I felt her spiritual resonance shiver over me, one of insatiable hunger and lust, but the shield forged of my will and magic held strong.

I grasped at the spirit trap hanging from around my neck, and lifted the twisted silver box. I focused my will, reached through the trap—

"Stop!" Mort called out, breaking my concentration. The spirit lurched forward, and I threw up my will again, stopping her reaching fingers less than a foot from my throat.

"Are you crazy?" I shouted, but realized Mort wasn't talking to me. The spirit looked from me to Mort, and her face rippled between demonic and beautiful and back again.

*La, I bet she's a demon in bed. Literally!* Alynon said.

*Stop distracting me, I need to focus!*

"Brianne, please!" Mort said, pushing himself weakly up onto his elbow. "Go!"

He was on a first-name basis with this thing?

Brianne looked at me, and I knew I had only a second to act. I raised the trap, and reached out through it once again to summon the succubus—

Brianne screamed—whether a cry of anger or a wail of despair I couldn't tell—and flew out of the window before my magic touched her.

"What the hell?" She should not have been able to pass through the wards that surrounded our home's exterior without being destroyed. They were meant to keep in the spirits we worked with as much as any enemies out. Yet I heard and sensed her fading away beyond the wall, fleeing.

*Clearly, your brother granted her free passage,* Alynon said. *And again, why did cruel fate trap me within the boring brother?*

Screw you, I thought at him.

*Promises promises.*

Mort slid from his bed and practically fell to his knees. He caught himself on the edge of the bed and pushed himself back erect, though thankfully only in posture. He looked terribly thin, less like early Spock now and more crow-like with his gaunt face and beak of a nose, and I thought I spotted a few glints of silver in his thinning black hair.

He glared at me. "What the hell are you doing?" he demanded. "Who said you could just bust into my room?"

"Are you kidding me?" I waved after the departed Brianne. "What the hell were you doing letting a succubus feed on you? And why are you on a first-name basis with her?"

"She's not a succubus," he said.

"I think I know a succubus when I see one," I replied.

"She's my—she's none of your business."

"Like hell she isn't! Even if I wasn't your brother and, for some weird reason, actually worried about you, I'm a necromancer. I can't just stand by and let a succubus run loose."

"She's not a succubus!" Mort shouted, his face flushing red.

"Then explain what I just saw."

"Get out of my room."

Sammy and Pete both appeared in the doorway behind me, Pete carrying the family's silver sword.

"What's going on?" Sammy asked.

I looked from her to Mort. "Just what I was asking. I came in and found Mort having sex with a spirit named Brianne who, as far as I can tell, was a succubus."

"Seriously?" Sammy asked Mort, disgust in her voice. "The Internet porn wasn't enough for you?"

Mort sagged down to sit on the edge of the bed, his head hanging as if too heavy to hold upright. "It isn't like that. Brianne is—she's my spirit wife."

"Your what now?" I asked.

"I—she's the spirit who possessed Mattie's mother during conception."

"What the hell?" Sammy said. "Did you use possession to rape Mattie's mother?"

"No! Finn can explain it."

"Um, no, I can't," I said.

Mort looked up, surprised. "You mean you don't know? You really don't know, about Mother, about the . . . ritual?"

I felt a sinking feeling in my gut as Sammy demanded, "What about Mother?"

Mort waved at me. "Why do you think he's got the Talker gift, and none of us do?"

*Hold, you truly did not know?* Alynon laughed in my head. *Oh Bright, that explains so much.*

"Stop playing Riddler and just tell us!" I snapped.

Mort sighed. "You know the Talker gift is rare. But if during . . . conception the mother is possessed by a spirit, it's much more likely to manifest." He raised his hands defensively as Sammy sucked in an angry breath. "It was totally voluntary on everyone's part, at least for us."

"You're saying . . . Mother was possessed by a spirit when I was conceived?" I asked.

"As far as I know," Mort replied. "For obvious reasons, it isn't something people talk about much, especially the older generations."

Pete dropped the sword and put his hands to his ears. "I don't believe you. This is another of your stupid pranks." He strode out of sight, singing "Rainbow Connection" loudly.

I put the thought of Mother being possessed out of my head— or rather, it leaped from my head like a stockbroker in a market crash, chased off the ledge by the danger of imagining my parents having sex at all.

"So where does your spiritual sex doll come in?" Sammy demanded.

"It's not like that!" Mort said. "I felt a connection to Brianne."

Sammy snorted. "I'll bet."

"I tried to make it work," Mort continued. "The women I dated after Mattie's mother, I tried to find someone open to a poly relationship, and—"

"Are you serious?" Sammy demanded. "That's not polyamory. That's just you getting your ghost fetish off. Did your spooky booty call ever contribute anything to the relationship, anything to your other partners, except to use their bodies?"

"You're addicted, you're not thinking straight," I said. "You *know* how a succubus is created. How can you not see what you've done? What you're doing to yourself?"

A succubus wasn't a born feyblood spirit, it was a human spirit twisted and transformed through the lust and need of a human necromancer, a creation born out of greed and fueled by self-destructive appetite, like Gordon Gekko, or boy bands. Sex with a spirit was supposed to be, well, a spiritual experience, leading to a kind of soul orgasm. But it was highly addictive for the necromancer, like coffee-flavored heroin, and being deprived of all other physical sensations, the spirit comes to hunger for it and for the life energy fed on in the process.

"You know what?" Mort said. "I wanted to give my child the best gift I could. And I fell in love with Brianne. So sue me!"

"Wow," I said, realization hitting me. "You really did just have Mattie to secure your place as head of the family business."

"No," Mort said. "I had Brianne possess her mother so that she'd have the best possible—"

I heard a swallowed sob behind me.

Smeg.

I turned to see Mattie staring at her father with wide, tear-filled eyes.

"Is Uncle Finn right?" she said. "Did you—is that why Mother left?"

I didn't *want* to be right. But Grandfather did make clear in his will that he wanted leadership of the family business to go to someone with children, and that the Talker gift was equally important.

Mort pushed weakly to his feet. "Matilda, honey, I—"

Mattie shook her head, and fled back through the door up to her attic bedroom.

"You bastard—!" Mort yelled at me.

"Yell at me later," I said, feeling pretty damn horrible. "Your daughter needs you."

Mort began to stand, then slumped back down onto the bed, his eyes closed, his body swaying. "She's angry. She won't want to talk to me right now."

"You still need to try," Sammy said.

"I will, when she calms down," Mort replied.

"You're a coward," Sammy said. "And I'm pretty damned ashamed to be your sister right now." She followed after Mattie.

"Dude," I said. "Seriously, you need to get your act together. Mattie needs you. And . . . I hate to see you like this."

Mort laughed. "Whatever. You're just determined to make me look bad, in front of Mattie, in front of Pete, in front of clients. You want to take my place? You think you could? You don't know half of what it takes—" He began coughing, and it went on far too long, escalating into body-racking convulsions. Just when I moved in to help, however, he regained control, and waved me off. "Go . . . away."

"Mort, we need to summon Brianne. We need to dissipate her spirit, send her on. And then, you need to talk to Mattie."

"No!" Mort said. "No. I—I don't want your help. I'll take care of it." He cleared his throat, looked up at me. "I need to take care of it myself. Or it won't mean anything."

There was so much pain and emotion swirling in his eyes, I felt tears spring to mine and didn't even know why.

"Okay. Okay, but you need to do it soon. And then rest. You look like hammered troll poop, Brother. Seriously."

"I will. Now give me some privacy. Please."

I sighed. A huge part of me doubted him, that he would do what needed to be done, or even that he wanted to. But I also needed to give him the chance to do the right thing. For Mattie's sake and his own.

I nodded, and left the room, closing the door behind me.

I opened the door to the attic stairwell. Sammy stood at the top, and I could hear Mattie's sobbing voice from above.

"I thought Mom left because I'd clung to her too much. I know Dad had to cut the spiritual cord and . . . and . . ."

I started to climb the creaky stairs. Sammy glanced down at the sound, gave me a quick frown and shake of her head. Not a good time, then. I nodded, and went back downstairs.

I found Pete back in the kitchen, Vee holding him and making soothing sounds.

"Pete, you okay?" I asked.

Vee looked at me. "Are *you* okay?" she said.

"I'm just Grape Ape," I replied. "Pete, I'm sure Mort was talking out his butt, as usual. Mother and Father wouldn't have done what he said."

*You know but the half of it,* Alynon said.

Pete looked up from where he had his head buried in Vee's shoulder. "You don't think so?"

"Absolutely not," I replied, as much to reassure myself as Pete. *And you can shut it,* I thought at Alynon.

*Ah, willful ignorance and denial,* Alynon replied, *the engines of romance, egos, and spandex sales.*

I heard the back door open and close. "Hello?" Dawn called out.

"Okay," I said. "Dawn and I are headed to the local ARC head-quarters. You guys want to come with? Pete, I know you love the lighthouse."

Pete and Vee exchanged glances. Vee squeezed his shoulder, and said, "Actually, we just made an appointment with our counselor. Pete's feeling a bit . . . upset with everything that's happened this morning."

"Oh. I'm sorry. Maybe I can—"

My cell phone rang. I pulled it out and looked at it. Reggie.

"Hello?"

"Finn, hey. Look, if you're going to question that dead feyblood, you'd better get over there and do it fast."

"What's going on?"

"Someone's ordered the body burned, and I'm not sure how much I can delay the order."

"Frak. Okay, thanks." I hung up, and looked at Pete. "I'm sorry. Maybe we can talk when I get back? I really need to go."

Pete shrugged, but did not meet my eyes. "Sure."

I crossed to him and gave him a tight hug, and said, "I love you, Brother." Then I nodded to Dawn, and we headed out the back door.

# The Way It Is

The closest ARC facility sat hidden beneath the New Dungeness Lighthouse near Sequim, located halfway between my home and the Elwha feyblood steading. Most ARC facilities were either under moving water or near a power plant of some kind, or ideally both, since the shifting nature of water and the electromagnetic waves interfered with scrying magics.

The town of Sequim was an extremely flat and sprawling collection of fancy homes and small trailer parks, marked by metal art installations of elk, a prominent Walmart location, and proximity to camping and fishing sites. Dawn drove us through it, and parked in the day visitor lot of the Dungeness campground. A short hike along a forest trail brought us down to the beach.

The lighthouse sat far from shore on an incredibly long spit of rocks and sand, and the only way to reach it, beside by boat, was to walk nearly five miles along that narrow strip. This made for great protection against land assault, but was a pain in the butt when you're in a hurry to question a dead feyblood before she gets cremated.

Dawn normally kicked my butt at hiking, proving to me again and again that being fit and being skinny were not always the same thing. But as we marched along the spit she stopped frequently to take pictures with her phone, breathing heavily, and I could soon tell she was far from fully recovered from the injury and blood loss of last night. I kept looking at the distant lighthouse, wondering if the feyblood's body had been destroyed already.

"Dawn, why don't you stop and rest. You'll be safe here."

"You know what?" Dawn said, leaning against a driftwood log, "I think maybe I'll stop here and rest." She set the bag with food and sparkling cider she'd brought down on the sand.

"What a great idea," I said, smiling. "And feel free to eat if you're hungry. I'm going to be a couple of hours."

"Don't go sneaking off on any adventures without me," she said.

"I won't. I'm done with adventures, trust me."

We kissed, a soft, lingering kiss, then she slapped me on the butt and sent me on my way.

It took nearly forty-five minutes hiking at my best speed along the sandy spit to reach the lighthouse, which rose from the center of a bright white house, and was accompanied by a couple of smaller outbuildings with matching red roofs, all on a perfectly maintained green square of lawn. It looked very Technicolor and pristine. I moved to the smaller outbuilding, no bigger than a tool shed, and went inside. I knelt down and pressed my persona ring against the concrete floor. *"Aperire Ostium."*

A passage opened up, revealing a descending stairwell. I followed the stairs down, and the entrance closed behind me.

A young enforcer in his black suit waited for me at the bottom of the stairs. He had the traditional enforcer moustache, but the silver beads were woven into a braid behind each ear. It must be the new fashion.

"Finn Gramaraye," he said. "We weren't expecting you for a couple of hours."

"Yes, well, you know, I was just wandering along the spit anyway, had some seashells to pick up, thought I'd drop in."

"Right. I'll need you to put this on." From inside his suit jacket, he pulled out a black blindfold that had thaumaturgic symbols sewn in silver thread across it.

"What? Why?"

"It's just a precaution, sir," the enforcer said.

*I don't think you are their concern,* Alynon said.

"Oh." Of course. I had a Fey spirit stuck in my head, and the ARC didn't want him learning the layout or details of the facility.

I sighed, but took the blindfold and put it on. Just to try, I reached out with my arcana senses to detect magic, and then my spirit senses to find the enforcer's spirit, but both senses were as blinded as my eyes.

"This way," he said, grabbing my elbow firmly and pulling me forward.

We walked a series of halls, turns, and stairways, until the enforcer had me stop and remove the blindfold.

I blinked against the yellow light. Arcana avoid using fluorescent lighting since discovering that it slowly leaches away both one's magic and life energy. In fact, some prominent arcana are still trying to prove that both fluorescent lighting and cubicles—which box in and prevent the natural flow of energy—were introduced to our world as part of a Fey conspiracy.

We stood in a small morgue, where the ARC brought bodies for autopsies and magical investigation. It looked much like my family's own body prep room: stainless steel tables with drainage channels, machinery for draining and pumping fluids, glass-faced cabinets with medical equipment and supplies. Containment rings. Spirit traps. A captive bolt pistol in case of zombie emergency. The usual.

On one table lay a naked woman with skin that appeared pale and rubbery like raw calamari, and dirty blond hair that had an almost greenish tint to it and might have been wild and curly in life, but now wilted limp and stringy onto the metal table. I focused on her face out of habit and respect, but nothing I'd seen of her body gave me sufficient clue as to her magical nature.

Surrounding the table were a number of artifacts and devices covered in thaumaturgy symbols, or holding vials of alchemical potions, whose purpose were beyond me but probably had some investigative purpose.

Or experimentation purpose.

"That's the feyblood killed at the alchemist shop?" I asked the enforcer. "Veirai?"

"Yes. And we have instructions that nobody's to mess with the body until they cremate it. Now, if you'll excuse me, I'm going to step outside and be distracted for exactly ten minutes."

"Oh, uh, thanks?"

"Don't thank me. Thank Knight-Captain Reginald, and the fact that I trust his judgment more than a feyblood's orders."

"Feyblood's orders?"

"Yeah, it was the local Silver Court Archon who ordered the body destroyed."

I frowned. "Has anyone else Talked to her?"

"No," the enforcer said. "What necromancer would want to give up some of their own life to verify the guilt of an already dead feyblood?" His tone suggested he had the same question for me.

"Right." I didn't feel like explaining myself. "Thanks."

The enforcer shrugged and left the room, and I crossed to the table and the dead feyblood, running through the mental exercises Grandfather had taught me to clear my head of distracting thoughts, to bring my emotions to a neutral hum. I saw the note on the toe tag—SIREN.

That was lucky.

Each feyblood was a blending of an "earthly" spirit from our world and some diluted, descended form of Fey spirit from the Other Realm. But when necromancers summon the spirit of a dead feyblood, what comes through is only the "earthly" spirit tied to the biological part of their nature. Any Fey aspect tied to their magical nature is missing. This sometimes had little effect, especially in feybloods whose magical natures weren't as critical a part of their existence—a siren, for example, who was largely human except for the power her voice held. Try to summon the spirit of a goblin or chimera, however, and you got a mad entity too damaged or incomplete to safely communicate with or command. Imagine Animal in *The Muppets Take PCP*, and you start to get the idea.

I looked at Veirai's face and touched her hand. I could feel the resonance of her spirit. Her human spirit, at least.

"Veirai, I summon you, and compel you to speak true."

I felt an immediate connection.

Veirai wailed, though her mouth remained closed, her body unmoving. The sound was despair given form. It failed to compel me or drive me mad, thankfully, with the Fey siren power being absent.

"Veirai, I need to ask you some questions, and quickly. Silene sent me."

Veirai's wail died away. "Silene? I must warn her! I—wait. Am I, like . . . dead?"

"Yes," I replied. "And I need to know what happened. How did you die?"

"I—it is coming back. I think . . . oh my gods. Silene. She pulled me aside, and told me to drink a potion, said it would allow my powers to, like, work on the alchemist through whatever protections he had. I could totally persuade him to confess his crimes to the ARC and give us—" She fell silent.

"Give you the cure to Grayson's Curse."

"Yes."

"So what happened?"

"I . . . I think I went a little crazy, like full on diva-meets-bridezilla. I remember wanting to smash up his shop, to sing and make him drown himself in his own potions. I charged into his shop, but . . . as soon as I passed through the doorway, the crazy feeling just, like, went away. I started to turn back, to leave, and . . . the alchemist, he totally fired some kind of tranquilizer gun at me! Except it wasn't tranquilizer—wait, if Silene sent you, are you here to destroy my spirit, to silence me?"

"No. She sent me to Talk to you." Actually, I had offered, Silene hadn't asked. But she'd said yes. Which still didn't make sense if she was the one really responsible for what had happened. Perhaps she'd just wanted to get me out of her steading, and then had done what she could to prevent me from Talking to Veirai. Either way, I'd gotten what I could out of Veirai, and time was life.

"Veirai, thank you. May your spirit find peace."

"Wait!" Veirai said. "I finally got an audition for Rent on Sunday. Isn't there some way you can just, like, animate me or something?

Even for a day? If Jenny gets that part, I'll just kill myse—oh my god, well, you know what I mean."

"I'm sorry," I said. "I can't. And I must release you now. Go in peace."

I released my summoning. Dizziness rushed over me. Thank goodness I hadn't eaten yet.

I took several deep, slow breaths until the worst of the dizziness passed. Had Silene been willing to sacrifice Veirai for her cause? Was she willing to sacrifice the four feybloods that the DFM arrested as well? She'd said the lightning strike woke her up, changed her. Had that change made her a cold, determined militant?

Whether or not Silene had intended for Veirai to attack the alchemist, it seemed the alchemist had killed Veirai after all. Even if in self-defense, there were a thousand things a skilled alchemist could have done to defend himself short of killing, especially in a shop filled with his own potions. He needed to be held responsible for that at least, especially if he was working with the Arcanites to produce Grayson's Curse.

"Something still doesn't feel right, though," I whispered.

*What doesn't?*

"I don't know. But the last thing I need is for the ARC to go starting a war with the feybloods because I shared what Veirai said, especially since I suspect that's exactly what somebody out there wants."

*You think Silene's being set up?*

"Maybe. Or used. Either way, I want to know more before I throw her to the wolves."

I needed to force the hand of whoever was behind all of this. At this point, all signs pointed to that being Silene, or perhaps her Archon. If it wasn't them, then I'd need to prove that, too. And I needed to do so where I'd have both enforcer and feyblood witnesses.

I had an idea. A dumb idea, but then, I excelled at dumb ideas.

Two g-mails—gnome mails, I had to remember not to call them g-mails anymore—and an exhausting hike later, I found Dawn making a small sculpture of driftwood, stones, and seashells on the narrow strip of beach, next to a collection of empty Tupperware and an equally empty bottle of sparkling cider.

"How'd it go?" she asked, putting the final stone on the stack and taking a picture with her phone.

"Three guesses."

"You left with more questions than you came here with?"

I sighed. "Yup. Come on."

"Where next?" She gathered her things.

"We're going to get yak slobber on your car."

"Ugh. You're determined to make me regret coming along, aren't you?"

"I hope not," I said as we began the trek back to her car. "Hopefully, the only thing we'll have to regret is getting milk shakes on the way home." Oh deadly dairy delight, how I craved thee.

"Holy frell, a milk shake does sound good," Dawn said, shaking her head. "And full of delicious creamy regret indeed, especially if I get stuck in a close space with you."

What can I say, the ill-effects of milk shakes were just one of the many sad realities I'd had to adjust to after returning to a forty-year-old body.

*You're just determined to ruin all my hard work,* Alynon said.

I sighed.

Alynon had done a nice job of keeping my body fit while I was in exile, but I hadn't done much to maintain the results of his hard work and was, admittedly, getting a bit of a spare tire.

*Whatever,* I thought back. *Milk shakes are totally worth a little flab.*

*You could have milk shakes *and* do sit-ups, you know.*

*You could be quiet* and *do shut-ups, you know.*

*We shall see if you still feel that way when next your back is aching. Or you get punched in the stomach.*

"We built this city—" I sang to Dawn.

"We built this city on rock and roll," she sang back.

*No!* Alynon said. *Okay, I'm sorry, don't—*

"We built this city—" I continued, and Dawn picked it up. She understood exactly why we were singing it.

We continued to sing the song together as we held hands and strolled along the spit, with Alynon screaming protest in my head, then begging mercy, then finally falling silent.

The Olympic Game Farm was just a few minutes' drive from the Dungeness spit, and provided a convenient cover for the ARC's Department of Feyblood Management. Founded in partnership with Disney as a home for the large animals, such as bears and cougars, featured in their nature films, the farm now held public driving tours. The true highlight was the near-death thrill of being surrounded by herds of buffalo and other beasts standing taller than your car and with enough mass to knock it over if they wanted. Mostly, however, they just wanted bread, and left a generous dose of slobber all over your vehicle in exchange. For the waeryak, that joke never got old, I guess.

The waerbears, however, lauded as the "waving bears" for their "amazing" ability to wave at the tourists, mostly preferred to play endless rounds of Chinese checkers and watch soap operas, with their game boards and televisions hidden from public sight deep inside their man-made caves.

We bypassed the normal tour loop and took an AUTHORIZED PERSONNEL ONLY road up to a stone retaining wall. I hopped out, and said, "Feel free to take a spin around the loop. I'll be here when you get back."

Dawn sighed. "Seriously, why can't I just come inside, and then we can do the loop together? Who am I going to tell about any of this?"

"I'm sorry," I said. "They don't even trust me as long as Aly's in my head. And we don't want to remind them—"

"—that I know about them, or they might decide I'm a risk," Dawn said. "Yeah, yeah. Okay, I'll be back in a bit."

Her car rattled off, Dawn's disappointment trailing palpably behind her like the car exhaust.

"You can come out, Sal," I called.

Sal the sasquatch stepped out from behind a nearby tree, the shimmer of his glamour fading away.

"Why did youself send gnomebright for I?"

"Because," I said, "I'm about to get your future love out of this place, and I thought it might look good to her if you helped free her." And because it never hurt to have a friendly sasquatch around when facing a group of potentially hostile feybloods and Department of Feyblood Management enforcers together, regardless of the DFM's protections.

"I trusting youself," Sal said.

"I give you my word," I replied. "I brought you here to help me, not to be arrested."

Sal grunted agreement, and I opened the hidden passage in the stone wall leading to the DFM facility. Once again, an enforcer greeted me, this time Knight-Captain Reyes, the leader of the group who'd arrested the feybloods at Elwha. Without her helmet on, her short-cropped silver hair and crooked nose gave her the appearance of a female Mexican boxer in her early fifties.

"You need to put this on," she said, offering me a blindfold.

"I figured," I said, and sighed.

She held up a silver collar to Sal. "And you will need to wear this."

Sal looked angrily at me and took a step back. "Youself give word I not being badgrabbed."

"We're not arresting you," Reyes said. "It's just the rules. No feybloods are allowed in this facility without a suppression collar on. As a sasquatch, it will inhibit your strength. But it will not be used to shock or subdue you, unless of course you attack an enforcer or attempt to free one of our guests."

"It's okay, Sal," I said, and felt an uncomfortable feeling in my stomach. I hoped they would not make a liar of me. "You're protected under the Pax. You'll be able to leave whenever you want. Correct?" I asked, turning to Reyes.

"Correct."

Sal eyed the collar sideways, but allowed Reyes to put it on. I slid the blindfold on, and Reyes led us through the facility, this time climbing rather than descending. We finally passed through what sounded like a bank vault door. I felt the tingle of wards wash over me, and then the weak warmth of sun on my skin.

"You may remove the blindfold."

I did so, and found myself outside, in an open bowl-shaped area the size of three football fields within a ring of forested hills. A landscape of tall grass, boulders, shade trees, and the occasional single-room cabin surrounded a large pond that appeared dull and lifeless beneath the gray sky.

A fence ran around the entire perimeter that I could see, and a chain-link tunnel led from where I stood to a small bunker of concrete blocks and barred safety glass about twenty feet inside the circle, with locked security gates at either end.

A metal sign hung on the fence that read: Warning! *Dangerous feybloods. No weapons, active spells or potions allowed beyond this point except by DFM personnel. The following may also cause undo danger to you or the feybloods: mana, meat, muffins, music players, silver, iron, virgin blood, salt licks, wine, mead, extreme sorrow, red cloaks, broken shoes, mirrors, riddle books, or firstborn children. See duty captain for any special restrictions.*

Reyes punched a code into the keypad lock, then pressed her persona ring against the metal plate above it.

The gate clicked open. Reyes led us down the tunnel, the gate closing behind us.

A jackalope bounded up and sniffed at us from the other side of the chain-link before loping off again into the tall grass, its antlers bobbing above the grass as it hopped.

We entered the concrete structure. It was a single, open room with several square plastic tables spaced throughout. Near one table stood the four Elwha feybloods—Frog Face, Faun, Dunngo the dwarf, and Sal's potential soul mate, Challa.

Zenith, the changeling who'd offered Vee a place with the Silver

Court, stood among them with her fitted suit and short bobbed hair. As I entered, she finished speaking to the feybloods in a low tone that suggested she was giving instructions.

Dunngo spat dust when he saw me. "Gramaraye. Come to laugh at brightbloods."

"No," I said. Hopefully, I'd have a chance to speak with Dunngo alone, to tell him how sorry I was about his son and assure him I would do everything I could to find a cure for Grayson's Curse. I couldn't blame him for his anger, but I didn't like the idea of someone hating me, especially for the wrong reasons. "Silene asked me to help you." I glanced at enforcer Reyes, wary of how much to say in front of her. "I Talked with Veirai, but I need to ask a couple of questions."

"I'm not sure that's a good idea," Zenith said. "I'm here to protect the rights of these brightbloods under the Pax articles."

"That's okay. I have questions for you, actually. What do you know about the attack on the alchemist, and the death of Veirai?" She wasn't the Silver Archon, but she was in his counsel. If the Archon was involved, maybe I could get Zenith to reveal what she knew, or to lie about it in front of these enforcers with their truth-sensing.

Or at least I could stall long enough for Plan B to arrive.

Zenith's eyebrows rose. "I am a changeling, Gramaraye. Even if I did know something, you have no right to question me unless I've broken the conditions of my visit."

"If you are protecting those who knowingly caused an attack on an arcana, or ordered the destruction of a witness, then that breaks the conditions of your visit."

Zenith crossed her arms. "And if you had proof I did such a thing, then you could ask me if I did such a thing."

I could hear Alynon chuckling in my head.

*I'm glad you're enjoying yourself.*

The door opened, and a DFM enforcer who looked like a buff Anthony Michael Hall with spiky hair led Silene and Romey inside.

"Captain," the enforcer said.

"Lieutenant Cousar," Reyes replied with a curt nod.

Silene pulled away from enforcer Cousar's touch as if it made her ill, but Romey's young face was a mask of proud defiance, and she smiled at me with her waerfox grin as if I were the one being led in at her orders. I hadn't asked for her, only Silene, but we'd see how long her arrogance lasted.

"Good," I said. "We can get some real answers now."

Romey simply brushed at her fox-red dress and patted at her hair as if she'd been led into a nice restaurant. But Silene practically squirmed, causing her green dress to shimmer. She looked like she'd been drinking all night and then had the chili-dog with extra onions for breakfast: fidgety and sweaty and miserable. It was possible her discomfort was simply at being in a warded space cut off from any plant life. It was also possible her discomfort had a deeper reason, like guilt.

She glanced at Sal, and raised one eyebrow. "So they finally arrested you for yarn bombing innocent trees?"

Sal crossed his arms. "So *youself* gotten badgrabbed for being a big iceheart?"

Silene sniffed. "You've been doing the arcana's bidding too long if you believe every scrap of lies they toss you. I've done nothing wrong," she declared to the room.

"Maybe you believe that," I said. "But one thing I've learned from the enforcers is that almost nobody thinks what they're doing is wrong, even when it is."

"Romey was right," Silene replied. "I should never have trusted your offer of help."

Romey's fox smile widened.

"Right," I said. "What you mean, I think, is you didn't expect I would actually try to help, and discover the truth."

"And what truth is that?" Silene said.

"That you tricked Veirai into attacking the alchemist, and then had your Archon try to cover it up."

"What?" She sounded genuinely startled, and slightly alarmed, glancing from Sal, to me, to Reyes. "I had nothing to do with the alchemist murdering Veirai," she said. "And I only just spoke to our Archon this morning. He does not wish to get involved."

I glanced at Reyes questioningly.

"I detect no lies," Reyes said.

I frowned, confused. "But then—"

I saw Romey touch enforcer Cousar. It was subtle, and from my angle of viewing I doubted anyone else noticed. Cousar shuddered, reached into his jacket pocket, and threw what looked like several thumb-sized teeth onto the ground. As they struck the concrete floor, he shouted, "*Spartoi adorior!*"

Knight-Captain Reyes extended her baton with a flick and leaped at her fellow enforcer, but it was already too late. Even as Cousar swung his own extending baton up to block Reyes' strike, the dragon's teeth took root in the floor, and four spartoi grew up in their place faster than the Road Runner high on Jolt Cola.

The spartoi were not Ray Harryhausen skeletons in hoplite armor. Rather, they were living breathing warriors who looked more like naked male underwear models, if those models were thrown into a pit and told the last survivor would get the Calvin Klein gig—heavily muscled and with a murderous light in their eyes.

Romey shouted at Dunngo and the rest, "The arcana are trying to frame us! Fight for your freedom!"

The feybloods growled and hissed and, in the case of Dunngo, ground stony teeth.

The spartoi raised their hands like claws, and let out a murderous war cry.

I stood between them, and gave out a small squeak.

*Oh, shazbot.*

# (You Gotta) Fight for Your Right (to Party)

Dunngo flexed his stony muscles as his obsidian eyes turned to me. Frog Face blinked rapidly, the faun shuffled his hooves sharply in preparation to charge, and Challa's fur-armor fluffed up as her beady sasquatch eyes narrowed in my direction.

"Wait!" I shouted, and then thought better of trying to convince them Romey was the real problem here, and thought even betterer of getting my butt out of there in one piece.

Unfortunately, between me and the exit were four summoned spartoi, two battling enforcers, and one evil waerfox minus a pear tree.

Dunngo charged at me on his rolling torso of rocky soil across the concrete floor.

The spartoi leaped at the feybloods.

I spun to get out of their way, tripped over a plastic chair and fell hard to the ground. I scrambled back as the feybloods and spartoi crashed into each other at the center of the room in a flurry of limbs, fur, flesh, and spattering blood. One spartoi leaped at Dunngo, getting between him and his obsession with hurting me.

Sal stepped between me and the battle, his fur fluffed up and his hands flexed into fists the size of small bowling balls.

In front of the exit to my left, Reyes exchanged a rapid series of blows with the enemy enforcer, Cousar, like two dueling Jedi on fast forward, their batons now glowing with blue fire and sending sparks flying with each strike and block.

My back hit the cinder-block wall.

This was insane! Romey, Cousar, and his spartoi were the real enemies in the room, but the feybloods thought the arcana were the enemies so were as likely to kill me as Cousar. The only beings in the room I could count on not to kill me were Sal, and maybe Reyes, assuming she didn't think I was somehow responsible for this.

My hand went to my chest, to the skeleton key hanging beneath my shirt. If I could reach the exit, I could get out.

Frog Face screamed in pain as a spartoi warrior slammed him to the ground. The collar prevented him from paralyzing the spartoi with his poisonous skin, and he was the weakest of the feybloods here.

Smeg.

I couldn't just escape. I had to help if I could.

I pushed myself up. Zenith had Silene's hand to my right, also with their backs to the wall. Our eyes met, and Silene's eyes narrowed into a murderous stare.

"No!" I said, holding up my hands. "Romey, she did something to enforcer Cousar!"

I realized then that Romey was nowhere to be seen. She'd fled somehow. But not before sticking a knife in Reyes' back, I saw. The handle jerked and wobbled as Reyes exchanged blows with her fellow DFM enforcer, and I could tell it was slowing her down, hampering her movements.

Double smeg.

Zenith glanced at Reyes and Cousar battling each other, then back to me. "If you're not behind this, then get us out of here."

"No!" Silene said, yanking her hand free of the changeling's. "I won't abandon my cousins."

Sal, still standing as a wall of defense between us and the spartoi, looked back at me. "Use arcana lightnings or fires!"

"I'm not a wizard!" I replied.

We could definitely use a wizard about now, though.

Frog Face leaked greenish blood freely as his spartoi kicked him. The second spartoi had the faun suspended a foot above the ground by a death grip on his neck, the faun's legs unable to kick far enough forward to do much damage. The third had gone in low against Challa and was lifting her off her feet like a wrestler, seemingly oblivious as she shredded the flesh along his muscular back with her claws—if she fell, she'd be vulnerable, and the collar kept her from using her full strength to prevent that.

Only Dunngo seemed to be holding his own. The spartoi's blows and grasps crumbled and broke off chunks of dirt and rock from Dunngo, and the collar prevented the dwarf from regenerating or taking new material from the concrete floor. But the spartoi was a mass of bloody flesh where stone had scraped away skin. And was that a rib poking out of his side? It was a race at this point to see which of them lost too much of their body to function first.

I had no weapons, no artifacts, and if I got close enough to use my necromancy effectively on a spartoi, he'd break my neck before I could exorcise the tiny spark of dragon spirit that animated him.

I still gripped the slender skeleton key in one hand, however, and it gave me an idea.

"Sal! Hold still!"

I reached up and touched the enchanted fingerbone to the back of his collar. The collar opened with a click, and fell to the floor.

The spartoi kicking Frog Face stopped and turned toward us. But he took only a single step before Sal charged in with a roar and his arm swung around in a windmill uppercut.

The spartoi's head snapped back and his jaw ripped free, flying across the room as his feet flew out from beneath him. He slammed to the ground, most definitely dead.

I touched the key to the changeling's collar, and then Silene's, as Sal moved in on the spartoi choking the faun.

"Is there anything you can do?" I asked them both.

"Not in here," Silene said, tears of frustration building in her eyes.

"You know magic is forbidden me," the changeling said, and her tone suggested I was still trying to trick or trap her. "But I am well skilled in physical combat."

"Well, that makes one of us," I said. Everything I knew about hand-to-hand combat I'd learned watching movies, and what I'd learned from Mister Miyagi was that if I tried to pull an amateur karate move on one of these spartoi, then Finn-san would be squashed, just like a grape.

*I have urged you to learn krav maga or some such art,* Alynon said. *If you get us both killed—*

*Now is not the time!* I thought back.

*It never is.*

Cousar's baton connected with an audible *clunk!* to Reyes' head, sending her spinning to the ground.

Not good.

"Sal!" I shouted, trying to get his attention as I sprinted at the enemy enforcer. Sal grabbed the head of the faun's spartoi in his massive hands, and twisted.

Maybe I could distract Cousar long enough for Sal to get to him, before—

The enforcer shouted something, a tattoo glowing around his throat. Lightning leaped from his outstretched baton in a concussive, blinding flash, filling the air with the smell of ozone and lifting the hairs on my head and arms as it arced past me. I tried to intercept the blast—not entirely a suicidal act given a certain Fey tattoo that Alynon had left me with, handy against direct energy attacks and not much else—but I was too slow and only caught the edge of the lancing arc. Just enough to leave me collapsed on the ground, my muscles twitching spasmodically.

The lightning struck Sal in the back. His arms flung out, and he slammed forward into the far wall of the room. Black curls of smoke rose from a circle of blackened fur as Sal fell to the ground.

Silene ran to Sal, and the changeling followed her.

I blinked away the purple-and-green afterimage of the blast, and struggled to my feet.

Cousar kicked me in the gut, knocking the air out of me and doubling me over in pain. I retched and gasped for breath.

*I told you!* Alynon said. *If you had done sit-ups—*

*SERIOUSLY?* I thought-screamed at him. I threw my hands up

defensively and backed away, grasping blindly for any physical contact with Cousar I could use to summon his spirit. Pain exploded in my left hand as the baton smashed into it. I screamed and jerked both hands in, cradling the blazing supernova of agony against my chest.

A ululating war cry echoed from the concrete walls, and Zenith leaped over me in a forward dive, rolled, and came up under Cousar's next swing of the baton to punch him in his baby-making parts.

His uniform must have taken most of the force of the blow, because he barely flinched, and instead brought the baton back in a return swing for the changeling's head.

She dove to the side, rolled again, and came up holding Reyes' baton. "Go help Silene!" she said without taking her eyes off the enforcer. She smiled a wicked grin, and said, "All right, wizard, let us see what you can do."

My hand still screamed pain at me, but it was now merely a small nuclear detonation with throbbing aftershocks. Sweat stung my left eye, and I rubbed at it as I looked around me.

Challa's spartoi had her down on the ground, and tickled her feet—the surest way to render a sasquatch helpless long enough to do real harm.

Dunngo and his spartoi were now staggering around each other like two drunks, both looking horribly beaten and broken. I considered trying to reach Dunngo, to unlock his collar so he could regenerate, but getting past the spartoi would be difficult, and Dunngo was just as likely to crush me as thank me.

The changeling gave another ululating cry and leaped at the enforcer, raining a series of blows at him. She seemed to be holding her own, at least for the moment.

I staggered around the perimeter of the room to join Silene and Sal.

Silene looked up at me. "There's nothing I can do. I'm too far from my tree to heal him. But I have . . . eased his pain."

Sal gave a low moan, and it sounded more like pleasure than pain. Nymphs could bring near-orgasmic pleasure with their touch.

Silene looked down at her hands. "I thought—I thought I'd lost it, after the strike."

Challa's spartoi stopped tickling her feet, and stood.

"Frak," I said. "Stay back."

I ran at the spartoi as he moved toward Challa's head. He turned at the sound of my shoes slapping the concrete. I tried to do a jumping kick thing at him. He hopped back and to the side, waited for me to land, grabbed my arm, and spun me around. I went flying back to crash into the ground, hitting Sal and almost knocking Silene over.

Squash, like grape.

The spartoi advanced on me, limping, looking as determined as a Terminator sent back to kill the inventor of Teddy Ruxpin before the horrible chain of events leading to human destruction could unfold.

And I lacked a large hydraulic press with which to destroy him.

I tried to push myself upright, both hands grasping at Sal's wiry hair, my left hand screaming in pain. Something sharp pricked my right hand. I glanced at it. Another damn burr.

I blinked, and yanked the burr free from Sal's hair. I held it up, a small prickly brown ball of Velcro pain on my palm. "Silene! Can you—"

She grabbed it from me and threw it at the advancing spartoi.

The burr stuck to his hairy chest. And sprouted.

Blood ran in rivulets down his chest and stomach as roots dug into his flesh. Broad green leaves sprouted out, and stems poked outward, then bloomed into small burr-like flowers.

The spartoi grabbed at his chest, tried to tear the plant out. He jerked once, twice. On the third jerk, his entire body spasmed, his eyes went wide, and he fell to his knees. His hands fell to his sides, and then he crashed face first to the concrete floor.

"Go team!" I said, turning to Silene. She gave me a weak smile, then slumped gracefully to the side, her eyes fluttering closed to the continuing *clang clang clang* of striking batons.

Shoot.

Dunngo managed a blow to his spartoi's kneecap that dropped the warrior, and Dunngo collapsed on top of him, burying the spartoi's face in dirt. The spartoi tried to kick and push himself free, but his movements grew less and less forceful, until he lay still. Dunngo did not rise.

Cousar shouted a shaping. I looked over, fearing another lightning bolt flying my way. He had managed to disengage with Zenith long enough to cast his spell. Concrete flowed up from the floor and over his clothes and flesh, forming a skin that I knew from previous experience would absorb any physical blow yet flow like sand when he moved.

Zenith's left cheek was swollen practically over her eye, and her left arm hung limp at her side. She blinked against the sweat and pain and advanced on Cousar.

She wouldn't last much longer, not against an enforcer able to wield his magic when she could not. I struggled to my feet. If I was going to get close enough to summon his spirit, it would have to be while he remained distracted—

A large section of wall between me and the two duelists collapsed with a loud *THWUMP!* Dust rose from the pile of sandy debris, and several DFM enforcers in full protective gear streamed over the pile and into the room. Knight-Lieutenant Vincent, the DFM enforcer who'd given Pete and Vee their ultimatum, entered last with a protective vest poorly fitted over his belly.

"Drop your weapons!" Enforcer Vincent shouted.

Zenith stepped back, the baton held above her head in both hands. "I claim the rights of—"

"Drop it!" Vincent said again, as he and two of the other DFM enforcers moved to surround her. The fourth moved in my direction, a tattoo glowing around her throat ready for invocation. I held up my empty hands.

"Brad, report," Vincent said to enforcer Cousar, the man who'd started the fight.

"Arrest them all," Cousar said. "A feyblood started this whole riot, and the captain is seriously hurt." Both statements true, technically. Cousar moved to Reyes, who lay unmoving. As my DFM enforcer moved behind me, and grabbed one wrist to force it to my lower back, Cousar knelt beside Reyes and placed a hand on her neck.

There were a thousand ways he could kill her if she wasn't already dead, and then we'd be truly screwed. "Wait!" I shouted. "He's going to kill your cap—!"

"Shut it!" my enforcer said, yanking up on my wrist so that my shoulder screamed in agony.

"Stop!" I said, and tried to pull free, to get them to listen. "Cousar is the—"

The *clunk!* of a baton hitting the back of my skull knocked my next words free of my brain before they could reach my mouth. I didn't see birds or stars, but the pain silenced me long enough for my enforcer to finish binding my wrists and drag me from the room.

# My Prerogative

I sat in a small gray room with the generic one-way mirror, gray metal table, and two chairs. Unlike the cliché interrogation room, however, it had a line of embedded metal runes and symbols running across the floor and under the middle of the table, splitting the room in half. Wards which, if activated, would prevent most arcana or feybloods from crossing it unless permitted. They were currently inactive, but that didn't mean much. An enforcer could more than handle me without the need for wards, especially in my current state.

My left hand throbbed, swollen and stiff, as I turned it over to check my watch. 1:43 P.M. Lances of pain shot up my arm as I flexed it. And I could feel a lump on the back of my head slightly smaller than an egg and slightly larger than my hopes I'd get out of here without heading straight to an ARC trial for sentencing if Reyes hadn't survived to clear my name.

I hoped Dawn had the sense to just leave when I didn't emerge. I hoped Sal was alive, and that the feybloods were okay.

I hoped they brought me some really good pain-killers.

"What in all the hells did Romey hope to do?" I muttered.

*Perhaps she thought you too slow at completely screwing everything up?*

I looked with one eye at my reflection in the mirror, held up my hand, and pinched the image of my head between my fingers.

*What are you doing?*

*I'm crushing your head!* I said. *I don't suppose you have any real suggestions?*

*No. Except that Silene has brought much trouble upon her clan with her little rebellion, as I told you she would.*

*I don't think the trouble's her fault. If she was going all Charles Bronson on black market alchemists, and was willing to sacrifice her own clan to do so, why did she risk her life to help her feybloods today? Or help Sal? Why'd she heal the wisp back at her tree? I really don't think she's the Big Bad here. Romey is. Or whoever Romey's working for.*

*La, I did not think even a fox crazy or clever enough to attack enforcers in their own home.*

*And I've never heard of waerfoxes being able to control*—The door buzzed, and opened. Enforcer Vincent walked in and crossed to the other chair as the door clicked closed. He adjusted the ill-fitting black tactical jacket as he sat down.

"Gramaraye," he said. "I'll be questioning you under ARC Law regarding the attack on our facility."

"The others," I said, "are they okay?"

"I'll ask the questions," he said. "That's what questioning means. Let's start with you telling me your version of events?"

At least he wasn't trying to silence me forever, or using the term "confession," so that was good. Probably. I still didn't know if I could trust him.

I leaned back in my chair and sighed. "Okay."

The real question, as always in my dealings with enforcers, was how *much* of the truth to tell them. This guy would know if I lied about anything, and would press me for details. I had to find the balance.

"Well, for starters," I said, "I know the alchemist shot Veirai with something lethal, when he could have easily tranquilized her."

"Arcana have the right under the Pax to defend themselves against feyblood attacks with all necessary force."

"Believe me, I've been attacked a few times myself, and I'm all for self-defense," I replied. "But killing Veirai wasn't necessary force. An alchemist, in his own shop? He had options. And did your crack investigators notice she'd been shot in the back? As in, she was leaving his shop on her own?"

"The alchemist isn't on trial here, necromancer."

"Why not?" I asked.

*Because arcana do not consider the death of a brightblood as important as the death of a human,* Alynon said.

"The reasons are not my concern," Vincent said. "And therefore certainly not yours. What I want to know is what exactly happened in the visitation room?"

Was this really just a case of "not my job" disease, or were he and the alchemist in the same group of feyblood haters? He hardly seemed the empathetic type.

And this was the guy in charge of Pete and Vee's case. Not that he'd seemed all that supportive to begin with, but this just made me itch all the more to find some solution to their problem. They were running out of time and if they were declared rogue, then jerkheads like this could do whatever—

"Hello, Gramaraye?" Vincent said.

I had to get out of here. I had to make this enforcer decide he didn't want or need to question me further.

"There was a fight," I replied.

"Cute. Who started it?"

"You know, that's the problem with violence, it's so hard to tell where it started. Perhaps with enforcer Cousar's parents raising him on macho stereotypes of masculinity, or—"

"You do realize the seriousness of the situation?"

"You do realize I have an injured hand and raging headache because one of your enforcers unleashed spartoi in a small space without proper ventilation, and then another hit me on the head without first supplying a proper safety helmet? One call to the Department of Safety, and I could have you guys shut down."

"And you realize we have your girlfriend in the next room?"

Dawn. My heart clenched. "Is that a threat?"

"It is a reminder that we are not here to joke."

Ah, crap. It was so much easier to be a smartass when other people's lives weren't at stake.

"Look," I said. "A waerfox named Romey did something to your boy Cousar that made him go crazy and toss spartoi all over the place. Cousar is the one who struck down Reyes. The feybloods were only fighting in defense of their lives. And the changeling, Zenith, only fought Cousar to protect Reyes and the rest of us. That's the facts, plain and simple."

I waited as Vincent leaned back and sighed. It was less a tired sigh and more like I'd just given him the bothersome job of killing me and disposing of my body to cover up whatever plot or conspiracy I'd stumbled into this time; or, and I preferred this version, perhaps simple disappointment that I'd not given him some reason to beat a confession out of me.

Then Vincent raised his eyebrows, as if what I'd said fully registered.

"So you're saying it was really the fault of this Romey creature, and not Brad—enforcer Cousar?"

Ah. There it was. No enforcer wanted to believe their fellow knights, or the ARC, could be corrupted or even make mistakes for that matter. And I'd just offered a way to shift the blame back onto the feybloods. But that meant—

"Wait, you knew Cousar caused the fight?"

"I know that Knight-Captain Reyes said that Brad attacked the feybloods and knocked her out. But I never believed it was his fault, and you've just confirmed that."

"Yes, well—" I stopped myself. His smug confidence made me want to point out this could all still be the fault of some arcana conspiracy, that maybe his buddy Brad wasn't as innocent as Vincent wanted to believe and certainly the alchemist was not. But I wanted to be free more than I wanted to score imaginary points just then.

"'Yes well' what?" Vincent asked, leaning forward again.

"Well, uh—you're an enforcer. Obviously you'd know if someone was guilty or not. And on that note, mind if I leave? I have a splitting headache and need to get this seen to." I raised my injured hand and waggled my ring finger, flashing the persona ring that now bit painfully into my swollen finger, conveniently giving a reminder that I was an arcana and had rights.

*La!* Alynon said. *Looks like someone dislikes the idea of being outside the comforts of arcana privilege after all.*

*Stuff it where the bright don't shine.*

"Focus," Vincent said. "Is there anything else you can tell me about the attack today? Why this Romey creature might have caused the attack, or how she controlled Brad, perhaps?"

I hesitated, forming the thought firmly in my head that I "can't" tell him, because if I did I'd have to talk about Grayson's Curse, and Veirai's accusation against Silene, and other things that would get me held for further questioning, and I needed to get out of here. "Nope," I said as calmly as I could, and waited for his lie detector alarms to go off.

His eyes narrowed for a second, then he shook his head. "Very well, Gramaraye. You're free to go, for now."

"And the others?"

"Your 'squatch friend, the nymph, and the changeling will all be released if they clear questioning. The faun and Kermit's body will be released to the Silver feybloods for proper disposal. But the dwarf and girly 'squatch will still be held as we continue our investigation into the attack on the alchemist."

"But—" I took a slow breath. Stay cool. "Okay." Challa and Dunngo were not in immediate danger of being sentenced for anything. I could still get them released. What was important was making sure they weren't released into the control of some evil puppet master.

And even more importanter was getting out of here myself.

"One last thing," Vincent said. "You've done your brother and his girlfriend no favors today by giving your family even more of a reputation for trouble." He stood, and I followed.

I remained silent as Vincent led me from the room and down a hallway with numbered steel doors.

Gods, I hoped Dawn was okay. Best case, they'd tried to bully her into giving them information, knowing she was ignorant of any Pax and ARC rules protecting her. Worst case, they'd wiped her memory of everything related to magic, and she was sitting in an interrogation room terribly confused and afraid.

We stopped in front of room 82, and the enforcer opened it.

Dawn sat on a bench beside Silene, braiding her hair.

"Uh, hi," I said. "You okay?"

"As right as rain on a Tea Party convention," she said. "Silene, it was a pleasure to meet you. You keep fighting, sister."

"Thank you, Dawn," Silene said. "And you as well."

Dawn glanced at me, and smiled her wicked cat smile. "Oh, I will. So, we free to leave?"

"You and your boyfriend are," Vincent said. "We have more questions for your feyblood friend there."

"*Bright*bloods," Dawn replied.

"Whatever," said Vincent, and waved her out.

"Thank you, enporker."

"En*forcer*!" Vincent replied with an angry snap. "Show some respect."

"Earn it," Dawn muttered.

Dawn and I were blindfolded and led from the facility a bit more roughly than necessary. We were left blinking against afternoon light as the secret door closed behind us in the rock retaining wall.

"Come on, before they change their mind," I said, and began walking down the gravel road toward the game farm parking lot.

Dawn caught up and asked, "Should we wait for the others? Silene and Sal at least? Give them a ride?"

I shook my head. "I don't know how long the DFM is going to question them. And besides, they wouldn't accept a ride, especially Sal."

"Wait, why wouldn't they accept a ride from me?" Dawn asked, clearly offended. "Because I'm a mundy?"

"No. If we got in an accident, and Sal were injured or killed, it'd raise all kinds of questions with the paramedics and police. Besides, they have their own ways of traveling quickly between places."

"What, like fairy paths? Why the heck are *we* driving then? Gas is crazy expensive."

"Trust me, it would cost a lot more than some gas money for us to travel the Fey Ways. Feybloods are protected somehow by their Fey spirits, but we would be . . . changed."

"You mean like, 'sometimes dead is better' changed?"

"I mean that circus freak shows and the *Weekly World News* were invented to cover up the results of people stumbling across the fairy paths."

"Ah. Well, I don't mind driving then, I guess."

We reached Dawn's old Woody station wagon, and climbed in. Dawn wasted no time in pulling out of the Olympic Game Park and heading back through Sequim toward the 101.

As the park receded in the sideview mirror, I said, "You really okay?"

Dawn smiled. "I'll be better if we can get those milk shakes you promised." Her smile melted into a frown. "What I don't get, though, is why they threw me in a room with Silene. I thought they wanted to keep mundies like me away from the magical world."

"Good question." I mulled it over for a second. "They probably hoped she'd attack you." Anger flared as the truth of that hit me. "They were just using you to try and incriminate her. They want to blame the feybloods—"

"Brightbloods," Dawn said. "They call themselves brightbloods."

"It's the same thing," I said. "They've been called feybloods since, well, ever."

"Uh huh. Let me ask you, how does it feel if I say Pete's a feyblood?"

Not happy. "He's still an arcana as far as I'm concerned."

"See? 'Feyblood' means something negative to you. And when you use it, they hear every meaning it's ever had."

"I don't—" I began to say I didn't use the term in a negative way, certainly not toward feybloods themselves. A non-Fey voice in my head argued that the feybloods were just being too sensitive, that they could simply choose to understand the term was just a name, not an insult—it had been around a long time, like calling the native tribes Indians. It wasn't like the N word.

But Dawn had a point about my not wanting to call Pete a feyblood. And it felt . . . uncomfortable to question why.

I'd told quite a few feyblood jokes in my youth. They were the arcana equivalent of Polack jokes. Mother had seriously disapproved of them, so I'd stopped telling them, but never really gave much thought about why until now.

"Okay. I guess I get it. I'll try to remember."

"Thank you," Dawn said. A minute later, she sighed. "Those enforcers aren't going to help Silene and her brightbloods, are they?"

"Probably not. Not unless someone can prove the feybl—the brightbloods are innocent, and who's setting them up."

"*Some*one?" Dawn asked.

"Yeah."

"Huh." Dawn drove in silence for a minute, then said, "Not that I think it's a bad thing, but I'm kind of surprised you care. I didn't think you liked the Fey or brightbloods all that much, not after your exile, and what happened to Pete and all."

"That's not—I don't know." I watched the wooded hillside zip by. "It would be easier to be angry at the Fey, or the brightbloods, but they weren't the bad guys. Not really. My grandfather was. If not for him, I wouldn't have been in exile. If not for him, Pete would be fine."

*Truly?* Alynon asked, his tone surprised.

*Yeah, really.*

*I'm—thank you,* Alynon said. *It was not comfortable being inside someone I thought hated my kind.*

*Hate? No. But I still find you incredibly annoying.*

*I do try my best. Wouldn't want you to get too comfortable having me around.*

Dawn reached over and squeezed my leg. "I love you. I'm sorry your grandfather was a dickhead, and I know he caused a lot of damage, but I'm just grateful he didn't make you a dickhead in the process. I'm kind of partial to you being non-dickheadish."

"That's me, Sir Non-Dickhead."

"So if your ARC won't help Silene, don't the brightbloods have their own council or something?"

"There's the Archons, who're supposed to represent them, but I'm not sure if they can be trusted to help. The Silver Archon for the area seems to be distancing himself from the whole affair. And from the rumors I've heard, he's one of the most self-serving Archons they've had in generations, anyway."

*La! 'Twould little surprise me to learn he truly destroyed Veirai's body to cover his own ass.*

"It sounds like you're saying Silene's screwed?" Dawn said.

"Pretty much." I looked out the window a second. "And if I get Silene condemned by sharing what Veirai told me, Pete will be even less welcome within the Silver Court than he is already. Much as I don't want them to pledge to any Demesne, if they have to, the Silver's by far their best choice."

*La! Look who's finally embracing reality.*

*Sit and spin, Ralph.*

Dawn drove in silence again for a mile before sighing, and saying, "Then I guess 'someone' should help her. If you can."

"Yeah."

"Just, don't be stupid about it."

"What's that supposed to mean?"

"Dude," Dawn said. "If you don't know what 'stupid' means, well, I don't know if I can explain it to you without creating an infinite loop of stupidity that would destroy the universe."

"Very funny."

"What I meant was, don't go trying to fight that spider creature or do anything noble-but-dumb and get yourself killed. Because, you know, I kind of like you and all."

I smiled. "Aw, that's sweet. I kind of like you, too."

"And, of course, it would be really inconvenient if you died. I'd have to spend, like, all week finding a new boyfriend."

*I'm sure Barry would console her.*

*Double dumb-ass on you, too.* "I don't plan on being stupid."

"Nobody *plans* on being stupid. What *do* you plan on doing?"

"I guess I'll talk to the alchemist," I said. "He's the only lead I have left."

"Ooo, listen to you talking all *CSI*."

"CSI?" I asked.

"Yeah. Cute, Stupid Idealist. What can I say. I have a type."

"Thanks, babe. That makes me one lucky idiot, I guess."

"Got that right."

I hung my old Chuck Taylor hightops on the line between my bedroom and Dawn's house to signal for Heather, then sat on my windowsill to relax for a minute. My Star Wars alarm clock said it was 3:17 P.M. We'd stopped at the walk-in clinic to get pain-killers for what turned out to be a bruised bone in my hand, and at Fat Smitty's for milk shakes, both of which had left me feeling much improved. I looked across our yards at Dawn's house. I missed her already. It was weird, this feeling of absence after being with her for hours, like the whole world had gone dead silent. But she'd passed out as soon as she got home, and would probably sleep for hours. Just as well, I supposed, given what I had planned for the evening—and who I planned to do it with.

I grabbed the Simon artifact my father had made me off the nearby shelf, and turned it over, revealing thaumaturgic runes painted in silver. I lifted the battery panel, and saw that the batteries were wrapped in hair dark like mine. I replaced the cover and turned it on. The four colored buttons lit up in a sequence of six flashes, and the beeps that accompanied each flash caused the crystals to hum in a building resonance I could feel in my teeth . . . and in my spirit. I quickly turned it off as its possible uses began to solidify in my mind. What had Father said? *Over there, other there, criss-cross spirit sauce.* Something to do with the Other Realm perhaps? Or the other side of the Veil? I looked out of the window, letting my mind drift.

Late afternoon light played across the pine trees that swayed in the breeze and the madrona trees that shimmered. Finches sang, and somewhere a crow gave its sharp barking caw. The breeze up here, above the treetops and the low-hanging smells of dried grass and warm pavement, still held faint hints of the ocean's cool crisp scent.

I flexed my hand slowly, then set an ice pack on it.

*How's the stomach?* Alynon asked. *Are we rethinking the whole 'no sit-ups' policy?*

"I'm rethinking every life choice that stuck me with you in my head, not to mention a jorōgumo and crazed waerfox on my butt. But no, my stomach's not bothering me half as much as this whole situation with Silene."

*The jorōgumo attack, the orders to destroy Veirai's body, Romey's attack in the visitation room: your Arcanites could have orchestrated all of that, especially if they are using Grayson's Curse.*

"They aren't *my* Arcanites. And this feels too sloppy and exposed for them."

*Mayhap. Your Arcanites do tend to be more obsessed with slaughtering we Aalbrights than stirring up trouble in your world.*

"They're *not* my—never mind. There are plenty of other groups, both arcana *and* Fey, with their own grand plans for world peace or world domination. I just don't know enough to even guess at who's behind these things. Any real thoughts you're willing to share that *aren't* just to annoy me?"

*Alas, no. That would be boring.*

"Fine." So I would focus on what I did know, what I could control.

I loved my brother, Petey. That was an unshakable certainty. And . . . I might not be able to keep him from being declared a brightblood. But I could help make sure that whatever choice he made, wherever he made his home, he would be welcomed rather than hated because of his family name.

A fluttering outside my window made me look out just in time to see a crow lifting my shoes off the line and descending to the back of the house, toward the garden.

Heather's doing. Or the crow just had good taste in shoes.

## Keep Your Hands to Yourself

The garden filled a good portion of our backyard. Mother had tended it with skill and care before her death, filled it with her love and energy so that it truly lived. Not in an Audrey II "Feed me Seymour" kind of way, but the garden had a definite life and personality to it. After Mother's death, Felicity, our au pair, had also tended it with skill and care, but with the added element of witchcraft at my grandfather's guidance, using Mother's lingering love and energy to control her ghost and, through her, control my father.

I'd destroyed the garden's heart that had animated it to that evil purpose, and now the garden hunkered down like a wounded lion in a bramble, tangled and wild and uninviting, but still holding a savage beauty.

I picked my way carefully along a path cut through plants that might have been tomato vines, or perhaps rose bushes, or possibly triffid-spawn, pushing through to the center of the garden. The green smell of tomato vines and the cool musk of shaded soil hung in the air.

Heather stood there, beside the garden's dried husk of a heart, water pistol in hand. She still wore the long black coat and short black hair, and looked like she'd been trapped on the set of Richard Simmons' *Sweatin' to the Oldies* for two weeks without food or sleep—exhausted, gaunt, and deeply haunted.

"Could you maybe point that away from me?" I asked, nodding at the water pistol.

She leaned to the side, glancing past me to make sure I was alone, then lowered the plastic gun. "So you thought of something I could do to help?" she asked.

"Have you been working on a cure to the mana drug?"

"I told you, I can't," she responded in an agitated voice.

"You mean you won't."

She sighed. "Is this why you signaled for me, to have the same argument?"

"No," I said. "I need your help."

"With what? A potion?"

"With talking to a fellow alchemist."

Her eyes narrowed. "What's the catch?"

"He's a black marketer," I said. "And possibly working for the Arcanites."

"Oh, is that all?" she asked. "You want me to reveal myself to the group of arcana most likely to want me dead?"

"Uh, yes?" I replied. "Please?"

She gave a sharp exhale of a laugh, and said, "You're determined to make this hard on me, aren't you?"

"I didn't make you a fugitive," I said pointedly. "I'm just asking for your help. And sometimes helping the people you care about isn't about what's in it for you."

Heather looked up at the house, its upper floors and tower visible above the shifting leaves of the garden, and scowled in silence for a minute. "How's Mattie?" she asked finally.

"Doing okay," I replied. "She's pretty mature for her age, definitely more than I was at that age."

Heather snorted. "More than you are now."

"Yeah, probably. But she's still a teenager. I don't think any of this has been easy on her. And her father—" I shook my head. "She has her family, and Vee now. But I know she misses you." I looked down at the trampled stalks and vines. "We all do. You threw away a lot when you made the choice you did."

"I didn't have—" Heather stopped and shook her head, and then looked to the side, raking her bottom lip with her teeth.

"Fine," she said finally. "I'll help. But we're doing it my way."

◪

I stepped through the doorway beneath a sign that read TRADI-TIONAL MEDICINES. The jangling of a bell welcomed me, followed by the nose-tickling smell of herbs and spices, and the tingling of magic as a fine mist drifted up to brush my hands.

Heather had warned me of the mist, rising up from a thin grate that ran across the doorway. It would neutralize any active magics working on me, such as potions or spells that might gift me with abilities that could be used to hurt the alchemist or give me an advantage in price negotiations. It was the reason that Veirai had "woken" from the effects of the rage potion as soon as she entered the shop. Woken, and turned to leave.

The shop looked much as I'd expected, with lots of tins and bottles holding traditional herbal medicines staged on shelves and small tables in the shopfront. I'd waited until the shop appeared empty of customers, so aside from me the only person in the shop was the man who stood behind a counter of dark wood, in front of a wall covered in small drawers with handwritten labels.

The infamous black market alchemist.

If you shaved Santa Claus, laid him off from his Christmas gig due to a drinking problem, and made him work double shifts as a salesperson at Toys "R" Us for the holidays instead, you'd get a happier, healthier looking version of this guy.

"Can I help you?" the alchemist asked.

"Just wanted to check out your shop," I said.

*La, I'd wager he has some draught to clear up your little performance issue with Dawn.*

*I don't have a performance issue! I have an annoying Fey in my head.*

*That is *your* problem. When a naked woman lies in your arms, you're supposed to think with your other head.*

*And you've lain with how many naked women?*

That shut him up.

I fished a gremlin bone out of the coin pocket of my jeans. Technically, it was a rat bone about the size of a toothpick, carefully carved and prepared. Gremlins were not lizard-like creatures that sprung out of a mogwai's back if you got him wet or fed him after midnight. If you got a mogwai wet, all you'd have is one irritated mogwai and a room that smelled like asparagus. No, gremlins were Fey spirits from the Chaos Demesnes who slipped into our world to possess and twist other beings into serving their desire for mayhem and mischief. Rats were among their favorite, present almost everywhere, small enough to get into tight spaces but big and strong enough to cause some real damage. Raccoons were another favorite.

And very rarely, a gremlin chief would be strong enough to control a human to sow the seeds for real lasting chaos, mayhem, and annoyance, such as the one who possessed Alexander Graham Bell. True, the phone was a fairly useful device on the surface, but that prescient gremlin chief laid the groundwork for telemarketing, automated help lines, and groups of people all sitting around staring at mobile phones instead of each other. Please push 1 for chaos, annoyance, and disconnection.

After the Black Death, gremlin bones had been common trinkets, often used by children to play pranks. During the past several Fey-Arcana wars, however, a lot of them were used up or lost in sabotaging enemy equipment, and they were now much more rare.

I rolled the gremlin bone back and forth between my fingers, then let it drop through the grate at my feet.

"Looking for anything in particular?" Alchemist Claus asked, suspicion creeping into his tone as I continued to linger by the door.

"Just browsing," I said. "Thanks."

A horrible whine and clanking noise came from the vent. The mist stopped rising.

I opened the door, and Heather strode in.

She had applied some kind of cream to her face that made it shimmer and waver as though seen through thick, turbulent water, so that it was impossible to make out more than a face-shaped blur.

"What—" the alchemist began as Heather raised a SuperSoaker and fired a stream of liquid that glowed hot pink and smelled like the ball pit at Chuck E. Cheese's.

"—the—" the alchemist finished as the potion stream hit him in the chest, spattering up over his face and raining down onto the dark wooden counter.

His eyes took on a distant glaze as the effects of the potion flooded his brain with happy chemicals and played havoc with his emotions.

I don't know which made me wince more—the difficulty he would have getting that smell out, or the risk I knew Heather took on my behalf. The potion even now filled Alchemist Guy with a desire for Heather's approval and happiness, which would eclipse all other passions, all other cares, all other personal dreams and motivations he might have had. Love potions were illegal for a good reason. People did crazy things when they got jealous or insecure about their love. A love potion didn't make someone good, it just made them in love, and not everyone knew how to express love in the healthiest way.

I tried to feel better by reminding myself that I hadn't chosen the potion, or pulled the trigger. And that this dude was a bad guy.

And the choice made sense, as much as I might dislike it. A truth potion would make him tell the truth if we asked a question, but wouldn't make him cooperative. He would still fight us, attempt to mislead with half-truths or to flee and resist, and unless we asked the right question we could miss important information. A love potion had the opposite problem, potentially—it would make him very cooperative, but some people would lie so as to try to impress the person they loved, or to not reveal anything they feared would lessen them in that person's eyes. The trick was to make them believe you would like them more for telling you the truth, and make sure they didn't think "truth" meant saying just what you wanted to hear. It was a trickier enterprise than a priest working in evolutionary biology.

Alchemist Guy blinked at Heather, then turned his eyes on me, and a look of complete worship swept across his features.

"Uh—" I said.

"He can't imprint on me because of the mask," Heather said, her tone suggesting she enjoyed this.

"Great."

*Don't be such a prude,* Alynon said.

*I'm not a prude,* I replied. *I'm worried he will want to wear my skin.*

*I don't know why he would,* Alynon replied. *You haven't exfoliated once since taking back ownership of your body. Again, all my hard work gone to waste.*

"Are you okay?" the alchemist asked me, real worry in his tone. "I can give you a little something to make you feel better. Just tell me what's wrong."

"I'm fine," I said. Heather nudged me. "I, uh—Ralph, right?"

"Yes!" Ralph said, ridiculously pleased that I knew his name.

"Right. I'm, uh, worried about you. I heard you had some trouble with feybloods the other day?"

The alchemist frowned. "That's what they tell me."

"You mean you don't remember?"

Ralph glanced around as if someone might be listening, and beckoned me closer. I approached the counter cautiously. He leaned forward, and said in a low voice, "You wouldn't betray me to the ARC, would you?"

"What do you think?" I asked, not wishing to lie to him. That was another thing about love potions—whatever happened to the person while under the influence of the love potion would leave a real psychological impact after the potion wore off. And funny thing was, people who used love potions rarely did so only because they wanted the best for whomever they used it on. So it was not unusual for the impotioned person to develop issues with things like trust or physical contact afterward. I might not think much of this guy, but I wasn't going to be the one to ruin love for anyone if I could help it.

Ralph worked his lower lip with his teeth for a second, then said, "I think . . . of course you wouldn't betray me. The thing is, I use a potion to wipe recent memories after my more . . . sensitive transactions, to protect the identity of my clientele and suppliers and such." He motioned to a couple of hourglass-shaped bottles on the shelf behind him, filled with a milky fluid. "I guess . . . I must have taken one after whatever happened, because I don't remember it."

Or the Arcanites had forced him to do so, or wiped his memory in some other way to protect themselves as well as their valuable potion maker from potential questioning.

I glanced at Heather, but her mask made it impossible to read her expression.

"And I'm guessing you don't have security cameras or anything like that?" I asked.

"No. I have more active measures against troublemakers and thieves. Besides, everyone likes me," he said. "I'm a fun guy, really! Watch this!"

He grabbed three potions off the nearby shelf, and began juggling them. "Do you juggle? I'd love someone to practice with. I don't want to brag, but I'm kind of ambidex—"

One of the bottles fell and crashed to the floor with the sound of shattering glass. Ralph fumbled with the other two to keep them from falling, then quickly stepped away from the fallen potion. "Uh, you're not allergic to goblin blood, or have the power to project nightmares, do you?"

"No," I said.

"Good, good. Perhaps we should just step over here for a bit anyway." He moved down to the end of the counter. "I like to, uh, smash a potion every once in a while, just to test my shop's filtration system. You know, in case a customer has an accident."

"Well, yeah," I said. "Very smart. Look—"

He smiled as if I'd just announced he won the lottery. "Thanks! Not as smart as you, I'm sure."

I shot a quick glare at Heather, who was doubtless smirking like an idiot beneath her masking spell. I was so going to repay her for this. I turned back to Ralph, a smile on my face. "I don't know. I couldn't make a potion to enslave feybloods to my will, for example. I heard you were working with certain mutual friends on that."

"Mutual friends?" he asked, and sounded more hopeful than suspicious.

"Friends who know the real danger the Fey represent," I whispered conspiratorially.

He put his hand over mine on the counter. I had to resist the urge to jerk away.

"I knew there was a reason I liked you," he said, and smiled.

"Uh, yeah, me, too." I patted his hand as I carefully pulled my trapped hand free. "I just hope you keep the cure safe. We wouldn't want the feybloods getting hold of that."

He frowned. "There is no cure."

"Right," I said, doing my best to hide my disappointment, and slapped him on the arm. "I was making a joke."

"Oh! Got it!" He laughed.

"So you have no idea who might have wanted to stir up trouble between you and the feybloods?"

"Naw. Just the feybloods themselves."

I lowered my voice. "Maybe our mutual friends did it?"

Ralph shrugged, his eyebrows raised. "Maybe. Don't seem like them, though. Why would they want the ARC sniffing around here?"

"Right."

It seemed I'd reached another dead end. And what little I'd learned was not good. No cure for Grayson's Curse. And if the Arcanites weren't behind recent events, then I really had no clue who was.

"Well, I should go," I said. "I have some things I need to do." I nodded to Heather, and started for the door.

"Wait!" Ralph said. "I don't even know your name. Or where you live. Let me just close up the shop and we can go get some food, or—"

"That all sounds really great," I said as I continued edging toward the door. "But I really need to run some errands first, on my own. It's what makes me happy."

Ralph looked at Heather with narrowed eyes. "But she gets to go with you?"

"No," I said. "I'm going alone."

"Maybe she should wait here for you then. Any friend of yours is a friend of mine."

His tone suggested otherwise.

"No, I wouldn't want to burden you," I replied, putting my hand on the door handle. "And this way, when I come back, you and I can hang out alone."

"I suppose," he said uncertainly. "I can wait here then, if that's what you want. But hurry back."

"Thank you," I said and opened the door. "Take care of yourself."

I slipped outside, followed by Heather. The gray clouds building overhead made it feel closer to dusk than the 4:30 my watch claimed. A couple of seagulls fought over a food wrapper in the Starbucks corner lot across the street, and a crow cawed from the power line above us.

"Well, that was no help," I said.

"Maybe," Heather replied in a distracted tone. "Maybe not." She pulled a tranquilizer gun out from beneath her jacket, and shot the crow before I could—

The large black bird fell to the ground.

—even ask her, "What are you doing?"

"Lone crow, so I'll bet he has a nest in the area," she said. "Good chance he saw what went down with your feyblood friends."

"Maybe, but—oh!"

Of course. The ARC had sorcerers who could read the memory of birds and animals. If this bird really did see what went down with the brightbloods, then it might be enough to prove their innocence. Or it might prove Silene had pushed Veirai into the attack.

"Here," I said, motioning for the bird. "I'll take it to the ARC and—"

"No," Heather said, holding it closer. "What if the Arcanites have someone on the inside, or the ARC chooses to have the bird destroyed to avoid scandal with the Fey?"

"Well, what then? Do you have a potion—"

"No," she said, and gave the bird's head a sharp twist. There came the *snap crackle pop* of delicate bones, and the bird went limp. "I have a necromancer."

I stared at the now-dead crow.

"And what am I supposed to do with it? Even if I can Talk to its spirit, I don't exactly speak crow."

"For that, I *do* have a potion." Heather produced a strawberry milk bottle. "Sort of. It's how I give them commands once I've enchanted them. But it works more by passing images back and forth from mind to mind."

I sighed, and took the offered bottle. This was a bad idea. But I didn't have any better ones.

I slammed back the contents of the bottle, which tasted less like strawberry milk and more like the ashes of burnt foot fungus. I coughed some up onto Heather's jacket, but managed to choke down enough to do the trick. I hoped.

I shuddered, and shook off the effects of the taste. Then I focused my will, calmed my mind, and summoned the crow's spirit.

It rose up with a fluttering of ghostly wings and an indignant cawing. Images formed in my mind as the caws thrummed across my consciousness like the vibrations of a guitar string, images as if seen through a fisheye lens in black and white, of me and Heather emerging from the alchemist shop, and Heather firing her tranquilizer gun.

I was Talking to a bird.

"I am Dar," I said, in my best Beastmaster barbarian voice. Except my words came out as harsh caws.

I put my hand to my throat, and turned a questioning look to Heather.

"It wears off quickly," she said. "Don't freak."

"Caw caw caw," cawed the crow's spirit. Images flashed across my mind—of a soaring crow, and a McDonald's sign. I frowned in confusion for a few seconds, then the magic translated the images into the crow's name—Soars over Golden Hills.

"Soars over Golden Hills, I need to know what happened two days before today, when a group of brightbloods gathered here, and one was killed by the man inside that shop behind me."

Soars' spirit cawed. More images: Dunngo, Challa, Frog Face, and Faun gathering outside the alchemist shop, their brightblood nature masked from mundane sight by the shimmering of glamours. Their trying to discourage arcana from entering the shop while Soars cawed at them to either drop some food or go away. Veirai charging from the alleyway across the street, plowing through her fellow brightblood and the opened door of the shop. Veirai facing back out of the shop, a confused look on her face. Veirai falling forward with an expression of surprised pain.

Veirai on the ground, dead.

My brows furrowed. "Did you see anything in the alley from where the brightblood charged, before or after the attack?"

Soars cawed again. This time, I saw Silene watching from the shadows of the alleyway. Silene with her face blurred as if by a heat shimmer.

And then Romey stood in her place.

Holy Batfey! Romey wasn't just a waerfox, she was a true shapeshifter!

There weren't many brightbloods who could shift shape at will *and* choose the shape. Doppelgangers. Trickster gods.

And of course—

The jorōgumo leaped out of the alley across the street, taking form from the shadows not in a memory but in the here and now and oh crap. Her human body swayed side to side as she skittered forward on the spider legs that grew out of her back.

"Caw caw!" I shouted, releasing Soars' spirit.

*Oh shite,* Alynon agreed.

## If You Don't Know Me by Now

Heather, thankfully, reacted to the look on my face before my second "caw" had even escaped. She dropped the crow's body as she spun. In the same motion, she grabbed a bottle from an inside pocket of her long jacket, and flung the bottle back at the jorōgumo.

"Cawm on!" I said, my ability to speak returning as I grabbed Heather's arm and pulled her in the direction of the alchemist shop. The jorōgumo half-caught half-swatted the bottle to one side with a human hand as she continued to advance on her long spider legs. As I swung open the shop door, the potion struck a Toyota Prius and exploded in white fire. The explosion blasted us through the doorway, and caused the jorōgumo to stagger and scream in pain.

I slammed the shop door closed just in time. The jorōgumo smashed into it. Her screams sounded like Mothra being kicked out of a textile factory.

"Are you okay?" Ralph asked.

"No!" I said. "There's a jorōgumo about to break down your door."

He reached beneath his counter, and closed his eyes a second, then said, "Not now. My wards are up. And I imagine she's not too eager to strike my door again anyway. I mixed a little something with the paint on this building that's extremely painful for most feybloods to touch. A necessary precaution in my business."

Indeed, there were no further strikes against the door, and the jorōgumo's furious cries faded into the distance.

"Well, thank you," I said.

"You're not injured, are you?" he said, sweeping out from behind the counter and striding toward me. "I have healing potions, and antivenins."

"No," I said. "I—"

"But he might in the future," Heather said to Ralph. "I'm sure he'd really appreciate it if you gave them to him anyway."

I shook my head at Heather. "I can't afford healing potions, and I'm guessing neither can you."

Heather shrugged. "And I'm guessing he'd be willing to give them to you for free, or at least very cheap."

"Absolutely," Ralph said. "Anything I can do to help you out." He winked at me. "Being my friend has its advantages."

"Uh, maybe if you have something I can use to protect myself against a jorōgumo, something that is cheap even without your friendship discount? All I have on me is forty bucks, and a quarter Thoth of mana."

"I have just the thing," Ralph said, eagerness in his tone. He turned and hurried though a curtained doorway to the back of his shop.

I looked at Heather. "I won't take advantage of his 'friendship.'"

"Why not?" Heather replied. "You don't think he takes advantage of other people? Or feybloods?"

"We're already in dangerous territory legal-wise," I said. "But so far, all we've done is ask him some questions. When the ARC busts him, and they will, I won't have him telling how we used the love potion to steal from him." And I wasn't going to leave him believing love had made him a fool.

"You need to wake up," Heather said. "You've got not just one world but three working against you—the human, the feyblood, and the Fey—and you need to look out for yourself, because nobody else is."

"My family is."

"More like you're looking out for them. Which is why you should do whatever is necessary to protect yourself, and them. Just think of it like one of those video games you love, where you go into a shop and take whatever potion you find in the chest. You need to take the merchant's potions to help you survive."

"Life isn't a game," I said.

"Shows how much you know," Heather said. "Life is a game, and believe me, we're not the players, we're the pawns."

"And all is fair in love and war. I get it. If we're done with the cliché-a-thon, can we discuss what we're going to do?"

"We?" Heather snorted. "I plan to get as far away from this disaster as I can, right after I send a message to the ARC turning this guy in as an Arcanite and black marketer. Hopefully, that will earn me a little credit toward avoiding exile, at least. I have no clue what you're going to do."

"That makes two of us," I said. But even as I said it, I realized what I had to do.

The crow was probably toast after that explosion, and if not was hardly a credible witness. I had no evidence of what I thought I knew; and what I thought I knew still didn't make any sense. I'd learned Romey was the jorōgumo, and she clearly wanted to cause Silene's brightbloods some trouble with the ARC, if not kill them outright. But why? And who was helping or controlling her? Was this tied to the Arcanites in some way after all, with the mana drug, or was that a coincidence? I just kept coming up with more questions.

I'd learned just enough to know how screwed I was, but not enough to get unscrewed, or help anyone I'd promised to help. And I only knew one way to get the answers I needed, to truly clear Silene and her brightbloods, to get me and my family free of the danger of an unknown enemy, and gain my brother some good will.

I had to capture and question the jorōgumo.

"Most heinous," I whispered.

Ralph returned. He held a jar of what looked like Pepto-Bismol. "Are we still going for lunch, just you and me?" he asked, an edge of jealousy in his tone as he glanced at Heather.

"Uh, what do you think?"

"I think we definitely are," he said.

"Well, there you go then," I replied.

Ralph's face lit up, which given its florid state looked like a very pink and unhealthy glow. "I know this great new Mexican place. You're going to love it."

"Sounds great." I sighed.

"Unless you don't like spicy foods. I know another place—"

"No, that's fine," I said. "I love spicy. Look, I—"

"Oh man, I'm the king of spicy," Ralph said. "I can eat practically anything! Here, uh, watch this!" He grabbed a nearby candle, and shotgunned the melted wax down his throat.

"Ahhhmmmphh!" He exclaimed, and began coughing and turning bright red, dropping the bottle he'd brought for me onto the counter rather than the floor, thankfully.

I looked to Heather. "Can you help?" I asked.

She shrugged. "I could."

I rolled my eyes, and started to move toward Ralph to slap his back; but he waved me away, and fumbled at the potions on the shelf behind him as he continued to cough and gag. He found a bottle he liked, pulled the cork, and downed the potion with a good deal of gagging and spitting.

Finally, his breathing and color returned to relatively normal.

"You okay?" I asked.

"Hundred percent," he said, his voice a bit scratchy. "It, uh, just went down the wrong tube."

"Uh huh. Look," I said. "You don't need to prove anything to me, really."

He flushed pink. "Oh man, you must think I'm pathetic, desperate. I'm not, I swear. I have lots of friends. And I'm very confident. Here, look," he said, turning and starting to unbuckle his belt. "I even got a tattoo—"

"Stop!" Heather and I both said at the same time.

I raised my hands. "I believe you. Really. So is that the jorōgumo potion?" I pointed at the bottle he'd dropped on the counter.

"Oh, yes!" He rebuckled his pants, and grabbed the bottle. "Here, it's a gift."

Heather moved close to the door, and cocked her head as if listening.

I took the potion from Ralph. "I can't accept it as a gift. But I will pay for it, as agreed."

"I think it's safe to leave," Heather said, her tone one of mixed amusement and disgust. "Or at least, to make a run for it."

"Wait!" the alchemist said, and grabbed my arm. "You can't just go out there. You should wait until we know for sure it's safe. We could . . . talk more."

I shot Heather a desperate glance. I had reached the limit of my tolerance.

She shrugged. "Love isn't a game, remember?" she said.

"Clever," I said, annoyed. "But you didn't seem to think that when you seduced me for Grayson." I winced inside as soon as I said it. I knew it was a jerk thing to say.

Heather stiffened. "Hey, potion pusher," she said without turning her face from me. "Your wards only work against feybloods?"

"The ones I have up, yes," Ralph said.

"Great. Good luck," she said to me, then turned and left.

"Heather, wait! I'm sorry—" I moved to follow.

"Let her go," Ralph said, and grabbed my arm again. "She's obviously high maintenance."

I shrugged off his hand. Guilt, weariness, and irritation all conspired to put patience in a choke hold. "Bad news," I said. "I called 1-900 Corey and Corey, and they're my new best friends, so we'll have to take a rain check on the whole lunch thing."

"What?" Anger swelled up in Ralph's voice. "You can't just go changing plans like that."

"Watch me." I turned to exit the shop.

"No, I—!" Ralph grabbed me again, spun me around, and kissed me.

He smelled of cigars and love potion, and tasted like ashes.

I jerked away, and wiped at my mouth.

He fell back a step, a confusion of emotions warring across his expression. "I—excuse me." He fled through the doorway to the hidden back of his shop.

*Shame, I thought things were about to get interesting at last,* Alynon said.

*Now is not the time for your jokes,* I thought.

*I was not joking. Far as I have observed, sex is sex and it all feels good. Don't be so repressed.*

*I'm not repressed. I'm worried* he *is.*

As a rule, arcana weren't particularly religious, but that didn't mean we were immune to all the other ways in which people were made to feel shameful of their natures.

Throw in a love potion, and things could get ugly. If someone had been repressing certain urges they thought were "wrong" or "sick," and the love potion caused them to act on those urges, then when the potion wore off they could experience the kind of deep shame and self-loathing that results at worst in serial killings, and at best in fanatical campaigning against any sex that didn't involve the missionary position between a married man and woman for the sole purpose of procreation (and possibly birthdays).

I sighed, and headed to the back room to reassure Ralph he'd done nothing wrong.

Ralph stood with tears streaming down his jowls, his head tilted back as he drank milky fluid from an hourglass-shaped bottle. A forgetting potion.

It probably wouldn't counter the lingering power of the love potion. But it might reset the effects, so that Ralph would fall in love with the first person he saw after forgetting about me.

I quickly closed the curtain, dropped payment for the potion on his counter, and flipped the OPEN sign around to CLOSED on his door. Hopefully, he wouldn't go out, and nobody would come in, until the love potion wore off.

I stepped out into the early evening light, the jorōgumo potion held ready.

Unfortunately, Heather was nowhere to be seen. Phew! Fortunately, neither was the jorōgumo.

I called Reggie on the drive home.

"Finn?" he said.

"Yeah, hi. I—"

"Son, I think you must've been cursed at birth or something the way you attract trouble."

"I see you heard about the fun at the DFM holding area," I replied.

"For starters. Someone also just called in an incident with some Greek Fire over by an alchemist's shop—the same alchemist involved with your feyblood friends. Please tell me that's a coincidence?"

"Well, I can tell you I didn't throw any Greek Fire," I dissembled.

*Indeed,* Alynon said. *You would throw Geek Fire, inflaming a burning desire to play those terrible fantasy movies and computer games you inflict upon me.*

"That's a pretty specific answer," Reggie said. "Which tells me you're hiding something."

"And that's why you're an enforcer," I replied. "I was attacked again by the jorōgumo."

"Damn it. We've been trying to locate her, but shapeshifters are hard to get a lock on normally, and this one, well, for some reason she's more slippery than most. She may even be unregistered."

I told him about her being Romey, and of my need to question her.

"Well," Reggie said, "that explains some things. And she seems keen on you. Maybe she wants to make you her next slave."

"Slave?"

"Yeah. Remember Enforcer Cousar? She must have black-widowed him. Well, jorōgumo-style anyway. That explains why he attacked you all like that."

Of course. Jorōgumo were rumored to be masters at condition-

ing men and women to be their slaves. It usually involved seduc-
tion, though sometimes it was more a case of torture, and either
way was said to include using their venom somehow to enhance
the effects.

"I don't think she wants to make me her slave. I think she just
wants me dead."

"Well, then, maybe we should set a trap."

"With me as bait?" I said. "Um, I was more hoping you could
check out the local Shadows steading for me and see if you can get
a lead or something?"

"I tried that and didn't get far. But with you there, we might get
lucky."

"We?" The Shadows brightbloods would be even less happy to
see me than the Silver had been. Words like "evisceration" and
"marrow-sucking" ran through my head, leaving little bloody foot-
prints and the echo of mad laughter behind.

"You've seen the jorōgumo. If you're there to stand as witness,
I can justify really questioning them, and I can do an unmasking
to see if she's hiding among them."

"Of course." I sighed. "Fine, let me stop home and grab a couple things. Where should we meet?"

"The Shadows steading nearest to you is out on Bainbridge."

"Okay. See you there in . . . two hours?" That would give me
time to eat some dinner at least.

"So if you didn't throw the Greek Fire, who did?" Reggie asked.

"What?"

"You were clearly avoiding my question earlier. What aren't you
telling me?"

"How about you ask me that question in, say, two days?"

Reggie was silent for a long moment, then said, "Fine. Probably
better for my blood pressure if I don't know anyway. Certainly
better for the paperwork. See you soon."

I touched my coat pocket for the hundredth time to confirm the
anti-jorōgumo potion had not somehow disappeared. I regretted
for a second leaving payment for it. If Heather turned Ralph in like

she'd said, it wasn't like my forty bucks was going to help him much.
But I still felt better knowing I hadn't cheated him.

Even fake love was complicated.

It was just shy of five thirty when I entered the house through the
back entrance and into the smell of hot oil and garlic.

My stomach growled.

I strode up the hall and pushed my way through the swinging
kitchen door.

Mort flipped a perfectly golden tortilla in a cast-iron pan. It took
me a second to understand what I was seeing, but he was actually
up, dressed, and cooking food.

"Uh, hi!" I said. "What's cookin', doc?"

"Me," Mort said. "And don't make a big deal out of it."

"I wouldn't dream of it. Okay, I lied. Wow, this is kind of a big
deal! I don't think I've seen you cook once since I've been back."

"I'm making vegetable quesadillas, with Mother's tortilla recipe.
They're Mattie's favorite."

I don't know why, but I was surprised that Mort was actually
right about that.

"That's awesome," I replied. "She'll love that. Though I'm not
sure she likes *huitlacoche*." I nodded at the opened can on the
counter.

"The *huitlacoche*'s for me and Petey," he said while sautéing vegetables in a second pan. "And I'm so glad I have your approval."

"Look, I'm not the one—"

The door to the dining room swung open, and Mattie fairly
bounced into the kitchen. "Hey Uncle Finn! Wow, smells good,
Dad. So what are you two talking about?"

"Nothing," Mort said.

"Uh huh. You two should totally go out soon and do something
together."

"Like what?" Mort asked, obviously not thrilled at the suggestion.

"I don't know," Mattie said. "Brother stuff! What do brothers do?"

"Ruin your fun," Mort said.

"Bully you," I replied. "Until Kelly Lebrock turns him into a pile of poo."

"Plot to seize the throne from you," Mort said.

"Or seize control of your starship to visit God at the center of the universe," I added.

Mattie rolled her eyes. "Maybe you two should watch some different movies. Like . . . *Step Brothers*, or *Darjeeling Limited*. Have you ever done mini golf?"

"No," Mort and I said at the same time.

"All right then, I'm going to look up the closest mini-golf place while you finish making dinner."

"It's almost ready," Mort replied.

"Did you make enough for Uncle Finn?"

Mort sighed as Mattie bounced back out of the room.

"She seems back to her normal self," I said. I wasn't entirely sure that was a good thing. It made me wonder how much of her "normal" self had always been a mask.

"Yep. What do you want on your quesadilla?"

"The works, no *epazote*, thanks," I said. "So . . . you're down here hanging with the living. Does that mean you diffused Brianne's spirit?"

"I noticed you're running around with Heather," Mort said without turning around. "Does that mean you're going to have Dawn's memories wiped?"

"What? I— How do you know who I've been running around with?"

"I saw you two, in the garden, out my window."

"Well, there's nothing going on anyway. I just needed her help with something."

"I'll bet you do."

"It's not like that. Not that it's any of your business, but—"

"Exactly!" Mort said. "Just like Brianne is none of your business.

So why don't you stop getting in my business, and I won't share yours with Dawn."

I sighed. "Look, I'm just trying to help. Honest, bro. You know how succubi work."

"She's not a succubi. And I'm not addicted."

"All I'm asking is that you take a step back and just consider the possibility that you can't see things clearly, not where Brianne is concerned. And that you might be in danger."

Mort did not respond, did not look at me, but just continued his cooking.

*I understand sibling rivalry. Believe me,* Alynon said. *But can you two not engage in a fistfight or something more interesting? All of this trying to help someone who does not wish your help, 'tis boring.*

*Well good thing I'm not here to entertain you then,* I responded.

*Apologies. You are right. I could be more helpful, I suppose.*

*That might be a nice change.*

*La. Then here is my advice. You sleep with Brianne. Then Mort will see her for what she truly is.*

I sighed. *Nice try.*

"Maybe," Mort agreed finally. "Maybe things *have* gotten a little out of control with Brianne. I'll consider it."

I stared. Wow.

"That's all we're asking," I said.

"Dinner is ready," he replied. "You can do the dishes, since I cooked."

I rolled my eyes. "So great to have you back."

# Who's That Girl

The local Forest of Shadows steading was an estate lurking about an hour and a half's drive south on Bainbridge Island.

From Dawn's description, Bainbridge had become a forested island struggling to retain its soul. Located a ferry ride away from the heart of downtown Seattle, it attracted commuters and retirees, and others torn between the desire to get away from the bustle of the city versus the need or desire for the city's amenities. Mansions dotted the hillsides, their perfectly landscaped and decorated façades often inhabited by lonely women whose husbands lived and worked in the city in order to afford the house, the landscaping, and the decorations. A small native presence, a well-supported artist community, and the "locals" filled modest homes, apartments, and trailers tucked back in forested vales and side roads, well hidden yet slowly being pushed out by the effects of gentrification and development.

I arrived at the Shadows steading at about a quarter after seven, less than two hours before sunset. Secluded back in the forest surrounding the Gazzam Lake Preserve, the steading held an old barn-like home with outbuildings, and easy access to woods, lake, and the Puget Sound for the brightbloods whose natures required it. I stopped by the side of the forest road, and parked behind Reggie at the foot of the driveway leading up to the steading's buildings.

Reggie dismounted his Harley, a fancy beast with more chrome and detailed flare than a disco ball falling into a supernova.

"Let me do the talking, Gramaraye," he said as he pulled off his helmet and ran a hand across his bald head. A middle-aged black man dressed FBI-style with the attitude to match, Reggie wore the traditional enforcer moustache with silver beads woven into the ends, and had a pale scar across his scalp from the battle three months ago in which he lost both his rookie partner, Jo, and his ex-partner (and ex-lover), Zeke.

That had not been a great day.

"Please, talk away," I replied. "Just, uh, maybe don't mention my last name in front of them."

He raised his eyebrows. "Why's that?"

"The Gramaraye name seems to be unpopular among the brightbloods these days. I'm trying to change that, though."

"Brightbloods, huh?" He set the helmet on his motorcycle, and we strode up the driveway. "Well, let's go make some new friends."

A Japanese girl, maybe ten years old and wearing a dress printed with butterflies, jumped rope at the top of the drive as we approached.

"She could be Romey," I whispered.

"Close," Reggie whispered back. "She is jorōgumo, and she's had a number of complaints. Name's Kaminari though, and she's the one that gave me the runaround last time."

The girl smiled as we drew closer, and started speaking to the rhythm of her jumps, "One, two, three, four, why'd you come back for?"

"I want to talk to whoever's in charge here," Reggie replied.

She gave me a quick glance, then looked Reggie up and down, her eyes lingering on his enforcer moustache.

"I'm the girl who's on top. Whatchu want, Tootsie Pop?"

"Great," Reggie muttered. His right hand pushed back the edge of his leather jacket and came to rest on the baton holstered at his hip. "What I want is to know why one of your fellow jorōgumo's been running around causing trouble, and why I shouldn't just stomp on her spider ass?"

Kaminari smiled, her mouth stretching just a bit too wide. In a voice as sweet and chilling as an Icee brain freeze, she said, "Harm my sister and I'll kill you, mister."

Sister? Awesome.

Not.

"Well, that's progress," Reggie said. "Thanks for confirming she comes from your steading. Now maybe you can tell me why your sister has been attacking arcana, or tried to sabotage a feyblood protest at an alchemist's shop?"

"Cin-der-ella, dressed in yella," she replied. "Take off or I'll kiss you fella."

"I'd like to see you try," Reggie said.

The girl blinked, and her eyes went all black.

Crap.

I clapped my hands to the rhythm of her jumps, and said, "I went downtown, to see Miss Brown. She gave me a nickel, to buy a pickle." Kaminari looked at me and blinked as though surprised, and her eyes returned to human. "Uh . . . your sister's no bug, but she's in danger, she might be drugged, and—" I looked at Reggie. One of his wizard tattoos peeked out from beneath his shirt. "He's quick to anger."

Kaminari laughed, and continued skipping rope. "I like you, arcana, you've got style. But my sister's been gone a while. She broke all ties with our clan, so really I can't help you, man!"

I exchanged looks with Reggie. He gave a slight nod. She was telling the truth.

It was extremely rare for a brightblood to break allegiance with a Demesne once they'd pledged. There were the occasional *Romeo and Juliet* cross-clan affairs, or *Falcon and the Snowman* cases of disillusioned brightbloods acting out. But the costs were usually too high to the brightblood, not just in lost protections and mana, but in lost trust and companionship, and any real break always required the permission of their Fey patrons.

"Why'd she leave?" I asked, forgetting to rhyme.

"Dum Dum dodo, catch her if you can, she'll stick you and lick you and make you her fan."

We clearly weren't going to get any more out of Little Morphin' Canny here.

Reggie said, "I come with a witness and claim the right of

inspection. We're going to take a quick, quiet look around, just to make sure your sister's not hiding here. Give us any trouble, and this place will be swarming with enforcers."

"Big wizard with a little gun," Kaminari said. "Just hurry up and be done."

Reggie pulled what looked like a small eight-sided mirror out of his pocket and held it up, facing Kaminari. "*Detego!*" he said.

Kaminari wavered as if seen through a heat wave, and I saw her true form—a young Japanese woman with spider legs coming out of her back. But she was not the jorōgumo I'd seen at the post office.

"That's not her," I said.

Reggie nodded, and we proceeded up the drive to the main building. Reggie swung the small mirror around like a flashlight, revealing the true forms of the feybloods we encountered, and unveiling some who'd attempted to mask themselves entirely from sight. We moved quickly so that Romey would, hopefully, not be warned of our coming, though I had little hope we'd actually find her.

The steading's main building was like a giant dorm or barracks house, room after room with basic amenities. The air smelled of animal sweat, blood, and dirty socks. Chore charts, house rules, and curfew times were posted, and it was clearly the job of a few of the more powerful brightbloods to keep the others in line. There was an uneasy tension in the air that felt like it went deeper than our presence. With so many Shadows brightbloods being predatory or violent in nature—ghouls, redcaps, waerwolves, trolls, lindworms, wendigos, unicorns—it was not surprising.

We finished our sweep of the steading building without any luck. Many of the brightbloods were out roaming the woods or working whatever jobs they'd been permitted. The only thing we learned from the ones we met was our jorōgumo's real name: Hiromi. And every feyblood we spoke to said the same thing, that Hiromi had never been around much, and she disappeared entirely several months ago.

I also learned enough to confirm that I never wanted Pete or Vee to pledge to the Shadows.

We walked back to the driveway, where Kaminari still jumped rope.

"Thanks for coming, wizard boy," Kaminari said. "Being hassled's always a joy."

Reggie grunted. "Don't worry. I'll be back if I find out this is all somehow a Shadows game."

"Eat you later, alligator," she replied, and stuck her tongue out at us.

"Come on," Reggie said, and we left. Reggie walked backward with his hand still on his baton until we were a safe distance from the jorōgumo, then turned to walk beside me.

When we reached our vehicles, I noticed a piece of paper had been slipped beneath my wiper. I looked around, surprised, and pulled it out.

"What's that?" Reggie asked.

"A note," I replied, and showed it to him just in case anyone was listening. It asked us to go to the Japanese American Exclusion Memorial.

Reggie frowned. "It could be a trap, or a game. Or could be someone doesn't want little Miss Rhymes back there to find out they spoke to us."

"Are we going?" I asked.

Reggie smiled. "Of course. Worse that happens is I get to vent a little on someone's head."

The Japanese American Exclusion Memorial sat nestled in the woods near the island's original ferry dock, the spot where nearly three hundred local Japanese-American men, women, and children were forced from their homes and shipped off to internment camps by the U.S. Army to join thousands of others. Not one of the brightest moments in American history. Or arcana history for that matter—few had fought to protect their Japanese brethren; most were too afraid of exposing our world to the mundies, and just as susceptible to the fears and prejudices of the day.

The entire area had been turned into a memorial park, with raised wooden pathways winding through the forest to the dock site, and a small mock village at its heart. Curved wooden walls above river stone bases displayed art that captured the memories and feelings of those who'd been imprisoned. Fear and regret had left their marks on the spiritual resonance of the land. The place felt no more haunted than most to my necromantic senses, but I knew that sorcerers with strong empathic ability avoided the area.

Reggie and I moved cautiously along the wooden path, the slanted streamers of evening light casting the trees in stark profile.

As we neared the final bend before the memorial village, something hissed at us from the trees.

Reggie's baton extended in a flash.

"Don't attack, arcana," a voice whispered from the shadows, and two yellow eyes blinked. "I claim Pax truce."

Reggie lowered his baton. "Step forward. I won't attack."

Ferns and huckleberry branches shifted, and a man stepped out beside the path, looking furtively around him and sniffing at the air. He was sturdily built, with a beer gut, a buzz-cut mohawk, and a goatee of copper-colored hair almost lost in the stubble surrounding it. He wore a Kingston Lumber T-shirt with the sleeves cut off, and blue jeans covered in paint splatters. His feet were bare.

"Who are you?" Reggie asked.

The man replied, "Ned. I'm Hiromi's boyfriend. She's being set up."

"Yeah? By who?" Reggie asked.

Ned leaned in and whispered, "I think the Bright Lords sent her on some kind of suicide mission."

"To do what?" Reggie asked.

"I don't know. She got a message from them, and next thing I know, she's leaving the clan."

"Maybe your Archon kicked her out?" I suggested.

*Never happen,* Alynon said. *Shadows don't go free, they disappear.*

"Never happen," Ned echoed. "The Archon liked her. I know. He had her doing some kind of secret mission for the past two years, so she was hardly around. But these last orders, they came from the Bright Lords, not the Archon."

"What was her mission?" Reggie asked.

Ned growled low in his throat. "Wouldn't tell you if I knew, Enforcer." He looked down, and flinched as if suddenly pained. "But she would come home smelling of sex sometimes, and human sweat, or cedar. When she didn't come back this time, I worried maybe she'd left me for another woman, but then I heard she was in trouble, and realized it had something to do with that message."

"Another woman?" Reggie asked. "I pegged you for a waer, not a full shifter."

Ned shrugged, and I could tell this was a topic that had brought him discomfort in the past. "My wolf spirit and form is a she." He looked up. "You should understand, Enforcer. I saw your show at Le Fey Faux once."

I looked at Reggie with raised eyebrows. "Show?" I asked.

Reggie just shook his head.

"Yeah," Ned said. "He did a pretty good Tina."

"We're not here to discuss me, or get chummy," Reggie said. "Where is Hiromi now?"

Ned looked around him again. "Well, to be honest, I kind of hoped she'd show up here. This is like sacred ground to her, she used to come here a lot to be alone and think and stuff. Her foster parents were taken away, left her and her sister alone when Hiromi was just a teen. She pretends it don't bother her anymore, but, well—"

Reggie lifted his baton, his eyes scanning the forest warily. "If she's on a secret mission, she wouldn't likely come back to someplace familiar."

"Don't know," Ned said, and waved at us, "I thought if she knew you guys was here, she might show. She wouldn't be happy she finds out her enemies were tromping around this place."

I felt suddenly exposed on all sides. "You invited us here as bait?"

Ned shrugged unapologetically. "That would be wrong," he glanced sideways at Reggie, "and possibly illegal. I knew you were looking for her, and she was looking for you, and I thought I'd just help you all out. But it don't matter. She didn't come."

Reggie scanned the trees above us. "You're sure of that?"

"Yeah, I'd smell her. But you're here, so I'm asking you to help her."

"Excuse me?" Reggie asked. "Why would we do that, exactly?"

"Because you're all about justice and protecting your precious ARC and all, and Hiromi can help you a lot, figure out what's really going on before more folks get hurt."

"Gee, I never knew a Shadows feyblood to care if an arcana got hurt."

"Oh, there's plenty of us'd be fine with every one of you being corpses or changeling puppets. But me, I don't want to lose Hiromi just to see that happen. If I lost Hiromi, well, that would suck the joy right out of my world, whether you were alive or dead."

"Aw," Reggie said deadpan. "That's so sweet."

Ned growled. "Don't mock me, arcana. Your kind take enough from us, you have no right to mock what little good we have." Ned's fingernails grew half an inch and darkened at the tips.

*He has a point,* Alynon said. *Several of them, in fact.*

*As if your kind treat them any better.*

*'My kind'? How rude. I'm one of a kind, don't you know?*

*Uh huh.*

*But if we Aalbrights ruled this world, all brightbloods would benefit.*

My level of discomfort jumped higher than a Super Mario Brother on the moon. It was bad enough to have another being inhabiting your head. But it was easier if I could just think of him as annoying and forget that a large portion of his race wanted to use us all like meat puppets at worst, or slaves at best. Alynon usually complained about his poor treatment at the hands of his Fey kin rather than speak as one of them.

Reggie flicked his baton in Ned's direction. "How about you put away the claws, and tell us how we might find your girlfriend?"

"If I knew, I wouldn't need you," Ned said. "Hell, if I even thought she might return a year from now, I wouldn't so much as talk to you. But I'm . . . scared she ain't coming back from whatever the Bright Lords have her doing this time. If you do find her, don't kill her, arcana. She's just following orders."

"Everyone has a choice," Reggie said. "But I won't kill her unless forced to. Not because you ask, but because that is Pax law."

*And because sometimes a dead brightblood can't be interrogated.*

"Well, guess that's about the best I could hope for from an arcana," Ned said.

"You ever try luring me into another trap, and that's the *least* you can hope for," Reggie said. "Now why don't you just stay right there where I can see you until we're gone."

Reggie waved me back, and we retreated back down the wooden walkway. Reggie didn't put his baton away, even when we passed an elderly Japanese couple going in the opposite direction. They skirted nervously around us.

"What next?" I asked as we walked.

"Next, we find this jorōgumo and figure out what the hell the Shadows Fey are up to. I have a bad feeling about this whole thing."

"*You* have a bad feeling? I feel like John McClane being called to a disturbance at the Empire State Building on Christmas Eve."

"Well, prepare to feel worse. I'm afraid Ned had the right idea."

"What's that?" I asked.

"Like I said before, spider woman seems to have a thing for you. We can maybe use that to draw her out. The trick will be making sure she gets the message. And keeping you alive until then."

"Uh, I hope you plan on keeping me alive *after* then, too."

"Of course," Reggie said.

"So are you planning to call in some DFM reinforcements, then?" I asked hopefully.

"I could," Reggie said. "But you and I both know the risks."

"Frak. Right." If whoever was behind all of this had ears inside the Department of Feyblood Management—guys like Cousar, and maybe Vincent—they might warn off Hiromi. Or ambush our ambush with their own reinforcements. I sighed.

Reggie slapped my shoulder gently. "It's your butt on the line. I'll let you make the call."

"Yeah. Great."

*I vote against poking the angry jorōgumo with a stick. Just inform your ARC, that changeling Zenith, and the Silver Archon that Silene was set up, and I'm certain someone shall clear her.*

*You know better than I do how unlikely that is. And if whoever's behind the jorōgumo sends her after me in the meantime to eliminate Silene's one witness? Or after my family to make me back off?*

*You hole up at home behind your wards.*

*That's not going to help Pete and Vee's situation. And I can't keep my entire family locked up at home for who knows how long. Better to go on the offensive, and take on the jorōgumo on my terms.*

*Sure thing, Rambo. I don't suppose you'd reconsider exorcising me first?*

*Sorry. But if I'm going up against a jorōgumo, I'd kind of like to have my brain intact and working and all.*

*Why? That hasn't stopped you before.*

"All right," I said. "I think I may know how to 'leak' word to Hiromi about where I'll be. Here." I stopped by the exit from the path to the parking lot, where two stone lanterns stood near the path like mini gray pagodas. I turned to the one on the left, and glanced around to make sure we were alone before saying, "Konbanwa, Burabura."

Two eyes blinked open on the lantern, beneath the shade of its hat-like top.

"Konbanwa," it responded.

I had sensed the spiritual resonance in the lantern as we passed it. A burabura was a type of Tsukumogami, a race of objects that had come alive. Like the Port Townsend Post Office, the object had gained something of a ghostly resonance after years of attention by human owners, but unlike the post office, this object had then become a kind of simple brightblood, possessed by a sprite-like Fey spirit from the Other Realm who was too weak to bond with a true living being.

Thankfully, it took at least a hundred years in most cases for an object to gain the kind of spiritual resonance that allowed possession, and modern societies rarely kept objects around for more than a decade or two at most. I didn't even want to imagine gangs of animated New Kids on the Block action figures running rampant in the streets.

"Can you get a message to the local gnomes?" I asked the lantern.

*"Hai."*

"Excellent." Tsukumogami tended to be helpful creatures, eager to feel useful. Except Bakezōri—living sandals—who usually just complained about being walked all over. I patted my pockets. "Uh, Reggie? Do you have a pen and some paper?"

Reggie produced a small flip tablet and a pen.

I wrote two messages, one for Sal and one to Silene, and an offer of payment for delivery.

Contacting Silene would get the jorōgumo's attention, I felt pretty certain. Hiromi had infiltrated Silene's steading as Romey, and seemed to still be tied in to whatever was going on with Silene. And by getting Silene and the jorōgumo together in one place, I figured I'd get some straight answers from both of them about what the heck was going on, one way or another.

As for Sal, well, much as I trusted Reggie to watch my back, I'd had enough adventures these past few months to know that things rarely went as expected, and it never hurt to have a friendly sasquatch around if things went south, or went any direction but home safe, for that matter.

I requested that they both meet me out at Fort Worden at dawn the next day. That seemed as safe a place as any, at least any place the jorōgumo might show herself: neutral ground, with plenty of escape routes—or ambush spots.

I carefully tipped the stone lantern back, causing it to giggle, and placed the notes underneath as I explained their contents to Reggie.

"That should work," Reggie said as we walked to our vehicles. "The trick will be to capture the jorōgumo alive."

"The trick will be not getting *anyone* killed in the process, especially me," I replied.

"Sure thing," Reggie said, and grabbed his helmet off of the back of his hog.

"So, Tina, huh?" I asked. "As in Tina Turner?"

*La!* Alynon said. *He is clearly the type to start things easy, then finish rough.*

"Let it drop, Gramaraye," Reggie said, sliding the helmet on.

"I'm just hurt you haven't invited me to one of your shows, is all."

"I haven't performed in years," he replied, his voice slightly muffled. "It was a different time in my life."

"Because you wanted to be a private dancer?" I asked.

"Because I just don't wear the mail well anymore," he said as he put his key in the ignition and flipped up the kickstand.

"Oh!" I nodded approval. "So you were *Thunderdome* Tina." Everyone made a big deal about Leia in her slave bikini, but I'd always thought Tina in her chain mail was the hotter, hands down.

"Obviously," Reggie said, "you don't think I'd go up on stage in front of a bunch of feybloods and other strangers without armor, do you?" He pressed the ignition button, and the motorcycle roared to life. "See you at dawn," he shouted. "Stay safe until then."

Reggie rode off.

*Speaking of Dawn,* Alynon said. *If you want to stay safe, you won't tell her you're going to play bait for a deadly trap. I'm pretty sure she asked you exactly *not* to do something that stupid.*

Oh. Shazbot.

## It Takes Two

It was just past nine and the sun fully set when I reached home. I entered through the side door, and made my way to the dining room.

The entire family sat around the table, eating ice cream: Father, Mattie, Mort, Pete and Vee, and Dawn as well.

And Barry "ear massage" McSchmoozy sat at the table next to Dawn. He grinned up at me with his perfect charming smile when I entered. "Hey, brah!"

Pax Laws and necromancer ethics be damned. I reached out with my spirit senses to see just what, if anything, Barry was besides the mundy he appeared. I didn't trust this pretty boy with his—

"Hey!" Dawn said, and stood to give me a hug and kiss, breaking my concentration. I tasted sugary sweetness on her lips.

There's just some things that make life bearable, particularly after a really crappy day. Fresh baked cookies. A long hot shower while blasting your favorite music—well, when you aren't terrified of water. And the embrace of someone who loves you. I let myself fall into that embrace, into the warmth of her kiss, and wished I could just stay there a while.

"Get a room," Mort said.

*Yes, please!* Alynon added.

I sighed through my nose, and then leaned my forehead for a second against Dawn's.

"Tell him your news!" Mattie said to Dawn as we stepped apart.

"News?" I asked.

Dawn shrugged, but I could tell it was more an embarrassed shrug than an indifferent one. "Sheila Weisman from Volvur Records heard my last show, and messaged me. She wants to hear more."

"What? Oh my god, that's awesome!" I said. "I mean, it is, right? Is Volvur a good record company?"

Barry patted Dawn's back. "They're great," he said. "And obviously they know groovy music when they hear it."

"They're an up-and-coming label," Dawn said, her tone modest. "But I like their music. They really support a positive message, and female artists."

"But I thought you were a positive artist with a female message," I said, and nudged her.

"Damn straight I am, but they're willing to experiment," she replied.

I frowned. "So why don't you seem totally excited?"

Dawn shook her head. "I am. I just—we can talk about it later. How'd your thing go? Get your answers?"

"Uh, no." Reality slammed back into me like a badly timed commercial break. I glanced at Barry, then said, "Can I talk to you real quick in the kitchen?"

Dawn arched her pierced brow, then looked to Mattie. "What do you think are the odds he's got a giant cake in there for me, and Hugh Jackman is going to jump out of it?"

Mattie shook her head. "Since he doesn't know who Hugh Jackman is, pretty slim."

"Yeah. I was afraid of that." Dawn waved from me to the door. "Lead the way."

As we passed into the kitchen, I heard Barry saying, "I met Hugh Jackman once, when I was backpacking down the coast—" The door swung closed.

"So what's Barry doing here?" I asked, and winced. That wasn't what I'd intended to say.

Dawn arched her eyebrow again. "Mattie invited him, actually. She's a huge Boingers fan, and Barry roadied for them a couple summers ago. She wanted to ask him questions. Is that really why you brought me in here?"

"No." I took a deep breath. "I need to reschedule the volunteering session, for the animal shelter."

"Okay," Dawn said, and crossed her arms. "And what will you be doing instead?"

"Well, you know that spider creature you told me not to fight? I, uh, need to help capture her."

Dawn considered me in silence for several long, loud heartbeats.

"Alrighty then. I can have Bear cover my shift, and go with you."

*Bear? Sounds like someone's getting cozy with the nicknames and all.*

*Shut up, Wesley!* "Tomorrow could get ugly," I said. "If anything happened to you because I allowed you"—Dawn's raised eyebrow made me change quickly—"because I agreed to take you, well, it would kill me."

"Look, I know you said the ARC wouldn't help Silene's brightbloods, but this creature attacked *you,* and you're one of their arcana, right? So shouldn't the ARC or whoever send an army after her ass?"

"Whoever's giving her orders may have ears in the ARC."

"Uh huh," Dawn said. She crossed her arms, and frowned, rolling her healed shoulder. "And?"

"And, we need answers that only she can give us. We don't want her being warned away. Or disappeared."

"And?" Dawn said.

I shrugged. "And that's it."

"Really?" Dawn said. "How about *and* you're trying to make up for every sucktacular thing your grandfather did to the brightbloods?"

*Wise woman,* Alynon said.

*Nobody asked you.*

*Uh huh.*

"This isn't about me trying to balance my family karma or whatever," I said. "Or at least, not mainly. It's about helping Silene, and helping Pete and Vee, not to mention the fact this jorōgumo has come after me twice, almost getting you and Heather killed in the process—"

"Heather?" Dawn asked.

Frak.

*La, you screwed up now,* Alynon said.

"Uh, yeah, I was going to tell you, but things have been so crazy—"

"You've been seeing Heather?"

"I haven't been *seeing* her. She came to me, asked me to help her find a way to avoid exile. So I asked her to help me deal with the alchemist who killed Silene's clan-mate. But—"

Dawn shook her head. "You're the butt, butthead."

"Yeah, I know."

"Damn you, why do you have to be so difficult?"

"I'm sorry, Dawn, really. You know I'm not interested in Heather."

"Damn you again," Dawn said. "I trust you, that's not the problem. You don't trust *me*."

"Yes I do. I—"

"No. You don't, not really. Maybe you don't trust what you feel for me. Or maybe you think I'm in love with some Finn that doesn't exist anymore, and don't trust that I love you for you. I don't know. And I don't know how to get past whatever it is."

I blinked, surprised. How did she do that? Was there anything about me she didn't know?

"I've had a lot to figure out since I've been back, I know. But I'm getting there, I swear. And a lot of that is thanks to you."

Dawn rolled her eyes, then sighed. "Well, they did rename the self-help section of the library after me for a reason. But Finn, I've barely got my own crap together, I shouldn't be anyone's therapist."

"And I'm not asking you to be. I just need a little more time, that's all."

"Time for what exactly?"

"Oh, you know, to figure out who I really am, and what I really want to do with my life. The easy stuff."

Dawn snorted. "Sure. So, say, until tomorrow?"

"I was hoping more like Tuesday. I also wanted to solve world hunger." I took her hands in mine. "Really, just . . . give me a couple of days to get this mess with the brightbloods all settled, and then I'll be one hundred percent focused on getting my crap together."

"I just wish you realized you don't have to do it alone. You idiot." She pulled me to her, kissed me on the corner of my mouth, and rested her cheek against mine for a second. As we parted I felt a cool spot high on my cheek where the wetness of a tear had pressed between us. "Go deal with your monsters," she said. "All of them. You know where I'll be when you're done, or really ready for my help."

She turned and left out the back door.

I stared after her a minute.

*Go tell her you love her.*

"She knows I care about her," I said.

*Perhaps. But perhaps she needs to know that *you* know. Perhaps she needs to know you *understand* how your decisions have put you in different worlds—*

"Uh, are we still talking about me?"

There was a slight pause. *Do what you will. You never heed my advice anyway.*

*Yeah, that's because your advice is usually to have sex with whatever is moving.*

*And what is wrong with that? Someday, when this bag of meat you call a body gets old, you're going to regret that you ignored my urgings.*

*Yeah. I'm sure that will be my biggest regret.*

I considered going after Dawn, not because of Alynon's words, but because having her unhappy with me felt like a heavy shadow had fallen over my heart, leaving a cold and uneasy feeling where her light normally warmed me.

But if I died tomorrow, maybe this would make the choice to have the ARC remove her memories of all of this, of us, easier for her.

I shivered for some reason, then pushed my way back through the swinging door into the dining room.

Barry, thankfully, was gone.

Pete looked up at me, his face a cherubic model of guilt. "Hey Brother. Um, there was only a little bit of ice cream left, and it was melting, and I didn't think you'd want it if it melted, so I ate it."

I smiled. "That's fine, Petey."

"You okay, Uncle Finn?" Mattie asked.

Vee looked past me. "Where's Dawn?"

"She went home," I said. "Everything's fine." I looked at my family, gathered around the table. In the three months since my return from exile, I'd adjusted to the differences between who they were before my exile and who they were now. I still felt out of place most of the time, or perhaps out of time most of the place, but damn it if I didn't love them all. Even Mort, though I still couldn't say why.

"Who wants to play a game of Monopoly?" I asked.

Mattie wrinkled her nose. "That game's boring."

Fifteen minutes later, we were playing Cranium, and I was trying to make a dinosaur out of purple clay and laughing, my many problems and coming dangers not forgotten, but pushed briefly to the corners of my mind at least.

It wasn't the same without Dawn, though.

Morning mist clung to the trees and ferns that covered the hillsides above Fort Worden, rolling in off of the Salish Sea. It clung to the clusters of evergreens and twisty madrona branches as if snagged in passing, stretched and torn into thin wispy clouds. It was perfect cover, and the kind of fog that fills epic 80's music videos. I would not be surprised if Hiromi leaped out of the trees looking like Prince doing the "Batdance." Terrified, yes. Surprised, no.

I parked at the top of the hill behind the rows of officer housing now turned vacation rentals, and hiked up into the forest. It had not escaped my notice that several of the madrona trees that lined the entrance to the park had been "yarn bombed," their trunks wrapped in patterns of colored yarn.

The trail was an uneven path of dirt and stone and the occasional tree root, rising steeply up until it branched out. One branch would continue on to the concrete bunkers, and eventually meander down the far side of the bluff to the coastline. The other branch did not want to be seen. I felt a compulsion to continue along the mundane path, to look up at the distracting beauty of fog and light playing in the treetops. But I focused my will, and the hidden path became clear. I turned down it, and hiked until it opened up onto a grassy bluff with a stone ring near the edge.

The ring looked like it might have been a giant fire pit, with blocky stones each the size of a basketball forming a wall around the edge, stacked high as a man's knees. The stones look charred as if by a fire, the runes covering them long obscured.

This ring of stones had been part of the spell Katherine Verona used to end the last Fey-Arcana war. There were other rings and structures like it around the fort, one of which being the place I'd first met Sal several months ago, but this one I knew was special. Perhaps that was why I'd so rarely visited it. The magic around these sites that compelled anyone nearing them to take a different path was, in some ways, tied to the emotional energy of the site, almost like a ghost, and there were few sites in the fort where I imagined the emotional resonance was as strong, or as full of pain and loss, as here.

Between that, and the active wards the ARC maintained on the ring to prevent any brightbloods desecrating it, Hiromi should not be able to touch anyone inside the ring, which made it an excellent retreat option if things went sideways.

I stepped out of the tree line onto the dew-soaked grass. My jeans quickly became damp up to my knees as I strode through the uncut grass and weeds and stopped at the near edge of the ring. I held the bottle of jorōgumo protection potion in my left hand. My right hand rested on the nylon pack strapped to my waist, and the hard outline of the family's revolver—which I was in theory allowed to use in self-defense while officially assisting Reggie in the capture of a dangerous criminal brightblood. I would have actually preferred a good wand, something certain to freeze or bind Hiromi in one shot without killing her. But wands were outside my price range, bullets were not.

I turned and faced the forested hillside, and uncorked the potion.

The jorōgumo could be anywhere in those trees. But then, so could Sal. A sasquatch's glamour was strongest in the forest, working with the natural patterns of light playing between branches and leaves, using the beautifully chaotic architecture of nature to trick the eyes of observers. A jorōgumo's glamour played more on shadows and darkness, on the unpleasant or frightening corners of the landscape that thousands of years of evolution conditioned us to avoid for fear of deadly creatures, poisonous gasses, and foul stenches.

Looking at a glamoured jorōgumo was a bit like popping in a movie and finding your parents had recorded a sex tape over it in which they vigorously role-play Jabba and Leia: your eyes turn away before your brain can even fully register what you've seen, and you feel a sudden dark stain on your soul and the urge to flee.

A dryad's camouflage, on the other hand, was simplicity itself.

Silene emerged from a cedar tree on the edge of the clearing, shimmering into site.

"Greetings, dryad," I said.

Silene crossed the grass to me and the stone ring. "Your message said I might confront the one responsible for Veirai's death?"

"Yes," I said. "Though I worried that Romey might've been waiting at your steading to finish what she started at the DFM compound."

"If she had, I think she would have been disappointed."

"Would I?" Romey said, and emerged from the shadows of the tree line.

Now we come to it. "I thought you might show up," I said, and rested my free hand on the reassuring cold steel of the revolver.

Romey sneered. "You remain clueless, arcana. I told you to stay out of brightblood affairs. Now, you will pay the price."

"Let me guess," I said. "Just three easy payments of nineteen ninety-nine?"

For response, Romey transformed. Except she did not change into a large fox. She became the jorōgumo. Spider legs burst out of her back, growing out and down to touch the ground, then lifting her body up suspended in the air even as that body itself transformed, the waist narrowing, the hips widening, her face molding into the features of a beautiful Japanese woman.

A look of fury swept across Silene's features. "A shadowbright spy?"

Hiromi leaped at me.

I drank the alchemist's jorōgumo protection potion in quick, desperate gulps.

Reggie stood and leaped out from the stone ring behind me, his camouflaged uniform making the world seem to bend around him, and threw his arms around Silene.

My mouth went dry. A bone-like crust sprang up over my skin, a thousand shards of razor-sharp fossils overlapping like scales. My clothes shredded, and the belt holding the pack and revolver fell away. I tried to grasp it, but my thickened, crusty fingers were too clumsy.

The jorōgumo crashed into me, her arms wrapping around me. We tumbled across the wet grass.

She screamed in pain, and flung me aside.

I hit the ground hard and rolled to a stop, tearing up grass and mossy sod, the fossilized skin protecting me from abrasions but not from bruising. My shredded clothes formed a trail behind me.

I pushed myself to my knees.

Reggie had pulled Silene back within the protection of the stone ring, granting her passage through its wards.

Hiromi twitched to her feet, her skin lacerated, oozing dark fluid from countless small cuts—fluid she needed to operate her spider legs, if I remembered my biology lessons correctly.

She lifted up on those legs, not injured enough to be out of commission yet. But she did not leap at me again. She skittered sideways, away from the rune circle and Reggie, her black eyes fixed on me.

"Clever defense," she said. "But that will not save you."

"Hiromi," I said, rising to my feet. "Why are you doing this? We don't need to be enemies." I moved slowly to place Hiromi between myself and the tree line.

"Of course we do," she replied. "We are different, and difference always leads to conflict. Or enslavement."

I eyed the pack with the revolver, and then flexed my fossil-covered hands. I wasn't sure I could fit my finger through the trigger guard even if I could reach the gun before Hiromi struck me down.

"You sound like my grandfather," I said.

"Then he is right," she hissed back.

"He's dead. He tried to start a war, but arcana and brightbloods, we fought together to stop him."

"Then you only delayed the inevitable!" Hiromi flicked one of her legs up, and a stone the size of oh-my-god-that's-going-to-hurt flew at me. I tried to dodge, but it slammed into my gut like a dodgeball from hell.

A great cloud of white dust and the sound of shattering fossils exploded up from the point of impact, and I flew off my feet. The impact with the ground knocked out whatever air I had left, and pain flooded my chest and abdomen. I curled up on the damp grass and moaned, clutching my stomach.

*Get up!* Alynon screamed in my head.

I groaned, and struggled up, expecting to see another stone flying at my head and not sure I could dodge it any better than the last.

Instead, I heard Reggie shout *"Dormio!"* and the jorōgumo dis-appeared with a *Thwump!* of imploding air as a glowing missile like a miniature photon torpedo flew through the space where she'd been standing.

I blinked, and looked over at Reggie. He stood inside the rune circle, a wand pointed where Hiromi had been. He cursed and tossed the wand aside, drawing a silver automatic pistol from beneath his jacket.

"Where'd she go?" I managed to say, and thought better of say-ing anything more as the pain of speaking burned in my chest. Had she gone invisible somehow?

*She transformed into a true spider,* Alynon replied.

Ah crap. I took a step back, looking down at my feet, though I knew she could not have covered the distance to me so quickly, not as a tiny spider.

There was another pop of displaced air, and Hiromi reappeared several feet to the side of where she'd been. She made a flinging motion, and from her belly shot streams of glistening, milky threads at Reggie.

I expected him to counter with a fireball, or lightning, or some-thing equally devastating. Instead, he fired the pistol at her, and Hiromi jerked and screamed in pain, but her webbing struck Reggie and entangled him. Hiromi gave three hard pulls on the threads, and Reggie jerked forward to slam into the edge of the stone ring three times. His suit flashed with blue light at the impacts and pro-tected him from the worst of the damage, but his eyes still fluttered closed.

Reggie slumped down into the pit, entangled in webbing, and didn't move. A jorōgumo's webbing sedated its victims.

Hiromi turned to me, and her smile did not promise anything pleasant.

## Heart and Soul

Hiromi shifted on her spider legs to face me, her grin spreading wide.

Oh, crap.

A roar of challenge rang across the hillside, and Sal charged from the tree line at Hiromi's back, his long fur-covered arms swinging like opposing pendulums and his head thrust forward. Hiromi only just managed to turn when he plowed into her, his fist pummeling into her stomach so hard she lifted up off of the ground and fell back in a tangle of spider legs and human limbs.

Thank the gods.

I ran toward Reggie to help him, and saw that Silene had already begun to tear at the webbing with a sharp stone, though with little obvious effect.

"No!" another voice shouted from the tree line, and Ned, Hiromi's boyfriend, ran across the grass toward Sal, pulling his sleeveless T-shirt up over his ginger mohawk and tossing it aside as he ran.

"Sal!" I shouted, but he was already turning.

Ned leaped forward, and transformed into a gray-haired she-wolf the size of a small bear. Even in motion and from a distance, his—her—long yellowed fangs and heavily muscled chest, neck, and jaw looked like a vicious locomotive train of pain. She looked less like a common wolf and more like something He-Man would ride.

Sal roared a challenge and leaped forward into the attack.

The two giant creatures crashed into each other. Sal managed to get his arm up between his throat and Ned's snapping jaw. Ned's teeth clenched down on Sal's arm, and Sal turned, swinging the giant wolf around. I doubted Ned's teeth could penetrate Sal's armor-like fur, but a waerwolf that size had enough strength to bite through steel, and Sal's fur wouldn't long keep his bones and muscles from being ground to pulp beneath.

Hiromi rose unsteadily to her feet. Sal swung Ned around to put the waerwolf between him and the jorōgumo.

My skin tingled, and the fossilized bone began to flake off in small patches. I would be able to use the revolver soon—and be completely naked and vulnerable. And I was not a trained fighter like Reggie. I glanced from Reggie back to where the small hip pouch lay in the crushed grass. Silene had given up trying to free Reggie from the webbing and was instead trying to reach safely past the webbing to touch his head, I assumed to heal him with her touch and try to counter the sedating poison of the webbing.

I ran for my gun.

Hiromi tried to skitter around Ned to reach Sal, but Sal swung Ned around, the wolf's rear legs and bushy tail flying through the air and keeping the jorōgumo at a distance. Sal let out a sudden howl of pain and fell back a step. Ned's grinding bite must be doing serious damage. Sal brought his other fist around in an arching hammer-like blow for the waerwolf's back.

Ned released his bite and dropped to the ground, in perfect position for a good kick from Sal that would send her flying like a football.

Sal retreated in a low crouch instead, holding his injured arm close to his chest.

Blast. Sasquatches never kicked. Too much danger of having their foot caught, or their legs swept out from under them, exposing their most vulnerable point—the bottoms of their enormous feet. Even with his combat boots, Sal's conditioned instincts had cost him a chance to take Ned out.

I reached the waist pack, and fumbled at it as the coating of thick bone continued to crumble and flake off my fingers.

Hiromi sprayed Sal with webbing, entangling him.

Ned turned, her tongue lolling out to one side, and spotted me. Her mouth stretched into a wicked, snarling grin, and she began loping in my direction. Saliva ran in steamers from her gaping mouth.

If Ned wasn't Fettered, then one bite from that mouth could infect me with the waer curse—a bit of Fey spirit that would take root in me and grow into a full animal Fey spirit. I would become a waerwolf, like Ned. And like Pete.

More likely, though, she'd simply tear my throat out.

I raised the revolver in both shaking hands and fumbled back the hammer, causing the chamber to turn and click. Each chamber held a hollow point of iron with a silver-filled tip. They served well to stop most brightblood creatures.

The trick was getting the bullet in the creature.

Ned loped side to side, speeding at me in a zigzag pattern.

I squeezed the trigger. The gun jerked violently, pain shot up the back of my of my hand where the enforcer had smashed it yesterday, and the explosive bang rang in my ears.

I wasn't sure where the bullet went, except not in Ned, who continued loping at me uninjured and definitely unfriendly.

I cocked back the hammer again, and did my best to still my shaking hands and ignore the pain, to point the gun straight and steady. Ned had crossed more than half the space to me.

I fired.

Ned yelped, and stumbled, but quickly recovered and continued to run at me, now with a slight limp to her gait. I'd grazed her front right leg.

I carefully squeezed the trigger again, not bothering to cock back the hammer.

Ned leaped at me, her yellow teeth and massive paws filling my vision.

The gun fired.

Blood sprayed hot across my skin. Ned yelped, and inertia carried her into me, slamming me to the ground. I flinched, expecting the pain of teeth digging into flesh, but Ned tumbled off of me and across the thick grass.

I moaned, my cheek pressed to the damp ground.

Ned coughed.

*He's not dead. Get up!* Alynon said.

"I'm trying!" I snapped back.

I rolled away from Ned, and pushed myself to my feet. The gun had flown off into the tall grass, and I couldn't see where.

Ned transformed back into his human form and held a hand against his left shoulder. Blood oozed out between his fingers. He snarled at me, and tried to sit up, but collapsed back and closed his eyes, his snarl turning into a growl of frustration and pain.

The silver inside him would keep him from transforming, and hopefully knock him out. If not removed, it might even kill him in time, but I would have the DFM take him into custody well before that happened.

If I survived Hiromi.

Sal stood wrapped in webbing, his arms trapped and pushing against the cocoon of milky white ropes as he tried to break free through sheer strength. His fur must protect him against the web's sedating poison.

One strand of webbing broke with the loud *Twang!* of a snapping steel cable.

Hiromi advanced on Sal, black pincers growing from the corners of her mouth.

"Hiromi!" I shouted. "Stop, or I kill your boyfriend!"

I held my hand behind me, raised and pointing at Ned as if holding a weapon or wand, my body hiding the lie from Hiromi.

Hiromi turned and hissed at me. I prepared to dodge webbing. Hiromi wouldn't come attack me directly. She knew by now that my most powerful weapon, my necromancy, would only work if I could touch her. If I were powerful enough to summon her spirit from a distance then I would have done so already.

I just needed to buy Sal and Reggie a little time to get back into the fight.

Hiromi raised her hands in preparation to cast webbing at me. "Don't do it!" I said, waving my hand behind me.

"It is not in your nature to kill," Hiromi said, taking a step toward me, though she lowered her hands. "Not a defenseless being."

*She has your number,* Alynon said.

"You have no idea what I'm capable of," I replied to them both.

*Says the man pointing a pretend gun rather than using his real power.*

Hiromi's eyes narrowed, then she laughed. "Your time has come, meddler," she said.

I glanced behind me. Ned grinned back at me, one trembling hand held up in some kind of sign. He had signaled my bluff to Hiromi.

Smeg.

Hiromi raised her hands again.

Vines snaked up around her legs.

She twitched back, but the vines held fast.

"What—?" she said, and pulled harder at them, but the leafy green vines continued to snake up and over her legs in a thick, writhing mass.

We both looked at Silene.

The dryad stood at the edge of the stone ring, leaning forward with her hands both planted in the grass, her chopped bangs only partially hiding eyes closed in concentration.

"Silver Court bitch!" Hiromi screamed. "I'm going to burn your tree down!"

"You can try!" Silene shouted back, and lifted her head. "If you can get free of *my* web." Silene raised one hand, and clenched it into a fist.

The vines contracted, pulled downward, and Hiromi's scream echoed across the bluff, filled with more pain than any single scream should hold. I heard several loud snaps and pops, and Hiromi collapsed down to the ground, three of her spider legs broken free and spurting dark fluid, the remaining legs bent at extreme angles.

"Holy—" I said.

*Shite,* Alynon agreed.

"Hiromi!" Ned screamed, and struggled to his knees. "Hiromi!" he said again, and tried to rise, but fell back down. He looked at me. "Damn you, Gramaraye! Stop that dryad bitch before she kills my Romi!"

I shook my head. "I—I think it's too late." But I walked toward Silene anyway. "Silene, that's enough. She's not going to hurt any-one else."

Silene looked at me, her face wild, feral. I became keenly aware of the fact that I was stark naked. I held my hands self-consciously in front of my private area, but Silene's eyes never left mine.

"She pretended to be one of us," Silene said. "She betrayed us, and she tried to kill us. Don't interfere, arcana. This is brightblood justice."

"You're within your rights," I said. "But killing Hiromi isn't going to help your cause, or yourself. Capturing her, helping us to prove she set you up for the attack on the alchemist, that will show the ARC you can work with us toward our common goals."

A fresh wave of fury swept across Silene's features. "This crea-ture is the one responsible for Veirai's death?"

*Smooth.*

Crap.

"Someone else told her to do it, and that someone's the real en-emy here. But if you kill Hiromi, we won't find out who, or why."

"Not true," Silene said. "You can ask her after she's dead."

"Maybe, but—"

Silene raised her hand, spread-fingered, her eyes fixed on Hiromi.

"Please, don't," I said. "Talking to her spirit will drain me of life. And if Hiromi's orders came from the Fey Lords themselves, we need her alive to prove it. You know my word alone won't be enough to accuse the Forest of Shadows of breaking the Pax."

Silene stared at Hiromi for a long minute, then slowly lowered her raised hand back to the grass, and shuddered. "It matters little anyway," she said. "She will not live long."

She slumped down to rest against the ring's edge, appearing suddenly exhausted.

I looked at Hiromi, weeping and twitching on the ground.

"Can you heal her?" I asked Silene.

Silene looked from me to Hiromi. "I will not finish her life," she said, her voice heavy now with weariness. "But neither will I save it."

I sighed. Why couldn't anything be easy?

I would need to get Reggie free of the webbing, and have him question Hiromi before she died. Reggie probably had come prepared with a potion or spell to melt jorōgumo webs, but he was the one person who couldn't help free himself.

Of smeggin' course.

I hurried to my pile of shredded clothing, and salvaged what I could, tying the remains of the flannel shirt around my waist to drape down like a loincloth.

*Waste of time,* Alynon said. *You have nothing to be embarrassed about except that gut, and sorry to say your loincloth does nothing to hide that.*

*I'm not embarrassed, I'm cold,* I lied, and began searching for the revolver. Well, I was cold, too. The misty breeze coming up off of the ocean prickled over the goosebumps on my skin, and my feet had long gone numb in the cold grass.

"You're wasting time!" Ned said as I continued searching the tall weeds. He tried once more to get to his feet and collapsed as if extremely drunk. "She needs a healer!"

I ignored him, and found the revolver. I picked it up, and crossed the grassy bluff to Hiromi.

"Help me," she cried.

"I'll do what I can," I promised, and looked at Sal. He had broken several strands of the webbing around him but still remained entangled from the waist down. "You okay?" I asked.

"Iself's arm big hurts. But spiderbright webs almost gone."

"Okay. Hang in there, and we'll see about your arm."

I kept clear of Hiromi's front, where she might still somehow spit webs or lunge at me. I wrapped a shredded jeans leg around one of her detached limbs to protect my hands from the wire-like hairs, and tugged it free of the vines. The leg was as wide around as my calf, ending in a curved, talon-like tip with a wicked sawed edge. I dragged it over to Sal, and sawed at the webbing with the claw. Hiromi's claw passed through the strands like hot drool through cotton candy, and the webbing fell away from Sal.

"Keep an eye on them," I said, nodding to Hiromi and Ned, then strode over to Reggie and cut through the webbing covering him.

"Can you revive him?" I asked Silene.

She blinked at me, then at Reggie. "I—maybe." She kept one hand on the grass, and placed the other on Reggie's head. After a second, he stirred, and then jerked awake, raising his baton as if to strike me.

"It's Finn!" I said. "You're safe."

He scrambled to his feet, and took in the scene. He looked from Hiromi to Silene. "Your work?" he asked her.

Silene nodded.

"Well done," he said, and climbed out of the ring, glowing baton in one hand, pistol in the other. Silene climbed out after him.

"We don't have much time," I said. "We need to get Hiromi to a healer, or get one here."

"Not sure it would help at this point," Reggie said. "Those are mortal wounds for a jorōgumo. Stay here," he said to Silene, then strode to Hiromi. I went with him. He glanced at me sideways. "Nice look by the way, Tarzan."

I sighed. "Thanks. Why didn't you just blast Hiromi with some wizard magic?"

"Reasons I don't feel like discussing," Reggie replied. He stopped in front of Hiromi. "Hiromi Haraguchi, you are hereby accused of breaking the rules of the Pax Arcana by inciting war between arcana, feybloods, and the Fey through acts of deception and terror. Tell me your orders, and who gave them, and you may be given asylum in a DFM holding facility. Otherwise, you will face sentencing under Pax law."

Hiromi hissed a laugh, but it was weak now, and her eyes drooped. "You're too late, Enforcer," she said, her words slurred. "I am free. As will all of my brothers and sisters be soon enough."

She slumped down, and shuddered.

Her remaining legs curled inward.

"No! Hiromi, no!" Ned shouted.

I turned, raising my revolver, and Reggie did the same with his pistol.

Ned rose to his feet, but remained where he stood, swaying slightly.

"You bastards!" he said, tears running down his cheeks. "You took her from me! You took the only good thing in this stinking human world." He wiped at his face, smearing the blood from his wound across it. "You will all face the Shadows someday." He turned to Silene. "And you, Silver whore, you will be among the first to suffer." Then he lurched into a stumbling run at Silene, screaming.

Silene tried to re-enter the protection of the stone ring, but the air flashed orange above the stones. Silene bounced back into the grass. She couldn't re-enter it without Reggie's help.

"Stop!" I shouted at Ned. With Hiromi dead, Ned was our best chance for a living witness to hand over to the ARC.

Reggie didn't bother with a warning. He aimed and fired several shots in rapid succession.

The first two hit Ned in the arm and side, causing wounds to blossom like roses. Ned jerked, but did not fall, continuing his charge at Silene. She retreated but did not run, her expression one of determination. The next two shots missed.

The third hit Ned in the head.

His head jerked away from us, and his body followed the direction of his head, wobbling like a marionette operated by a drunk.

Ned tumbled from the edge of the bluff.

I ran to the edge and looked down. Ned lay in a contorted, bloody mess among the rocks and ferns at the base of the cliff.

A seagull cried as it rode the wind in from the Salish Sea.

*Well, that could have gone better,* Alynon said.

## I Know You Got Soul

I turned away from the bluff's edge, away from the view of the sea, away from the sight of Ned broken and dead on the ground far below.

"What now?" I asked Reggie as he stepped beside me and glanced over the edge.

"Now we take them both to the local DFM headquarters," he said.

"Will the ARC at least have a necromancer Talk to them?" I asked, remembering how the DFM hadn't even bothered Talking to Veirai.

"Yes," Reggie said, and rubbed vigorously at the top of his bald head. "But the ARC isn't going to care too much about clearing your feyblood friends. They're just going to wanna know about any threats to arcana security, if any of the Fey Demesnes are actively working against us. They may not ask the questions you want asked, and if they do, well, I guess it will depend on who's doing the asking whether the answers leave the room."

I felt a chill that had nothing to do with the wind. "So, in other words, if I want to prove Silene and her brightbloods are innocent and make sure they aren't still in danger, I'll need to Talk to Hiromi myself."

" 'Fraid so," Reggie replied.

Veirai's spirit had been largely intact, her personality whole, because her nature had been largely human, and her Fey nature minimal. But Hiromi, she was as much or more a product of her Fey nature as any human aspect. Whatever of her human spirit I was able to summon, I did not expect it to be entirely whole, sane, or safe.

So not only would getting any answers from Hiromi be much harder—and more draining—but if I got possessed by such a spirit, I'd go all Jack Nicholson, *Shining* style, and that was if I was lucky.

Thinking about her dual nature, half Fey spirit, half earthly spirit, I had a sudden lightbulb moment about the nature of that Simon artifact Father had given me. But that would have to wait for later.

"You're going to want to do it soon," Reggie said in a prodding tone. "All this magic and death, enforcers are going to be here soon."

Perfect. "*Carpe* frakking *diem*, oh captain my captain," I muttered, and strode back to Hiromi's body.

She lay on her back, curled in on herself. Her human arms were tucked in close and crossed over her chest, her hands curled up into half fists. The pincers had retracted from the corners of her mouth, leaving only her red lips in a small pout, and strands of long black hair fell over her face. If you could ignore the spider legs that surrounded her like a curled cage, she looked asleep, peaceful. Beautiful.

I reached out and placed a hand on her arm. With her being so recently dead, at least, there might still be some life energy in her body to help fuel the Talking.

I concentrated, called up my magic, and summoned Hiromi's spirit. And even as I did so, my free hand grasped the spirit trap that hung around my neck, prepared to force Hiromi into it to prevent a second and potentially deadlier battle with her.

"Hiromi," I said. "I must ask you some questions, and I compel you to answer true."

"Ask ask asking ask," she responded in a voice that only I could hear, and sounded . . . unsettled. "Answers are mine, you cannot have." She giggled.

I felt life energy trickle from me as she spoke, a wider flow than normal as I opened up the summoning so that Hiromi's voice echoed out of her body and could be heard by Reggie, Sal, and

Silene as well, though the effect only went one way. While I could make others hear a summoned spirit, the spirits I summoned could only ever hear me.

"Refusing to help me will only hurt your brightblood brothers and sisters," I replied. "Help me prove who's behind your actions and I'll explain to the ARC you were only following orders."

Hiromi's laugh did not hold the hissing it had in life, but was the mad laugh of a woman who had lived long years filled with more tragedy and pain than a human soul was meant to bear. "Following orders, borders orders soldiers badges bridges ferries fairies forts. Yes! Oh yes! Brightbloods murdered herded hurted, war is over never over never over. Any excuse you will use abuse I refuse—"

"Hiromi, focus, please," I said. "The DFM won't show you patience, or mercy. But I do want to help. So help me understand. Help your sister."

"Sisssster. Oh pretty sister. Poor little sister."

"I met her you know," I said. "Kaminari? The girl who likes to make rhymes. You do realize the ARC is going to come down on her and her clan for your actions? They won't believe you were acting alone."

A sudden, wild surge of will and energy from Hiromi's spirit pulled my mental feet out from beneath me like a vicious riptide and drowned me in an ocean of madness before I could block it or use the spirit trap.

Emotions crashed over me. Fear and fury, pain and love. And images began to smash into me, the fragmented wreckage of her memory, upon which my own mind somehow enforced a kind of order and sense.

*Hiromi huddled in the tree line, barely eighteen, and held eight-year-old Kaminari in her arms as they watched the American soldiers directing their mother and father toward the ferry.*

*Adopted parents, and arcana at that, but the couple had raised both of the girls since an associate found the sisters stowed away in a Japanese cargo ship. Jorōgumo were prized for many reasons, few of them good for the jorōgumo, but the couple had not sold them to alchemists, or the underground fight pits, or the brightblood brothels, or any of the other possible fates that awaited them. And as sorcerers, the couple had been able to work with Kaminari's fits, calming her mind and her fears. They had helped Hiromi learn control of the crueler instincts her Fey half inspired. They had shown the girls love. It might have been out of sorrow for their own daughter at first, lost to polio and pneumonia, but the reasons mattered little to Hiromi. The love had been real.*

*Now those parents were the ones being shipped off, treated like animals. Hiromi didn't understand why they didn't just use their power on those stupid mundy soldiers, why none of the Japanese fought or resisted losing their homes, their businesses, their freedom. "We are loyal Americans," her father had said. "Fighting will only prove their fears."*

*A U.S. soldier stopped her parents, and pinned dangling paper tags onto their jacket collars. The way her parents had tagged objects to be sold in their antique shop. Hiromi's hard-won control began to slip, her spider legs itching to come out—*

*Kaminari stirred restlessly in her arms.*

*She had to protect Kaminari. She could not risk exposure, or her own life, not when she was all that Kaminari had.*

*Hiromi squeezed her little sister, and said, "Calm, little Kami. It will be over soon. Send them good thoughts. Remember they can feel us still."*

*But as her parents boarded the ferry, what she felt was a growing anger. They were leaving her, leaving Kami, when they could have fought, should have fought, to stay.*

*But they would rather abandon her than upset their mundy oppressors.*

*Hiromi did not trust the old unicorn, standing there in his gray suit amidst the squalor of poorly maintained steading housing. There was something in the way he looked at her and Kaminari with those silver-blue eyes that caused the spider in her to stir, to want to bite him, and—*

*She shook herself. The power of unicorns to seduce was a rival to that of a jorōgumo. But he had assured her she would not have to bed him. More importantly, she had little choice.*

*The brightblood clans were preparing for war against the arcana, and with the Silver and many rogues siding with the humans, few other clans were willing to trust a rogue brightblood who suddenly wanted to join them. Kaminari needed mana for her Fey spirit to grow healthy, not damaged or stunted, and they both needed protection from the arcana.*

*This small clan pledged to the Hidden Vale was the only who'd been willing to take them both.*

*"Don't worry," Antipas said, flashing his white, perfectly even teeth. "I will take good care of your sister, if you but fight for our clan."*

*Hiromi paced her cell in the processing facility at Fort Worden. The war had been lost. The Hidden Vale destroyed in the Other Realm by some arcana superweapon. She had been captured, and held for nearly six months. Three months since, she'd earned communication privileges, though she'd still had to dictate the letters to one of the newly minted Department of Feyblood Management enforcers. No response from Antipas, or her sister, in all that time.*

*She had used the skills taught her by her parents to survive the endless questioning, the "conditioning," the subtle hints that perhaps she would be happier if she simply killed herself. She had endured the news that her mother had died in the internment camp from illness; and her father, upon being informed by the oh-so-helpful enforcers that Hiromi had fought for the Bright Lords against the arcana, had refused her letters. Even though they had no evidence that she'd killed a single human.*

*Why was Kaminari not responding? That question filled her days and nights with fears, tested her control over her more violent impulses. Why was Kaminari not responding?*

*Hiromi decapitated the redcap she found on top of Kaminari, and pulled her sister free of the tangled and bloodied bedsheets, lifted Kami in her arms. She stepped back out into the hall, and over Antipas's body. Kaminari moaned but did not give any other sign of awareness that Hiromi now held her safe.*

*"Shhhh," Hiromi said, "I'm here now, Sister."*

*Kaminari only stared at her with the slack face and dull eyes of someone dead.*

*"Come back to me, my little Kami. Please come back to me."*

*She rummaged through the filthy housing units for food, and mana, and gently washed her sister's face with a cool wet cloth. As she did, she sang one of the rhymes her mother used to sing to them:*

> *"The itsy bitsy spider went up the water spout,*
> *down came the rain and washed the spider out,*
> *out came the sun and dried up all the rain, and—"*

*Kaminari stirred, and sang in a weak voice, "The itsy-bitsy spider climbed up the spout again."*

I felt like I was drowning in Hiromi's pain, her sorrow, her memory as her spirit overwhelmed me.

I panicked. And in that panic I scrabbled to the surface of the chaos, found the shape of my own will again, and imposed it on Hiromi's mad spirit.

I regained control.

"Are you okay?" Reggie asked. "Are you . . . you?"

"Yes," I replied. "I'm not possessed. Well, Alynon notwithstanding. I just need a second."

I took several deep breaths, and considered breaking off the summoning. But I still had not learned what we needed to know.

"Hiromi. Focus! I want to help little Kami, but you need to help me. Tell me what your mission was?"

"Ghost talkers death walkers Gramaraye curse bringers!" her voice echoed out of her body. "Liars liars blood buyers curse hawkers!"

"I'm not—" I stopped. I was getting nowhere. But I knew from her memories that she was still in there somewhere.

"You need to threaten her," Reggie said.

I frowned. Tradition held that threats against the dead were bad luck. That might just be a necromancer superstition, but I preferred not to test it out if I could help it.

*Use Ned,* Alynon said.

*What? How? Ned's dead.*

*There are few tortures more cruel than to be separated forever from the one you truly love,* Alynon replied, his tone subdued.

I tried to think of an alternative. But time was my enemy, and Hiromi was not exactly a friendly ghost.

It seemed I had no choice but to invite bad luck after all.

"Hiromi," I said. "Ned is dead. He sacrificed himself to be with you in the afterlife. If you don't tell me what I want to know, I—I will destroy his spirit, scatter it to every part of existence. Everything that was Ned will be lost, and his death will be for nothing. You will never be together."

Hiromi did not respond. If I did not feel the cold presence of her spirit, and the continual draining of my life energy, I might have thought the summoning lost.

"Hiromi, I swear I will—"

"Assssssk," Hiromi hissed, and her voice quivered with fury.

I exchanged glances with Reggie, then said, "You were responsible for Veirai attacking the alchemist?"

"Yesssss."

I waited for her to expand, but she was obviously not going to offer any information freely.

"You infiltrated Silene's group posing as Romey, a waerfox?"

"Yessss."

"Did you do these things under orders?"

"Yessss."

"Who gave you the orders?"

"Little gnomes naughty gnomes."

I frowned. "You took your orders from gnomes?"

"Yessss."

"But—" Oh. I rolled my eyes. "You mean the gnomes handed you the actual orders. Who gave the orders to the gnomes?"

Hiromi was silent.

"Hiromi? Were your orders really from your Forest of Shadows patrons?"

"Yesss. I obey obey betray the betrayers all will die die die."

"Can you tell me why they ordered you to cause so much trouble for Silene?"

Hiromi went silent again.

"Hiromi, I *will* destroy Ned."

"I won't betray, I won't betray, go away away away," Hiromi cried.

"Hiromi, does your Archon know why you were sent after Silene?"

Hiromi wheezed a laugh. "No no no no. He sends bends me uses me but he sees nothing nothing you all are blind little blind fools. You won't see your death death death."

*The Shadows would not work directly through a vassal without informing the Archon,* Alynon said. *Unless—*

*Unless what?*

*Unless they are not just trying to create conflict between our brightbloods and arcana. The Shadows are preparing for a war against the Silver Court itself.*

"A war?" I said out loud.

"War?" Silene asked, alarm in her tone.

The summoning began to wear on me. Dizziness and nausea lurked on the edges of my senses.

"Hiromi, I release you!"

"Ned!" She pleaded, her voice distant.

"He'll be waiting for you," I said.

*You do not know that.*

*I choose to believe it.*

Hiromi's spiritual presence faded.

I wavered, and Reggie put a hand on my back. "Steady there."

"Thanks," I said, and swallowed back some bile that rose up sharp in my throat.

"You spoke of war!" Silene said. "Please, what did you mean?"

*We must needs warn the Silver Court,* Alynon said. *If they are not aware of this—*

"Everyone, remain where you are," a voice rang out, and three DFM agents strode out from the tree line.

"Yay," I said with a complete absence of enthusiasm. "We're saved."

## Don't Dream It's Over

I paced the interrogation room of the Department of Feyblood Management compound, back and forth over the line of ward runes embedded in the floor, watching myself in the one-way mirror. I wore a gray jumpsuit loaned to me by the enforcers and had a nasty bruise on one cheek, and still kept finding chalky bits of powdered fossil in my hair and the lines on my skin.

The fact that I was becoming familiar with an interrogation room, I thought, might suggest that I really needed to reevaluate my life choices.

Interesting fact: thaumaturges once had a booming business in inventing clever magical interrogation devices. Once such devices were no longer needed or as popular due to truth spells and ethics and such, many of them ended up being reimagined for commercial use by the Arcana Ruling Council in much the same way NASA gave us freeze-dried ice cream. But, you know, less delicious. The most successful adaptations were toys and board games. Mouse Trap was based on an interrogation device, of course, but so were Mr. Mouth, Don't Break the Ice, and Hungry Hungry Hippos.

But one of the most effective and insidious devices was reportedly turned into the See 'n Say. Its use as a magical brainwashing device apparently had something to do with mixing up the pictures and the sounds and forcing the victim to play them constantly Clockwork Orange style, until they accepted their torturer's new reality. To this day, there are believed to be sleeper agents out there ready to do whatever "The Farmer" tells them if triggered with a bit of magic and the correct phrase, such as "The *Cow* says . . . Oink Oink Oink!"

Thankfully, we now lived in more civilized times.

Enforcer Vincent had simply asked me probing questions—minus actual probes—for nearly an hour, while Reggie, Sal, and Silene were presumably being served a big heaping plate of the same with side dishes of hostility or suspicion in varying portions. And now, hopefully, the DFM had necromancers Talking to Hiromi and Ned to verify my story.

"I still don't understand," I said, rubbing at my bruised hand. Just being in this place seemed to have made it flare up in remembered pain. "Why would creating tensions between arcana and brightbloods mean the Forest of Shadows is preparing for war against the Silver, and not us?"

*'Tis not just that they create tensions, but that they keep such actions hidden from their own Archon that is a telling clue. The Archons in the end are but powerful brightbloods, ever concerned first for their own kind above even their Aalbright masters, and would not willingly follow a plan that would sacrifice their clan in this world simply to gain advantage in the Other Realm.*

*Okay. Then what is their plan?*

*They wish to weaken the Silver Court before attacking, by removing our sources of support. We need to warn my Demesne. You need to have your enforcer friend get a message to Zenith, and the Silver Archon. He will not dare ignore a direct message from me to the Court.*

*I can try,* I thought. *But first, I need to understand what the hell is going on.*

*I have already told you.*

*You've told me what you think is happening, but I don't understand why you think it, or why it's happening.*

Alynon gave a frustrated sounding hiss, then said, *In short, all the ways the Silver Court has benefitted in your world since the last Bright War, including our much greater number of brightblood vassals, has added to our power and helped us to gain position in the Colloquy.*

*That's kind of like your United Nations in the Other Realm, right?*

*Something like, insomuch that representatives of the Demesnes do meet there. And there's a kind of game of power and position that is played within the Colloquy, much as is played in your Congress or ARC, though not to such self-destructive ends.*

*Okay. And Hiromi's attacks on Silene would change that how?*

*The Forest of Shadows and the Hidden Vale were the Aalbright leaders in the last war. The Vale was all but destroyed by the weapon sent in by Verona, but the Vale's destruction only served to strengthen the Shadows. They gained both sympathy and respect from the other Demesnes for the penalties placed on them by the Pax, and for having led the charge against an enemy who, in the end, proved the Shadows' fears true through use of the spirit bomb.*

*Verona was only trying to—*

*Reasons matter little. The results were the downfall of an entire Demesne, and the loss of a war the Aalbrights thought all but won. The Silver Court and the Forest of Shadows have since become the two most powerful Demesnes, at least in the area of the Other Realm closest to this land. As long as the Silver Court has the support of the arcana, and the greater number of brightbloods, the Forest of Shadows cannot be guaranteed a victory in any conflict.*

*I don't suppose you'll tell me what exactly you Aalbrights get from your brightblood vassals if not memories?*

*No.*

I sighed. *Fine. So if the Shadows drive a wedge between the Silver Court and the ARC, and remove the Silver brightblood's greater number and freedoms—*

*Then the Shadows shall gain true advantage.*

Gods. If there really was a Fey war, even just between the Silver and Shadows, Pete and Vee would be forced to align with a Demesne if they hadn't already, or be held in an ARC compound.

Neither the ARC nor the Fey would tolerate undeclared bright-bloods during a real war. And whatever Demesne they aligned with would expect them to fight for their new Aalbright masters if needed. Lose lose.

*Please,* Alynon said. *You must help me warn my Demesne.*

"Yeah, I got that."

The door buzzed, and Reggie led Silene into the room. A DFM agent closed it from outside, locking us back in.

Reggie shook his head at the door. "Beast cops. They just love when they get to play at being real enforcers."

"Beast cops?" Silene asked, her tone dangerous.

"Shit, sorry," Reggie said, looking at her. "It's just a name that we Pax enforcers use for the Department of Feyblood Management sometimes. I shouldn't have used it."

Silene gave a dismissive wave. "I would expect no better."

Reggie opened his mouth as if to reply, then sighed, and just said, "Yeah, I guess not." He crossed to me. "So, you figure out what's going on?"

"Maybe."

I explained to Reggie and Silene what Alynon had shared with me.

Silene's eyes widened. "So it is war for true? Bright, I pray you are wrong. It would mean death and suffering for too many bright-bloods. We cannot let this happen."

Reggie grunted. "Well, I'll talk to my commander. Frankly, we've already noticed a pattern of Silver feyblood troubles, and thought it might be a sign that the Silver were getting a bit cocky and testing their strength. We can flag them for deeper investiga-tion though, look for signs they were set up like that alchemist attack. But——" He hesitated.

"What?" Silene and I asked together.

"Shit. To be honest, if the Fey are fighting amongst themselves, and the feybloods, too, well, the ARC might see that as a good thing. I mean, long·as it doesn't interrupt the flow of magic, and no arcana get hurt by the fallout, they're likely to just let it play out, at least until they see a way we can gain something from interfering."

"Are you kidding me?" I asked.

"You are surprised?" Silene asked. "Then you do not know your own kind well."

"Maybe not," I replied. "But how is it in arcana interests to let the Shadows wipe out the Silver Court? Don't they remember the last Fey-Arcana War, when the Silver helped us?"

"Of course," Reggie said. "But friends and enemies change, villains become allies and allies turn enemy. Avalon. The Germans and Japanese. The Hidden Vale. Al Qaeda, the French Canadian unicorns—"

"Okay, I get it," I said. "But the Shadows Fey, they aren't Germans or Japanese, or any of those others you named. They're the darkest side of every culture they drew their existence from."

Reggie raised his hands. "Hey, preaching to the choir, man." He glanced to the mirrored wall, then leaned in closer and said in a low tone, "I'm just saying, the ARC are all about protecting arcana interests. And letting the Fey weaken themselves in an internal battle will seem like a great idea. Hell, there may even be some who will try to help speed up the process."

I knew from experience that was true. And having spent twenty-five years being fed on by the Fey, a part of me understood that sentiment. But knowing what it would mean for Petey and Vee, not to mention Sal and Silene and the other brightbloods I'd met— I sighed. "We have to at least try to stop it."

"Sure," Reggie said. "But I suggest you don't try to save the world. That's too much. Just focus on what's in front of you: freeing these brightbloods, and protecting your family."

Silene shook her head. "I am losing sight of what we fight for. We may free Challa and Dunngo only for them to die in pointless battle with our Shadows cousins."

She went to the mirror and looked at her own reflection, but her expression and manner were more ones of trepidation than vanity.

*Hello?* Alynon said, his tone frustrated. *I know one thing you could do.*

"Oh, yeah," I said. "Alynon wants to get a message to the local Silver ambassador, and the Archon if possible."

Reggie frowned a second, and said, "I'm not sure that would work."

*Damn it!* Alynon screamed in my head, causing me to wince. *I'm not trying to plot against the ARC here, I'm just trying to warn my people!*

"Why wouldn't it work?" I asked through gritted teeth.

"Well, something this big, I don't think a secondhand opinion from a changeling is going to get the results you want, and especially not from Alynon. No offense, but from what I understand, he isn't exactly held in high regard to begin with."

I knew from hints Alynon had dropped that he wasn't a favorite child of the Silver Court. And under other circumstances, I would have jumped at the chance to have Reggie share what he knew. But I was more worried about what Reggie had implied.

"What are you saying?" I asked.

Reggie rubbed at his head, obviously not happy at the thoughts running around inside it—not a good sign. "Shoot. I don't see many options, son. If you really want to stop the Shadows, and protect your brother and Vee from being drafted into a Fey war, you're going to need to go into the Other Realm and convince the Fey directly."

My knees went wobbly, and I fumbled the nearby folding chair out from beneath the small steel table just in time to collapse into it.

No no no. This couldn't be happening.

*He's right,* Alynon said, eagerly. *We—you have to present your evidence directly to the Colloquy!*

Of course Alynon would be all for it. But if we went to the Other Realm, there was no guarantee I wouldn't be trapped in his body.

"No," I said, my voice barely above a whisper. "There has to be another way."

"It sucks, no lie," Reggie said, "But you'd be going as a free arcana this time. You would be in control of what memories you shared, and when."

I shook my head. "The Archon could go. Or . . . Silene," I said, looking up at her, feeling a bit of a coward for saying it. But she was a vassal of the Silver Court, after all. Didn't it make more sense for her to go?

"Feybloods cannot share their memories," Reggie said. "If they could, there would be no need for the Fey to feed on human memory."

"I thought they could," I replied, "but it just didn't give the Fey whatever . . . essence or whatever they needed."

"It goes beyond that," Silene said. "It is a very . . . sensitive matter that we do not like to talk about."

"But—"

*Let it go, Finn,* Alynon said. *Do not shame her to satisfy your curiosity.*

I blinked, surprised at the sharpness of Alynon's words.

But I wasn't ready to jump into the Other Realm either. Whatever Reggie said about me being free this time, once there I would be at the mercy of the Fey, who apparently still blamed me for the death of their wardens killed during my transfer from exile. They might find some excuse to hold me in exile yet again, to feed on my memories—

The door buzzed, and Sal was led inside before the DFM agent left and the door closed again.

Sal tugged unhappily at the collar around his neck. The DFM had confiscated my spirit trap and skeleton key this time, so I couldn't remove it if I wanted to. Silene's collar had been removed already, either because she wasn't considered a threat here sealed away from any plants, or they hoped she'd *prove* herself a threat.

"Arcana have bad manners," Sal muttered, and shuffled uncomfortably. I realized he did not have his combat boots on. The DFM agents must have removed them to make sure they hid no weapons or artifacts. Or perhaps just to make Sal feel more vulnerable during questioning.

Sal's feet were, well, not big feet.

They weren't small by human standards. He would probably stretch Pete's shoes. But for a sasquatch, they were absolutely tiny.

Sal caught my glance, and his face blushed red where it was not covered by hair.

"You sound surprised," Silene said, still looking in the mirror. From that angle, she probably had not noticed Sal's feet. "Did you expect better treatment?"

"No." Sal sighed. "But still it makes I heartsad. And bad-mad."

"I'm sorry, Sal," I said, still hunched over in the chair. "You didn't ask for any of this. I was supposed to be helping you, not getting you involved in more trouble."

Sal grunted. "Iself be Seeahtik. Weself be bear-strong and rock-tough, so allfolks only bring us trouble, or ken that war-making is all-and-every Seeahtik are liking." He shrugged, and I saw his gaze flicker briefly over to Silene, who seemed still fixated on some aspect of her own appearance. "Even otherself brightbloods think so."

Silene blinked, turned to Sal, and said in a defensive tone, "Well, it *is* all your tribe seems to do, fighting, and destroying."

"No," Sal replied. "War-making is all otherselves will give Seeahtik the bright to do."

Silene crossed her arms. "Well, maybe if you refused, and—" She stopped, her gaze falling on Sal's feet.

Sal blushed red again, and shuffled uncomfortably, looking down at the ground. "I not wanting to bigfight with youself," he said.

"No, of course," Silene said. "I just—" She put a hand on her chest. "I understand what it is to have others expect only one thing from you, to prune and bind your life to fit their design. It is not easy to set your own path, sometimes."

Sal looked up, and gave Silene a grateful smile.

Silene turned to me and Reggie. "We shall be set free, shan't we?"

"Yes," Reggie said. "We were within our legal rights to defend ourselves. And once the DFM's necromancer Talks to Hiromi and

Ned, and confirms my report, they should release your clan members as well."

"Good," Silene said, and put one hand to the smooth glass of the mirror. "I do not like being so separated from the growing, living world."

She did look pale, and weary. She had not been given time to recover from her healing of Reggie and the battle with Hiromi before being cut off from the natural world.

"I am having smallgift for youself," Sal said, and crossed to Silene in two great strides. He dug into the fur above his stomach, and then held out his hand. He held a twig with dried flowers on it.

"What—" Silene began, then blinked, and looked up at Sal's eyes with a surprised expression as he hunched over her. "Is that a brightlily?"

Sal shrugged, an expression more of shyness than uncertainty. "It was in sister-mine's remember box. I heart-wished to give youself bigthanks for healing Iself."

Silene gently took the dried flowers from Sal's hand, and closed her eyes for a few seconds.

From one of the dried flowers grew up a single, long stalk, and six pink and lavender bell-shaped flowers grew from the end.

Silene opened her eyes, and a tear ran down her cheek as she looked at the flowers. "I thought the last brightlily had been destroyed years ago." She looked up at Sal again. "Thank you." With her free hand, she took his shoulder and pulled him down, and gave him a quick kiss on the cheek.

Sal blushed red yet again, although this time he definitely didn't look miserable. He shuffled, clearly uncertain of what to do or say.

"Brightlily?" I asked to break the tension. "Does it have a Fey spirit in it?"

Silene's gaze lingered on Sal a second as if trying to puzzle something out, then she blinked, glanced at me and held up the lily.

"What? Oh, no. But when consumed by a brightblood, it allows us to more clearly . . . feel the bright within us. Some used it to gain a greater wisdom about ourselves, about what of our natures is the bright and what is other. Some used it to gain greater harmony with their bright nature."

"Wow, sounds like therapy in convenient and tasty flower form," I said.

"If you say." She looked down at the plant. "But it was never an abundant plant, and it was greatly consumed once its nature was learned. Much of it was destroyed as the human cities spread up into the hills. And some of the . . . darker-natured brightbloods, who did not like what the flower showed them and resented or feared that others might grow stronger or wiser from its use, they destroyed what little remained. It is always a sad thing when a green cousin is lost to us forever, but doubly so when its life brings good into the world."

The door buzzed, and Vincent entered the room still dressed in his ill-fitting tactical gear as if we might suddenly attack him. Which, I guess, wasn't an unreasonable concern given recent events. He set a duffel on the table and opened it, revealing Sal's boots, my necklaces, and Reggie's gear.

"You're all free to go," he said, sounding as disappointed as a destitute dentist who'd just learned Halloween had been canceled.

"What about my clan—" Silene began.

"The other Silvers are free to go as well. However, we have sent a bill to your Archon for the damages and time resulting from your actions, as well as the costs for our investigation and necromantic questioning. Whatever the jorōgumo may have done to incite violence in the siren, you and your feybloods were not forced to threaten the alchemist's business and life to begin with."

"We threatened no one!" Silene said. "We are within our rights to protest—"

Reggie put a hand on her arm. "A fight for another day," he said. "You and your feybloods need to return to your steading and heal."

I turned to Agent Vincent. "Is the Silver ambassador here? Zenith? We really should warn the Fey about what's going on."

Vincent scratched at his crew cut. "She's not stepping anywhere near this place. The Silver's trying to play that we are conspiring against them."

Reggie slid his pistol into its shoulder holster, and said, "Another bluff for negotiating purposes, or for real this time?"

"For real. They know we've begun reducing their freedom of movement and access to resources, given the recent troubles. And then, of course, there was the attack on that Zenith chick, and the fact their Archon's now claiming he never sent any order to ward and burn that siren's body."

"Why am I not surprised," I muttered, then asked, "If the Archon didn't, then who did?"

"That's for the Archon to figure out," Vincent said. "It's his communications that's been breached, and his feyblood who got burned up. And his purse that's going to pay, regardless."

*Could be Hiromi faked the message somehow,* Alynon said. *To cover up what she did to Veirai.*

*Maybe.*

Vincent looked at Reggie. "It'll be for the ARC to deal with the Fey anyway. We just deal with their stepkids here." He nodded in the direction of Sal and Silene.

Sal growled.

"Right," Reggie said. "Come on, Finn, we've still got work to do."

Frak. This was supposed to be the end of the job. The jorōgumo threat was ended. Challa was free for Sal to pursue, and we'd cleared Silene's name. Everyone was supposed to be happy, and Pete ideally welcomed to join the Silver. Instead, we now faced war.

I followed Reggie out into the hallway. Silene followed gracefully behind me, and Sal ducked through the doorway, with Vincent bringing up the rear. I was blindfolded, then led by Reggie with the others.

"Maybe we should go visit the Silver Archon," I said to Reggie as I followed blindly through the hallways. "He might find it hard to stick his head in the sand with your boot on his neck. He could speak to the Silver Court, convince them of what's going on."

Nobody spoke for a minute. Finally, Reggie replied, "Sounds like the Silver Archon ain't exactly feeling trusting of arcana right now, but for all we know the Archon really did order the siren burned and is attempting to use this situation as some kind of power play. He didn't exactly move heaven and earth to handle this situation with Silene's clan, or the jorōgumo. But even if he is legit, he'd be putting his own position on the line to accuse the Shadows of conspiracy, not to mention raising questions in his Fey patrons of whether he can handle the position given him. I just don't see how you could trust him to help."

We reached the exit. Vincent pulled off my blindfold, removed Sal's collar, and waved us out the door to the Game Farm loop road. Late morning sunlight slapped me in the eyeballs. I blinked at my watch: 10:45 A.M.

So far, not my favorite Monday ever. I wanted to just shoot the whole day down.

And Pete and Vee had only one day left to find a solution that didn't suck.

As my sight adjusted, the others joined us outside, and I saw that Dunngo and Challa waited for us. The dwarf moved back and forth along the road, and the sharp gravel wriggled up into place along his skin to form a spiky exterior. Challa paced anxiously near the entrance, waiting for us, her glamour shimmering around her like a heat wave, making her appear like a bear to anyone without the ability to see through it.

"Brightsister!" Silene said, and embraced Challa. She stepped back. "My heart shines to see you. How do you fare?"

Challa looked at Reggie and me before saying, "Iself not hurt. But big-need home."

"Yes. I think we all could use some rest," Silene said. Dunngo rode his dirt wave up beside Challa, his mosaic head of colored stone level with Silene's chest. Silene put a hand on his shoulder. "I think we shall take a break and think again on how best to fight for our cause. And—" She glanced at me. "We may need to prepare for greater troubles to come."

I couldn't meet the question in her eyes, and looked away.

Damn it, I was not responsible for every person I met. Not even those affected by my grandfather's legacy.

There had to be a better way to help Petey.

Dunngo grumbled, and I saw he was staring at me. "Is Gramaraye trouble?"

"No," Silene said. "No. He helped to free you. As did our Silver cousin here." She motioned Sal forward. "Challa, this brightblood is named—" She glanced at Sal.

"K'u-k'a Schken'ah Saljchuh," Sal said.

"Ah," Silene said. "Perhaps it is time you claim a new name for yourself. You have risen above those . . . . challenges given you at birth."

Sal shrugged, but he blushed slightly.

Challa glanced down at Sal's feet. "Youself cover greatfeet with human clothings."

Sal shrugged again. "Protecting against much bad."

Challa gave two sharp, rapid cough-like barks that sounded dismissive and disapproving. "Youself hide Seeahtik pride like rabbit-heart." She turned away. "I return home-safe now." She strode in the direction of the nearby woods.

"I not—" Sal began, his voice tinged with anger and defensiveness. But Silene put a calming hand on his chest.

"I told you when we met, Challa has her own wounds. Her father, he gave her to a mate when she was very young, a mate who badly abused her. It will take time for her to trust any male of her kind."

Sal growled low in his throat. "Herself not know true-good Seeahtik then."

"Sadly," Silene said. "But, I shall speak to her of your kind deeds and good heart." She sounded oddly unhappy, and looked after Challa. "But for now, you may need to give her time. We all need time, I think." She looked at me again. "I will speak to my Archon, for whatever good may come of it, and do what I can for my clan and cousins. I wish you luck in whatever you choose."

"Thanks," I said. "I—good luck to you, too."

Silene gave a single nod, then said to Dunngo, "Come. Let's return home."

They followed after Challa, across the gravel road and up the hill toward the forest, headed for the nearest fairy path.

"You know," I said. "I'm beginning to think Challa's wasn't the spirit at Elwha that the Kin Finder pointed to."

*Brilliant, Sherlock,* Alynon replied.

"What youself say?" Sal asked, his gaze still following after Silene and her party.

"I said, that Silene is pretty amazing, huh?"

Sal nodded, then blinked, and looked down at me. "Herself is like summer storming. Warm skywater and pretty sunglow, then youself get badhit by lightning."

"Uh huh," I said. "Well, I don't have my equipment, so I can't know for sure, but—you know what, never mind. I think you're doing just fine without my help. Sal, I think if you follow Silene—and Challa—back to her steading and spend some time there, you will find the love you were looking for. You don't need me. None of you do."

Reggie gave me a skeptical sideways glance, but didn't say anything.

Sal shrugged. "I will try. It not be so bad maybe to stay with other brightbloods for a shortwhile."

"There you go," I said, and slapped him on the back, which was a bit like slapping a wool-covered boulder.

Sal followed after Silene, and Reggie led me back to the parking lot of the Game Farm, where we found his motorcycle waiting, but not my hearse. Was that professional courtesy for Reggie or dislike for me?

"Need a lift?" Reggie asked.

"Looks like," I said.

Reggie straddled his motorcycle, and grabbed his helmet off the handlebar. "Look, Finn, I understand why you don't want to go back to the Other Realm," he said. "Hell, I wouldn't go. But don't fool yourself. If you don't go, if you just let Silene give her story to the Archon and leave it up to him to do something about it, then you're putting the life of your brother and Vee in his hands. And if war does break out, will you be okay knowing you might have stopped it?"

"There's got to be a better way."

"Name it," Reggie said.

"We could . . . . take off and nuke the Other Realm from orbit?"

*Not funny. At all,* Alynon said.

Ah, hells. "Fine," I said. "I can't think of anything better. Yet."

*YES!* Alynon shouted. *I'm going home!*

"Yippee ki yay." I sighed.

Mother frakker.

## Miss You Much

Waterfront veggie pizzas covered our dining room table, my first choice for a last meal. Their delicious smell filled the room and made my stomach rumble as I said good-bye to my family again, and for possibly the last time.

Of course, I didn't put it that way. I just informed them that I would be going into the Other Realm to speak with the Silver Court.

Silence fell around the table.

Dawn sat on my right. I couldn't tell if she was still upset with me or not. She'd played it cool when I first walked in, as if there'd been no doubt I'd survive a confrontation with a jorōgumo, but she hadn't been overly affectionate, either. I worried the news that I would be leaving again, risking my life yet again, would not help the situation, but couldn't bring myself to face her yet. I turned and looked in the other direction instead.

Mort appeared confused. He wore one of his fifty-dollar black T-shirts that normally fit him as if tailor made, and I couldn't help but notice how loose it hung on him, how unwell he still looked. Who would kick him in the butt when I was gone? Who would keep him from driving himself or the family business into the ground out of some impulsive need or fear?

Father put olives on two of his fingers and waggled them at each other like finger puppets. And Mattie looked angry, as if I'd broken a promise to her. She stabbed in a distracted but forceful manner at her food with her fork, and wouldn't meet my eyes.

Gods, what would happen to them if Mort lost the family business, or worse, his life? Mattie had taken on much of the responsibility for Father before I'd returned. Hell, she'd taken on most of the responsibility in the household, period. I'd tried to take some of that off of her so she could enjoy more of a normal teenage life— or at least as normal as a teen in a family of necromancers can have—and Pete helped out as well, but neither of them were exactly in a position to take responsibility for Father if anything happened to me and Mort both.

Sammy pushed up her thick-rimmed black glasses. "There's got to be a better way," she said, and the light from the chandelier glinted off her nose stud as her nostrils flared. She leaned back and crossed her arms, giving me a stare that said I was a sucker, or an idiot, or possibly both. She might look after Father, Mattie, and Pete, but she would resent it and it would be from a distance. Putting aside her allergy to magic, she would not be willing to leave the city and move back to Port Townsend, two hours and a ferry ride away from her friends, her job, her girlfriend.

Pete and Vee exchanged worried glances, and Pete's brow furrowed. "You said before you couldn't go back there even if you wanted."

"Yeah, well—" I had no response.

I turned last to Dawn, and met her eyes.

She took my hand and squeezed it. "Finn, if you were going off to fight another monster, I admit, I'd probably kick your ass myself. But if there's one thing I know, it's that you wouldn't be going anywhere near that Other Realm place if there was any friggin' way in hell to avoid it. So I'm guessing there's a pretty damn good reason?"

I managed not to look at Pete and Vee, and just said, "Yeah. A lot of lives may depend on it."

Sammy made a disgusted noise. "So let the ARC handle it. Hell, they should be kissing your ass after exiling you and all that's happened, not making you do their job for them."

"The ARC isn't making me do anything," I said.

"Yes, they are," Sammy said. "By not doing anything, they're making you do something."

"Yeah," Mattie said. "Auntie Sam's right. If there's really lives at stake, why aren't *they* going into the Other Realm?"

"Because," I said, still avoiding Pete and Vee's eyes. "It's not arcana lives at stake. It's the Fey. And brightbloods."

"Oh," Vee said.

"What does that mean?" Pete asked.

Sammy looked from Pete to me, and her expression softened as she uncrossed her arms. "Shit." She sighed. "You're sure there's no other way?"

"Not one that I can trust and sleep okay tonight. None that I could live with if—" I glanced at Pete, and quickly away again. I shrugged.

Mort shook his head. "I know this may sound a bit insensitive, but, well, have you considered that a few Fey and feybloods losing their lives isn't necessarily the worst thing that could happen?"

"What the fuck, Mort?" Sammy snapped.

"Dad!" Mattie said.

He raised his hands. "Look, I'm just saying, for all we know, worrying about the Fey dying is like, well, worrying about the characters in your dream dying because you woke up. But they sure as hell want to kill us, and that's real."

*Your brother is a cretin,* Alynon said.

*Grandfather's influence,* I thought back.

"It's not just about the Fey," I said.

"So?" Mort said. "Feybloods aren't much better. Well, obviously, I don't mean Pete and Vee and folks raised normal who didn't choose to be infected. But real feybloods? How many times in the last three months has our family been attacked by them? Those witches, the sasquatches, the waerwolves, that jorōgumo—and that's just us. I think maybe there's getting to be too many of them if the DFM can't control them anymore. And, well, I know this might sound cold or whatever, but let's face it, if a bunch of feybloods were to pass on, that wouldn't exactly be bad for business."

"Dude!" Sammy said. "Every time I start to have a little hope for you, you go and pull some messed-up junk like this."

"Seriously," I agreed. "Mother taught us better than that."

Mort looked offended. Oh the irony. "*Seriously,* you're all going to pretend like you haven't had similar thoughts? What, you all love the Fey and feybloods now?"

"Some of them," I said. "The ones who deserve it."

*Aww, thanks,* Alynon said.

*Don't make assumptions,* I thought back.

Mattie nodded agreement. "Dad, I know you're not trying to be racist or anything. You're just, uh—" She looked to me for help. But I had nothing, and gave her an apologetic shrug.

Mort snorted. "Racist? Seriously? Come on, let's just be honest for a second. If Mother had gone through what we've gone through, even she—"

Father suddenly stopped playing with the olives and looked at Mort, his face serious. "Go to your room."

Mort looked at Mattie. "Get him some candy." He turned back to face me. "I don't think you all—"

Father slapped the table, making the dishes jump.

"I said go to your room!"

Mort turned an annoyed expression toward Father, but the expression faded when their eyes met. There was an awkward moment of silence, then Mort snorted. "Whatever." He grabbed his napkin from his lap, and tossed it onto the table. "I don't feel like sitting here anyway, not with you all pretending like I'm some kind of monster for speaking the hard truth." He gave me a dismissive wave. "I was just trying to keep you from throwing your life away for a bunch of homicidal half-bloods. Sorry for caring."

He strode from the room in classic pout mode.

"Wow," Sammy said. "Every time I think he's outdone himself—" She shook her head.

I leaned toward Father, putting my hand out to him on the table though he was too far to reach. "Father? Are you okay?"

Father looked at his hands, and the broken remains of olive that clung to his fingertips. "They're falling apart," he said. "Why can't all my fingers be on the same hand?" He wriggled his fingers.

"It'll be okay," I said. Gods, I'd need to have Mattie watch him, make sure he didn't try to invent a way to sew his hands together or something.

Father looked up at me, and grinned. "Okee smokey artichokey, you better learn to dance the polky."

I tried to keep the tears back. But they broke free, and then I began sobbing in a series of explosive releases as though I were being punched in the gut. It was as raw as the roof of my mouth after a box of Cap'n Crunch, and unexpected as the Spanish Inquisition.

Dawn made reassuring sounds, and pulled me into a hug. Mattie, Pete, and Vee all asked if I was okay, and what they could do.

It was all too much. My family's needs. My father's madness. The uncertain promise of me and Dawn. The unbelievably suck-a-rific choice I faced: to return to the Other Realm and risk potential destruction or permanent exile; or to possibly allow the Shadows to start a war that would destroy thousands of lives, including my brother's and Vee's? And I hadn't really had time to process or recover from the fighting and Talking drains of the past couple of days, which probably didn't help.

I felt embarrassed, and frustrated, and nothing like a champion of the brightbloods or leader of my family. I wanted to just go to my room and curl up in my bed, to spend the next week eating junk food and playing games on my Commodore and leaving everything and everyone else be. But the love and comfort of my family helped quiet the chaos in my head and heart, and I soon regained control. I rubbed at my eyes and nose.

*I am sorry, truly,* Alynon said. *You know I wish to go home, but, well, I understand. I think I may even miss your family.*

I laughed, and wiped apologetically at the wet spot on Dawn's shoulder. "I'm sorry," I said to everyone. "Not exactly the manliest reaction."

Dawn snorted. "Are you kidding? That was damn sexy. Especially the boogers you left on my shirt."

"Gee, thanks!" I said.

"You have nothing to be embarrassed about," Sammy said. "It's better than getting drunk and making an idiot of yourself, which is my normal reaction to stress."

Pete nodded. "Doctor Weirmedice says what you don't let out in a good way now will just come out in a bad way later."

Mattie looked up in the direction of our bedrooms. "I'm sorry my dad is kind of a jerk sometimes. He just—" She shrugged, and I felt fresh tears building at the clear disappointment on her face. How much must it suck for a child when they can't make excuses for their parent's bad behavior anymore, even to themselves?

"We know, Mat-cat," Sammy said. "Now, hero boy, is there anything we can do to help you get ready?"

"Actually," I said, "I do need to do a couple of things. Vee, maybe we can work a little on recovering my memories before I leave?"

"Oh! Sure," Vee replied in a surprised voice.

And I would need some time to absorb some magic from the family's stores of mana. It would be nice to test out my theory about the Simon artifact as well—"over there, other there" Father had said—but I couldn't risk it. I'd arrange for Pete to test it once I was gone.

One memory session, three-fourths Thoth of mana absorbed, and lots of family hugs later, Dawn and I made our way to her house to get her car keys.

"Thank you for not trying to leave me behind," Dawn said.

"Of course! I'm just glad you want to go with me at all, after last night, and everything that's happened." It would be nice to not be alone with my thoughts and fears for the ride there.

Dawn halted, and pulled me to a stop beside her in the noon warmth. "About last night, it wasn't just about us, or Heather, or—" She stopped, and shook her head, and tears built up in her eyes.

"Dawn, what's wrong?" I asked, stepping closer and putting my hands on her arms.

"I tried playing guitar yesterday, and I couldn't. Not for long." Her hand went to her shoulder. "I don't know if it was the damage, or the way it was healed or what, but this is tight, and hurts when I try to strum for long."

"Oh. Oh shit. Dawn, I'm so sorry. And then that record company wants to hear you play—"

She nodded. "I was just upset, and scared. And a little angry at you. But it wasn't your fault."

"No, I don't blame you. If I hadn't gone sticking my nose where it didn't belong—"

"Stop," Dawn said. "I'm proud of what you're doing, it makes me love you more. I just needed a little time to process is all."

I pulled her into a hug. "Still, I'm sorry." I stepped back. "Maybe Amber can play while you sing, just for a while? She's always joking about forming the New Dawn cover band."

"I've already talked to her," Dawn said. "She's going to help with my gig Tuesday night. And the ladies at the massage school said they'd help with some massage, and pointed me to a physical therapist who might take barter. I'm not asking you to fix this, Finn, I'm just letting you know what's going on so you understand."

I nodded. "Okay." We continued walking to her house. "You really sure you want to come with me? I'd understand if you wanted the time to rehearse with Amber."

"Nice try, baby, but I'm taking you there, and you're going to hold me in front of that friggin' romantic waterfall, and rehearse something a hell of a lot better than a song."

"As you wish," I said, and smiled.

The regional ARC headquarters was located beneath Snoqualmie Falls and the hydro-power plant, on the "mainland." It was to the lighthouse ARC facility what a state supreme court was to a local county court.

Western Washington isn't so much an area of land as a collection of hills, plateaus, peninsulas, and islands—not to mention political, cultural, and economic islands—divided by inlets, lakes, straights, wetlands, and valleys, with countless bridges, ferries, and narrows connecting them all. So it took almost three hours, a ferry ride, and crossing a floating bridge to reach the Snoqualmie Falls.

Dawn excitedly informed me during the drive over that Snoqualmie Falls Lodge—or Salish Lodge, as I guess it was now called—had been featured in a show called *Twin Peaks*. I didn't know about that, but I did remember that they made an amazing breakfast. I hoped that was still true. And that I had a chance to test it out when I got back from the Other Realm.

We pulled into the parking lot just after 3:00 P.M., then strolled to the Falls viewpoint.

We had an hour to kill before I was to meet Reggie. Per Dawn's plan, we kissed in front of the waterfall long and passionately, at least until the unhappy looks from passing families made us grin at each other and wander off to explore the paths and displays on the history of the falls, the power plants, and the Snoqualmie tribes to whom the land was held sacred.

The time of simply being a happy couple came to an end, and time to face my choice arrived. We walked to the restaurant and gift shop that overlooked the falls. The place looked nothing like I remembered. It had been completely remodeled shortly after my exile, replacing its old rustic charm with a more "upscale lodge" look. Oak wood support and ceiling beams framed honey-colored walls, tasteful art displays, and items for sale.

I felt a bit lost.

"Ready?" Reggie said behind me, making me jump.

"Hey!" I said. "Uh, yeah, one sec."

I gave Dawn a last long kiss, PDA rules be damned, and held her tight. "I'll be right back," I whispered to her.

"You'd better," she replied, her voice thick. We stepped apart, and she cleared her throat. "Make sure he doesn't do anything stupid," she said to Reggie.

Reggie shrugged. "I'll do what I can."

Dawn nodded, and headed toward the exit. She glanced back when she reached the door, and said, "Have fun storming the castle." And then she was gone.

"Come on," Reggie replied. "We only have a small window between shifts."

He led me downstairs and to a door with a security keypad on the handle. From his jacket pocket, he pulled the now-familiar black blindfold with thaumaturgic symbols sewn in silver thread across it.

"Sorry, Finn. I need you—"

"Yeah, yeah, I know." I sighed, and slid it over my head, covering my eyes and dulling my arcana senses.

I heard Reggie punch in a code on the door lock. "This way," he said, and guided me with a hand behind my shoulder.

We walked a short distance, then stopped, and Reggie said, *"Aperire Ostium."*

I heard the grinding of a door opening in concrete or stone, and then we proceeded.

The air grew instantly cool, and smelled like a spice cabinet where all the spices had long ago gone stale. We were descending beneath the lodge, into the ancient network of tunnels and caves that ran behind the waterfall. We took several turns, and at one point the roar of the waterfall and chilly blanketing of mist on my skin told me we passed the original "hidden" entrance to the tunnels; then the sound of a metal door opening, and the ground became smooth. We'd entered the more recently built tunnels of the Regional ARC Headquarters, an underground, multi-floored complex of concrete and steel.

The ARC complex held a number of departments: Department of Mana Management (typically called MaMa, especially by those who felt the department was like an overbearing mother); the Department of Arcana Justice that oversaw the enforcers; the Department of Magic Administration that approved new spells, potions, and artifacts and said what magic usage was legal versus illegal; and many more, including, obviously, the Department of Interdepartmental Cooperation, and the Department of Department Departmentalization and Administration. And then there were fun little features like the Crucible, the small amphitheater-style courtroom where they had sentenced me to exile twenty-five years and three months ago, or the rumored "Cruelcible" dungeon where the more dangerous criminals were questioned.

Reggie led me down several flights of stairs, through a couple more doors, and finally said, "Okay. You can take off the blindfold."

I blinked against the lights, and took in what looked a bit like my father's basement thaumaturgy laboratory, but five times the size and, if appearances were any indication, joint-funded by DARPA, the NSA, and George Lucas's Industrial Light & Magic.

A woman stood blinking at me through bottle-thick glasses, her hair a wild silver nest held in place by pens; her lab coat had a giant ink stain on the pocket that was matched by a small smear on her nose.

It took me a second, but I recognized her. During one of the many visits I'd had here after learning of Alynon's presence, she'd suggested the possibility of using a modified brain scanner to magically dissect my brain and identify exactly how I'd managed to "trap" a Fey spirit without being susceptible to his commands or influence on my body.

"Uh, Reggie?" I asked. "What's going on?"

"Hi," the lady said. "I'm Verna. I—oh, wait, *he* can hear us. One second."

"Reggie?" I asked again.

"Just be patient," he said. "Everything will be fine."

So why did his voice hold a slight edge of doubt?

Verna fumbled around in a cabinet for a second, then another cabinet, and finally pulled out what looked like a Mr. Microphone with a series of crystals and wires stuck along the outside. She then grabbed an old radio boom box off a nearby shelf, and set it down on a lab counter near me.

"What —?" I began, but she raised a warning finger and shook her head, then turned on the radio and adjusted the dial until soft static hissed out of the speakers. She scurried across the room, and looked at me, her manner excited.

"Hello," she said, or rather, she spoke softly into the microphone, and her voice came out of the radio.

"Uh, hi?" I replied loud enough for her to hear me.

"If I'm right," she said, "your Fey should not be able to hear what I'm saying, as it is resonating at a frequency that is painful for Fey spirits."

*Ahhh!* Alynon said. *What's she trying to do, serenade a fax machine?*

"Is it working?" Verna asked.

"Well," I replied, "either it's working, or he's faking a reaction."

Verna made a "darn it" fist in the air, and said loud enough that I could hear her without the microphone, "Stupid, Verna, stupid. I should have asked him to describe the result, not tell him what was expected." She sighed, then spoke into the microphone again. "Well, we shall just have to hope it is working, I guess. Reginald tells me you want to see if your control over your Fey guest would carry over into the Other Realm. I think this would be an excellent experiment. The potential of your unique situation as a way to travel the rainbow roads again, or explore the Demesnes—" She shook her head. "Of course, I'm sure the ARC will find some way to use it as a weapon, but there's no helping that if we're going to get your pass validated."

I turned to Reggie. "What is she talking about?"

*She's talking?* Alynon asked.

Reggie cleared his throat. "It's not like getting passage into the Other Realm is an easy thing. You haven't committed a crime worth exile, and as far as the ARC is concerned, there is no imminent threat to the Pax or arcana security that would warrant sending a special ambassador over, and you would not be their first choice of ambassador anyway. So—"

"An experiment?" I asked. "Is this really the only way? To shoot me off into the Other Realm like a monkey in a space capsule?"

*If the jumpsuit fits—* Alynon said.

"We tried monkeys, once," Verna said. "Or rather, chimpanzees. Given their higher cognitive function, both we and the Fey wanted to see what would manifest, and whether the Fey could feed on their memories."

"What happened?" I asked, curiosity getting the better of me.

"It failed," she said. "The chimpanzees lacked whatever higher function allows humans to retain their identity and adapt to the Other Realm. Though, surprisingly, one did manifest a copy of Hamlet. Still," she said, her voice becoming excited again, "that did give us the opportunity to advance our brain resonance scanning technology. You know, since you're going to be technically comatose while your spirit is visiting the Other Realm, I was hoping we could revisit the possibility of doing some scans? Well, comatose assuming your changeling doesn't just remain here and regain control of your body, but even then—"

"No!" I said, then continued in a calmer voice, "I appreciate your wanting to help, but I'd rather not have anyone poking around in my head when I'm not home."

*What is this noise?* Alynon demanded. *It's like electric bagpipes set to overload!*

*I don't hear it,* I replied honestly.

*You are clearly holding a conversation without me, which is rude enough, but if you're talking about trying to zap me out of your brain then I really should be part of the conversation!*

*You're not going to get zapped, Scott Fey-o. Just relax for a second and trust me.*

Verna sighed. "Very well," she said. "But I must say, very disappointing. We really have worked out the bugs. Or most—"

A knock on the lab door, and it opened. An enforcer led Silene inside, blindfolded and collared.

"Wait," I said. "What's she doing here?"

The enforcer removed Silene's blindfold, and she gave him an irritated glance as he left before saying, "I asked to go with you. This matter affects the brightblood greatly, and our words together are more likely to find fertile soil than yours alone."

*She is in for a rude awakening,* Alynon said. *But she could prove helpful. Especially if you—* He stopped.

*If I don't survive the trip?*

Alynon did not respond.

Reggie shrugged. "You're only going to have one shot at this, we should give it the best chance of success."

Verna patted at her hair. "Yes, yes. Everyone's here. We should get moving now. We don't have much time."

"Wait, why is that?" I asked, looking between her and Reggie.

"Well," Verna said, and blushed lightly, "the clerk at the Department of Portal Management is a . . . friend of mine. He may be willing to give me the portal pass if his bosses aren't around. But we have to get there during their lunch break."

"Oh."

Verna hurried from the room. Silene followed, and Reggie motioned for me to join them.

"Don't I need the blindfold?" I asked stupidly.

"It's a short walk," Reggie said.

Indeed, we only went a few doors down the same hallway, and into a room that had been divided up into smaller offices. The entrance area formed a small waiting room with a counter. A man perhaps a couple years younger than me sat behind the counter, typing on a computer. He looked up as we entered.

"Verna! Hello." He leaned his head to the side to look past the monitor, taking in myself, Silene, and Reggie. "What have we here?"

"Lucius," Verna said. "I have a tiny favor to ask." She glanced toward the offices, then leaned closer and spoke in a voice too low to hear.

*La! Good for her,* Alynon said. *You see? Even Grandma Verna is getting more action than you. He is at least twenty years her younger, she must truly know how to—*

*Do you mind?* I asked. *You're about to go home to the Other Realm, so maybe you could give up harping on the whole sex thing? It's obviously not going to happen at this point.*

*I don't know. From where I'm standing, I would bet Verna might give us a quick encounter.*

*Seriously? If I wouldn't make love to Dawn with you around, what make you think I'd cheat on her with Verna?*

\*I understand why you might not wish me to witness your own woman in such intimacies, but why should you care if I see Verna knocking boots? She clearly has the experience to teach you a few things that would make Dawn happy. In fact, the more I think about it, the more I really think you should explore this idea for your own sake.\*

*I'm sure you do.*

\*No, truly. Ask her, I'm sure she would say yes, perhaps even perform the act as we are transferring. Tell her it's an experiment, to see how your body reacts to stimulation before and after transfer, tra la la.\*

*You really are unbelievable,* I thought.

\*Aw, thanks.\*

*Well, thank you for one thing. You've actually made me eager to get this over with. I can't be separated from you soon enough.*

\*La! Always happy to help.\*

I sighed. Verna smiled, and gave the clerk, Lucius, a kiss on his cheek.

Reggie and I both held our persona rings over what looked like a slab of oily gray stone with a cord running from it to Lucius's computer, and then made Silene place her hand on the same slab. Lucius typed a few things in, printed off a form, and stamped it with a rubber stamp.

Verna turned to me. "You'll need to pay the fee."

"Fee?" I asked, looking from her to Lucius.

"Nine hundred ninety-seven," he said. "Dollars. For processing and administrative fees on two spirit transfers, material costs, etcetera. And two hundred Toths of mana for energy expenses."

"Oh," Verna said. "The mana will come out of my department's cost code."

"Sure," Lucius said. "So just the nine ninety-seven then."

"But—" I sighed. "Never mind. Do you take American Express?" I asked, pulling the necrotorium's business card out of my wallet.

"Of course."

Five minutes later, I had a receipt and two round-trip tickets to the Other Realm.

Well, if things went poorly and I didn't come back, at least I wouldn't have to explain the credit card bill to Mort. That was not a conversation I felt like having.

"You're the best, Lucius," Verna said as I looked over the receipt and paperwork.

"Dinner soon?" he asked.

Verna pushed up her glasses. "That would be groovy. Take care."

We left the office, and Verna said, "Well, we can do the transfer from my lab, which is probably for the best if we're to avoid inconvenient questions and uncomfortable pat downs and such. I have all the necessary equipment. And I have a memory-blocking helmet I've been meaning to test out. It should target and block—"

"Uh, no offense," I said. "But I don't want any experimental artifacts messing with my memory."

"Oh poo. Fine. I'll have a sorcerer come down from the Department of Information Management."

Thirty minutes later, Silene and I were strapped into reclining chairs, with a slew of medical equipment meant to keep our bodies alive (and a necromancer on call to do the same just in case of equipment failures, Verna assured me), my memories of necromancy training and other sensitive arcana information locked up to prevent the Fey from accessing them illegally or otherwise, and a feeling in my stomach like I'd swallowed a burning chunk of charcoal and then tried to douse it by chugging a jar of pickle water.

Facing us was a vertical stone ring with an opening the size of a standard window, mounted on a metal stand with rollers. The stone band itself was about six inches thick with runes carved all along it, and what looked like a flux capacitor hanging off of the bottom. A disc of cold iron covered the hole until Reggie lifted it off.

"Here we go," Verna said. She struck a crystal hanging in a triangle with a tiny silver hammer, and read an incantation from our travel paperwork.

Portals between the worlds required coordination and approval from both sides after the establishment of the magical barriers—or a major assault on the barriers that was unlikely to happen short of war. Each portal required what was essentially a password agreed on by both sides, and each password was used only once.

The stone ring began to hum in a deeper tone sympathetic to the crystal triangle, and purple lightning began to dance within a window on the flux capacitor.

*Chevron one, locked,* Alynon said, excitement in his voice.

*What?*

*Nothing. La! Perhaps when we reach the other side, I shall be able to gift you all those memories you were to get in our last transfer, and you shan't be so clueless!*

*I'm beginning to question whether I would've wanted those memories,* I replied, *given your clear obsession with the sexual habits of humans.*

*Me?* Alynon said. *La, I may have been hoping for Vala and SG-1 to find themselves on planet PX-0RG1—*

The stone ring rang like a gong, and a portal opened up within it, a glowing watery view of what appeared to be a room made of white marble.

"Wait," I said to Verna. "Where exactly are you sending us?" A few feet in our world could be the equivalent of miles in the Other Realm, or could be inches. The Portal Room in each ARC facility was built to deliver transfers to a specific point in the Other Realm, but there was no knowing how leaving from this room, several floors and who knew how far away, would place us over there.

"Oh, don't worry," Verna said. "I built a shunt artifact that should in theory slide you along the quantum substrate on this side before piercing the barriers, so it will be just like leaving from the Portal Room."

"In theory?" I asked, panic rising.

"A strong theory," she said. "I did the math and alchemical equations myself."

She struck the chime again, and my spirit lifted out of my body and flew through the portal, falling forward into the one place I'd hoped never to return.

Alynon laughed madly the entire way.

# Paradise City

I opened my eyes. Except they weren't eyes. They were glowing crystals floating in a body that looked like a semitransparent blob, a life-sized gummy bear left on the dashboard in the sun too long. I was back in the body of an unshaped Fey.

I looked around me. I stood on what appeared to be a balcony made of granite, with gargoyles crouched in the corners, attached to a curved white wall with gargoyles crouched in the corners. An open arch led from the balcony inside, though I was at a bad angle to see through it. And beyond the balcony lay the chaos of the unshaped Other Realm's unshaped wildlands, where the sky and land melted together in a shifting rainbow mess I imagined must be like watching *Fantasia* through a prism after eating acid-laced Fruity Pebbles.

Two more blobs began to move on the balcony beside me. The first took on the same semihuman shape as my own. But the other shimmered, and truly transformed.

Within seconds, the second blob became a naked man who looked like Ziggy Stardust's taller, even more beautiful and decidedly fit brother, his hair flowing in metallic silver waves past his shoulders. He looked down at himself, and spun around with a loud "Whoop!"

The second blob looked between us, then at its blobby appendages. Much more slowly than with Alynon, the body took shape, shrinking in and blooming with color until Silene stood there in her green dress, looking much as she had in our world.

I tried to speak, but wasn't surprised when nothing happened. This body didn't have lungs or vocal chords, and even if it did I wasn't sure that there was even really air here. I focused, tried to make my own body take shape, but nothing happened. Whatever was in Alynon and Silene's Fey natures that allowed them control over their bodies here, I lacked.

I looked at the man. *Alynon, I presume?* I projected the thought at him by power of will.

"Indeed," he said, and gave a sweeping bow. "In the flesh, so to speak. Holy Bright! I can finally clothe myself properly!" He frowned and tapped his chin for a second, then snapped his fingers. "Got it!"

Clothing sprang into being around him. Ruffles, tight pants, ornate buttons, bright colors. Prince would have wept with envy at the sight.

Alynon swayed, and put a hand to his head. "Whoa."

"A foolish waste of energy," a man's voice announced in a thick French accent. "You make a poor spy, *monsieur.*"

I turned to find a small, weasely-looking man standing in the arched exit from the balcony, dressed like a French aristocrat going to a goth concert: tall boots, fitted calf-length jacket, and tri-corner hat, all black.

"We are not spies," Alynon replied.

"Indeed, then I beg your pardon, sir," the man said. "But when a Silver aristocrat shows up uninvited on my balcony, I assume he is either a spy, an idiot, or entirely mistaken as to my proclivities. Are you an idiot then?"

"La, I have been called worse. I am Alynon Infedriel, Knight of the Silver Court," Alynon said, and bowed. "We have just arrived from the Human Realm, and clearly did not arrive where expected. If you could but tell us where we are, happily will we depart."

"You are in the Colloquy," the man said. "In my private quarters. I am Ganel te'Chauvelin, Proxenos for the Greatwood. And if you have newly arrived, and clearly not where expected, that begs the question of whether anyone knows you are here? And more to the point, from what I know of your reputation, Alynon Infedriel,

Knight of the Silver Court, I wonder if anyone would miss you should you never arrive?"

As Chauvelin said this, a second man the size of a professional football player who'd eaten a professional weightlifter appeared in the doorway, wearing nothing but a loincloth and a grin.

"Uh," Alynon said.

I moved to the edge of the balcony and peered cautiously over it. We were in a tower that appeared to be made of some black, rough stone at the base, and blindingly white alabaster at the top, with a slow gradient of brightness and smoothness between. And unfortunately, we were at least a dozen stories above the rainbow fractal landscape that swirled below.

"But come, such concerns are yours, not mine," Chauvelin continued. "We are here at the Colloquy to foster good will among our Demesnes, are we not? So let us guide you safely back to where you belong, and we will consider this only a minor infraction of Colloquy Law, worth barely a mention. And of course, you will owe me only the smallest of obligations."

"Of course," Alynon said, and sighed an unhappy sigh. "Perfect. Thank you."

"Do not mention it," Chauvelin said. "And to your human companions, my utmost respect and welcome. May I be so bold as to ask your identities, and what brings you to the Colloquy?"

I hesitated before responding.

I didn't trust Chauvelin, utmost respect or not. The Greatwood was what the Shadows called their forest. And the only Chauvelin I knew of was Armand Chauvelin from *The Scarlet Pimpernel*, a ruthless, fanatical patriot and politician.

Chauvelin was a fictional character, but he had clearly lived in enough detail and richness within someone's memory for that memory to form the basis of a Fey's identity. In fact, there might be a thousand Armand Chauvelins running around the Other Realm, each unique due to the mix of other memories they'd incorporated and their own actual experiences.

Hence the te'Chauvelin, to announce the root of his identity, a kind of self-proclaimed heritage, without claiming to be *the* Chauvelin. In the end, though, I still found it easiest to drop the "te'" and think of a Fey as the person they most represented. Unless I knew them as individuals, or had to deal with multiple Fey of the same origin at once, it just made life easier.

And regardless of how unique a snowflake this particular Chauvelin might be, a Fey who chose to look and act like Chauvelin and represented the Forest of Shadows was not someone I would trust with the life of my pet rock.

*I've come to speak with some of the Aalbrights here,* I projected at him.

"Obviously," Chauvelin said. "That is the purpose of the Colloquy. But if you give me some clue as to your purpose, I may be able to help speed your success."

*I'm pretty worn out from the transfer and all,* I said. *I'd rather not discuss official business until I have a chance to recover.*

"Of course. Though I did not catch your name?"

I hesitated, then replied, *Phinaeus.* I didn't want to risk a lie even to Chauvelin, not when I had come here to ask the Fey to take me on my word.

"Well met, Phinaeus. And your beautiful companion?" he asked, turning to Silene.

"Silene Treebright," Silene replied, her tone proud.

"Indeed? A tree bright. I should have realized. Well, this is a most unusual party that has appeared upon my doorstep. Come."

Chauvelin stepped aside, waving us through the doorway. Silene and I both looked to Alynon, who stood up straight and tugged at his paisley waistcoat before giving Chauvelin a quick bow of the head and proceeding through the doorway.

Chauvelin led us through chambers furnished in a Spartan fashion with dark wood furniture and silver fixtures. But there were clear signs we were no longer in Kansas. A lava lamp floated in the air, slowly turning. A harp played itself beside the crackling blue fire in the silver fireplace. And gods, was that a nude painting of Chauvelin on a bearskin rug? Winking at us?

Yep. Evil.

The barbarian warrior trailed behind us, not quite herding, but still uncomfortably close.

I willed my blob-hand to form into a point, discreetly. Nothing happened. Blast it. It seemed I truly had no more control over my Fey body than I'd had in exile, which is to say, I could move around by willing it, but that was about it.

As we passed through the chambers, Chauvelin looked back at me and said, "I noted you admiring this building's structure. You may be interested to know that it represents the Creation, when all that was light and pure rose to create the Aal, and all that was, shall we say, less light and pure sank to create the human realms."

*Very impressive,* I said with less sincerity than a senator apologizing for an affair with a televangelist. *Build it and Fey will come.*

Chauvelin looked confused, but gave a curt nod.

We exited the chambers into a hall of white marble that curved slightly in either direction. Light appeared to come from the marble itself, illuminating everything in an even, soft glow.

"Now," Chauvelin said, glancing back at me and Silene as we walked the hallway, "your first time to the Colloquy, I sense?"

*Yes,* I projected back. *Though I would be missed if I did not arrive.*

"You wound me, *monsieur.* I was merely asking out of politeness." He waved at the hallway. "The Colloquy is a mighty achievement indeed, a monument to the power of the Fey citizens who cried out for true governance."

*It's a regular Ministry of Love, I'm sure,* I replied. *But I don't need a tour, really.*

Silene quickly added, "Excuse him, Bright Lord, like all arcana he has little appreciation for the accomplishments of anyone not human. I would like to hear more."

I held in my protest.

"Happy to oblige," Chauvelin said as he continued to lead us down the hallway. "The Colloquy was established to negotiate trade and truces between the Demesnes, discuss together issues of common interest or concern, and settle disputes or matters of justice that extend outside our own Demesne. Many of our greatest diplomats reside here, if I may be so bold as to say so, as well as great heroes of our wars who lend status and influence to their Demesne, such as Volruk there." He motioned to the tower of barbarian muscle behind us. I could only assume Volruk had been the champion, or perhaps myth, of some tribe whose shaman traveled into the Other Realm long ago.

The walls changed. Where once they were smooth, now they were covered in bas-relief figures of thousands of Fey, each about six inches tall and incredibly detailed.

"I am interested in politics myself," Silene said.

"Indeed?" Chauvelin said. "Fascinating. Please, tell me more. We have so little opportunity to speak with our brightblood vassals directly."

*Silene,* I tried to send to her in a warning tone.

"I don't know that—" Alynon began.

"Come," Chauvelin said. "I have always said the reason we cannot hear the needs of our cousins more clearly is because we do not allow them their own voice." He looked at Silene. "But if you feel foolish or ashamed about your interests, you need not speak of them."

"I have no need for shame," Silene said defensively. "I am happy to speak of my cause with any who will listen."

"Then please do," Chauvelin encouraged.

Silene spoke to Chauvelin of her awakening and decision to fight for fairer treatment and the equality of her brightblood cousins. She spoke for several minutes until Chauvelin stopped, and raised a hand.

"Pardon me, but this is our destination: Nibiru, what you would name the Room of Arrival." He stood before double doors ornately carved with hundreds more of the small Fey figures. "Do you like the doors?" he asked me. "A bit more decadent than I typically enjoy, but nonetheless, quite lovely work, no?"

*Yes, very detailed,* I projected back.

"Each one of the figures here, and along the hallway, represents one of the Vale's Aalbrights that were lost to the terrible arcana weapon that ended our last war," Chauvelin said. "Observe."

Chauvelin placed his hand on one of the door handles of woven silver bands. It glowed bright for a second, and then the light rippled out from it, sweeping across the doors and out along the walls. All of the figures touched by the light cried out in silent agony and then melted away, leaving the wall smooth.

"A bit dramatic, perhaps," Chauvelin said as the first figures erased by the door handle rose up out of the wall, reforming, followed in a slow wave by the figures around it. "But it does serve as one small reminder of why we are here."

*To avoid another war?* I asked.

"Of course, that is it," Chauvelin said, and pulled the left door open. "Now, I will leave you to announce your arrival officially. And may I be the first to say, welcome to the Colloquy. I hope your visit is of value to all."

*Uh, thank you,* I said.

Chauvelin turned to Silene and gave a small bow and flourish of his hand. "I look forward to our next encounter, lady."

"As do I," Silene replied.

"And Alynon Infedriel, Knight of the Silver Court," Chauvelin said. "Should you find your homecoming as . . . disappointing as your departure, you are always welcome in the Greatwood."

"Thank you for your kind offer," Alynon replied with a curt nod of his head. "But I have sampled the Shadows' hospitality, and it left a bitter taste."

Chauvelin gave a sad shake of his head. "Do not let the unfortunate difficulties of your situation color your views. Should you join the Shadows, what cause or power would any have to deny you your happiness?"

Alynon did not respond, but just looked away, his jaw clenching.

"Well, farewell friends, until we meet again." Chauvelin gave a courtly bow, and departed, Volruk lumbering along in his wake.

*What was that all about?* I asked Alynon.

"My affairs are no longer yours," Alynon said. "Let us get this over with."

I pulled open the door, and we proceeded inside.

The Room of Arrival had, I could only assume, been created in an attempt to make a space humans would find familiar for traveling between worlds.

A counter divided into five stations greeted us as we entered, with numbers floating in the air over each station. A ticket dispenser to our right distributed numbers that I assumed went with those floating above the stations, and looked suspiciously like one I'd seen at a Department of Motor Vehicles. In front of the counter was a waiting area. It looked very much like the Milk Bar from *A Clockwork Orange,* or perhaps had been inspired by a memory of Caligula's party room, with sculpted naked figures of white marble bent over and laid out as tables and decoration. Maybe the Fey had intended to make humans feel comfortable while waiting, but lacking context they had been about as successful in their intent as an uncle giving a *Penthouse* magazine to his eight-year-old nephew for Christmas.

If *Logan's Run* had an airport scene, it would have looked something like the remaining room behind the counter, where a half-dozen freestanding doorways like metal detectors each stood before an obelisk with a different color crystal on top. Silver doors lined the wall between the obelisks.

Only one person stood behind the counter, his skin and long braided hair both as white as the marble forms of the waiting room. He smiled at us with teeth that flashed gold, and said, "Greetings, travelers! I am Ulfrik te'Heimdallr. Take you a number, and quickly shall I send each on his way."

*Uh,* I projected. *We're not here to travel anywhere. We just arrived actually, and kind of got lost.*

"Oh, I am quite aware of who you are and how you arrived," he replied, his tone disapproving. "Now, please take you a number and have a seat."

We took numbers, and were called up one by one. Alynon was sent off through one of the silver doors for a debriefing of some kind. Silene received a bracelet and was told to wear it at all times, then returned to the waiting area.

"Here," Heimdallr said as I stepped up to the counter, holding out a silver band. "Hold out your arm."

I hesitated, then lifted the blob-like extension that was my arm. Heimdallr locked the band around it, and after a second my body transformed to resemble my real-world self.

"That is better, is it not?" Heimdallr said. "Now, your name?"

"I thought you knew who I was," I said, distracted as I flexed my arms and legs. It was better than better, it was awesome beyond words to feel like myself and not the shapeless form I'd been trapped in for twenty-five years.

"I know who you are," Heimdallr responded. "But it is always good to make sure *you* know who you are, especially after leaving your true body behind."

Fair enough. "Phinaeus Gramaraye."

"Well met and welcome back, Magus Gramaraye. I would not have expected you to return to our realm, especially after the way in which you left."

"I never intended to come back, especially after the way you all treated me like a memory vending machine for twenty-five years. But here I am."

"Indeed. And what purpose brings your return, may I ask? Though you used an ARC password, I received no official notice as to your purpose."

"I'm here to warn the Silver Court of a serious threat to their safety and the safety of their brightbloods."

"I see. I suppose the matter is urgent, or you would not be here?"

"Exactly."

"Very well, I shall assemble a Demesne Quorum. You will have the chance to present your case to them."

"I really just wanted to speak with the Silver Court—"

"This is the Colloquy, arcana. Here, all Demesnes have equal right to hear whatever a human ambassador has to say. Now please return you to the waiting area until your companion returns."

I rejoined Silene in the waiting area. Somehow, I didn't think this was headed in a good direction.

Alynon emerged from the silver door, but he strode right past us to the room's exit.

"Going someplace?" I asked.

"Yes," he said, turning his silver eyes to me. "I am done with living your life. I go now to live mine."

"Look, I get why you'd be eager to do so, but can't you at least wait long enough to back me up with the Colloquy?"

Alynon put his hand on the hall door. "I would only hurt your case," he said. "The other Demesnes will assume I have influenced you. And the Silver Court, well, my word will lend no assurance to their belief."

"But—"

"Farewell, Finn," Alynon said. "I cannot say it has been fun, but I can say it is over."

Alynon opened the door and left.

I stared at the door a second, and said, "Well, that's great."

Silene shook her head. "The Bright Lords are not what I expected."

"Well, I'm hoping the rest aren't like Alynon," I said. "Though I get the feeling he was never exactly a model Bright Lord to begin with."

Yet I'd really been counting on his help with the Colloquy.

A soft tinkling of bells, and Heimdallr said, "The Quorum will see you now."

# Eternal Flame

Silene and I were led through the halls of the Colloquy by an armored guard who looked like one of the slayers from *Krull,* dressed entirely in black insect-like armor. I named him Herman.

Occasionally a Fey would pass us, or I would spot one in a cross hall, and I tried to identify them from history, myth, or pop culture. They were not the actual figures, of course, just Fey who'd taken the core of their identity from memories of the figures, but it was fun trying to identify them regardless. I spotted Abraham Lincoln, and someone I thought might be Prometheus carrying a scepter with fire dancing on its end. A blond-haired blue-eyed Jesus, a black Jesus, and a Middle-Eastern Jesus stood huddled in a corner in passionate debate or negotiation. And, in the distance, I could have sworn I saw C-3PO briefly. Which made sense, I guess. With the Fey coming in all shapes and sizes, and each Demesne having its own rules and traditions, a protocol droid would be a handy thing to have around. Then again, perhaps it was just a Fey in golden armor.

When I bumped into a Fey resembling Ambassador Sarek in the hall, however, there was no mistaking Spock's father. By the time I thought of what to say, he'd already swept off stoically down the hall. Granted, he wasn't really Sarek, or even the actor who played Sarek, but I still had a tiny nerdgasm.

I wondered if he had been created out of my own memories of Sarek, fed upon during my exile. Would that make him my child in a way? Like the child of a sperm donor?

"We have arrived," Herman the death-guard announced, and

stopped before double doors that narrowed at the top to form an obelisk shape. Herman opened the doors, and waved us through.

We passed down a short hall into a dark circular area lit in the center by a single sharp shaft of light. Above and around us sat a circle of Fey representing the various Demesnes, their faces lit dramatically from below, each paired up with a banner hanging before them showing their Demesne's sigil.

I could hear my grandfather rattling off the Demesnes in my head:

The Islands of the Blessed, known as the Demesne of
    harmony and community.
The Summerland, Demesne of creativity and art.
The Emerald Fortress, Demesne of order and logic.
The Vale of Revels, Demesne of games, commerce, and
    thieves.
The Mountains of the Mind, Demesne of knowledge,
    research, and strategy.
The Eternal Fields, Demesne of the hunt, exploring, and
    wanderlust.
The Shores of Chaos, Demesne of change, entropy, and,
    well, chaos, and beyond whose borders was rumored to
    seethe the Primordial Chaos.
The Forge of Creation, Demesne of crafting and invention.
The Everchanging Gardens, Demesne of the seasons,
    nature, and rebirth.
The Heart Lands, Demesne of passions, lusts, and desires.
The Forest of Shadows, Demesne of cunning, deception,
    and power.
And the Silver Court, Demesne of wisdom and justice.

Some of the figures above those banners I recognized from my history lessons, or from playing the game Diplomacy—I'd relived the memories of those lessons and games enough times in exile to actually remember them—diplomats like Klemens von Metternich,

Theodore Roosevelt, and Cyrus the Great. Some were mythic or religious figures known for their diplomacy, such as Athena in her golden aegis, and Oshun in flowing gold robes and a peacock feather headdress, both representing the Silver Court. And some I recognized as inspired by fictional characters, such as Damien Thorn, our good friend Chauvelin, and a man I felt pretty certain was Brigadier Sir Alistair Gordon Lethbridge-Stewart.

Some I felt less certain of, but thought might be modeled after Sun Tzu, Yudistira, and the Mouth of Sauron. That left several of the Quorum I did not recognize, unsurprising given the breadth of cultures and span of time from which the Fey had been pulling memories.

I also noted there were, in fact, two Metternichs representing opposing Demesnes, which was not surprising. Given the way Fey identity worked, it would be possible to have good Kirk, and mirror universe Kirk, and both transporter accident Kirks all on the same Quorum, all equals and representing a different Demesne most aligned with their nature.

A kingly Viking-looking man rapped on the railing with a fist, bringing silence to the murmurs of the other members. My best guess was Bragi, the Norse god famous for being welcome in any of the realms, a diplomat who sought peace. He'd be a perfect choice to lead a group of disparate Fey. And I took it as a positive sign, since I'd come here precisely to ensure peace.

"Fellow Proxenoi," Bragi said. "We have been summoned to hear the words of a visitor from the human realm, Phinaeus Gramaraye." That caused a stirring of the Quorum members. Bragi looked down at me. "Speak your words, arcana, that we may judge their import. But be warned that this chamber has the power to detect untruth, and any lie shall bring great and immediate pain to the deceiver, be they human, brightblood, or Aalbright."

"Uh, sure," I said, and cleared my throat. "I came here to make you aware of some upsetting events in my world."

I told them about Hiromi. That she had been working to infiltrate and sabotage the Silver Court brightbloods. That she'd allegedly received orders directly from the Forest of Shadows to frame the Silver Court for an attack on the alchemist. That Veirai's body had been destroyed on orders supposedly from the Silver Court Archon and yet the Archon denied giving any such orders, suggesting that someone had forged them. I told them of the attack at the game farm by Hiromi that attempted to pit the Silver Court brightbloods against the arcana. And I shared Alynon's theory that such acts were meant to help drive a wedge between arcana and the Silver Court.

Athena glowered in the direction of the Shadows proxenoi.

"What defense can the Shadows give?" she demanded. I was sad to see no mechanical owl on her shoulder.

Chauvelin whispered something to the Damien Thorn knockoff, who disappeared. He then leaned forward, a calm smile on his face. "I assure you, to the best of my knowledge no such orders were given to our vassals. This human's story is just that, one of their fictions, though clearly even he is deceived to speak such untrue words here without consequence."

That gave me pause. I had expected some elaborate deflection, but not an outright denial.

The Fey never lied, not outright, though this seemed due more to a fundamental psychological trait or principal than an actual inability. They could play with the truth, however, twist it and reshape it with unparalleled skill—Zeno's paradoxes were said to have been created by a Fey as the equivalent of kindergarten lessons for his offspring. I tried to find the evasion in Chauvelin's words. But his denial seemed pretty forthright, and Bragi had said the chamber would punish anyone who lied.

Perhaps the problem was in Athena's question. She had not asked him directly about Hiromi's actions, but rather to defend himself. I looked at Chauvelin. "Then tell me, what was the purpose of the Forest of Shadows in ordering Hiromi to set up the Silver Court brightbloods for attacking the alchemist?"

In explaining the reason, he'd be acknowledging that they ordered it to begin with.

Damien reappeared next to Chauvelin, and whispered into his ear. Chauvelin smiled, like a cat who has spotted a caged bird, and looked down at me.

"Unfortunately, your question is based on a wrong assumption, and that is that the Forest of Shadows gave any such orders."

I frowned. "Just to be clear, when I said the Forest of Shadows, I wasn't referring to the Greatwood, saying that a bunch of trees gave the order, I meant some representative of the Forest of Shadows Demesne."

Chauvelin shrugged. "Oh, I took the question as such, and still my answer remains the same. No representative or leader of the Forest of Shadows gave any such orders to the jorōgumo Hiromi, nor in fact have ever given any direct orders to her except through her Archon. Is that clear enough?"

"Uh, I mean no offense, but, well, is it possible you weren't informed of this particular communication?"

"Yes, it is possible," Chauvelin replied. "But we have ways of knowing what messages have been sent to our vassals, and I've just confirmed that no such messages were sent to Hiromi, with or without my knowledge. At least, not by the Forest of Shadows."

Shazbot.

If there was some deception or evasion in his replies, I wasn't smart enough to spot them. And if he was telling the truth, if the Forest of Shadows truly was innocent, at least of sending Hiromi against the Silver brightbloods, then I'd hit yet another dead end.

Maybe that was a good thing? If the Shadows really weren't behind Hiromi's actions, maybe that meant they were not plotting war.

But if they weren't, then was someone else setting them up the same way I'd thought the Shadows were framing the Silver brightbloods?

"If the Forest of Shadows didn't give Hiromi her instructions, who did?" I asked.

A Chaos Proxenoi, Set, scrunched his curved snout and said, "Let not our feet be set down paths of speculation, for that way lay danger to the purpose of the Colloquy."

Chauvelin gave a nod of his head. "Well said. None here would benefit from such conflict." He frowned, and looked thoughtfully to the side. "Except the Silver Court, perhaps, sacrificing their pawns to set up the Shadows for a greater fall?"

Athena stood up, her face flushing red.

"How dare you accuse—!"

"PEACE!" Bragi said, and turned to Chauvelin. "You shall refrain from guesses and wild accusations and speak only that which is certain and true, is that clear?"

"Of course, my apologies," Chauvelin said, giving a slight bow of his head in Athena's direction. She hardly looked mollified, but she sat back down, appearing a bit unsteady as she did.

Chauvelin smiled down at me. "Now, arcana, let me ask *you*: what could you hope to gain by coming and laying such false accusations against us? Or is this some kind of joke? You'll have to forgive me, we Aalbright do not have your human proclivity for playing with the truth."

Silene prickled at Chauvelin's words—thorns literally grew along her limbs—and she said, "Finn speaks the truth. I bore witness to many of the events he describes, and to the confession of the jorōgumo."

"Indeed?" Chauvelin said. "Tell me, vassal, to whom is *your* allegiance pledged?"

Silene's back straightened, and her chin lifted. "I am pledged to the Silver Court."

"Precisely. So you claim that Hiromi, a Shadows vassal, forced you and your followers to protest the actions of this alchemist?"

"No, she—"

"Perhaps you can share with us then why your followers were in the alchemist's domain to begin with?"

I took a step in Chauvelin's direction. "Silene didn't come here to be put on trial. She came here to be a witness, to prevent countless brightblood and Fey from dying—"

"Is that a threat?" asked an Indian man in loose flowing robes.

"What?" I said. "No! I—"

"Proxenos Kautilya, if I may," Chauvelin said. "Their accusations were against the Forest of Shadows." He looked back down on Silene. "I repeat my question. Why were you there if not forced by Hiromi? Are you ashamed to say?"

The thorns on Silene grew longer. "I have no reason to be ashamed. It is the alchemist and those who protect him who are to be ashamed. We were seeking to end the unfair exploitation of our kind by the alchemists and others, to gain the respect we deserve and greater equality—"

"In other words," Chauvelin said, "you pledged allegiance to the Silver Court, and yet are seeking to upset the carefully established balance between the arcana and your Bright Lords and Ladies. You did not trust in the Silver Court to protect you, or address your grievances, and so took the matter into your own hands?"

Silene shrunk in on herself. "No, I—" She turned toward Athena and Oshun, a pleading look on her face. "Believe me, Bright Ladies, I meant no disrespect or—"

"Enough!" Athena said. "You are—"

Oshun put a hand on Athena's arm, and smiled down at Silene. "Peace, child. And hold your thoughts within." She looked to Chauvelin. "Whatever is the point of your questioning, come to it swiftly."

"With pleasure. My point is simply this," Chauvelin said, and waved at me. "We have here an arcana once exiled by his own kind, one with reason to resent both our kind and his own, an arcana involved in the death of two Bright Guards at the end of his last visit."

"That was not my fault!" I said.

"Pardon me," Chauvelin said. "An arcana present when two Bright Guards were killed with magics that left him entirely unharmed and conveniently trapped one of our own within his body as a prisoner—"

"Hey, if you think I *wanted* Alynon stuck in my head, you're crazy!"

"And yet, Alynon Infedriel, of the Silver Court, *was* 'stuck in your head,' present throughout these events you describe, no doubt telling you what to think of them, how to interpret them, for all we know making you see and hear whatever he willed—"

"It doesn't work like that."

"Would you know if it did?" Chauvelin replied. "Clearly you believe these accusations you've leveled against us, but just as clearly they are false, and a human's capacity for self-deception and willful ignorance is famous, especially when such deceptions feed into their natural desires and prejudices."

"I don't—" I began, but Chauvelin continued over me, turning to Athena and Oshun.

"My *point,* fellow proxenoi, is that we have a story of Shadows conspiracy against the Silver Court. And who offers this story? An arcana who has something of a reputation for causing trouble. We have a Silver Court lordling who has an even greater reputation for the same, and could not even be bothered to speak here, perhaps not wishing to further tarnish his name. And last and certainly least, we have a half-bright vassal pledged to the Silver Court who dares to think herself not only our equal, but better than both us and the system we work so hard to maintain—"

"No!" Silene shouted, frustration clear in her tone. "You're twisting—"

"Child," Oshun said in a warning tone.

"A vassal," Chauvelin projected over her, "who cannot do what little she was made for, so would rather see us all burn, her own cousins die, than—"

"Stop!" Silene cried out. A tangle of thorny vines each as thick as my wrist shot out from Silene's feet in a line toward Chauvelin, springing up out of the smooth floor as if molded from the marble itself and turning brown and green as quickly as the eye could follow.

"Cease!" Oshun shouted.

A wall of light sprang up in a line from Athena's aegis across the Quorum chamber. The racing thorns slammed into the wall and withered away, melting back into the floor.

Two Fey who looked like meaner cousins of Chauvelin's barbarian brute ran into the circle and grabbed Silene's arms, apparently immune to the thorns. The Quorum burst into angry and excited arguing.

"I'm sorry!" Silene said. "I didn't know I could—I didn't mean—"

"Order!" Bragi said, pounding on the banister. "*ORDER!*" The second shout echoed directly in my head, ringing loud.

The Quorum quieted.

I cleared my throat. "Your, uh, Honor, that was an accident," I said. "Chauvelin clearly provoked—"

"Please be silent," Bragi said, and turned to the Silver Court proxenoi. "The brightblood is your vassal. You must choose her fate."

Athena and Oshun exchanged words, then looked down at Silene. Oshun gave a sad smile, but Athena's eyes held no compassion as she said, "Vassal, you have shown little of the dutiful devotion owed your patrons, and have violated the sacred peace of the Colloquy with your attack on a Proxenos. However, we do believe your intent in coming here was to prevent conflict, not cause it"—she looked up at Chauvelin—"and it is due to your lesser nature and poor control of will that this offense has been given."

Chauvelin opened his mouth to protest, but Oshun raised her hand and shook her head. He raised a single eyebrow but did not speak.

Athena continued, "We therefore offer you a choice. You may forfeit your life for this offense, and word of your sacrifice to honor your patrons shall be passed to your followers as a source of inspiration to them; or you may return to your world alive, and you and all those who followed you in your foolish quest for power shall be stripped of our patronage and protection."

Silene closed her eyes, but she barely hesitated a second before saying, "I offer my life, Bright Ladies, and beg the forgiveness of all the Bright Lords and Ladies here for my offenses."

Chauvelin grinned.

"What?" I said. "No!"

Bragi said in a warning tone, "Ware, arcana, you have no authority here."

"Screw authority, what about what's right?" I asked, my voice growing louder. "Silene came here to try and keep you all from killing each other, and instead you're going to punish her? How is that right? And you," I said to Chauvelin. "You tricked her into losing control, and you know it. You want us to stop our accusations and leave? Fine, we'll leave. But Silene doesn't deserve to be punished for doing the right thing."

Chauvelin raised his hands in an innocent shrug. "I'm afraid it is out of my hands. She is not my vassal, and her actions cannot be wished away with insulting accusations against me."

"Finn, please," Silene said. "You must stay, and discover the truth of Hiromi's plot. My life is not as important as the lives of all who will be lost if war comes."

I looked up at the Quorum. "What if—I will share my memories. Finn's Brain Buffet is hereby open and it's all you can eat. You'll have all the evidence you need of Hiromi's actions, and Silene's virtues. But you have to let Silene go without punishment."

"You do not understand," Oshun said, sympathy in her tone. "There is an imbalance and great offense here that must be addressed. Silene represents the Silver. You do not."

"Indeed," Chauvelin said. "And sadly, the Pax forbids such sharing of arcana memory outside of exile."

Yeah, he was clearly all kinds of sad about it.

"Forest of Shadows," Athena said. "Do you accept the punishment as satisfying the offense?"

Chauvelin gave a regal nod. "We do."

Athena stood. "To that end, and by the Law of the Quorum, a Proxenos of the offending Demesne may upon their self take the chosen punishment of any vassal. I so exercise that right now."

That caused a wave of murmurs to pass through the gathered proxenoi, and Chauvelin stood as well, his eyebrows raised. Then a smile spread across his face like the joker spotting Batman entering a porta-potty.

Bragi shook his head, but said, "This is as the Law allows, but seems ill-advised. Your voice adds great value to this Quorum, your life has burned bright. The life of the tree-bright, as much as any vassal is a valued cousin, holds but a spark of the Aal, her function but a fraction of your service."

"Nonetheless," Athena said. "And as is also my right, I choose the manner of death. I shall die that Silene Treebright may share her memories with the Quorum."

Chauvelin's smile faltered somewhat, but only for a second. He apparently did not fear Silene's memories as much as mine, and still felt he'd won whatever game he was playing.

"Very well," Bragi said, and waved his hand. The brutes holding Silene released her, and withdrew from the circle of light. A minute later, Athena and Oshun strode out of the darkness to join us. Oshun looked like Naomi Campbell's prettier sister, and strode with a serene grace as the circle of light shimmered off of her flowing gold robes and peacock feather headdress.

Athena looked like a tall Drew Barrymore dressed in white robes, and from her focused intensity she was *definitely* more in her "goddess of courage and strategy" mode just now than goddess of wisdom and the arts. As she drew close, however, something about her looked . . . off. It was hard to put a finger on, but it was almost like her skin held a slight translucence, her starts and stops a little stilted.

Silene fell to her knees before Athena, bowing her head.

"Bright Lady, it is too much. I cannot let you make this sacrifice for me."

"Peace, child," Athena replied. "You have no power to let me nor prevent me. This choice is mine, and freely made. There is more here than you could possibly know or comprehend, but understand this: I believe your memories important for many reasons beyond your current cause, and I can think of no greater way to end my service to my Demesne than to do so protecting and aiding such a brave vassal in the cause of saving lives."

I cleared my throat. "Excuse me, I'm sorry, but I don't understand. How is sharing Silene's memories a death sentence for Athena?"

The two Fey ladies exchanged glances, and Oshun said, "For reasons unknown, when an Aalbright feeds upon the memories of a brightblood, it . . . undoes our nature rather than adds to it. It is a most delicate matter, one that our brightblood vassals find shameful for fear that it means they are somehow unworthy of merging with the Aal." Silene blushed, and Oshun continued, "But I find this reasoning unlikely."

Silene shook her head, but before she could speak, Oshun put a hand on her shoulder and said, "Come, stand, child. Whether you will or not, the choice is made. It is now for you to ensure Athena's sacrifice be not in vain."

Silene rose unsteadily to her feet, and looked at me. "What memories should I share?"

"I don't know," I said. "Memories of Hiromi, of how she tried to frame you and your brightbloods?"

"That will be important," Athena agreed. "But Chauvelin has tried to turn the Quorum against you by questioning your motives, painting you as a rebellious and ungrateful vassal. You must show them your true quality, and why you are here in truth. Make them *feel* that truth, feel your love and fear for your brightblood family, make them understand your motives, and they will more readily believe the rest."

"I—I'll try," Silene said.

"That is all that may be asked of anyone," Athena replied, and placed one hand upon Silene's head as Oshun placed her hand upon Athena's shoulder.

"Are you ready?" Athena asked.

"Yes, Bright Lady," Silene said, and a tear slid down her cheek. "I—you are all that I believed a Bright Lady to be."

Athena smiled. "I am honored you think so."

Oshun looked up to the gathered proxenoi. "We are ready. With your permission?"

Bragi nodded. "Proceed."

Silene and Athena both closed their eyes. Then Oshun closed hers, and Silene's memories were projected into the air, filling the space.

## Janie's Got a Gun

*The projection immersed us in Silene's memory, like a hologram except that every sense was engaged, the emotion of the moment palpable as it wrapped the entire Quorum in its spell. . . .*

Silene stood naked before her tree in the silver moonlight, swaying with the great cedar as if in a wind, though the trees of the surrounding forest barely stirred. A true being of beauty and sexuality, her movements were hypnotic and full of promise. She was, in that moment, to an erotic dancer what a lioness is to an alley cat.

There were few beings said to dance with the grace and allure of a dryad. That's why so many famous arcana dancers studied the moves of dryads, including Josephine Baker, Mikhail Baryshnikov, and the Solid Gold Dancers. Even Michael Jackson, a mundy, was actually investigated by the ARC under suspicion of having a dryad lover, though the case was quickly dismissed.

In the field before Silene's tree, a collection of brightbloods also sang and danced, clapped their hands, and stomped their feet. Some I recognized—Frog Face, the faun, Veirai the siren alive and well, and a few others from the Elwha gang—but I did not see Dunngo, or Romey, and there were many more that I did not recognize.

Some danced with simple, wild abandon. Some moved in stepping pose-like motions that reminded me of Native American dances. And a few demonstrated the influences of their lives hidden among humans—I spotted some folk dancing, a bit of salsa, Veirai bopped back and forth in a Molly Ringwald–style 80's move, and a tall lanky sasquatch did a fair imitation of John Travolta in *Saturday Night Fever,* his long fur-fringed arms pointing and swinging.

Challa played the part of a wallflower, her sasquatch form staying in the shadowed edges of the clearing, and I realized after a minute that she watched the male sasquatch warily, moving to always be on the furthest edge from him.

Silene raised her hands, and as the singers grew quiet she said, "Soon, the great Thunderbird will sweep down the river, driving the salmon before him with his lightning. Who will join with me on the river's shore and taste the joy of life?"

Her voice took on a silky, sultry quality that made clear what she meant by "join with me." Several fauns, nymphs, and other brightbloods broke from the dance and gathered around her, and she laughed in delight as they approached, her arms spreading in welcome.

The forested hillsides upstream flickered with light, heralding the Thunderbird's position.

A third sasquatch came roaring out of the tree line wielding what looked like a length of rusted rebar in each hand. The dancers were taken by surprise, scrambling out of his way, and Silene and her love gang spun to face him with startled expressions.

"Challa'vel'Vek!" the new sasquatch roared, looking around him. But Challa had ducked behind the ten-foot stump of a tree, and I noticed that the other male sasquatch who'd been dancing slipped away into the forest. "Challa, come here now and fast!"

Silene floated forward across the muddy earth. "Friend, welcome to our revels. Come, set aside your weapons and your anger. It is a time to celebrate light, and love, and the creation of life." She motioned to the flashes of light illuminating the river valley, growing ever brighter and closer.

"Nymph-bright," the sasquatch growled. "Youself is one telling Challa to leave I!"

Silene's smile never faltered. "No, I told her to seek out happiness and love. And I tell you the same. Come, let me show you the joys—"

"Youself try to split apart Challa and I hearts. I show youself how badhurt feels!"

He raised one length of rebar like a club, and stepped toward Silene.

"No!" Challa shouted, and ran out. "Iself am coming ourhome. Leave the treebright alone." She stood stooped over in a submissive posture, her hands raised, her eyes lowered.

The sasquatch growled. "Youself need to learn I strongest of all brightbloods, youself lucky to be one of Iself's mates." He moved past her toward Silene. Several of the brightbloods with Silene moved between her and the sasquatch, though none looked certain it was a wise move.

Challa grabbed the sasquatch's arm. "No! Youself are strongest—"

The sasquatch struck her in a backswing across the head, the rebar bending. Challa's knees wobbled, and she fell to the ground.

"Youself stay down until I say standing good," he said, keeping his attention focused on Silene and her protectors. He raised the other length of rebar again.

Challa screamed, a scream that contained years of pent-up anger and pain, the scream of someone pushed well beyond her breaking point, and she leaped on the male sasquatch's back. One arm wrapped around his neck, the other began pounding at his chest and punching at the side of his face while she continued screaming.

He howled a battle cry, dropped both rebar poles, and grabbed Challa's arm from around his throat with both hands. He spun, and she flew off, but he held onto her arm. There was a terrible, crunching pop, and Challa screamed out in pain, then the sasquatch slammed her to the ground like a giant doll. She lay in the dirt, whimpering, her arm bent at an impossible angle.

Lightning danced over the nearby bend in the river, announcing the arrival of the Thunderbird.

"Youself listen next time I saying stay down, Iself thinking," he said, and snatched up the nearest piece of rebar. He looked at Silene. "And youself, try to take I heart, Iself take youself's heart instead." He took a half step back, hefted the rebar, and threw it like a spear.

It plunged into the trunk of Silene's tree with a loud "Thunk!", and quivered there.

Silene staggered and put her hand over her left breast.

"Stupid nymph-bright," the sasquatch said. "I think *youself* listen next—"

His words ended with an explosive cough of blood as Challa slammed the other piece of rebar through his back and out of his chest, her scream one that would haunt even a banshee.

The Thunderbird swept by, a magnificent bird the size of a pterodactyl, lightning dancing from his wings along the river below him. In the flashing, strobe-like illumination, the sasquatch seemed to fall forward in slow motion.

An arc of lightning leapt from the Thunderbird and struck the rebar in Silene's tree, drawn by natural attraction to the metal. Not a deliberate act by the great bird, but devastating all the same. There was a terrible scream of metal heating and wood splitting, and the smell of char.

Silene howled in pain. When the flash faded, her left breast had been burned away, leaving an angry red scar that ran from just below her shoulder down to her abdomen.

Silene swooned, then fell face first into the mud.

Many of the brightbloods panicked and fled. Others rallied. A pair of kelpie channeled a fountain of river water onto the tree, sending up a burst of steam from the rebar and quenching the glowing coals around the strike before they could burst into flame.

Several brightbloods carried Silene to her tree and lay her against it, and someone shouted for word to be sent to the Archon of what had happened.

*The memory blurred, and then resumed.*

The sun shone down across Silene's tree in faint columns that shifted as thick groups of silver clouds moved swiftly across it.

Silene sat against the fuzzy red cedar trunk, her face a mask of grief. She now wore the familiar green dress.

The snapping of branches beneath boots announced the arrival of someone. Silene looked up as a DFM enforcer stepped out of the trees. He did not wear riot gear, just a camo uniform, and no helmet hid his spiky blond hair or enforcer's moustache.

Brad Cousar. The man who attacked the gathering at the Department of Feyblood Management farm under Romey's influence.

"Bradley!" Silene said, and stood. "Thank the Bright you came."

Brad grinned as he crossed the clearing. "Every time, you say never again, but I always get another message asking for mana. What sad feyblood pulled your heartstrings this—"

He stopped, and looked from the damaged cedar to Silene. "Jesus, Silene, your tree—" He shook his head. "You okay?"

Silene's hand began to go to her chest, but stopped. "Please, I have need of mana that I may heal my tree."

Brad's eyes narrowed. "How about you do *me* a favor. Take off that dress and dance for me, the way I like."

Silene glided up to Brad, and put a hand on his arm. "I don't need to dance to make you feel good." Her voice held a ghost of the seductive quality she'd spoken with during the revel. "Just lay back in the grass, and—"

"Why don't you not tell me what to do. Are you going to dance for me or not?"

Silene raised her arms, and began to wave her hips. "If dance is really all you want—"

"Naked." Brad crossed his arms. "I didn't come here to see a fashion show."

Silene stepped back. "I—please, Brad. I don't want to—"

"But this isn't about what you want, is it? It's about what I want if you expect me to pay you. You know how this works." Brad pulled out a stainless steel mana vial, its brushed silver surface covered in runes.

Silene looked from the vial to her tree, and her hand went to her left breast now. She turned so that her back was to Brad, slid

the dress from each shoulder, then let it fall to her feet. She began
to dance, sinuous, seductive.

"Turn around," Brad said.

"You can take me from behind," Silene said. "I know you like
that."

"Turn around, Silene, or I'm leaving."

Silene stopped dancing. She turned, tears running down her
face.

The scar had begun to heal, but it remained a pink, puckered
line where her left breast had once been.

Brad winced. "Damn. What a waste." He shook his head, and
his expression softened. "Are you okay? I mean, does it hurt?"

"My tree takes the pain," Silene said. "Please, if I can just heal
her, maybe—"

Brad sighed. "Shit, Silene. I'm sorry. It's been fun, no doubt about
it. And we both got something out of it. How about we don't make
this hard, huh?"

He turned, and began walking back toward the forest.

"Brad, wait! Please! I—"

Brad turned back. "Don't. You'll just be embarrassed later."

"If I can just have some mana—"

Brad shook his head again. "Sorry, babe, but a little magic ain't
going to fix that. Besides—look, I might as well tell you now, I
got another feyblood girl now, I was going to stop our little visits
regardless. And you've got bigger problems than some burns anyways."

Silene's head shifted back. "What do you mean?"

"You haven't heard? They're tearing down the dams. When they
do, there's a good chance you and your tree are going for a swim
down the river."

Silene looked to the river. "I—I didn't know. I am happy for the
river and its spirits, but—" She began to sob.

Brad sighed. "Damn it, don't cry like that. Okay, look, I know
an alchemist, he'd pay good money for certain fluids and . . . parts
of you and your tree, and he has a drug that can unfetter you.

Give him whatever you can live without. Maybe you can get enough mana to, you know, make a little Silene cutting or seed or whatever it is dryad mothers do, and plant it above the waterline, closer to the lodge." He waved up at the hillside.

Silene's brow furrowed. "Sell my—?" She wiped roughly at her face with the back of her hand. "Go impale yourself."

"Now what kind of talk is that from a creature of pleasure?"

"I do not exist just to give pleasure," Silene replied, standing straighter. "I bring health and happiness to my tree, and all beings within these woods. I am not a cow to be milked and cut up in pieces and—"

"See, I tried to be nice," Brad said, walking back to jab his finger at Silene's shoulder. "But you want the hard truth, babe? Your value to us and your mighty Fey masters is in distracting all those wild feybloods out there, so they are focused on your tits and ass and not thinking about fighting or causing problems. That is what you do to earn your place around here, and guess what? You can't do that anymore. And nobody's going to give you mana just because you're a sweet girl. So if you want my advice, you'll sell what you can to the alchemist while it still has value, take the drugs, and make yourself a baby while you can."

"Screw you!"

"Sorry, sweetie, but you got nothing I—"

Silene punched Brad. Not some offended princess slap. An Ellen Ripley punch that sent Brad stumbling back to fall on his ass.

Brad shook his head, and leapt to his feet. Blood trickled from a split lip, and he rubbed it away. "You little—" He advanced toward Silene, who raised her fists. She held them in front of her like a shield, looking more awkward than imposing.

Brad stopped, and suddenly burst out laughing. "Okay. I probably deserved that." He shook his head. "But you hit me again, and I'm going to have to arrest you, and that's a whole lot of paperwork and questions I don't want to deal with. Don't forget your place Silene. Now good-bye, for real."

Brad turned, and marched away. As he did, he rubbed at his jaw again and said, "What a waste."

Silene watched him leave, then turned back to her cedar. She rubbed at her fist.

Challa appeared out of the forest, her natural glamour making her seem to materialize out of the light and shadows.

"Yonman badheart," she said. "Is what heself say about stonedams breaking real-true?"

"Maybe," Silene replied. "Probably. I know the Klallam firstmen have been fighting to free the river for many years."

"This is true-bad," Challa said.

"No, it is good, it should be a cause to rejoice. But we must also prepare." Silene touched her chest, and glanced in the direction Brad had left. A look of determination settled on her face. "It is no coincidence that all of this change has happened at once. The Aal wished to awaken me, to remind me I am a vassal of the Silver Court, the Demesne of justice. There is a time for revels, for dancing and loving and tasting of joy, for the healing and strength they bring. But today I understand that a slave dancing is still a slave."

"So . . . what youself doing now?"

"Now?" Silene asked. "I shall rest, and heal. Tomorrow, however, I shall begin to gather those of the Silver who would share in the purpose the Aal has revealed to me. And then? Then, we shall fight for the respect we are owed."

*Blur* . . .

Silene stood within the protective stone circle on the bluff at Fort Worden, hacking at the strands of spider silk around Reggie as she watched me struggle to my feet, the white crust of the jorōgumo protection potion flaking from my skin. Hiromi faced us across the dew-soaked grass, swaying on her spider legs.

"Hiromi, why are you doing this?" I shouted. "We don't need to be enemies."

"Of course we do," she replied. "We are different, and difference always leads to conflict. Or enslavement."

"You sound like my grandfather."

"Then he is right," she hissed back.

"He's dead. He tried to start a war, but arcana and brightbloods, we fought together to stop him."

"Then you only delayed the inevitable!" she said, and attacked.

*Blur . . .*

Silene stood beside the curled-up, still body of Hiromi as I questioned the jorōgumo's spirit.

"You were responsible for Veirai attacking the alchemist?" I asked.

"Yesssss."

"You infiltrated Silene's group posing as Romey, a waerfox?"

"Yessss."

"Hiromi? Were your orders really from your Forest of Shadows patrons?"

"Yesss. I obey obey betray the betrayers all will die die die."

*Blur . . .*

Silene, looking like a young teen girl, stumbled backward through a moonlit forest. Bright flashes, explosions, and screams deeper in the forest announced a battle drawing ever closer. Silene's hands trembled as her fingertips sought out the comforting feel of the ferns and shrubs that surrounded her.

A mixed group of arcana and allied brightbloods began to appear from between the trees, retreating toward Silene. Soon, enemy brightbloods could be seen pressing them back, bolstered in strength and ability by possessing Fey.

Silene tried to stem the tide of enemy brightbloods, tried to weave tangled walls of vines and branches to slow them. But the enemy brightbloods were too many, and too strong.

Allied brightbloods—dryads, satyrs, sasquatches, gryphons, leprechauns, and others—fought a desperate but clearly losing battle against waer creatures, ghouls, trolls, lindworms, wendigos, unicorns, and other dark brightbloods fighting for their Fey masters.

Arcana fought side by side with the allied brightbloods. Wizards wielded wands and rings, or fought with tattoos and swords. Sorcerers cast illusions to frighten and confuse, or controlled the minds of the less intelligent enemy brightbloods and turned them against their own. Thaumaturges crushed and broke the enemy lines with prepared boulders or tree trunks by moving a resonant pebble or branch across their palm. Alchemists lobbed gas grenades, or splashed healing potions on the wounded. And necromancers darted forth to rip the spirit from enemy creatures, or snag the magic from both ally and enemy fallen in order to fuel the living arcana's spells and weapons.

They continued to retreat, emerging from the forest onto a grass clearing.

I recognized it. The bluff at Fort Worden. This was the final battle of the last Fey-Arcana war, just before Katherine Verona used her daughter's spirit as the equivalent of a nuclear bomb.

The chill evening air reeked like spoiled steaks being charred over a dung fire as bodies were shredded, chopped, burned, boiled, putrefied, and disintegrated. The only sounds louder than the explosions were the screams.

And then, the night was banished by a blue-white flash from the edge of the bluff—

The memory ended, the projection faded.

"This is what my brightbloods may face, what we all may face, if we let war happen again," Silene declared to the Quorum.

I blinked, and looked from Silene to Athena.

The Fey lady melted like a wax statue, collapsing to the Quorum floor, the runoff evaporating before spreading.

"Holy—" I stepped back, feeling a confusing swirl of emotions at the sight, but horror and sadness dominated.

Silene turned quickly away, shaking her head, her eyes scrunched closed.

Oshun stepped gracefully around what was left of Athena, and put a hand on Silene's shoulder. "You did well, child, and made her death a noble one. It is reason for joy, not sadness." She lifted her head, and raised her voice. "And we have great need for debate, I think, on recent events and their meaning."

I glanced up. Chauvelin looked anything but happy at what he, and all his fellow proxenoi, had witnessed. Many of those proxenoi nodded at Oshun's words.

Bragi stood. "There is truly much for us to absorb. We shall—" His words stuttered to a halt.

I began to melt. Not a disintegration like Athena, but my form softened and expanded, my hands and feet going globby and taking on the Jell-O–like appearance of an unshaped Fey.

"What the—" I said as my translucent skin began to glow with a bright white light.

"A spirit bomb!" Otto Von Bismarck shouted. "He intends to destroy us all!"

"The protections!" Bragi said. "It should not be possible."

There was a panicked scramble in the gallery as the members of the Quorum rose and disappeared in streaks of light, willing themselves far away without any pretense of walking the distance between. Even Chauvelin and Bragi disappeared.

Silene stared at me with a horrified expression, clearly uncertain what to think or do.

Oshun approached me as though I were a hissing snake, and placed one hand on my chest, her eyes suddenly the dark, swirling gray-green of a flowing river. She frowned for a second, then shook her head.

"I—I cannot stop whatever this is. I am sorry." She looked between me and Silene, then she too vanished in a streak of light.

"No!" I said. "I don't know what's happening! Come back! Help me!"

Gods, if my grandfather had survived our last encounter, he really could be using the spiritual connection between us to turn me into a weapon the way Katherine Verona had with her daughter. But this didn't feel like a buildup of energy so much as a fading.

I thought of Dawn, and wished I could talk to her one last time.

Everything went white.

## I Won't Back Down

I woke to the sound of Silene and Alynon arguing, and opened my eyes slowly.

The room looked like it could very well be the afterlife, with white marble floor and walls, and pillars like twined tree trunks rising up and fading into the bright blue sky of the ceiling. In between the pillars floated what looked like giant white leaves, which served as sofas, or hammocks, given that I now lay on one. An arched doorway stood in one wall, and a window on the opposite wall looked out onto the flashing colors of the unshaped Other Realm.

Not that I needed the window to know I wasn't really in the afterlife. If Alynon were here, I couldn't be dead. However thoughtlessly cruel the universe might seem to be at times, it could never be that cruel.

Oshun stood to one side of me, her hands folded within her golden robes and a look of amused patience on her face.

Alynon waved in Silene's direction. "If you could not control yourself, you should not have been there."

"At least I *was* there," Silene replied.

"Getting yourself condemned!" Alynon said.

"Hey!" I said to announce myself awake. "What's going on?"

Silene spun to face me. "Thank the Bright!"

Oshun nodded her head at me in the smallest fraction of a bow. "It seems that whatever force did hold Alynon within your body is still connecting you both," she said. "When he traveled too distant from you, both began to lose your form."

Great. "Well," I said, looking at Alynon, "at least we're alive."

Alynon crossed his arms over his ruffled shirt and looked downright petulant. "I question whether living is truly a reason for celebration if I must remain bound to you."

"Wow, thanks," I said. "You're no great prize there either, Hamlet McBlueballs."

"Fa!" Alynon said, and ran a hand through his spiky silver Ziggy hair. "Believe you me, I would that we were far, far apart."

"Speaking of which," I said, "where did you go?"

"Nowhere," Alynon replied.

"Hardly nowhere," Silene said. "The Bright Champions who brought him in said he collapsed on the edge of the Forest of Shadows."

"What?" I looked to him, surprised. "I thought you'd gone back to the Silver Court, or perhaps to whatever Demesne is the Fey equivalent of Reno. What the hell were you doing—" I glanced at Oshun. Had Alynon taken up Chauvelin on his offer to join the Shadows?

"My actions are no longer your concern," Alynon said.

"Fine," I said. "But maybe, if you'd let me, if you'd trust me, I might actually surprise you and help."

Alynon's mouth scrunched to one side, and I could see that he weighed my words. But then he shook his head. "It matters little. As long as I'm stuck with you—" He sighed heavily.

"You and your sighs," Oshun said, and turned to me. "My foolish brother went to the Forest to seek out his love."

"Love?" I said, surprised. "Wait, Alynon's love is in the Forest of Shadows?"

That helped explain his disfavor, and Chauvelin's attempts to have Alynon defect.

Alynon scowled. "Thanks, sister of mine," he said. "But you need not share my entire life story."

"Poor little Aly," Oshun said. There was a touch of mocking humor in her tone, but also genuine affection. "For true, I was happy to hear you had become stuck in the human realm."

"I'm sure the entire family was thrilled," Alynon said.

"You mistake me," she replied. "I hoped it was your destiny to find happiness there as you could not here, to be reborn into a new life. Never have you fit well within the . . . limitations of your position here."

"So you two are family?" I asked. "And the Athena who was in the quorum?"

"Yes," Oshun replied.

"Oh." I stood. "Alynon, I'm sorry about your sister. I wish—"

"Fa! It is my own fault for believing you capable of so simple a thing as speaking to the Quorum."

"Peace, Brother," Oshun said. "They comported themselves well." She turned to me. "And do not weep for Aalia te'Athena. She had recently given of herself to have a child, and grown unstable. It was but a matter of time before she returned to the Aal. You granted her a chance to give that parting greater purpose."

"Aalia branched?" Alynon asked in a surprised voice.

"Yes," Oshun said. "And she named her child Alynoniah te'Sophia."

Alynon turned away. "She . . . was never the wisest Athena."

"And you were never able to accept a gift, at least not from family."

There was an awkward moment of silence. I cleared my throat.

"So, if your sisters are Oshun and Athena, does that mean you're really part Orisha or god, too? Let me guess, Bacchus?"

"No," Alynon said with the same tone I'd heard Dawn use when someone asked to touch her hair. "I am me."

Oshun chuckled. "He is that. He is also a prince of the Silver Court."

"A minor prince," Alynon muttered.

"Even small rivers keep the lands green and the ocean wet," Oshun replied. "And had the nature of any godly spirit been part of your creation or makeup, it would be one of the tricksters I should think."

"He does have a kind of Loki vibe," I agreed.

Oshun smiled. "As lovely as this conversation is, now that I see you awake and well, I have matters of great import to attend to. I am to inform you, however, that your return home has been arranged. You may depart for your realm as soon as you feel strong enough to bear the strain of the transfer." She stepped closer, and put one hand on my shoulder. "And on behalf of the Silver Court, I wish to thank you for defending our vassals, warning us of the Shadows plots, and most importantly for putting up with my brother."

"te'Oshun!" Alynon said.

"Very well." Oshun smiled. "That last is from me personally. The Silver owes you both a debt," she said, and nodded to Silene.

"Uh, thanks," I said. "But do you really think it will be enough? Seemed like Chauvelin convinced everyone that we were just puppets of the Silver Court pretty easily, before Silene's memories. I'm guessing he'll try to do the same again."

"The Shadows have much power and influence, it is true," Oshun said. "Few are willing to oppose them directly or to openly declare sides until the outcome is most clear. But you have given us a foundation upon which we may build the arguments against them. And more than mere arguments, Silene has, I hope, reminded many of the proxenoi the true costs of this game we play."

"There's got to be something *I* can do," I said. "Make some promise or threat on behalf of the ARC?" And deal with the consequences when I returned home.

"No," Oshun said. "The Silver Court, more than any other Demesne, must now prove that it can achieve a victory without requiring the aid of arcana to do so." She turned to Silene. "And while you have given cause both in your world and ours for rebuke, know also that we see the value in your passion and your desire to protect your brightblood cousins. Such action, in spite of fear or consequence, brings honor to your clan and proves the quality of your nature."

"Thank you, Bright Lady," Silene said, and bowed her head.

Oshun returned the bow, then said, "Now, if you will excuse me, I must to these pressing matters attend."

A sad smile curved Oshun's lips as she stepped past Alynon, and paused.

"Brother, I wish you luck in your quest for freedom. Few desire for love to thrive as much as I, so though I doubt the wisdom of your choice, I do offer my truest sympathies for your heart's plight."

"Thanks. But if you truly wished my happiness, you would ask the family to keep me here until we figure out how to separate me from Finn."

"Uh, wait," I said. "What?"

"You know I cannot do that," Oshun replied.

"I know you will not." Alynon turned away from his sister.

Oshun sighed, and said, "Farewell, Brother."

"La. Thanks."

Oshun glided from the room, the door dissolving away from her, then returning once she'd passed.

"You know—" I began.

"Do not," Alynon said. "You are in no position to give me advice on family, love, or anything else."

"Fine."

I felt bad. I truly did. But our spirits were still clearly bound together somehow, and if distance in the Other Realm had nearly undone us both, I didn't imagine being in separate realms would end much better. I did not want to force Alynon to leave his own body and be trapped in mine again, and not just because he was an annoying brain-guest. But I also wasn't willing to be trapped in the Other Realm. "Look, when we get back, we'll double our efforts to find a way—"

"Just don't," Alynon said. "I don't care about your promises right now."

"I understand," I said.

And I did. Not just his anger about having to return with me, but that his family hadn't fought harder to keep him from exile. A feeling I could completely empathize with.

I summoned Herman the guard, and he swept ahead of us in his slayer armor, leading the way to the Room of Transfers.

Alynon looked absolutely miserable as we walked.

I sighed. "Is there anything I can do? You know, short of stay-ing? Maybe I can get Heimdallr to help you, give you a chance to see your true love or something?"

Alynon blinked at me.

"I—no, there's nothing you can do."

We reached the Room of Transfers. Heimdallr waited for us.

"The way is prepared," he said. "Upon your word, I shall open the way back to your home."

"Great," I said. "Three to beam up, Scotty."

Alynon gave a sharp nod to Herman behind me, and I felt a col-lar snap closed around my neck.

"What—!" I grasped at the collar.

"I'm sorry," Alynon said. "But only Silene will be leaving."

My body melted, lost its human shape, and returned to the blobby form of an unshaped Fey. The bracelet that Heimdallr had given me slipped to the floor. As my body changed, I continued clawing at the collar with both swelling hands. It felt all too famil-iar. I had worn one for twenty-five years, a representation of bond-age that allowed them to remove even my limited ability to move and project my voice.

I stepped away from slayer Herman, stepped back from every-one. As much as I had feared this might happen, had tried to prepare myself for the possibility, I still felt unreasoning panic scrabbling at the edges of my mind, threatening to overwhelm me. I tried to speak, but had lost the ability. *What are you doing?* I pro-jected.

"I am truly sorry, Finn," Alynon said. "But I cannot return to being a prisoner in your head. I won't."

Chauvelin entered the room, a smug smile on his face at the sight of me in my unshaped Fey body.

I looked from him to Alynon. *You made a deal with him, didn't you? What did you offer him?*

Alynon had the decency to look guilty at least, as he avoided my eyes. "You left me no choice. You, and my family."

Chauvelin gave a dismissive wave of his hand. "Alynon's choices are no longer your concern, arcana." He looked at Heimdallr. "You were told to send back the vassal, yes? We would not wish to add insult to injury for the Silver."

"Very well," Heimdallr said. He raised his hand and muttered some words in a language I didn't recognize, and a portal opened up within one of the gates, an oval window through which I could see Verna's laboratory in the ARC headquarters beneath Snoqualmie Falls. My body and Silene's lay in their chairs surrounded by equipment meant to keep us alive.

Though I knew better, I tried to reach out through that portal, not with my will but seeking out the resonance between my spirit and body, a path along which I might send my spirit back to my world. But it was like trying to see with my eyes closed.

Silene looked at me. "Finn?"

*Go,* I projected, though I wanted to scream 'help me.' *I'll . . . figure this out. But you should go while you can.*

Silene looked as if she might argue. Alynon stepped forward.

"Ware, vassal," he said. "The lack of inner control that led to your offense in the Quorum will only serve to lead you to mistakes in the human world, with equally disastrous outcomes. Do not waste the gift of life I give you now."

Silene looked from me to Alynon. "You have brought great shame to the Silver today, my *Lord.*" She filled that last word with all her disappointment and condemnation. Then she took Heimdallr's outstretched hand and let him guide her into the portal. She dissolved as she touched it, melting into the surface of the barrier between worlds like an ice cube on a hot glass pan.

I watched anxiously until Silene's real body stirred in the world beyond, and she opened her eyes.

"Close the portal," Chauvelin said.

Heimdallr waved his hand. The portal, my doorway home, began to close. Anxiety swelled within me, and I leaned back and forth as the portal shrunk, tried to see as much of the room beyond the portal as possible, and felt a huge surge of regret and sadness as it closed, cutting me off entirely from my world.

And then I realized why. I was hoping against all hope that Dawn would be there for some reason, waiting for me. That I would get one last look at her.

Trapped here, probably never to see her again, I realized I loved Dawn. Not just that I really liked her, and enjoyed the hell out of kissing her. I loved her. And I believed she loved me.

I'd been afraid I was incomplete, or not the person she loved. But if she didn't love who I was, she would have moved on. Dawn didn't waste time on pointless efforts, and certainly didn't open herself up to unnecessary pain.

I knew that about her. I knew that I balanced that out in her, just like we balanced each other in a hundred other ways. In fact, I knew a lot about her, and I wanted nothing more than to spend my life learning everything else.

Just as important, I realized that whether or not I knew who I had been with her before, I liked the person I was when I was with her *now*.

And wasn't that love? Not just the passing moments of affection and happiness, but the way that together you added to each other, brought out and nurtured and encouraged the best parts of each other? That was what Dawn did for me. And what I hoped I did for her.

I was perfectly able to love.

And I loved Dawn. I truly, deeply loved her. And all it took was the reality of losing her forever to make me admit it. Or, as Dawn would say, to stop being a friggin' idiot.

I laughed.

"I am glad you find this funny," Chauvelin said, smiling at me, "But I think you shall not be laughing for long, arcana. You are ours, now."

*Really? That's the best you can do?* I replied, determined not to give up yet. *I mean, there's so many more menacing things you could*

*say, like . . . 'and now you shall be doomed to relive high school algebra
forever!'* I shuddered. *Seriously, even Ed Rooney was scarier than you.*

Chauvelin's smug smile faltered slightly, then returned.

Alynon sighed. "Careful, Finn. Chauvelin is not likely to be as
patient with your idiocy as I was. He might just decide to absorb
your memories and learn to be as clever as you think you are.
Though that cleverness seems to have failed you, yes?" He looked
away again. "A shame."

Chauvelin stepped closer to me, grinning his weasily grin, and
said, "Phinaeus Gramaraye, I hereby place you under arrest for
multiple crimes against our Realm, including the murder of our
wardens on your previous visit, the death of multiple brightblood
vassals, and the involuntary holding of an Aalbright against his will
within your body."

*What? None of those things were my fault! And both the Fey and
the ARC cleared—*

"Your ARC claimed your innocence," Chauvelin said. "And
given our lack of jurisdiction in your world we had little choice but
to concede to their proposed solution. But now you are here, and the
Forest of Shadows will claim right to hold our own investigation
into your past crimes. As for the more recent crimes against our
own vassals—"

*Hiromi and Ned? They tried to kill me! I only defended myself!*

"—and your imprisonment of Alynon, the Colloquy shall determine your guilt."

*Wow. It must have really pissed you off to have your plot with
Hiromi exposed.*

"I spoke no lie in the Quorum. Whatever Hiromi's orders, they
came not from us. Though I cannot complain of their intent, and
we shall most certainly and swiftly find who did send those orders,
and they will regret using our vassals even more than you shall regret killing them."

I looked at Alynon. *Alynon, come on. I know you want to stay here,
I get that. And I'll do what I can to get you back here. But you know
what's at stake. Pete, Vee, all the brightbloods. You can't—*

"Don't," Alynon said. "Don't use your family and the bright-bloods to try and guilt me. This is about you and me. Here, at least we *both* have our own body, we can each live our own life. I gave you the chance to do what was right, what was fair, but you wouldn't."

*You think this is right and fair?* I asked.

"I released Silene, and have ensured your life," he shot back.

*Gods, Alynon! At least promise me you'll continue to look for a way to separate us. If I don't have to be here for you to survive, you will get me sent back home, right?*

Alynon looked between me and Chauvelin. "I have asked as much of them, and will do what I can. I do not wish you punished, I only wish to live my life."

Chauvelin smiled. "Indeed. Now, shall we take you to your new home, arcana?" He bowed his head at Alynon. "And inform the Silver of your new allegiance, of course."

*This is all part of your stupid game!* I said to Chauvelin. *Alynon's defection, your being the one to hold an arcana for trial, especially one who appears aligned with the Silver, it all makes the Shadows look just that much stronger, and the Silver that much weaker. And it will distract from all that Silene shared with the Quorum.*

"Will it?" Chauvelin said, all innocence. "Why, I suppose it might at that. But I do what I do for all Aalbrights, not just my own advantage."

A portal opened, several feet to the right of where Heimdallr's portal had been. Through it, I saw Verna's laboratory at the ARC again. She stood with Silene and Pete around my body on its reclining bed. Pete held against my chest the Simon game artifact Father had given me, its colored pads all lit up and casting the spirit trap in the center in a rainbow glow. Pete pushed a sequence on the colored pads, and his lips moved as he muttered something. I felt a tugging.

"What—?" Heimdallr said.

"Close it!" Chauvelin replied.

I felt my spirit lifting free of the Fey body, and as it did I projected at them all, *Too late*. I only wished I had enough control of my Fey body left to flip them off. I would just have to be happy remembering Chauvelin shaking Heimdallr furiously, his face going bright red. He was not an attractive screamer.

"Stop!" Alynon shouted frantically. "Stop! You bastard!"

*I know you are, but what am I?*

# The End of the Innocence

I flew through the portal, through the barrier between worlds, and back into my body.

I felt a sensation, like my spirit was a rubber band being stretched to the point of breaking. Somehow, it still clung to Alynon in the Other Realm.

And then it rebounded, and Alynon's voice shouted in my head, *Noooo!*

I'd played chicken with our lives, and won.

I could understand Pete's mumbling now. He was saying, "Two all beef patties, special sauce, lettuce, cheese, pickles, onions, on a sesame-seed bun." It was the mantra he'd used since childhood to help him put his mind in the zone for performing necromancy.

I blinked scratchy eyes slowly, and licked dry lips. "Well," I said. "That worked."

*Damn you,* Alynon said, his tone despairing.

"—Finn?" Pete said.

"Yeah."

"Oh gosh!" he said. "I was so scared I didn't do it right!"

"You did perfect," I said. "Close the portal, Verna."

"Done and done," she said. I could feel the change in the air as the portal closed, like a steady hum that was suddenly silenced.

*Why?* Alynon demanded. *Why couldn't you just let me stay?*

I held back my angry retort. *I don't want this any more than you. As soon as we return Silene to her tree and get back home, I will attempt the exorcism ritual.*

*But that might kill—* Alynon began, then fell silent.

I didn't want Alynon in my head. And whether I liked it or not, he *had* released Silene when he didn't have to. He wasn't evil. Demented and sad, but not evil.

"Finn?" Silene asked.

"What?"

"I asked, how did you get free?"

"Sorry," I replied. "Well, I was worried Alynon or the Fey might pull something—"

*If you hadn't forced me—*

"And so before I left, I gave Vee instructions on how to get me back using Father's artifact." Usually, summoning the spirit of a still-living person just resulted in a major headache. But the artifact made it so that my spirit being in the Other Realm was the same as if it were beyond the Veil. At least, that's what I'd hoped, and it seemed to have proven true. Over there, other there, crisscross spirit sauce. "Pete was able to summon me back as if I were dead. Thanks, Brother. I knew I could count on you."

Pete blushed.

Verna took the Simon artifact from Pete's hand, the lights now dim. "Quite clever, I must say. I would love to speak with your father about its design. It might prove quite handy should we ever need to pull someone else out of the Other Realm."

"I'm sure he'd like that," I said. "Assuming he was lucid enough."

*I never heard you give Vee instructions,* Alynon said. *And I hear everything you do.*

*Not my private thoughts and memories,* I replied. *Remember when I had Vee make one last attempt to help me recover my lost memories before we left for the Other Realm? I may have snuck in a message to her.*

*You—damn.*

Silene sank onto a stool. "Have we failed to stop the Shadows?"

"I don't know," I said. "Hopefully the Silver Court will be able to prevent war at least. They'll warn the Silver Archons of the Shadows' attempt to manipulate or frame their clans. And the ARC will be looking more closely at any supposed crimes by Silver brightbloods. I'm not sure there's any more for us *to* do. Awareness is our best defense now, assuming it isn't too late."

Our trip into the Other Realm had lasted half a day in real time. Cold moonlight and chill night air greeted us as we left the Snoqualmie Falls Lodge shortly after 11:00 p.m. Silene agreed to let Pete and me drive her to Elwha rather than traveling the hidden bright blood routes of tunnels and fairy paths, since we could not be certain of her safety from the Shadows brightbloods.

We piled into the old family hearse, with Pete driving. Despite my body having slept the day away while my spirit was in the Other Realm, I dozed for two hours on the drive. We reached the Elwha Dam trail at one thirty in the morning.

It was officially Tuesday now. The day Pete and Vee were expected to pledge to a Demesne or be declared rogue feybloods. And I still had no idea how to keep them safe, or what choice I'd make in their place.

Pete stayed in the car, since we couldn't be certain how the Silver brightbloods would react to a waerwolf at this point, and I escorted Silene along the path to her tree.

"Something is not right," she said as we walked.

I looked up into the tree-covered hillside. The moonlight gave the gently swaying evergreens a surreal halo, but most of the forest remained utterly black and held its secrets close. Below us, the Elwha ran merrily along its channel, splashing around rocks and the occasional fallen tree. I saw no other living creature except two clouds of gnats who chased each other across the faint dirt path in a swirling dance.

"What's wrong?" I asked.

"I do not know, but we should have been greeted by now."

"Maybe they're all waiting to jump out and yell 'welcome home'?" I asked hopefully.

"Unlikely," Silene replied.

"Yeah, I thought that was a stretch." I pulled the collapsible baton out of the back pocket of my jeans, but did not extend it.

Silene and I reached her clearing. Still no brightbloods in sight. Just her tree, swaying in the moonlight on the river's shoreline.

And her tree had been yarn-bombed. Dark yarn wrapped in tight lines from the base up the trunk at least six feet.

"Ash and fire!" Silene said, anger making her voice shiver as she marched toward the tree. "When I get hold of that sasquatch, I'm going to—"

The roar of a half-dozen battle cries cut her off as brightbloods charged out of hiding all around the clearing. Challa loped at us with a savage look on her face. Dunngo rode his wave of earth straight for me, because of course. And several others—two fauns, a man with buck antlers, and the waerbear—charged with them.

"Stop!" I shouted, and flicked the extending baton. Form Blazing Sword!

"Cousins!" Silene said. "Halt!"

Her words fell on deaf ears, most of them pointy or fur-covered ears and all of them mere inches away from eyes filled with Clubber Lang craziness.

Silene ran for her tree.

All of the brightblood altered their direction to intercept her.

The tree leaned toward Silene, and she lifted her hand. If she made contact with it, she could join with it and easily defend herself against the entire gang, except perhaps Challa.

I raised the now-glowing baton, ready to strike the first brightblood who attacked me.

Sal staggered out from behind Silene's tree, and then leaned heavily against the trunk.

He was naked.

By naked, I mean his fur had been shaved off, leaving only pale gray-tan skin, and a small strip of fur around his waist that hung down like a loincloth. And there were a number of nasty-looking cuts across his chest, arms, and legs that were far too large to be from shaving, even if he was as bad as me with a razor.

Sal shouted, "Stop! Herself be realtrue Silene." His voice carried over the shouts of the charging brightbloods, and their charge slowed in jerking strides until they closed around us cautiously. Silene stopped short of her tree as well, staring at the injured sasquatch.

"Sal!" I said, striding toward him. "You okay? What's going on!"

"And what in the moon's name did you do to my tree?" Silene demanded.

"He save tree," Dunngo rumbled, and stopped several feet away from Silene, his obsidian eyes narrowed. "You is you?"

"Who else would I be?" Silene asked.

"The jorōgumo," Challa replied. "Badbright spider came, looking like youself, and tried to bighurt youself's heart tree."

For a second, I feared that Hiromi had somehow, impossibly, returned. But then I realized it must be her little sister Kaminari, the girl who liked to jump rope, rhyme, and threaten to eat us. That made me feel no better at all.

"She attacked my tree?" Silene asked, true fear in her voice, and resumed walking briskly toward it.

Dunngo, Challa, and the rest followed her, and I trailed behind.

"Like say," Dunngo said. "Seeahtik save tree. He champion."

Silene reached her tree, and put her hand on the yarn. "This is your hair," she said to Sal in a surprised voice.

He nodded. "Seeahtik hair is bigstrong. Protects tree."

"You—" Silene looked at Sal. "Thank you. Your wounds, they are from protecting my tree as well?"

Sal shrugged, in that same self-deprecating golly-gawrsh way that Pete sometimes did, and looked down at his feet, still in their boots but looking even odder now with his stubbly legs. "Youself healed me. And went away to help all brightbloods. Youself have a bigbright heart, and I did not want heart to die."

"I—you are my champion for true," Silene said. "Come, let me heal your wounds."

Sal shook his head. "I not worst. Others need youself more."

"Others?" Silene demanded.

Dunngo nodded with the sound of scraping stone. "Take to cave. Two bad hurt. One very bad. And two dead."

"The jorōgumo did all of that?" I asked, surprised.

"No," Sal said. "The spider-shifter came first time and only tried reaching the tree by fake-facing Silene. But I know herself not be true."

"You—how did you know she wasn't really Silene?" Not even Veirai had realized when Hiromi had shapeshifted into Silene, and she'd known Silene well.

Sal looked embarrassed. "Silene smells like sunshine and . . . heart home. Jorōgumo smelled like moths and crazy. I not letting herself reach tree, so herself fled, and returned with many shadow-brights."

"But we fight!" Dunngo said.

"And Saljchuh protected tree," Challa said.

"The spider-shifter will come back with more shadowbrights," Sal said. "Herself seeks blood vengeance against Silene for sister's death. And many Silver brightblood are death-sick with Grayson's Curse, theyself cannot fight."

This was exactly the kind of escalation we'd been trying to prevent. I felt like I'd just Quantum Leaped into Sisyphus.

"Oh boy," I muttered.

Silene's shoulders slumped. "A shadowsbright seeking blood vengeance cannot be easily stopped."

"Stopped, no," I said, remembering Kaminari's crazy eyes. "But . . . maybe it can be deflected onto someone else. If she learns that someone faked orders from the Forest of Shadows and tricked Hiromi into trying to hurt you and your clan, maybe she'll see that you actually have a common enemy."

*La, what could go wrong, speaking to a revenge-crazy jorōgumo?* Alynon said.

At the same time, Silene shook her head. "Tricked or no, her sister died at my hands. I fear that words of peace or reason will take no root in her heart."

"What option is there?" I asked.

*If you wish to stop a jorōgumo seeking vengeance, her Archon must bring her to heel. You alone have neither the power nor the influence to hope for success.*

Ugh. "Alynon suggests having the Shadows Archon rein in the jorōgumo and her clan."

"Yes. That . . . may work," Silene said. "But if I attempt to address the Shadows Archon it will seem but an act of fear and weakness, and further open our clan to attack."

"Then have your Archon speak to theirs," I said. "That's what he's there for."

Silene nodded. "I will try, of course. Though . . . I fear our Archon may not be willing to pay the costs the Shadows would demand in exchange, not when I have brought such trouble to him and our patrons both. But I shall offer whatever it costs to protect my clan, even my life to the Shadows."

Ah, frak.

"Look," I said. "Maybe—"

"I thank you for all you have done," Silene said. "But you and your brother should depart quickly, lest the Shadows attack."

My brother.

Double frak.

"I'll go talk to the Shadows Archon," I said, words I could have happily gone my whole life without speaking. "It was my fault you faced Hiromi, anyway."

"I don't—" Silene began, then stopped, her shoulders sinking with resignation. "Thank you. I shall send word to the Silver Archon still, for what good that may do, and prepare for the Shadows' return."

"Then I stay, too," Sal said.

"That would make me—" Silene began, then frowned, and glanced at Challa. "That is, I'm sure you'd be welcome. But I alone may not decide, not when it affects others."

"Saljchuh deserve to stay," Challa said. "Besides, himself too strange to be scary."

"Umph!" Sal said in a sharp cough.

Challa shrugged, and walked away.

"That is . . . good to see," Silene said, though she didn't sound convinced of it. "You seem to have connected with her."

Sal shrugged. "Herself remind me of sister-mine."

"Oh? Well, that's—I should go and heal my wounded cousins," she said, and turned to follow after Challa.

"Wait," Sal said, stopping her. "Is not just brightbloods hurt by shadowbright attack. Is Grayson's Curse, too. Youself's clan not strong enough to stand against shadowbrights with so many bad-sick."

Silene looked to her tree, and shook her head. "I cannot heal them, too, not quick enough to be ready if the Shadows attack." She looked at me. "If you cannot gain us a cure, can you perhaps get us more of Grayson's Curse?"

"What?" I asked, shocked. "You want to drug your own bright-bloods?"

"They are drugged already. Without more, they will die before we can heal them. With it, they will at least be able to fight for their lives, and the lives of their fellow brightbloods should they need to."

I sighed. I could understand Silene's argument, but it still felt somehow wrong. It was not my choice to make, however. "I . . . may know someone who can make the drug for you," I said. "An alchemist. I will try and bring her to you, if you promise she won't be harmed."

"I would not harm someone come to help my clan."

"Okay," I said. "I'll try. I can't guarantee she'll come, though."

"Thank you. You are a true friend to the brightbloods," Silene said, and then hurried after Challa again.

Sal watched her leave, then said in a hesitant tone, "If youself need I for protection—"

I gave his arm a pat. "Stay," I said. "Probably best if no Silver brightblood go with me to the Shadows Archon anyway. I'll ask Reggie to go with me instead."

Sal shook his head. "The Archon would have to lock horns with enforcer to look bigstrong to himself's followers. Youself better to take wolfbright brother. Wolfbrights trusted by the Shadows."

"I'm not putting Pete in danger," I said.

Sal frowned. "Is himself not in danger go or not go? Why not let himself fight for life and clan, too? It is a big choice youself take from brother-yours, unless youself being true-sure can keep himself safe alone?"

"No," I said. Damn it. "But you don't know Petey. He's been through enough. And I don't want him to lose his, I don't know, his innocence. Not any more than he already has. Not if I have another choice."

Sal scratched at the stubble on his chest. "*Does* youself have other choice?" he asked.

I watched the river glinting in the moonlight for a minute. "I'll think about it," I said finally, though I already knew the answer. Taking Pete really would help, not only to be heard by the Shadows Archon, but to be trusted. And Sal was right. If Pete's and Vee's lives were at stake, I didn't have the right to leave them out of the decisions, or the risks. "Well, if I'm going to do this, I'd better get to doing it. I'll send word, whatever happens."

"And weself be ready," Sal said. "Whatever happening."

I started to turn away, then stopped. This whole thing had started with a promise to Sal, and I thought perhaps there was still a chance I could fulfill that promise at least. "Look, about Silene—"

"Yes?"

"I, well, if you like her, I think you should tell her so."

Sal blushed. "I don't think herself like I so much."

"I think maybe she does," I said. "Or at least, she will if you give her time. But she has reasons to think you won't like her, that she is no longer, uh, beautiful. You'll need to be patient, and make her understand the reasons you do like her. I mean, if you do."

Sal gave a shy shrug. I smiled.

"Okay. Well, good luck, and think about what I said. I'll keep in touch."

I made my way back along the trail, past the humming dam. As I marched along the trail, my phone began playing "Always on My Mind" and vibrating in a heartbeat staccato.

Dawn was calling.

*La! She will not be pleased that you are risking your life once again.*

I stopped, and pulled the phone out of my pocket, looking at Dawn's smiling face displayed on the screen.

*If she knows you are passing this close to home, she'll want to go along,* Alynon added in a warning tone.

She knew I was back, alive and well. I'd called her from the ARC facility to let her know. But Alynon was right.

If I answered, I would have to either lie to her about why I'd be delayed, or tell her I was going out to face the local Lord of Darkness, and neither was likely to lead to a good result in the end. I needed to speak with her in person. If I tried to explain the situation with the brightbloods over the phone, now, she might not give me the chance later to tell her my feelings about us, my decisions. Or I'd be forced to try and do so over the phone.

I was too afraid of losing her to risk everything on a phone call.

I pushed ACCEPT anyway.

"Hey," Dawn said. "Why aren't you in my arms yet, damn it?"

"Uh, well, I may not be back until the morning, actually. I need to take care of one more thing for Silene, something she can't do herself. Petey's going with me for backup, I think."

"What one more thing?" Dawn asked, her tone skeptical.

"Something risky and possibly foolish, but necessary."

"That's become the flavor of the week."

"No, you're thinking of Totally Fudged."

"Uh huh. Details?"

"I just need to have a talk with someone. I'd rather explain it when I get home. Do you trust me?"

Dawn was silent for a second, and then said, "Yes. Thank you for trusting *me*. I love you. Be careful. And hurry your butt home to me."

"I will. Good night."

"Like I'll be sleeping. Good luck."

Dawn hung up. I grinned in spite of myself. "I love her."

*Obviously.*

I reached the parking lot. Pete stood on a log facing in the direction of the Elwha steading, illumined by the yellow glow of a streetlamp and sniffing at the air.

"You okay?" I asked.

His eyes snapped to mine, and they were wolf eyes for a second, pale blue surrounded by black. He blinked and they returned to his normal warm brown. A confused expression crossed his big cherubic face before he said, "Finn? Sorry, I thought I smelled . . . other waerwolves have been here."

"Yeah," I said. "They attacked the steading."

"Two males, one female," Pete said. "Minerva, the one who came to the house. I felt an . . . urge to run into the forest, to find them."

"They're gone. I hope. But . . . I may need your help talking to their Archon."

Pete nodded earnestly. "I can do that. Thanks for not ditching me. I hate when you sneak off and get hurt."

I snorted. "Yeah, me too. Come on. The sooner we get this over with, the sooner we can eat."

"Waffles?" Pete asked, his tone hopeful.

"Der doy!" I replied.

The region's Forest of Shadows Archon operated from his estate on the slope of Cougar Mountain, just outside the city of Bellevue. The city sat on the far side of Lake Washington from Seattle, and though officially a suburb of Seattle, it had grown into a sizeable city in its own right. The Archon worked in the city by day, and by night held court over all of those voted "Most Likely to Be Evil" at Brightblood High.

He was, unsurprisingly, a vampire. And a lawyer.

Dawn had told me all about the vampire craziness in books and movies while I was in exile, but Sterling William Clay was not particularly sexy or glittery, nor mopey, moody, or broody from what I'd heard. He was a cold, calculating old bastard who'd lived centuries and generally saw humans as little more than cattle whose best uses were as food and to make him a profit.

It was a good thing for humans that vampires were notoriously territorial and not easily created. There were, as far as I knew, still only a dozen in the entire world.

And I had to convince this particular ancient jerkhead to stop his clan from attacking the Elwha steading.

It was still only 4:00 A.M. when we reached Bellevue, so we headed for Clay's estate rather than his law offices. Cougar Mountain was the first and smallest of the "little Alps," a range of tree-covered hills that loosely qualified as mountains and formed a circle of wilderness surrounded by sprawling cities.

The road up Cougar Mountain wound through forest, with the houses plentiful at first then coming further apart and growing larger and grander the deeper in we drove. By the time we turned up the paved side road that led to Clay's estate, we hadn't passed another house in over a mile. His property was backed onto hundreds of miles of protected wilderness, perfect when many of your clan preferred to run wild, or had a difficult time passing as human even with a glamour.

We were stopped by a tall iron gate across the road, and by the six-foot Crocodile Dundee–looking dude who stood in front of it with his bare arms crossed and his eyes shaded by an Aussie-style cowboy hat. As Pete and I got out of the car a safe distance away, he called out, "No visitors. Get back in and turn around."

Pete sniffed at the air, and cocked his head. "This is one of the waerwolves from Elwha," he whispered to me.

Great. I'd hoped against hope that the Archon had no knowledge of the attacks on the Silver, that he would be as furious about someone using his clan members to create trouble as the Silver were.

That seemed less likely now.

"Hello!" I called back, and held my hands out and open at my sides. I stayed close to the car. "I just came back from the Other Realm, where I had a nice chat with a Bright Lord from the Greatwood. I need to talk with your Archon about it."

Dundee dude's head tilted back, his nostrils flaring as he sniffed, and a golden hoop glinted in his left ear. "You're allied with that Silver tree bitch."

"No, not allied. I want to help you both."

He made a sound between a grunt and a growl, and said, "Rumor is a necromancer helped her kill Ned. He was my pack mate."

Crap.

"Look. If you can just get your Archon—"

A rustling in the undergrowth to our left caused me to take a step back and put my hand in my pocket, grasping the cool silver-plated steel of the baton.

A wiry old man stepped out of the forest wearing jeans and a dirty red flannel shirt, his white hair sticking out wild from beneath a fedora the color of drying blood.

A redcap.

He held a wooden staff in his left hand, his talon-like nails preventing him from closing his hand entirely around it, and in his right he gripped a wriggling rabbit by the scruff of its neck. He was busy tearing the throat out of the rabbit with his teeth when he stepped onto the road, and stopped short when he realized he was not alone.

He fixed his bloodshot eyes on me, and with a red grin he lifted the rabbit and let its blood stream down onto his hat. "Hallo, boys. What 'ave we 'ere?"

Why couldn't anything ever be easy?

Meeting a redcap without magical protections was about as lucky as running into Freddy Krueger in a knife shop.

I glanced back. I would not be able to get into the hearse before the redcap could reach me. And fleeing into the forest was not an option—this was their turf.

Dundee McWaerjerk smiled an unpleasant smile. "Good timing, Willem. This Shadows-murdering arcana and his friend were just trying to get at our Archon."

"Now wait—" I said.

"Funny thing," Waerjerk continued, "I don't see a single beaded moustache between them, and he ain't once gone all official talking about ARC authority and all. What do you think that means?"

Willem met his grin, and dropped the rabbit, his hat now glistening and bright red. "I'm thinking it means dinner, it does!"

"Don't do this—" I said, and stepped toward the car as I flicked my wrist. The baton extended and burst into fiery blue light.

Willem threw his staff at me, and leapt after it.

Why can't there be time-outs in real life?

## Devil Inside

I managed to turn enough that Willem's staff clipped my shoulder rather than punching me in the throat. It sent me staggering sideways, and my left arm went numb. I saw Waerjerk and Pete crash into each other, both punching and trying to knock the other to the ground.

And then Willem leaped on me, his eyes wide and wild and red as his fedora. I swung the baton with all my strength for his head.

He caught the edge of the blow on one forearm, but the baton still connected with his cheekbone, and flared white. The redcap crashed into me, and we fell to the cold concrete together. The baton jolted out of my hand as it hit the ground. Willem punched me in the throat, and I gagged. He straddled me, his bony knees pressing my shoulders to the ground, and leaned down, blood dripping from a nasty gash on his cheek.

I looked over, gasping for enough breath to call for help, but Pete had his own problems. Waerjerk leaped at Pete, transforming into a black wolf twice the size any wolf had a right to be.

The redcap pressed one hand over my mouth to keep me from speaking, jerking my head back to face him.

"No wizardy words from you, oh no," he said, a wicked smile wrinkling his old-man's face. His breath reeked of blood and decay, which only made me gag worse. He ran a talon along my cheek with his free hand. "Let us see what power there be in a wizard's blood, hey?"

I punched him in the side—and the redcap's pressing hand muffled my cry of pain. Willem might look like an old man, but he was solid as a log. He chuckled, and pressed his talon against my neck.

I grabbed his wrist, concentrated, and summoned his spirit.

Willem screamed, his body convulsing as the spiritual feedback set his nervous system on fire. I pushed him off of me.

My head rang from the feedback of the summoning as I scrambled across the carpet of pine needles and snatched up the baton.

"Mercy, mercy," Willem said, whimpering between words. "I meant no harm, only playing I was."

Yeah, right.

I crab-walked backward, and then pushed myself to my feet.

Willem pressed a hand to his bleeding cheek. His red fedora darkened around the edges, the blood draining away to sustain and heal him, leaving the rim dry and crusty.

I backed toward the car, the now-glowing baton held pointed at the redcap. "Don't move," I said, and looked over at the vicious sound of two wolves snarling and snapping at each other.

Pete had transformed into a wolf.

If Waerjerk was two times the size of a normal wolf, Petey was nearly three times. His coat shifted in a pattern of grays and light browns, and he had pale fur around his muzzle that was now spotted with red.

The dark wolf squatted low, growling. His gold hoop earring still glinted in his pointy ear. He limped to one side, and Pete growled and pressed in. Waerjerk snapped at Wolf-Pete, and Wolf-Pete launched into a crazed frenzy of barking and snarling. He bit at Waerjerk's neck and practically climbed on top of him before leaping away and stalking him again.

Waerjerk lowered himself to the ground, and belly-crawled toward Pete, whimpering.

Pete snapped once at him, then appeared to just lose interest. Waerjerk stood, and moved around to his side and slightly behind him.

"Pete?" I called. "You okay?"

Wolf-Pete's pale blue eyes snapped to me, and his hackles rose. He growled, and Waerjerk joined him.

Oh crap.

"Hey," I said. "It's me, Finn. Your brother?"

Wolf-Pete padded cautiously toward me, his lips pulled back to show all his teeth as he continued to growl.

I reached blindly behind me for the handle to the car door. If I couldn't get through to Pete, I'd have to try to escape and get help.

"Pete! Come on! Remember me! And Vee! You're going to marry her, remember?"

Wolf-Pete stopped, his growls dying down.

Then he barked at Waerjerk and bolted for the forest.

"It seems your wolf companion has abandoned you," a deep voice intoned. A man stepped forward from the gate as if he had passed through the metal bars, but I realized he'd probably been standing there for some time, glamoured, just watching our fight.

Sterling William Clay.

He looked like a man in his early fifties in constant and imminent danger of a heart attack; not obese, but not fit either, his pale puffy face tinged red as if he'd been running to the point of heat stroke. Some vampires might be vain, but Clay obviously fell more in the camp of those immortals who figured, what the hell, if cholesterol and alcohol can't kill you, why be moderate?

That didn't mean he was any less deadly, however.

Clay gave a smile stained nearly brown—I preferred to assume by centuries of tea, coffee, and tobacco rather than blood. "If the wolf has come to join us, he is most welcome," he said. "You, however, are most not."

"I came here to talk," I said. "I don't want to fight."

"And I do not wish to be disturbed from my evening walk by rude strangers attacking my home."

"Your clan mates attacked me," I said. "After I explained that I was here to help."

"Help?" Clay laughed. "We are not the ones in need of help, I think."

I heard a whisper behind me. I gave a quick look over my shoulder, but nobody was there. When I turned back, Clay stood close enough I could feel his breath on my face, and he wrenched the baton painfully from my hand. It flared white at contact with his skin, but he barely twitched, then slammed the baton closed. "And don't try to summon my soul, boy. I don't have one."

I swallowed. "Everybody has a spirit."

"You are twice a fool," he said, and walked back toward the gate. "Once a fool for coming here, and twice for not coming better prepared." The redcap rose to his feet, an unpleasant smile stretching his face as he lowered his hand from the now-healed cut.

"I came prepared enough," I said. "The ARC knows I'm here, for one."

"Do they? Or do they only know you intended to come here?" Clay asked. "Who's to say whether you ever arrived, the infamous Phinaeus Gramaraye, the necromancer who seems to find trouble wherever he goes? Perhaps you ran into a rogue redcap on the road?"

And me without my AAA redcap protection.

"Fine. But I came to tell you that someone is using your clan like pawns. That's what got Ned and Hiromi killed. If you don't care that someone is making a fool of you, go ahead and kill me."

Clay smiled. "Oh, I never said I was going to kill you. I was just offering advice, exploring hypotheticals. Willem, be a good lad and go inform Minerva that her boyfriend's off running with a new playmate. Have her bring them home?" He waved his hand, and the gates opened.

The redcap whimpered, and appeared to deflate, slumping forward into a dejected pose. "But I thirst."

"I've told you before," Clay said. "Do not pick fights you cannot win. Tell Consuela to give you a pint of blood before you dry out completely, then do as I requested. Now."

Willem glared at me briefly, a look that promised revenge, then he scooped up his staff and scurried off through the opened gates.

Clay watched him go, and shook his head. "Redcaps. So hotheaded. You wouldn't believe how much trouble he is, but I do what I can."

"Uh, yeah, it must be terrible."

"Ah, sarcasm. I remember when sarcasm was a killing offense. Better days. Come, let us go somewhere more comfortable to await the return of your brother, and discuss how you, the great necromancer, are going to help little old me." He turned in the direction of the gate.

"Uh, can't we just discuss it here?" I asked, glancing back at my car and the slim possibility of escape should things go sour.

"Come now, don't be a sissy boy. And do not fall behind, arcana." Clay began marching up the road. He looked to either side, and stage whispered, "There are bad things in the night." He chuckled, and continued his steady stride.

*I do not trust him.*

*If he wanted me dead, I'd be dead,* I replied. And really, I didn't have a lot of options.

I hurried to follow.

The road slowly curved and climbed up into the forested hillside. The climb gave Clay plenty of time to regale me with a long joke about a travelling unicorn who had to choose between the daughter of a Polish farmer, a Negro farmer, and a wizard.

Fun fact about vampires: they're mostly bigoted asses. It might have something to do with being privileged immortals, most of whom received their education and position centuries past. If the leader of the Ku Klux Klan hung out in a sauna with a bunch of rich old white dudes from corporate dynasties telling jokes about women, gays, and minorities, he would probably sound a lot like a vampire on a more polite day.

By the time we got to the top of the drive, I was winded, my legs ached, and I wanted to slap Clay into the twenty-first century.

Clay whistled what sounded like some Germanic opera tune as he led the way up the steps onto his pillared porch.

Clay's house was a house in much the same way the Pentagon is an office building. A grand, sprawling affair, I would not have wanted to enter without a map and compass. It looked like Frank Lloyd Wright had snorted coke and stayed up all night designing the Grandest. Home. Ever!

"Welcome to my humble abode," Clay said. "Excuse its poor simplicity, but I am merely a brightblood after all."

"It is no less than befits an Archon," I said.

"Well well, look who learned manners!" He motioned to the door. "Please, enter my home, and be welcome."

I cautiously opened the door.

A banshee scream blasted my ears. I jumped, my heart painfully skipping a beat and stubbing its toe.

Clay's face had an exaggerated expression of shock. "Oh, my, so sorry. That's our alarm system. I keep meaning to have that looked at."

Alarm, my ass.

Another fun fact: vampires love practical jokes. Apparently, practical jokes were one of the few things that made life less boring and predictable for them. They played them on anyone who came within their sphere of influence, which was annoying, but not usually dangerous.

The practical jokes that vampires played on each other, however, could be deadly to anyone caught in the crossfire. Being both immortal and virtually indestructible, a battle of practical jokes between two vampires could escalate over years, even centuries, to insane extremes. And with so much time on their hands, they were not above setting up jokes that took months, years, even decades to come to fruition, which made it difficult to end a battle since a joke whose foundations were laid decades ago might not bear fruit until years after a truce was called, triggering a response and starting the whole process over again.

Parking meters. Junk mail. Daylight Savings Time. All rumored to have begun as a vampire's practical joke. It's said one ancient vampire was responsible for both the invention of toilets, and of fireworks, just so that centuries later he could do the first cherry bomb in the toilet joke.

I stepped across the threshold, half expecting a trapdoor to open beneath my feet, but nothing happened. The entry hall alone was the size of a studio apartment, with walls of pale wood, stained glass windows, a pair of sofas, and a number of plants. More Martha Stewart than Transylvania Goth.

"You have a nice home," I offered.

Clay closed the door behind us. "Manners again! Quite refreshing." He proceeded across the grand entry to an arched hallway, and motioned for me to follow. "Redcaps, waerwolves, trolls, they can be quite cunning in their way, and excel at tearing out the throats of their enemies, of course, and yet I'm sure you will be quite shocked to hear they have terribly poor manners." His voice took on a low, confidential tone. "Frankly, not all brightbloods are created equal. Not their fault, obviously, but so many have the blood of animals, or the lesser races." He sighed. "It is rare that I have someone to chat with in a civilized manner. Ah, here, the den. This will be perfect for our talk, I think."

He motioned to the doorknob, and grinned.

"After you," I said.

"As you wish." Clay opened the door without any surprising results, and entered a room of deep greens and browns. I followed.

The den had been decorated to create a feeling of being in the forest. Dark green carpet, walls of brown stone hung with photos of trees, a polished table made from the gnarled stump of a tree, and more plants. A river-stone fireplace had a fake fire crackling on a video screen.

It would have been charming, if not for the lit display cases full of Mammy and Pappy figurines. The little black dolls with the giant red lips filled several cases spaced around the room.

"Ah, I see you've noticed my collection," Clay said. "I'm quite proud of it. Not as large as my collection of rubber ducks, but it is still growing."

*Careful,* Alynon said. *He's just trying to push you into re-acting out of anger, as either a strategy or a joke.*

*Or maybe he's just an ass.* "Actually," I replied with studied calm, "I've been thinking of collecting figurines myself."

"Indeed?"

"Yeah. You can apparently find all kinds of Count Chocula items on the web. Though I don't know if my collection would be as large as yours. Let's see. One, one offensive figurine, ah ah ah. Two! Two—"

Clay's red face got a bit redder. "You seem to have forgotten where you are, necromancer. And with whom."

"No. But I don't have to pretend to like your racism."

"But you do need my help."

"And you need mine," I replied. "Maybe we can get to the part where we talk about that?"

Clay ran a tongue over his teeth as he considered me. I felt quite proud at not bolting for the door.

"Very well," he said. "Please, have a seat. Would you like a drink?"

"Uh, no thanks." I sat on the sofa.

Clay cocked an eyebrow. "I do have something other than blood, of course. A soda, or ale perhaps?"

"Really, I'm fine."

"As you wish." He sat in an armchair on the far side of the tree-stump coffee table. "Now, you said something about my clan be-ing used as pawns?"

"Yeah." I told him about what I'd learned, and what Alynon had guessed. That Hiromi had been given orders supposedly from the Forest of Shadows Court, but that Chauvelin had sworn that the orders were forged somehow. That someone appeared to be at-tempting to upset the relationship between the ARC and the Sil-ver Court, and make it look like the Shadows were responsible and preparing for war with the Silver. Clay asked questions, and I answered them as best I could, or felt comfortable about.

When I finished, at least a half hour had passed. Clay tapped at his chin and stared thoughtfully at the fake fire. As he did, Alynon said, *You have made it sound that someone is doing him a favor by screwing over the Silver and handing the Shadows more power.*

*Maybe. But the thing about people in power is, they want control, that's why they have the power. So what good is power if someone else can just usurp or manipulate it at will? And get your minions killed in the process?*

*That's a pretty thin argument to lay your hopes on.*

*It's the only chance we've got,* I replied.

"There is an ancient proverb," Clay said finally. "Same crap, different day. I paraphrase, of course. But I have been through enough wars to question whether any power the Shadows gain in the Other Realm from such a conflict would be worth the lives of my clan here." He considered me for a few seconds, then said, "I cannot simply deny Kaminari her rightful vengeance. I may, however, be able to direct her anger at a new target. Say, whoever was behind manipulating her sister?"

"That's what I was hoping," I said. "Problem is, I don't know who really gave those orders. Isn't the knowledge that Hiromi was manipulated, that you and the Silver have an enemy in common, enough to at least call Kaminari off until you find the truth yourself?"

"Alas, no," Clay said, his tone lacking any actual regret. "What if we learn the Silver sent those orders to Hiromi in order to frame my clan as being dangerous and out of control? I would look the fool for letting them recover their strength before loosing Kaminari against them once more."

"Why would the Silver do this to themselves?" I asked. "They've suffered deaths, and lost trust—"

"Short term, perhaps," Clay said. "But you think on a mortal timescale. You do not understand the patient sowing of seeds that will bear fruit in decades, perhaps centuries."

I shook my head. "The Silver—"

A loud fart noise erupted from my seat.

"I say!" Clay exclaimed. "Are you sure you don't want a soda? It's quite good for an upset stomach."

I noticed Clay had his hand in his pocket, probably holding some kind of remote.

I gave him a level look. "No. I'm fine, thanks. But I don't think—"

Another fart sound erupted from my seat.

"Oh my," Clay said. "Clearly, attempting to think has upset your stomach. So allow me. You have overlooked one obvious option in discovering the identity of these supposed puppet masters."

"I have?"

"You have," Clay said. "The gnomes. You said they passed the secret messages to Hiromi. They further delivered the supposed message from the Silver Archon to destroy the siren's body, a message also forged, if your information is to be believed."

Great Scott! The gnomes. I could have saved myself serious time and trouble if only I'd thought of that.

Clay leaned back, lounging in the chair with his legs crossed. "I have taken the liberty of summoning a gnome. Let us hope he can corroborate your tale. I have high hopes for that waerwolf you brought, and would hate to start off our relationship by killing his brother."

"Yeah. That would be quite inconvenient for me, too. But you shouldn't make Pete angry. You won't like him when he's angry."

"I'll take my chances," Clay responded.

A knock on the door, and a Hispanic woman opened it to say, "A gnome to see you, sir."

"Well then, let him in, Consuela," Clay said.

"It's Corina, sir," she replied.

"Of course, of course."

Priapus, the leader of the most powerful local gnome family, entered the room. "Archon," he said as he entered. "You lookin for more cursed artifacts?" His Munchkin voice had the eagerness of an imminent deal. Then he noticed me. "Gramaraye," he said with much less enthusiasm.

Priapus stood about as high as my knees, not counting the blue pointy hat tilted jauntily back on his head. His dark beard was cut level across his gut ZZ Top style, and his green vest left bare arms covered in muscle and tattoos. One hand rested on the handle of a small hand scythe whose deadliness, I knew, could not be judged by its size.

Gnome families ruled the black market of the magical world. Stolen goods of a magical nature seemed to find their way into gnome hands—usually because the gnomes were the ones who stole them. They were also good at getting messages to anyone, anywhere. You could put a note requesting a good or service under any gnome statue along with an offer of payment, and if the gnomes accepted the deal you'd soon enough have the object in hand, or the service rendered, no questions asked.

I'd had dealings with this particular gnome leader shortly after my return from exile, dealings that had ultimately provided him with some wealth, but also got his gnomes tangled up in a couple of nasty fights.

"Priapus," I said. "Honor to your family."

"Thank you for coming, Priapus," Clay said. "I need the identity of whoever sent a message via the gnomes to the jorōgumo Hiromi. It was supposedly from the Forest of Shadows Court, but it was forged."

Priapus shook his head. "You wasted both our times then. Gnomes don't rat on our clients. It's bad for business. That protects you much as anyone, Archon."

"Really?" I asked. "You don't care that you were used like that?"

Priapus shrugged. "Hey, we don't never guarantee a message is authentic or nothing like that, we just promise that what you give us, we deliver. And we don't tell nobody who you are. Not less it's part of the message to tell them, capiche?"

"Priapus," Clay said. "Surely there is a clause in the rules that allows you to share such information, if it endangers your own family, for example."

"Yeah?" he asked. "If there was such a rule, and I ain't sayin' there is, how's this here endanger my family? I hope you're not threatening me, vampire."

"No threats," Clay replied. "But it appears someone is trying to start a war between the Forest of Shadows and the Silver Court, playing our brightbloods against each other."

"Well, that's rough," Priapus said. "But I don't see as how that's my business."

Meaning Priapus's clan wasn't Silver or Shadows sworn. "Wait," I said. "What Demesne *is* your family aligned with?" I realized I had no clue.

"The magical Land of Narnia," Priapus said. "As in Narnia Business."

"If allies are drawn into the battle," Clay said, "your family may have to fight nonetheless."

Priapus puffed out his cheeks a couple of times, clearly weighing our words. Then he spat. "Bah. Every time I get involved with you, Gramaraye, it ends with my boys in some kind of fight. You're bad luck, that's what you are." He paced for a second. "Tell ya what. I can't just give ya that information like it's your birthday. It has to be a fair trade. And that information, client information, that ain't gonna be cheap."

"Don't Jew me," Clay growled. "I could eat your entire family as a light snack, you Dago dwarf."

"Woah," I said quickly as Priapus's face grew red. "Archon, maybe dial down the insults? And Priapus, I'm sure we can negotiate a fair price. Let's not forget this information can help all of us, right?"

"Indeed," Clay said. "So if you have the information, gnome, I suggest you give it now."

"Yeah sure, oh lord of darkness," Priapus said. "But don't think I'll be forgetting this." He closed his eyes, and held up his hand for us to wait. "Let's see. Messages. Hiromi. Here we go, bada boom, bada—what in Hades?"

Priapus scowled, and cocked his head, eyes still closed.

"Everything okay?" I asked.

Priapus opened his eyes, and blinked. "Uh, tell ya what. How about I make ya both a new deal," Priapus said. "You name it. And I'll throw in free delivery of messages anywhere you want for the next year. But I can't give you the name of who sent them messages to the jorōgumo dame."

"I suggest you reconsider," Clay said. "If you are being threatened, I assure you, they are not as dangerous an enemy as I."

Priapus's scowl deepened. "Hey, if I had the info to give ya, you'd get it. But someone, they went and disappeared the information. I ain't never seen nothing like it." He shook his head. "It just ain't right."

"Who could have done that?" I asked.

"That's what's got me worried-like," Priapus said. "It has to be a gnome, someone in my own family. But I got no clue who. What kind of crazy palooka destroys information?" he asked. "Information's valuable!"

"What of the gnome who delivered the message?" Clay asked. "May he be questioned?"

Priapus shook his head. "That's the kicker. Looks like it was Tiny Tulips Tony, and we just found him yesterday, six inches under a garden townside."

"Well, this has been rather disappointing," Clay said, and gave a dismissive wave of his hand. "You may depart, gnome."

"Wait," I said. "That's it? There's got to be something we can do."

Priapus shook his tiny head. "Ain't no fast and easy options. I'm going to have to clean house, and do some digging, and that's gonna take time. And the sooner I get started, the better." He turned, and left the room, cracking his knuckles.

"But—" I said.

"Well." Clay stood. "It seems as though you've hit the end of your road, so to speak."

"Wait," I said, springing to my feet. "I know we didn't get a name, but didn't that show you just how dangerous and serious our common enemy is? Maybe just give me a little more time to discover their identity."

"I'm afraid I really can't keep my girl waiting forever," Clay said. "Have you ever tried to keep a jorōgumo on a leash? It never ends well for anyone, trust me. Now, unless I'm mistaken, Minerva should be back with your oh-so-dangerous brother now. Shall we?" He motioned to the door.

It was clear that Clay was done talking. Frustrated, and worried about Pete, I headed out into the hall.

I heard the high-pitched giggle of the brownies overhead a second before the bucket of ice water splashed down on me.

I screamed in shock from the cold, slipped, and fell onto my butt.

"You know," Clay said behind me. "I'm reconsidering your earlier threats. I see now I have serious reason for concern."

I shook off the water from my hands and arms, and prepared to grab Clay's leg, to test his claim that vampires had no spirit to summon—

*Think of Petey,* Alynon said. *And everyone else relying on you.*

I glared up at Clay.

*Fine,* I thought back. "You know, for someone with nearly unlimited time and resources, you have a pretty lame idea of jokes." I stood, and shook the water from my hair.

"Oh, I save the good stuff for those whom I do not like," Clay said. "Besides, this is entirely an accident. Clearly Consuela left her bucket laying around. It is so hard to find good help. It seems like anyone affordable is either foreign or ignorant, and quite often both."

I marched for the front door. "You know, my grandmother was Mexican."

"Really?" Clay asked, following at a casual pace behind me. "Is she good at windows?"

My hands clenched into fists.

*Don't!* Alynon shouted in my head. *You can't help anyone if you're dead!*

"You will die someday," I said over my shoulder. "And I have a feeling nobody will weep if your spirit is destroyed. By accident, of course."

"If I die, it will be long after you are dust," Clay said as I reached the front door. "And I already told you, I have no soul."

"You have a soul," I replied. "And—"

The floor gave way beneath my feet, and I dropped down into darkness.

# Wild Thing

I fell into some kind of tube slide. I slid for what seemed forever, unable to stop myself, the sense of time no doubt drawn out by the fact that I didn't know if I was being dropped into a pit of spikes or a tub of whipped cream. Either seemed equally possible at that point.

I slid around a final bend and shot out into the cool night air, slamming into a soft bank of earth and cedar fronds that knocked the wind out of me.

I stood, shaking from fear, and anger, and cold, and turned around to get my bearings. I saw lights not far off, and headed for them.

I emerged from the forest on the downhill side of the road to Clay's estate, just outside the gate. The hearse still sat there, waiting, and Pete stood there as well, wearing his recovered jeans and T-shirt. The jeans must have fallen free during his transformation, but the shirt had clearly not, and hung around him now like a ripped bib. But Pete himself appeared fully intact. Physically anyway; the shame and worry on his face were clear.

Minerva, with her spiky red hair and the physique of a professional women's basketball player, stood talking to Pete. Behind her, Waerjerk watched them both with an expression of naked jealousy. Appropriate, since he and Minerva remained actually naked. Well, except for Waerjerk's ridiculous pirate earring, and a matching ring on Minerva's—

"Excellent," Clay said, appearing out of the shadows near the gate again. "Enjoy your slide, Gramaraye? I assumed you would want to get here as quickly as possible, being worried for your brother and all."

"Thanks," I said through gritted teeth. "Pete? You okay?"

"Yeah," he said. "I want to go home."

Minerva touched his chest. "But you are home. We are your true family."

"I have a family," Pete said.

"You have people who happened to be born to the same parents. But you belong with us. You bested Georgio," she said as she nodded at Waerjerk. "You could be my mate, first mate to the pack leader. We could do so much more than run together."

Pete blushed, obviously struggling not to look at her naked body, though she kept moving to where he was looking.

"Back off," I said. "This isn't recruitment for college football. This is his life you're talking about, and his life is with us. And with the woman he loves. Right, Pete?"

Pete nodded.

"Minerva," Clay said. "Let the nice boy go. He'll be back, I'm sure."

A girl's angry voice said behind me, "I sent Georgio to seek aid, but find myself betrayed!"

I turned to find Kaminari, Hiromi's creepy little sister, looking between me and Clay, her face a mask of fury. Her ponytails twitched and jumped as if alive, and it looked like her ribs were pushing out against the sides of her flowered dress.

"Kaminari," Clay said, his tone dangerous. "You will mind your manners as long as these gentlemen are my guests."

She began spinning her jump rope around side to side, her eyes all black and fixed on me now. "You helped to kill my sister," she said. "I'm gonna destroy you, mister."

She whipped her jump rope at me, and it stretched out, becoming a stream of webbing. I threw up my arms to protect my face.

Clay blurred. One second he stood beside the gate, the next he stood between me and Kaminari, her web caught in his hand. With a jerk, he yanked it from Kaminari's grasp, clearly unaffected by its tranquilizing effects.

"You will obey!" he said. "You shall have your vengeance, but you will do so when and how I say."

Kaminari screamed, "No! No no no! I want to kill him NOW! I don't care about your when and how!"

Clay sighed. "Very well. You can kill him."

"What?" I said, and Kaminari smiled.

"But," Clay continued, "if you do so, jorōgumo, I shall kill you after. I'd have to make an example of you, you see. And appease their ARC."

Kaminari looked between me, and Clay, and then screamed, tearing at her hair and hitting herself in a wild flurry, and I could tell she was only working herself up to something far worse.

I felt as terrified as a man facing a tidal wave of blood seconds before it swallows him.

"KAMINARI!" Clay shouted, his voice echoing through the woods, and his mouth stretched, showing a mouth full of needle-sharp teeth.

The young girl froze, her eyes wide. Then she began to cry, the pitiful, heart-wrenching sobs of a young girl who is terrified.

"It is time you left," Clay said to me. "And face your fate with your Silver friends."

Kaminari stopped crying abruptly, and smiled a smile that would have made Nellie Oleson swoon with envy, a smile cruel and bratty and smug all at once.

"The Elwha are prepared for Kaminari to attack," I said. "It won't be like last time. Send her in and she'll die. A lot of your brightbloods will die."

"*The Elwha are prepared,*" Kaminari imitated me in a mocking tone. "More like they're scared."

I ignored her, and continued. "Sterling Clay, puppet, that's how history will record you. The fool who killed his own family because someone played him like a little bit—"

Clay blurred, and stood behind me, brutally squeezing my neck.

I screamed in pain. Pete advanced toward us, growling, but Clay gave a no-no-no waggle with a finger of his free hand, and squeezed so that I screamed again. Pete stopped, and Clay's grip loosened slightly.

"Manners," Clay said when I quieted. "No reason to be rude. Now look at my darling Kaminari. How can I deny her vengeance against those we know killed her sister?"

"But you know that Hiromi—"

"Yes, yes, it was all a terrible mistake, so sorry but you were tricked into killing her sister. Well, whoever has been manipulating events, my patrons and I shall find them and deal with them in time. But I'm afraid that you have proven of little use in this matter, and Kaminari does have a right to claim vengeance on you, your family, and that tree-bright's clan. So I'm afraid once you leave my property, I can no longer guarantee your safety."

Which meant I would likely be dead before I could reach help, or home. Or that she could instead kill anyone in my family to make me suffer as she had.

*Demand single combat!* Alynon shouted suddenly in my head. *Say it! Now!*

"Wha—uh, I demand single combat!" I shouted.

"Oh my," Clay said, and released me.

*What did I just do?* I asked Alynon.

*He said Kaminari has a claim of vengeance on you. That gives you the right to demand it be settled in personal combat rather than through clan feud.*

"Oh yes, oh yes, let us duel!" Kaminari said, grinning. "A mess a mess I'll make of you!"

"That was a lousy rhyme," I said, rubbing at my neck.

Kaminari screamed, and stepped toward me.

"STAY!" Clay snapped, and she stopped. "You've just agreed to fight a duel, dear girl, you may not harm him until then." He turned to me. "And if you would please cease provoking Kaminari, it will make everyone's evening more pleasant."

*You just got me into a personal duel with a jorōgumo?* I shouted mentally at Alynon.

\*Trust me in this. Declare yourself a representative of the Silver, by right of being my host.\*

*Why?*

\*Just do it! And dare her to accept it.\*

I looked Kaminari in the eyes. "I, uh, declare myself representative of the Silver, by right of being host to Alynon Infedriel, Knight of the Silver Court. I dare you to accept that, you little brat."

"Kaminari—" Clay began, his tone warning, but Kaminari hissed.

"I accept your dare, I accept your declare, it makes no change to how you'll fare."

"Well played, Gramaraye," Clay said, then sighed. "I am quite fond of my little Kaminari, not to mention darling Minerva. I suppose I should be grateful to you. But alas, you still shall die."

"Grateful?" I asked.

"Indeed," Clay said. "Kaminari, darling, you just agreed that Gramaraye here shall represent the Silver. That means that he is representing not just himself, but those Silver brightbloods homed at Elwha, including the little tree strumpet. When you kill him, you shall have no further claim of vengeance on her, and I'm afraid I simply cannot let you attack the Silver brightbloods without just claim."

"What?" Kaminari screamed. "No no NOOO! Their blood must flow!"

"Oh dear," said Clay, looking at me. "You do seem to have a most amazing skill at upsetting her. Kaminari, darling, settle down now."

"No no no NO!" Kaminari began beating at herself again.

Clay sighed. "Kaminari, go up to the house while I conclude business here. I grow weary of your tantrums. Minerva, Georgio, accompany her and see that she gets there."

The crying stopped on a dime. "You are so letting him go!" Kaminari hissed.

"Not that your obedience should require an answer, but I do not make Indian promises, dear heart. Hiromi shall be avenged by the next setting of the sun. If you do not do as I ask, however, you shall be in too much pain to enjoy it."

Kaminari glared suspiciously at me, but she turned and leaped over the gate. Spider legs sprang out of her back as she did so, and she landed on them, then skittered with the speed of a cheetah up the road. Minerva and Georgio Waerjerk sprinted after her, leaving Pete and I alone with Clay.

Clay waved nonchalantly in Kaminari's direction. "I meant what I said to her. You are going to die tonight. But since Kaminari is the one who claimed vengeance on you, you have the right to choose the method of combat."

Great. "I don't suppose a game of checkers would count?"

"Alas, no. It must be a physical contest between you."

"What about the whole dying tonight thing; I don't suppose we could really stretch the definition of tonight? Like, maybe, before sunrise?" That would give me time to support Dawn at her show, leave her with a good memory of me at least. "I have a prior engagement, you see—"

"No, I'm afraid I cannot do that," Clay said. "The most I can give you is the time it will take for me to arrange the duel. And just so you don't try to be clever and set it in China or some such nonsense to stretch this out, let's just say it will be held at the camp near your Elwha friends' steading, yes?"

Damn. There went my China plan.

"But I can pick the method?"

Clay sighed. "Yes, that is traditionally how it is done, though I must approve."

What could I possibly beat Kaminari at? She had more speed and strength than me. I wasn't an expert at any weapon, and the few I could use competently I imagined she would beat me at, even if she started barehanded. Pistols seemed the most likely to succeed, though I imagined with all her web shooting practice she had pretty deadly aim, whereas I was lucky to hit any target smaller than Godzilla.

I thought back to the battle with Hiromi. In the end, it had been Silene entangling her in vines that had made the difference.

"Gramaraye?" Clay asked.

"I'm thinking. Hold on."

"You cannot claim indecision forever. You must eventually choose, and die."

"Yeah yeah. I get it. Just hang on. Please."

What kind of weapon could I use to entangle Kaminari's legs that she couldn't as easily use to entangle me? A bolo? A rebel snowspeeder?

"Dance," I said, and the word registered in my brain after leaving my lips like the sound of a gunshot reaching the target after the bullet.

"Pardon me," Clay said. "But I thought you said 'dance.'"

*Please, no,* Alynon said. *This is our life. You need to be serious.*

Hey, dancing is serious, I thought back. "Yeah. We're going to have a dance-off," I said. "You know, a Saturday Night Fever fight. Breakin' 2 Electric Booga–duel. Winner takes all and saves the dance club. Or, you know, clan."

Clay arched an eyebrow. "You do realize, of course, that a duel to satisfy vengeance must be to the death, Gramaraye. You cannot have a dance off, or a cook off, or any other kind of off, unless it ends with a head off."

"I thought you were all about being civilized," I said.

"Indeed. And that is why when you lose your head, I shall discourage Kaminari from killing every person you love. We are not barbarians, after all."

"Obviously," I said.

*Finn! Damn it! Pick guns, or wands, anything that will give us an actual fighting chance.*

She'd kill me even faster if we used weapons, I replied. But I'm going to get that girl so twisted up she'll trip and fall, and it will all be over. Points deducted, head removed, problem solved.

*You're a fool.*

*A dancing fool.*

"Very well," I said to Clay. "Loser loses their head." Which frankly sounded quite preferable to any of the other ways I saw myself dying in a duel with a jorōgumo, all of them slow and painful and involving seeing parts of me no longer attached to other parts of me. A quick, swift beheading? Wham bam, thank you ma'am. "There can *be* only one," I added in my best Christopher Lambert impression.

And I fully planned to be that one.

"Excellent," Clay said. "One moment, please." He made as if whistling, though I could not hear anything.

*You are exorcising me before this fight,* Alynon said. *You have no right to keep risking *my* life like this.*

*We can talk about it after this,* I replied.

Clay whistled silently again.

"Summoning your dogs?" I asked.

"Just one, actually," Clay said. "I believe you know him. He's provided me with some wonderfully detailed stories about you, and your Negro girlfriend, what is her name? Dawn?"

The undergrowth rustled to my left, and a Yorkshire terrier leaped out of the forest and onto the pavement. Pete growled then stopped. He sniffed at the air with a confused look on his face, and sneezed. The dog padded toward us and transformed, rising up and shifting into a naked man among a cloud of patchouli smell that I now realized helped mask his scent from his fellow waers.

"Barry," I said, deliberately keeping my eyes on his. "Why am I not surprised you're a shadowbright?"

"Whoa, brah," he said. "No need for the heavy negativity. We're all friends here."

"Uh, no, we're not. So, what, you were sent to be a pain in my ass for some reason?"

Barry gave me a pitying smile. "Finn, my friend, you really need to step outside the circle of me me me, brah. One is a lonely number."

"Yeah, well, *tu* can be as bad as one. No, scratch that, you're worse. So, Duck Hunt, what *were* you doing sniffing around my girlfriend?"

Barry sighed. "You see what I mean?" he said to Clay. "My man here's totally insecure."

"Indeed," Clay replied. "But I didn't call you here for a reunion. 'Your man' has just challenged Kaminari to a dancing contest, and I would like you to stand in as her champion."

"Wait, what?" I said.

"Whoa," Barry said. "Totally flattered, Papa Clay, but won't Kaminari kill me after if I take her place? She's a little, uh, intense about this whole vengeance thing."

"Hey!" I said. "What makes you so certain you're going to win?"

Barry laughed. "That's the spirit, Fightin' Finn." He turned back to Clay. "Seriously though, what about Kaminari?"

"I will handle Kaminari. You handle Fred Astaire here."

"Sure thing, boss." Barry winked at me. "Should be fun, huh? When is it?"

"Tonight," Clay said. "I promised Kaminari that much."

"Whoa, harsh," Barry said, looking at me again. "Guess we're going to totally miss Dawn's show, huh? 'Course, she's likely to be more pissed at you than me. But don't worry, I'll comfort her after she's done yelling at your head and all."

My hands clenched into fists. "So how do we do this?"

## Giving You the Best That I Got

I didn't relax until the glow of Bellevue was behind us and we drove along the 405 north for Snoqualmie.

I glanced over at Pete in the passenger seat as the lights of passing cars and streetlamps cast his face in slow waves of light and dark.

"Hey," I said. "Are you okay? Really?"

"No," he said, his voice small.

"Oh." My heart ached for him. "That was your first time transforming in the wild, wasn't it? I mean, unbound, outside of the house."

Pete just nodded.

"Was it scary? Awful?"

"No," Pete said again. "It was—I don't know. Do you remember when we went to Disneyland, how it felt like . . . there was this whole other world that was just for us, that was like what we felt inside, and you just wanted to run away and live in the Family Robinson treehouse and spend every day running through the park having adventures?"

"Uh, sort of," I said.

"Well, it's a little like that," Pete said. "Beating Georgio in that fight, the run through the forest hunting food, and the, um, having Minerva wanting me, it all felt . . . good." He looked down at his hands. "Does that mean I'm a Shadows brightblood? Or that I'm . . . an animal?"

"No!" I said. "No. Pete, the wolf spirit didn't change your heart, it didn't change who you are. It just kind of lets your wild side out to play every once in a while. And that's not a bad thing, not by itself."

"But, I almost . . . I almost attacked you," he said.

"But you didn't," I replied.

He was silent for a while. "What if Vee had been there?" he said finally. "What if I had . . . hunted her."

"You wouldn't have," I said.

Pete began to sob. Great, shaking sobs that caused the entire car to bounce lightly and I would have had to shout to be heard, which I knew wouldn't be comforting at all.

I took the next exit and parked on the side of the road. I slid over on the seat, and held Pete, let him cry it out. When there came a lull in the sobs, where it sounded like he was hyperventilating, I said, "Petey, man, you would never hurt Vee. Don't you remember what made you stop growling at me? I mentioned Vee. Just her name was enough to calm you down. If anything, Vee is the one person you should always *want* to have around you. You love her. She loves you. We all love you, Pete, wolf or no wolf."

Pete's sobs settled into sniffles. "Really?"

"Really."

He sniffled a little longer, wiping at his face with his shirtsleeves, then said, "I still want to marry her."

"Well I should hope so. I've been thinking of what to do at your bachelor party."

"Oh. I forgot about that. I, uh, I'm not sure Vee would want me to watch naked women dancing. Not even nymphs."

"Well, you don't have to worry about that," I said. "I'm pretty sure there aren't any naked women at Enchanted Village."

"Enchanted Village?" Pete asked, perking up a bit. "Could we take Mort? And Mattie? And Vee? She's never been."

"Uh, sure. It's your bachelor party, I guess you can invite whoever you want." I smiled. "I love you, Brother. Everything's going to be okay."

He nodded, and I slid back into the driver's seat, buckled up, and drove north once again.

I hoped I wasn't lying to him, hoped everything really would be okay. I had to beat Barry in this dance off, and end this cycle of clan war before it escalated. Or instead of organizing a bachelor party, I might have to watch from beyond the cold distance of death's veil as Pete and Vee fought for their lives.

After a quick stop at the ARC headquarters under Snoqualmie Falls, Pete took over driving and we headed home with Verna in the seat between us. Her portal equipment rattled in the spacious back of the hearse.

*Thank you,* Alynon said for the fiftieth time.

*Stop thanking me,* I replied. *I want to send you home as bad as you want to go.*

Verna still wore her ink-stained lab coat, but had let her hair down into a wild silver halo. She blinked at the passing streetlights through her thick glasses, and rattled on about the exciting possibilities of Father's spirit-bridging artifact. I quickly learned that I didn't really need to do much to hold up my end of a conversation with her, just give the occasional sound of interest, or say "Really?" She apologized at one point for rambling.

"I just don't get out of the lab very often."

"It's okay," I said. "You're not rambling. Mattie, my niece, now she knows how to ramble."

"A niece! How nice," Verna said, pushing her glasses up. "Frederick, that was my husband, never wanted children, you know. I thought about trying to modify the portal magics to peek into parallel dimensions to see what my children might have been like, but the power requirements were far too great. And there was a small chance it would turn all life on the planet into eggplants. The equations were very tricky."

"Uh, well, that's too bad," I said, and wondered, had the power requirements not been so huge, might she have given it a try anyway?

Verna continued to ramble as Pete drove us over the floating bridge. The sight of Lake Washington passing beneath and ready to swallow us made me nauseous, so I closed my eyes and focused on finding a way to explain things to Dawn.

*Hi Dawn, I came home safe like I promised, but I'm going to be in a dance contest to the death with your good friend Barry the waerdog, and might miss your show due to my lack of having a head.*

No explanation I imagined led to a happy ending.

We arrived home an hour and a half later, just past 9:00 A.M. A dozen cherry walnut waffles from Hudson Point Café warmed my lap through the takeout boxes, their delicious scent driving me crazy.

I'd called home well ahead, so pretty much the entire family sat gathered around the long oak dining table. Sammy and Mattie looked up from working on their laptops, their expressions of relief bathed in the pale glow of the screens, looking like sisters rather than aunt and niece. Sammy's girlfriend, Fatima, sat barefoot and cross-legged on her chair, sketching in her sketch pad, and pushed her long black hair out of her face as we entered. And Mort had the necrotorium's appointment book and payment ledger on the table, frowning at them and making an obvious show of ignoring our entrance. Father was absent, most likely in his room.

Vee rushed to Pete with a worried expression and examined his torn shirt. "What happened?"

Pete gave an uncomfortable shrug.

At the same time, Dawn grabbed the takeout boxes out of my hand, threw them on the table, and punched me in the shoulder, hard, which wrenched the other shoulder that the redcap had struck with his staff.

"Ow!" I winced and held both shoulders. "What? I told you I was going—"

"That's for almost getting stuck in the Other Realm!" Dawn said. "But you're back now, and you took care of Silene's whatever issue, I assume. Mission accomplished, right?" She stopped and looked at my filthy clothes. "Why are you doing a Pig-Pen imitation?"

Vee pointed to Pete's shirt. "And why does it look like Pete transformed?"

"We, uh, went to the Shadows Archon about stopping an attack on the Elwha steading. There was a little misunderstanding with his brightbloods. But everything is fine now."

Dawn took a step back. "Define fine."

"Oh, sweetie," Vee said to Pete. "Come on. Let's get you cleaned up."

Pete gave a mournful look at the waffles. "But—"

"You'll get your waffles," she said. "But first you need to clean up, and give me a few minutes to appreciate you not being hurt." She took his arm and led him from the room.

Sammy crossed her arms and leaned back in her chair. "If everything really was fine, you wouldn't have called a family meeting after going to see that vampire. And who's your guest?"

"Vampire!" Dawn said as I looked at Verna, who stood holding a large piece of her portal equipment in the doorway.

"Oh geez. Sorry. Here, I'll take that." I lifted the portal equipment from Verna's hands and set it in the corner, then quickly introduced her to everyone. "Verna's going to help me with Alynon, hopefully."

"Hello," Verna said awkwardly.

Dawn crossed her arms. "Nice to meet you, Verna." She glared at me. "Now, back to how *you* got in a fight with a vampire?"

Right. "I think we managed to stop the Forest of Shadows and Silver Court from going to war, at least for now. But there's still some tensions between their brightbloods that needed to be worked out, so—"

Dawn sighed. "Why do I feel like you promised to try and fix it all again?"

"Uh—" I said. At the look on Dawn's face, I found I just couldn't tell her the truth about the dance off. If for no other reason than she might cancel her show to be with me, record company reps or not, and that was the last thing I wanted. Bad enough she couldn't play the guitar—*for now,* I willed to the Universe—I wasn't going to risk her dreams any further.

But she could tell I'd gotten involved somehow by my hesitation.

"Damn it, Finn!" she said. "I love you, but let's just recap previous episodes, shall we? You took Sal to meet his true love, and got caught up in Silene's troubles instead. So you just had to go talk to her dead friend real quick, and everything was supposed to get better. But then you got into a fight at the game farm and promised Silene—"

"You were there," I said. "You agreed I should help them."

"Help, yes. Use yourself as bait to catch a spider witch, hells no. And once again, that didn't solve the problem, so you decided to go to the Other Realm—"

"It's not like I wanted to!" I said.

"And now, the brightbloods are fighting, and you run off and get in a fight with Count Dracula? I love you and your big ole heart, but I'm beginning to think you really do have a problem here. So, out with it. What did you promise this time?"

I sighed, and looked between Sammy and Mattie. They didn't know Heather had returned yet, and now didn't seem the time to bring it up. "I, uh, promised I'd try to get an alchemist to go to the Elwha steading, to help them out so they can defend themselves properly."

Dawn looked at me for a second like I was that record company guy who'd passed on signing The Beatles. "I want to talk to you alone for a second," she said, and grabbed my hand.

"Okay, but—" I began, then was pulled after her.

Dawn led me back to the library. I felt a growing knot of discomfort in my gut as we walked. She'd finally had enough. I had to convince her that I loved her, that I knew she was right, that I wanted to be with her.

And that I still needed to do this one last thing.

"Close the door," Dawn said as we entered the library. While I closed the door, she went to the bookshelf nearest the door.

"Look, Dawn, I know—"

"Here," Dawn said, pulling a book off the shelf. "I got you a little present." She held it out to me.

I blinked at it. "You—oh, um, thanks?" I took the book. A thick, hardbound copy of *The Odyssey*. I quickly ran through possible reasons, including birthdays, anniversaries, and holidays, but I had missed none that I knew of. My relief was short-lived, however, when I considered it might be a fabulous parting gift. "Uh, what's this for?"

"Open it."

I opened the book. A square hollow had been cut out in the center of the book's pages, and within sat what looked like a *Star Trek: The Next Generation* phaser, and an amulet—a real amulet. I could sense the magical energy in it.

"What—where did you get this?" I lifted out the amulet.

"Sammy helped me get that. The Taser, I bought in Sequim."

"Wow. I don't know what to say." I held up the amulet and examined the wizard symbols engraved on its silver surface. Something to do with alchemy and balance.

Dawn stepped closer, looked at the symbols with me. "It's supposed to make it so people, or creatures, they can't mess with your body chemistry. You know, put you to sleep, or use love potions on you, that kind of thing. Sammy said it would need to be recharged after you use it. Like the Taser, I guess."

I lowered the amulet and looked at her. "I thought you were bringing me back here to yell at me. Which I totally deserve."

Dawn put her hands on her hips. "Damn straight you do. But I'm just too sweet to yell."

"Uh huh. And?"

"*And*, you may be risking your life more than I like, and getting into all kinds of trouble, but you're not doing it to hurt or disrespect me, I see that. You're doing it to help your family, and help others, and because you feel you have to."

"I really am," I said.

"I get that, Finn." Her hands dropped, and she looked less

confident now. "As for you and me, well, I also get that it's only been three months for you, and you've had a lot to deal with. I still think it was pretty sucky of you to let that anubis spirit take your memories of me—"

"I didn't know he would do that. I thought—"

"—he was going to take your Talker gift, I know. Still hurts though. And whatever you say, I think this magic stuff is going to keep putting you in danger."

"I don't plan—" I began, then stopped. I didn't plan to keep getting involved in these battles and conspiracies. Hell, I still dreamed, in my private quiet hours, of somehow leaving the necromancy behind entirely. But the Arcanites were still out there pursuing my grandfather's vision of arcana supremacy, and still using Grayson's drug. Hell, my grandfather might still be out there, alive. And if Pete or Vee, or even Mort, really needed my help, I'd give it, even if it was dangerous. "You're right. It's not what I want, but I have no idea what might happen in the future."

"Exactly. So, I can either decide it's too much for me and walk away. Or I can choose to look at this like I've learned my boyfriend's a spy, or better yet, Doctor Strange, and decide whether I want to go all in despite his need to keep running into danger."

"And which did you choose?" I asked, not daring to hope too much.

"Until you give me a real reason to think otherwise, I think you're worth going all in."

I felt as though the entire room, entire house, hell, the entire world had been holding its breath, and now let out a long sigh. I set the book and Taser onto the nearby table, grabbed Dawn around the waist with one hand, buried my other hand in the soft violet curls covering the nape of her neck, and pulled her into a kiss.

It was a long kiss, a perfect kiss, a homecoming.

When our lips parted, we stood a second with our lips barely touching, our eyes closed and warm breath mingling. I felt her lips curve into a smile.

I opened my eyes, and looked into hers. "I'm dang lucky."

"You're dang straight," Dawn replied. We stepped apart. I picked the amulet back up, slipped it over my head, then examined the Taser.

"These are great. Thank you."

"I expect you to gear me up, too, you know," Dawn said. "And I want us to take some classes together. Martial arts. And sword fighting. Or do they teach sword fighting in martial arts?"

*At last!* Alynon said.

"I don't know," I replied. "Maybe. I thought you wanted me to take that massage class with you."

"That too," Dawn said. "Like I said, I expect you to do your half here, dude. That move with the muse got you some major boyfriend points, but don't think you can coast on that forever."

"I won't," I said, grinning.

"Good. And you can start by not missing my show tonight. I'll need all the support I can get."

Crap. "Shouldn't be a problem," I said, and prayed to all the gods and goddesses that was true.

"Good. So," Dawn said. "I assume this alchemist you promised to bring to Elwha is Heather?"

"Oh, uh, yeah," I said, setting the Taser back inside the book.

"I don't suppose they have a sarlacc pit they plan to throw her into?"

I raised my hands. "I'm not her biggest fan either. But if she can undo some of the damage she caused, and help keep our family safe in the process, I'm willing to give her the chance."

"I guess," Dawn said in an unconvinced tone.

"And in the spirit of Finn Fantastic and Awesome Girl, I thought we could talk to her together."

Dawn frowned. "I'm not sure anything I'd say to her would be very helpful."

"You don't have to say anything," I replied. "I'll need to convince her to go with me to Elwha. But she was . . . not happy with me the last time I saw her."

"So?"

"So, you can be there to keep her from freezing me again, or talking me into doing some other crazy thing to win her help. I do seem to have a problem just saying no."

"Oh." Dawn went over to the fireplace, and pulled down the silver sword. "I can do that."

"I don't think you'll need—" I began, but stopped at the look she gave me. "Right. So, should we go have some breakfast? And I need to finish explaining the situation to my family."

"Right after you give me another kiss."

The kiss lasted several delicious minutes, and I felt a bit lightheaded when Dawn finally opened the library doors and we walked back to the dining room.

Pete had returned cleaned up and clothed, and he and Vee were making serious inroads into the waffles. Sammy and Mort were focused on their work, and Mattie chatted with Vera about one of the many crazy experiments she'd helped Father with.

Sammy looked up when we entered the room and noted the amulet hanging around my neck. "I see she gave it to you. She's better than you deserve, you know."

I chuckled. "Yeah, I know. Hey, Pete, I'll need your help with that exorcism spell if you think you're ready."

"I've been practicing and practicing," Pete said earnestly around a mouthful of waffle.

"I know you have. And I know you'll do awesome."

Sammy closed her laptop. "So, you going to tell us what's going on? Or do we get to wait for a phone call in the middle of the night announcing you've gotten our family in a clan war with leprechauns?"

"Well, you *are* always after their Lucky Charms," I replied. Dawn and I started dishing up waffles.

"Funny. But speaking as your sister and Mattie's aunt, it would be nice if you stopped doing things that put a target on your entire family."

"Hear, hear," Mort muttered.

"I didn't—" I began, and paused with a waffle dangling from

my fork. I sighed. "I'm sorry. That's the opposite of what I'm trying to do, I swear."

"I know," Sammy replied. "You were just trying to do the right thing. Which is why I'm here at all, and not heading home to prep for our *Game of Thrones* viewing party. But maybe next time try and 'do the right thing' a little smarter?"

"Gee, well, we can't all be as smart as you, sis."

Sammy shrugged. "Sad but true. So, give us the deets on your rollicking adventures."

We ate while I shared what I had learned in the Other Realm, and of the need to stop the fighting between the brightbloods before it escalated.

Mort exhaled sharply through his nose. "Yeah, well, good luck with that." He stood up, grabbing his ledgers. "I told you going into the Other Realm wasn't worth the risk. You need to cut your losses now. Let the feybloods have their little gang fight, and then they'll go away to lick their wounds."

"And if their fight escalates to all-out war?" I asked. "If Pete and Vee get pulled in? And little Miss Jorōgumo decides to come after my family for revenge?"

"Then it will be on your head, not mine," Mort said. "We'll fortify here until the danger passes. Meanwhile, I have to reschedule the wake for that fairy you left half prepped in the necrotorium." He left the room.

"Well, that was helpful," I said.

"He's an ass," Sammy said. "Though I hate that he's right about the fairy. You did have a job to do here."

"I know that!" I said. "I'm doing the best I can, but I'm only one person."

"Don't get your Underoos in a wad," Sammy said. "Just tell us, what do you need?"

"Mostly? I just wanted to make sure you were all together, and safe today. And of course, that you cheer extra loud at Dawn's show."

"Aw, thanks, honey," Dawn said. "My biggest fan."

"Naw, I'm just hoping you hit it big so you can introduce me to Susanna Hoffs."

"I catch you with Susanna, and she really will be walkin' like an Egyptian."

Pete swallowed a mouthful of waffle with a gulp, and said, "I can finish prepping the fairy."

"Thanks, Brother."

We finished making our plans for the evening, then I turned to Verna. "If you're ready, I'll introduce you to my father."

She patted at her loose silver hair and said, "Yes, quite."

I led Verna down the hallway to Father's door, and knocked before I cracked it open. Father sat at his desk, tinkering.

"Father?" I said, and opened the door. "I have someone who wants to meet you. Verna, this is my father, Arlyn. Father, this is Verna. She's an ARC thaumaturge."

Verna crossed to Father and held out her hand. "It's a real pleasure, Arlyn. I was quite impressed with the Summoning Simon artifact you created. I'd love to discuss it with you."

Father's hand twitched, and he said without looking up, "The secret's in the sauce. It has scrubbing bubbles!" He made popping sounds with his mouth.

"Bubbles?" Verna asked.

"I'm sorry," I said. "I tried to explain on the way here—"

"Oh, yes, I see." Verna cocked her head. "Are you referring to the phenomena of quantum-auratic foam, where the permeable energy layer of our universe is agitated by the product of magical decay in the Other Realm?"

Father dropped the object he was tinkering with and looked up at Verna. "Thirty-two flavors, scratch and sniff but don't go licking the jelly!"

Verna nodded excitedly. "Of course! A human spirit interacting in the Other Realm would create a different 'flavor' of auratic decay, and—brilliant. Oh, I must write this down." She felt in her hair, then in her lab coat pocket, but both were empty of pens.

Father held up a pen. He had tears in his eyes, and a huge grin.

"Oh perfect, thank you!" Verna said, and went to Mother's old desk. She pulled an old pad of stationary from the corner of the desk, and held it up. "Do you mind?"

Father shook his head, and she began rapidly scribbling on the pad. "This is quite exciting. I hadn't considered—" She looked up at me. "Oh, did you need help with the equipment? I really would love to speak with your father some more."

"I'll get it unloaded and set up as best I can," I said, my own eyes filling with tears at the look of joy on Father's face. "I'll come back when I'm ready to attempt the exorcism."

"Very good," Verna said, already scribbling again, her tone distracted.

I turned to leave, and Father said, "Finn Fancy."

I turned back. "Yeah?"

He went to speak further, but the left side of his face twitched and he shook his head. He just patted at his chest.

I nodded. "I love you, too, Dad."

I left quickly, wiping my eyes, and went upstairs to signal for Heather.

# With or Without You

I hung my pair of red Chuck Taylors from the rope between my bedroom window and Dawn's house. As I stepped back into the hall, I thought I felt a trace of spiritual energy, as of a disembodied spirit.

My eyes snapped to Mort's room.

I moved as quietly as I could up the hall, still sensing the spiritual presence.

*Please, tell me that Mistress Suck a Bus has returned!* Alynon said.

*Dude, you need frakking aversion therapy,* I thought.

The floorboard gave out a loud, obnoxious creak, as only real wood floors in very old houses can.

"Bat's breath." I hurried to Mort's door, and felt for the presence of a spirit, but detected nothing. I gave a gentle knock. "Mort?"

No response. Which meant he was refusing to answer.

Or incapable.

I tried the doorknob but it was locked. "Mort, if you don't let me know you're alive, I'll have to break this door down."

"Break down my door, and I'll break your face," Mort said from behind the closed door. "I'm trying to work."

His voice sounded off.

I pulled the skeleton key from around my neck, and touched it to the doorknob.

A ward symbol glowed orange on the door above the knob, and the door remained locked.

Crap.

"Mort, if you're still summoning that succubus, you're an idiot," I said. "And suicidal. Get some help before it's too late."

"I'm not—" Mort began, but I didn't stay to listen. There was only so much I could do to help someone who wouldn't help themselves. At least, not when I had a difficult exorcism to perform and a dance battle to prepare for. But even as I walked away I knew I'd be back to try and deal with Mort later.

Bat's breath.

I went downstairs, and Pete helped me to move Verna's equipment into the basement. We set up the containment circle, and the focusing ring from the Kin Finder 2000 that was meant to seek out resonance between two spirits from the same bloodline.

*Thank you,* Alynon said finally as I checked that everything was in place. *I—after what I did in the Bright Realm, I would have understood—just thank you.*

"You're welcome," I replied as I aligned the Kin Finder ring with the circle of Verna's portal equipment. "But mostly I'm doing this because I don't want to be responsible for your death if I lose to Barry."

*Whatever your reasons, I thank you,* Alynon said. *Though if I could ask but one more favor?*

I stood straight, and sighed. "What is it?"

*Could you perhaps use the other ring, the one meant to find one's true love? If I'm going to return to the Other Realm, I do not wish to show up in the Colloquy. At this point, I know not if any side will take me. I just wish to be with Velorain.*

I sighed. "I suppose it should still work, assuming Velorain really is your true love, and not just another true lust."

*It is true love.*

"Okay then. Love it is," I said. I swapped out the rings.

Pete returned with Verna.

"Your father is a brilliant man," she said. "And quite charming." She blushed a bit, and patted at her hair. "How he never worked for the ARC is quite beyond me."

"He just wanted to be with his family," I said. "I've set up the equipment as best I could, but—"

"Oh, yes, well, you have this backward." She hurried to her portal equipment and made some adjustments. "There. Ready to go."

"Thank you," I said. "I thought I was going to have to open an illegal portal, so this helps more than you can know."

"Oh, happy to do it," Verna said. "What you're doing could prove quite useful in banishing Fey spirits from our world should we need to."

*If it doesn't kill us both,* Alynon said.

*Do you want to try this or not?*

*Of course. I am desperate enough at this point that I'd try anything.*

*Okay, Mikey. Well, if it is any comfort, the changes I've made after seeing Father's Simon artifact in action should hopefully keep us both from being lobotomized.*

*Let's just do it before I talk myself out of it.*

"Here's to meddling with powers we can't possibly understand," I said, and settled cross-legged on the floor at the center of the circle. No need for big speeches or preparing my soul or anything. Like Alynon, I just wanted to get this done with, one way or another. "Pete, Verna, whenever you're ready."

"I'm ready," Pete said, holding the ritual in his hands. I'd typed it up in Paperclip and printed it out for him, just to be safe.

"Okeedokee," Verna said. "Here we go."

She flipped a switch. The lights in the basement dimmed and flickered, and then a portal opened up in Verna's rune-covered ring.

"Here's to not getting lobotomized," I muttered. Otherwise, Silene would have to choose a champion to take my place in the dance contest. And my family would have to get on without me once again. And Dawn—

I placed my hand on the crystal ball at the back of the Kin Finder 2000 before I could talk myself out of it, and looked at the portal through the KF2K's focus ring. I poured magic into it.

*Go into the light,* I thought at Alynon, and willed him to be gone from my body, to travel through the portal.

*I'm trying,* he said.

Pete cleared his throat. "Alynon Infedriel, Knight of the Silver Court, I summon you, and banish you to the Other Realm. By my will I compel you." He continued in Latin, using an incantation I'd tweaked for this purpose. I wasn't sure it would do any good, but hopefully it would make Pete believe it would work, and that could make all the difference.

I sensed something being drawn from inside me, like a rubbery membrane had been wrapped around my brain and was now being pulled toward the portal. But it felt like my entire brain was being pulled with it.

I pressed my free hand against my temple, tried to squeeze the pain away with counterpressure. "Something's . . . happening!" I said. "Keep going!"

Alynon screamed in my head, *Something's wrong! I feel like I'm being torn apart! I—Ahhh!*

The pain became unbearable, like someone was beating my head with a screaming baby made of blinding sunlight and steel. I felt myself fading.

My hand fell from the crystal ball. I closed my eyes, and threw up my barriers of will and spirit.

The world lurched, and the arcane energies surrounding me jumped.

There came a terrible, terrified scream. I opened my eyes to find Brianne, Mort's spirit lover, being drawn toward the portal backward, her hands scrabbling at the air as if trying to find some purchase in our world to keep her from sliding back into that pool of energy.

"Pete! Verna!" I shouted.

But it was too late. Brianne disappeared into the portal just as Verna slammed it off, and Pete stopped his incantation.

In the moment of sudden, complete quiet that followed, my mind raced to understand what had just happened.

*Alynon?* I asked.

*Still here,* he replied quietly, his tone a mixture of relief and disappointment.

When the summoning and banishment had lost its hold on Alynon, it must have jumped to the next nearest spirit not attached to a body. Which meant Mort had summoned Brianne, despite everything. And she had been pulled into the portal.

"Verna, is she—was she transported to the Other Realm?" I asked.

Verna, her wide eyes appearing owl-like behind her glasses, shook her head. "I don't know. They were expecting Alynon, but—" She looked at the portal.

Somewhere in the Other Realm, an insane succubus had just popped up in a Fey body. Or her spirit had been destroyed, disintegrating on the barrier between worlds. Only the Fey knew which.

A distant cry could be heard, a heart-wrenching howling. It took me a second to recognize it as human.

"Mort. Oh gods." I struggled to my feet, and almost fell back down. Wooziness from the botched exorcism and backlash of energies spun through my head.

Pete ran up the basement stairs. I led Verna after him as quickly as I could manage.

When I reached Mort's bedroom, Pete and Vee stood on either side of Mort's bed, trying to hold him down. Mort writhed, his limbs tangled in black sheets, his face pale and sweaty and his eyes wild as he bucked against Pete and Vee's hold. "Let me go! Let me go! I have to find her! Something's wrong!"

"Finn?" Pete called as I entered the room.

"Mort!" I said. "Mort, listen! You need to calm down."

"Where's Brianne?" he demanded.

Mattie rushed into the room and pushed a perfume spritzer into my hands. "Here!"

Calming spray. We used it to help calm grieving customers we thought might go wild in their pain. I went over and spritzed some onto Mort's pillow beside his head. Okay, I spritzed a lot onto his pillow.

"Mort, calm down!" I shouted. "You're going to hurt yourself."

Mort's struggles slowed, until he lay panting on the bed.

"Better," I said.

"Where's Brianne?" he asked. "I can't sense her."

I exchanged looks with Pete, and said, "We—I sent her away so you could get some rest."

Mort tried to look at me, but appeared unable to focus. "Sent her where?"

"Away," I said. "We'll talk about it more when you're better." From the looks of him, Mort was lucky that the accident happened. Luckier than Brianne.

His eyes drooped as he struggled against passing out. "If I find out you hurt her," he said, his words slurred, "I'll never forgive you."

I sighed, and muttered, "Get in line."

I glanced at the clock on Mort's bedside. I had maybe a few hours at most before I had to head out to the Elwha steading.

I turned, and saw the anguished look on Mattie's face. "Oh, Mat-cat, everything's going to be okay," I said, and pulled her into a hug. "We'll take care of your dad."

"I know," she said. "I know."

Verna stood in the doorway. "You have quite a . . . complicated family," she said. "A very chaotic system."

"Yeah," I said, and didn't offer any further clarification. "Come on, let's let Mort get some rest."

We all shuffled out into the hallway, and closed the door just as Mort began to snore.

Mattie wiped at her face. "I'll watch after Dad."

"You don't have to do it alone," I said.

Vee put an arm around Mattie. "Of course not." She looked at me.

Dawn put her hand on my shoulder. "But you have things to do, don't you? Like get your shoes back?"

"What?"

"Your shoes, that you left hanging outside," she replied. "They're gone."

"Oh. Right." Crap. "Yeah, I suppose I do."

Dawn hooked her arm through mine. "Don't worry, love, I've got your back."

"We've all got each other's backs," Vee said, pulling Mattie into a hug. "Come on, sweetie, let's go get you some tea."

I watched as Pete and Vee led Mattie down the hall to the stairs, pulling Verna along.

"So," Dawn said. "Let's go chat with your old crush, shall we?"

## Lips Like Sugar

We stepped out of the side door into late-morning light that appeared defiantly cheery and vibrant for a day already filled with so much darkness, though the temperature remained stubbornly cool. I tilted my head back, let the sun's promise of warmth soak into my face. Might as well enjoy it. I led the way around to the back of the house, and along the path into the heart of Mother's overgrown garden.

The center of the garden stood empty, just the crushed and chopped remains of entangled branches, thorns, and vines, and the scarred, twisted bush at its heart.

"Crap," I said. "Either we scared her off, or we missed her."

"Aw, you missed me?" The green tangled wall at the back of the clearing wavered like a Romulan cloaking shield being lowered, and Heather appeared, finishing off a vial of liquid.

She looked even worse than last time if that was possible, thinner, paler, the blue-gray shadows under her eyes practically bruises. Combined with the black hair and long black jacket, she might have been mistaken for a vampire groupie, except for the brightly colored SuperSoaker in her other hand.

"Heather," I said. "Thanks for coming."

Heather looked past me as she tucked the empty vial into a jacket pocket. "Dawn," she said. "I like the new hair color."

"Heather," Dawn said, and waved at the garden. "Have you just been lurking around here waiting for Finn's bat signal?"

"No. I have a . . . place, not too far away. When the crow called me, I snuck here as quickly as possible."

"Huh. Shouldn't you be in, like, Mexico or someplace?" Dawn asked, her tone skeptical. "Hiding out, putting the whammy on some resort bachelor or something, living the glamorous life of a fugitive and all?"

"You know, I tried," Heather said. "But turns out being alone, without family or friends, being hunted by half the people I knew, and hated by the rest . . . it just wasn't as exciting as the brochures promised." Her voice broke a little on the last word.

Ah frak. "Dawn, Heather, I—"

"But you've got all that magic," Dawn said. "Like love potions! You know, I just learned they're a real thing. So why didn't you ever use one on Finn?"

"Look—" I said.

"Because," Heather replied. "I didn't need it. And I would never use a love potion on someone I actually cared about."

"Ah. Okay," Dawn said as she slipped the sword in and out of its sheath a couple of times. "So you'd only seduce someone and try to kill them, but love potions, that's where you draw the line. Good to know your sense of right and wrong isn't completely bat-shit fucked up or anything."

Heather looked at me, and said in an exhausted voice, "Is this why you signaled for me, so your girlfriend can remind me what a horrible person I am?"

"No," I said, looking at Dawn to emphasize the point. "I need your help, to save the brightbloods."

"Damn it, Finn," Heather said, anger scrunching her face. "I already told you, I'm not going to make a damn cure for the mana drug. Even if it was possible, it would just put a bigger target on my back."

"I know," I said. "I want you to actually make the drug for them."

"Wait. What? Why in all the hells would I do that?"

"To at least keep them from dying while they try to find their own cure."

Heather gave a bitter laugh, and shook her head. "Jesus. You're just like your grandfather."

An unexpected rage flared up in me, and I took a step toward her, my hand going to the holstered Taser. "Take that back!"

Heather's eyes widened, and she said, "I'm sorry. Shit." She sighed. "I didn't mean that, really. It's just—no matter how much I try, I can't seem to escape my parents' life."

I relaxed. "You won't be doing this to control the brightbloods, or for profit," I said. "You'll be doing this to help. I'll escort you to their steading—"

"Their steading?" she asked. "Crap." Her mouth scrunched to the side for a second as she considered me. "Okay. I'll do it, but I want—"

"No," Dawn said. "No favors, no deals. Finn's not going on any more quests for anyone but himself."

Heather shrugged. "I don't see much reason to risk *my* life then, not for this."

"You get to help me out," I said. "And earn some good karma while you're at it."

"Good karma for making drugs?" Heather gave another bitter laugh.

"It's for good reasons," I replied.

"I need to earn points with the ARC, not some feybloods."

"Okay, fine. This isn't about you," I said. "Or me." I gave Heather the short version of recent events, and said, "I need your help to stop a clan war. And deal with the damage my grandfather, and you, have caused. For Pete and Vee's sake, and my own conscience."

"Shit," Heather said, and paced for a few seconds. "Look. I'm not proud of what I did. You know that. But, what you're asking me to do—" She shook her head.

I clenched my jaw in frustration.

*Remind her that a war between Demesnes would disrupt the ARC's flow of magic and profits. That won't look good for the current leadership,* Alynon said. *Helping to save their asses, or at least their assets, might earn her a little leniency.*

*I want to give her a chance to do this for the right reasons first,* I replied.

\*Right for you, or for her?\* Alynon said.

As if reading my thoughts, Dawn said, "Oh, well, we wouldn't want you to help just because it's the right thing to do."

Heather sighed. "Not all of us had the privilege of your carefree life, Dawn. Some of us had shitty parents, and then had to be parents ourselves, to—"

"You did a bang-up job of that," Dawn replied.

Heather looked as though Dawn had slapped her, and tears welled in her eyes.

"Crap," Dawn said. "How do you always bring out the bitch in me?"

"I'm sorry," I said, and looked at Dawn. "I know this is awkward, with all that's—"

"Oh, get over yourself," Dawn said. "This isn't about you."

"Yeah," Heather said, and gave a sad smile. "Dawn and I have disliked each other a long time without your help."

"That's the truth," Dawn agreed, but didn't sound happy about it, either. She poked at the ground with the sheathed sword. "I think—I guess I just resented how everything came so easy to *you*."

"Ha! Easy?" Heather said.

"Look, guys—" I said, trying to get back on track.

"Yes, easy," Dawn replied. "You'd show up at a bar and dance, and every guy there was yours. You got a great job—"

"Great? Teaching high school?" Heather said in a mocking tone. Then she seemed to deflate a bit. "Yeah, I guess it was pretty great. And you know, I may have gone home with plenty of guys, but it was always a mistake. At least you were free—"

"Oh yeah, I was so free, working crap jobs to support Phoenix just so he could dump me and run away."

"You were pursuing your dreams. That's more than I had the courage to do in the end," Heather said. "And you know, you didn't have to always go home alone. I heard guys admiring your . . . assets."

"Yeah, dude-bros who wanted to check off 'bang a black chick' on their fucket list." Dawn shook her head. "You know what, screw it, whatever. We're here now. We're both adults. Well, I am. You're running around in a Halloween wig and carrying a squirt gun."

A smile played across Heather's lips. "Cute." She lowered her water rifle. "I guess I can move beyond the past if you can."

"Sure," Dawn said, and smiled. "And that's the magic of nothing-to-lose conversations. Two women can talk through their personal crap." She raised the sword, and slapped the sheath across her palms. "But just to be clear, I still don't trust the woman who tried to kill my boyfriend."

The smile dropped from Heather's face, replaced once again by exhaustion and determination. And hurt.

Dawn continued, "This isn't about you and me, though. It's about protecting Finn's family from getting sucked into some crazy war. I know you care about them. I know you care about Mattie. So prove it. Help them."

Heather looked up at the house for a second. "I—I do still care about them." She closed her eyes. "If I do this, Finn, you have to swear to me on your magic that nobody will tell these feybloods I created the mana drug."

"I swear," I said. "We go in, make a bunch of the drug for them, and get out. That's the plan."

Heather was silent a minute, then said, "Where's this steading?"

"It's the Elwha Silver steading, upriver from the dams."

"Yay, hiking. I'll go get my equipment, and what ingredients I can. If—"

"Oh! wait," I said. "I, uh, also need two truth potions. Can you get those?" They were required for the duel, and I'd nearly forgotten them.

"I'll try," Heather said. "Meet at the trailhead in, say, two hours?"

"Sure, that should work."

Heather turned, and disappeared along the garden path.

"Damn," Dawn said after a few seconds. "I mean, she brought it on herself, but still. Damn."

"Yeah," I said. "That about sums it up." I shivered in the shade of the garden. "Can we go inside? Or at least back into the sun?"

"Big baby," Dawn said. "So what were the truth potions for?"

"Oh, uh, Silene asked for them," I lied. "I think maybe to make sure she doesn't have any more spies in her group."

"Makes sense." Dawn hooked my arm with hers. "Walk me home?"

"Of course, milady," I said.

"So you take Heather to these brightbloods, and then you're done, for real?" Dawn asked as we slipped through the break in the hedge between our properties, and walked toward her back door.

"One way or another, I will be done tonight," I replied.

*Nice dodge,* Alynon said snidely.

*Suck it.*

"And you promise you're not going to do something crazy and get yourself killed?"

"Well, I can't promise I won't do something crazy. But believe me, I'm not looking to get killed." Which was true. Not that it made me feel any better to lie to her.

We entered Dawn's house, and she led me into the kitchen to pour herself a glass of water. I leaned against the counter, and just soaked in the moment—the sunlight glowing through the kitchen window, lighting her profile, glinting off the glass of water. A beautiful sight.

"I love you," I said.

Dawn choked on her water, spraying it, and leaned over the sink to cough as I patted her back.

"I'm sorry," I said.

"What did you say?" she asked at last.

"I said I'm sorry."

"No, you idiot. Before that."

"Oh. I said . . . I love you. I really do. And, well, I'm sorry I haven't said it earlier. I was being an idiot."

"Huh," she said, and nodded. "Okay then."

She attacked me. In a good way.

*Don't ruin this,* I thought to Alynon as I consumed Dawn's kiss, was consumed by it.

And for once, Alynon, and the fates, listened.

I followed Dawn's lead, her kisses releasing a tidal wave of need in me. And I didn't even think about Alynon again until Dawn and I lay sweaty and naked and breathing heavy in her bed, at the end of a trail of clothes and several stops along the way. The thought that we might have damaged some of the family pictures we knocked from the walls getting here, and regret over the number of times I accidentally pinned her hair to the bed with my arm, also flickered across my drowsy mind. But such thoughts were pale, fleeting shadows on the glowing feeling that still pulsed through me like fading aftershocks.

I kissed Dawn's shoulder, and curled up against her.

"Mmm," Dawn purred, wriggling back against me. "You feel nice. Warm."

I kissed her neck, nuzzled up under the soft curls, breathed the coconut and slight chemical scent of her hair, tasted the salt of our earlier exertions. Where our kisses before had been wild, devouring, giddy, I now felt something more tender driving me: a desire to write poems with my lips across the smooth expanse of her skin; a need to speak the depth and truth of my love through my fingertips as they brushed gently down the path of her spine, over the curve of her goddamn beautiful ass, over her hip and down, under the fold of her belly. She moaned, and shifted onto her back, granting me access to her full beauty.

I painted a field of butterflies across her with my lightly brushing kisses. I gave a lingering kiss to the teeth marks on her stomach, where I had earlier bit into the ample flesh and had felt the animal urge to devour her, to growl and fuck and howl. I felt the urge rising in me again at the memory, but I moved on, exploring, following the lead of her quickened breathing, her soft moans, her writhing.

When I finally entered her this time, it was more than the joyous and mutual victory of the first time, it was returning home. I held myself over her, looked down into her eyes, into the dark heart of creation and life, the birthplace of stars and souls, and suddenly laughed a giddy, uncontrollable laugh as tears filled my eyes. She laughed with me, and pulled me down into her, into the world of her, our rhythm joined, our bodies molding to each other, and together we found completion.

We floated together for a time measured by the beating of hearts, warm breath on skin, sweat cooling degree by degree. And the fact that I had to do the impossible with less than a day to do it seemed in that moment the perfect reason to just go to sleep, holding Dawn close.

*WAKE UP!* Alynon shouted in my head.

I lurched awake. Dawn lay next to me snoring louder than anyone I'd heard except Petey.

*What the hell?* I asked.

*Time to make the donuts,* Alynon replied. *What do you think?*

I blinked crusty eyes to look at Dawn's bedside clock. The red digital numbers said 2:12 P.M.

*I am sorry,* Alynon added, and actually sounded genuine. *I wish I could just let you sleep. But you've got to prepare if you're going to win this contest and not get us killed.*

"Okay, okay." I sat up. Dawn looked so peaceful in the afternoon light. I gently shook her shoulder.

"Hey, beautiful. I'm really sorry to ruin the moment, but you've got a gig, remember?"

Dawn sat up, and rubbed at her eyes. "And you have to escort Ms. Breaking Bad to the brightbloods."

"Yeah."

Dawn pulled me in for a long kiss, then let me go. "Get going. Just don't lose your head and do something stupid to miss my show."

I felt a chill. "Hey, knock on some wood," I said.

Dawn rapped on my head, then gave me another kiss.

Pulling away from that kiss and the warmth of her bed, leaving behind the pleasure of her touch and the perfect contentment of her embrace to march off to my possible death in a cold damp forest was the most difficult move I'd made in my life.

# 32

## Sowing the Seeds of Love

Heather stepped out of the forest near the Elwha Dam trail, a large black duffel bag hanging from each hand like balancing weights.

"You're late. Where's Dawn?" she asked as I grabbed my boom box and backpack out of the hearse.

"Getting ready for a show tonight," I replied. "And that's as much as we're going to talk about Dawn."

Her eyebrows raised beneath the flat bangs of her wig. "What, you guys don't talk about *me*?"

"Not so much. And you don't have Girlfriend Confidentiality Privilege," I said. "Now come on, the sooner we get there, the sooner you'll be done." And the better chance the Silver brightbloods would be up to strength for the showdown.

"Aw, you're no fun."

"Uh huh." I marched down the trail of packed dirt, and Heather hurried to catch up. We followed the river for several minutes, then turned onto the hidden trail to Silene's clearing.

"Halt!" Don Faun stepped out of the trees wearing his camo vest, Utilikilt, and Budweiser cap, with his crossbow loaded and raised. "Gramaraye. Who's she?" He nodded his horned head at Heather.

"She's a friend," I said. "She's here to help you against the Shadows."

"Yeah? She got one of them riot shotguns she's willing to use?"

"You've been hanging around hunters too long, I think," I said.

Don spat. "Hunters. I've been watching drunk mundy idiots shooting up cans on hillsides—and sometimes themselves—with enough friggin' boomsticks to stop an army of shadowbrights. Meanwhile them DFM jerks won't let me use nothing but this—" He hefted the crossbow. "And that's only 'cause we managed to claim bows as part of our religious right or whatnot in the Pax."

"Uh," I said, "I'm sorry?"

Don took off his hat and scratched at his head. "Nah, not your fault. I just get a bit riled up at times like these, when an assault rifle or two'd come in pretty dang handy." He replaced the hat and turned away. "Come on, I'll lead ya'll in. The main path's trapped. And everyone you're wanting to see is up at the cave, anyway."

He led us uphill into the tree line, hopping easily on his goat legs up a path that Heather and I climbed with some difficulty. As the way leveled out, Don said, "I have to admit, Gramaraye, I'm a little disappointed you went and arranged to settle things with one little duel. Me and some of my boys, we were looking forward to giving them shadowbrights some payback."

I sighed. "Well, you might still get your chance."

"From your mouth to Ares' ears."

We passed a wooden signpost, long overgrown with ivy and worn by time and weather, but I made out the word LODGE and a sign pointing left.

"What's that?" I asked.

"Oh, that's from when the lodge was built. You didn't think we Silvers all slept in the woods and caves, did you?"

"I did wonder," I replied.

"Naw. Cave's just for safety. We got us a real nice place a bit further in. Built to be a hot springs lodge way back when, but it got claimed for the Silver as part of some pact or other. The ARC chased off all the mundies, erased the records of the place, and we put up our diversions so as nobody finds it. Place is old, though. Could sure use someone who understands plumbing."

"My brother's pretty handy with a wrench," I said.

Don frowned. "That'd be the wolf fella?"

"Yeah," I said.

Don was silent a minute as we continued marching, then said,

"Look, we appreciate you helping and all, and I can't lie, bright-bloods ain't easy on human plumbing so a handy guy'd be, well, pretty handy. But I just don't know as it would work so well, your brother living there, with being a wolf-bright and all that's happened."

I sighed. "Well, thanks for being honest."

*Perhaps his view is not the more common,* Alynon suggested.

*Yeah. Maybe.*

We reached a small bluff overlooking the river.

"There's the cave," Don said, and waved to a crooked, narrow gash wreathed in ferns in the side of the hill. "Good luck."

Don Faun tipped his hat at us, then disappeared back into the forest.

Heather eyed the cave entrance. "I'm pretty sure I've seen this in a horror movie. You positive we're not just walking into an all-you-arcana-eat buffet?"

"Fairly sure," I said, and led her to the cave entrance.

"Wait!" Heather said, looking at the pink and purple bell-like flowers growing along either side of the cave entrance. "Are those . . . brightlilies?"

"Looks like," I said. "Sal gave one to Silene. She must have grown these from the seeds."

"I—do you know the kinds of potions I could make with that?"

A hummingbird zipped in front of us, flitting up, down, over, its head tilting to examine us. It shimmered, and a fairy hovered between us and the cave entrance in a dress of glowing red and green feathers.

"You're Gramaraye?" she asked, her voice chirpy and sweet.

"As long as that's a good thing," I replied.

"Sunny! I'm Flidais. Everyone's inside. Well, not me. Or the others protecting the tree. But everyone else. I'll take you to them. I like your hair." She zipped to Heather, and flicked one of the black strands, then flitted back into the cave entrance. "Come on!"

We followed her into the narrow entrance, Heather gazing

thoughtfully at the brightlilies until they were out of sight. The cave opened up almost immediately on the other side, and a grizzly bear stood on his hind legs, one enormous paw raised and ready to rip our heads off. "Who's this?" he rumbled.

"It's Gramaraye," Flidais said, zipping behind me. "The arcana who's helping. I don't know who she is." The fairy flitted around in front of Heather. "Who are you?"

"Heather," Heather replied, her tone nervous. With her hands occupied carrying the duffels, she would have a hard time reaching a potion before the bear's claws shredded her. "I'm here to help, too. I'm with Finn."

Flidais clapped her tiny hands. "Yay! More help! This is Garl. He's nice. Except when he's hungry. Come on!"

Flidais flitted along deeper into the cave, and disappeared where the passage twisted down and around a pillar of rock.

"Wait," Garl garumphed. He plopped down on his rear, his back legs sliding straight out. He tugged a wool blanket over his legs, his paws settling on his lap with his Freddy Krueger–like nails crisscrossing each other, and Garl transformed into a man. For some reason I expected a chubby, hairy German-looking dude, but Garl was a leanly muscled and largely hairless Native American. He sniffed at the air. "Got any candy?" he asked.

"Oh, uh, no, sorry," I said.

Heather blinked as if Garl had hit her with a Waerbear Stare, and then said, "Oh, uh, I do. Here." She dropped a duffel, and pulled a Twix out of her jacket pocket. She handed it to him. "So, I've always wondered, do waerbears hibernate in winter?"

Garl laughed, the kind of genuine belly laugh that made you instantly like him. "No more than the rest of the year. I'm a big fan of naps."

"Right," I said. "Well, it was nice to meet you, Garl, but we really should get going." I motioned for Heather to follow after the fairy.

"Wait," Garl said again. "You guys watch *Downton Abbey*?"

"Uh, what?" I replied.

*"Downton Abbey,"* he said, carefully enunciating the words. "You watch?"

I looked to Heather.

"It's a TV show," she said to me; then to Garl, "No, sorry, we don't."

He grunted. "An old couple up at the RV park were watching it on their big TV, but they left. I'm dying to know what happens next."

"Uh," I replied.

Flidais flew back into sight. "Hey! Over here! Come on!"

"Sorry, Garl," I said. "We have to go."

We followed quickly after the fairy before Garl could ask anything more.

The passage went sharply downslope a dozen feet, the walls bumpy brown stone, then opened up again into a wide cavern. The smell of earth was quickly overwhelmed by the odors of sweat, animal fur, and sickness.

At least a dozen brightbloods lay on inflatable mattresses and sleeping bags around the cavern, some whose brightblood nature was obvious, such as the fauns, and many who appeared simply human. All looked in terrible shape. Those that didn't have clear injuries from battle moaned and twitched and sweated, the victims of Grayson's Curse.

Several brightbloods moved among those laying on the floor, men and women with hints of animal or elemental natures, offering water or clay bowls full of berries or what looked like raw meat, but most of the ill and injured seemed too far gone in pain or exhaustion to accept.

If Jim Henson had directed M*A*S*H, it might have looked something like that cavern.

In a far corner of the cave, Dunngo held a small man, pressing him down by his shoulders as he convulsed and kicked. No taller than three feet, the man's red hair and pointy ears marked him as a leprechaun, but he seemed a feral beast as spittle flew from his mouth and he clawed at Dunngo's arms. A gaunt man with antlers looked on, his body language saying he wanted to help, but had no idea how.

The leprechaun screamed a terrible, heart-wrenching wail. And then he collapsed, and lay still.

"Oooh," Flidais said, her tone deeply sad. "I don't like this. Excuse me." She flew back out of the cavern.

"Come on," I whispered to Heather, and we wove our way to Dunngo and Antler Head.

Heather looked from the dead leprechaun to another nearby brightblood, the young will-o'-the-wisp that the centaur had brought to Silene for help that first day I met them. She looked even worse than before, her delicate features now emaciated, her hair lank and lacking its normal shimmer, her lips cracked and brushed with flecks of blood.

"I—I can help," Heather said.

Dunngo rose up on a pile of dirt, his fists clenched and shaking. "Help? Finghin dead! Seven friends dead! Dunngo's son—" His whole body began to shake as if in an earthquake. I placed myself between him and Heather as he shouted, "Arcana no help! Arcana kill!"

"Dunngo!" I shouted back. "Stop! She *is* here to help. If you hurt her, you will be killing all the rest of your clan who are sick!"

Antler Head also stepped between Dunngo and us. "Dunngo," he rumbled in a James Earl Jones bass. "Go outside. Find your center."

Dunngo pounded his fist into the ground. "Dunngo want vengeance!"

Antler Head sighed. "You will have your fight soon enough, I fear. Save your anger for the Shadows. We will need it, my friend."

Dunngo rumbled in his chest like a rock tumbler, then grunted and left the cave, leaving a trail of loose dirt and an awkward silence behind him.

"Uh, thank you," I said finally.

Antler Head turned to me. "I did not do it for you." He looked after Dunngo again. "I fear he will seek out conflict until it brings him release from the pain of his son's death. Though even his own death may not be enough to bring him peace."

"I'm . . . sorry," I said, not sure what else to say.

"You have brought the alchemist?" Antler Head asked, looking at Heather.

"Uh, yes," I replied. "This is Heather. She has figured out how to make the drug and is going to give you guys enough to keep anyone else from dying. Help her get set up?"

Antler Head nodded.

I stayed long enough to make sure Heather would be safe with Antler Head, and had what she needed.

"I have to get going," I said, and turned to Heather. "Will you be okay?"

"Yes." She didn't face me, but looked again to the will-o'-the-wisp.

"Okay then." I turned to leave, but Heather said, "Finn."

"Yeah?" I stopped.

"I just wanted to say thank you."

"Oh. Well, you're welcome?" I replied. "Thank *you* for—"

"No, really, thank you. You could have reported me to the ARC after I showed up in your driveway. You could have probably hunted me down yourself, you and your family, even before that. And after the way I betrayed you all I wouldn't have blamed you. But you gave me a chance. More than one. And—just thank you for being a good friend, better than I deserved."

"I didn't have the heart to send you into exile," I said. "I'm not sure that makes me good."

"Yeah, you're not good, you're *grrreat*!" Heather replied, the way she would when we were teenagers. She smiled at me, her eyes glistening with tears.

"More like I'm coo-coo for cocoa puffs," I replied, and felt a sudden surge of my old affection for her. I pulled her into a tight hug. "Stay safe," I said, and let her go. "I'll be back."

"Okay, Arnie."

I gave her a smile that I almost felt, and headed for the exit.

Flidais waited outside, and happily guided me downhill through the various physical and magical traps that now surrounded Silene's clearing.

Silene sat, her back against the yarn-wrapped trunk of her cedar tree, shaded from the late afternoon sun and watching the river flow by. Sal sat cross-legged downriver a little ways, knitting with yarn from his satchel. Challa stood thigh-deep in the river near Sal, snagging passing fish and tossing them to the shore.

I knelt beside Silene. "I want you to know, whether I win or lose this duel, your clan will be safe."

"And leaves are green, today," Silene said. She gave me a doubtful look. "You must be a good dancer to have made such a challenge?"

"I'm good enough," I said defensively.

"As you say," Silene said. "I shall have my clan ready should the Shadows betray the peace of the duel." She closed her eyes as if nodding off while she spoke. She looked thin, exhausted.

"How are you doing?" I asked.

"I healed all those I could, until I collapsed. But I am recovering slowly." She placed a hand on her tree. "And with the alchemist's help, hopefully more of our clan will be able to stand in time to fight should the Shadows attack."

"I appreciate you giving her a chance," I said. "I know alchemists are not your favorite people."

Silene shrugged, watching Challa. Whenever Challa tossed a fish to shore, Silene's eyes followed its arc, then flicked over to Sal before quickly looking back to Challa. "Your friend is here to help. And Flidais said she sensed your friend is also . . . damaged."

"You do seem to attract those in need of healing," I said. "Challa. Sal."

"Sal?" she asked, looking up to me.

"Yeah. Not everyone affected by the mana drug are the ones addicted to it," I said. "His sister was used by the Arcanites, and died because of it. I get the impression he spent pretty much his entire life just trying to keep his sister out of trouble, taking care of her, and in the end he couldn't save her. He's still hurting from that."

Silene watched Sal knitting for a minute. "He should be seeking the comfort of his kin and kind."

"What he's seeking is a partner, someone who will judge him by his heart, not his physical appearance. Someone he can trust to return his love, and not just take it."

Silene looked back out at the river. "Perhaps he and Challa will be good for each other, then."

I looked at Challa. "I'm sure they could help each other," I said. "But I don't think they'd love each other, not as mates. Seems to me that Challa is still trying to figure out who she is. She doesn't want or need a partner right now confusing that. And I don't think Sal's ever had an easy time with the other Seeahtik, because of his feet."

"In time then," Silene said.

*Merlin's balls!* I thought to Alynon. *Are all brightbloods this stubborn?*

*Dryads live long lives,* Alynon replied. *For Aalbrights, sometimes long life means wisdom, and sometimes that just means you get really good at putting things off, since you'll always have more time. Perhaps 'tis true for dryads as well.*

*I don't think this is procrastination. I think it is fear.*

*Sometimes they are the same.*

I sighed. "It seems a shame if Sal had to just hold onto all that love he's got, waiting for a future that may never happen." I looked at my Pac-Man watch. "Shoot, I need to go practice before it is too late." I straightened.

"I wish you luck. Whatever aid we can give, just ask Flidais."

"Thanks. And good luck to you, too." I looked from her to Sal.

I walked over to the giant bare-skinned sasquatch, hunched over his pile of cedar threads. "Hey big guy," I said, stealing a glance back at Silene. She quickly looked away, but not quickly enough. "So I take it you haven't told Silene you like her yet?"

He lowered his head over his knitting, but I could see his blush nonetheless. "Herself is not looking for love."

"Everyone wants love," I told him.

He shrugged. "Herself keeps pushing Challa at I."

"Yeah, well, that's because she's being as dumb as you," I replied.

Sal looked up at me and growled. I shrugged. "Hey, you asked me to find you your true love. Well, I'm pretty sure Silene is the one. But you're not going to find out unless you take a chance and tell her you like her."

"I protect herself's heart tree, give Iself's own fur. I give herself brightlily. Herself still push Challa at I."

"What can I say, Sal. Never underestimate a person's ability to believe they're not good enough, or attractive enough, or interesting enough, to be loved."

Sal knitted in silence a minute, then said, "Is youself ready for the duel of dancing?"

"I think so. I just need to go loosen up."

"Youself a great dancer?" Sal asked, giving me the skeptical up and down.

Come on! Did I really look that uncoordinated or uncool? "I've got some moves," I said, perhaps a bit angrily.

"Is maybe goodsmart that youself go practice?" he suggested.

I sighed. "Yep. Okay. Fine. Take care, Sal. And good luck."

I whistled for the fairy, and had her lead me to a small glade in the forest that was nice and secluded.

Flidais watched as I practiced my dancing. She, at least, seemed to appreciate my moves. We chatted as I consumed a Subway Veggie, several Munch bars, and a couple bottles of Mountain Dew for fuel, and took frequent stretch breaks. It turned out Flidais was a distant cousin of the fairy whose wake my family was hosting. I promised her I would take special care with her cousin's body, and winced as I remembered removing the wings for donation.

Don Faun entered the glade several hours later. "The clans are gathered, the circle is set. I hope you are ready."

I grabbed my boom box. "Let's boogey!"

## 33

## Rhythm Is Gonna Get You

Elwha Dam RV Park was a magicals-friendly campsite near the Elwha path trailhead, where a large Greenman totem signaled the site as neutral territory. Near an ancient metal playground set was a small field where the Shadows and Silver brightbloods had gathered, two half circles facing each other. It was not an even match. The Shadows still had greater numbers, and the Silver side had many brightbloods obviously still recovering from illness or injury. But the Silvers had their home territory at their back.

Barry waited in the center of the circle, on a field of trampled grass, wearing his designer-distressed jeans and a faded brown flannel shirt that looked custom fit. He spotted me, and I couldn't wait to wipe that cocky grin off his face, with his perpetual five-day growth, and artfully messy blond hair that probably took an hour and a crapload of mousse to shape into that "I don't care how I look, I just look good" look, and—

I entered the circle with my boom box. Willem the redcap, Georgio Waerjerk, Minerva, they were all there leading the Shadows side. As was Kaminari, wearing a dress as shimmery black as her pigtails. She glared with frightening intensity at me as she gripped her gossamer jump rope in two white-knuckled fists.

Silene and Sal stood front and center for the Silver. Silene wore what looked like a green bodysuit covered in thorns. Sal had found a red plaid jacket just large enough to wear, at least once the sleeves had been ripped off. Between that, his fur kilt-like fringe, and combat boots, he looked like some mad Scottish giant.

And beside them stood Pete and Vee.

"What—you guys shouldn't be here!" I said, setting my boom box down beside them. Neither stood as tall as Sal, but still they were a head taller than most gathered there. Both wore jeans and leather jackets, and held hands. I would have found them adorable if we weren't surrounded by brightbloods on the verge of war.

"You can't make me go," Pete said, putting on his stubborn scowl.

Vee let go of his hand and slipped her arm around his waist. "What Petey means is, you shouldn't face this alone. And this affects both of us." She blinked and looked at the space beside her. "Yes, sorry, all of us." She looked back at me. "We're here, and we're staying. Deal with it."

I sighed, but it was as much from relief as resignation. "It *is* nice to have you here," I said. "Thank you. Wait. You didn't tell Dawn, did you?"

"No," Pete said, though he didn't sound happy about it.

"Okay, good. I don't want her distracted from her big show." I pointed down at the boom box. "Push play when I give the signal?" I asked Pete.

He nodded. "Good luck, Brother." Then he grabbed me in a sudden hug that felt like he was trying to squeeze the juice out of me. He let me go, and I almost fell backward.

"Uh, thanks, Brother."

Silene held out her hand, palm out. "Blessings of the Bright on you, Gramaraye."

"Thanks," I said. I fetched the two Mountain Dew bottles out of the duffel, the contents replaced with truth potion. "Okay. Guess it's time to boogie."

I turned, and crossed the grass to face Barry.

"Clay couldn't make it?" I asked, glancing past him at the gathered Shadows brightblood.

Barry shrugged, and announced loudly, "The local Archon for the Forest of Shadows regrets he could not attend, but it would be inappropriate for him to be directly involved in such an affair." He leaned in a bit, and said quietly, "I think it's just to cover his ass if things go sideways, dig?"

I glanced past him.

"Uh, if Clay's not here to control Kaminari, what's to keep her from throwing one of her temper tantrums?"

"Excellent question. If you somehow win, I guess nothing."

I frowned. "Are you telling me to throw the contest?"

"Naw. I wouldn't do that, brah! I'm just psyching you out. Papa Clay gave me a sleep potion to use on her if she goes all Veruca Salt again."

"Okay then. Did you bring the other potions?"

"Minerva's got 'em."

We each had brought two truth potions in matching sixteen-ounce Mountain Dew bottles. After checking the bottles for marks magical or otherwise, we mixed them up randomly, and handed them out to two of the Shadows brightblood chosen by Barry, and two of the Silver brightblood chosen by Silene.

"Okay," Minerva called out, her eyes glinting as they went wolf-yellow. "The four judges will drink the potions. Then the two champions shall dance for the length of a song. When the song ends, the judges shall pick which champion they felt was the greater dancer. If there is a tie, they will dance for another song, and shall continue to do so until a winner is chosen. The first dancer to win a majority of votes will be the victor. The one who does not shall lose his head. Any protests or questions?"

The gathered brightbloods shifted uneasily, but nobody spoke out.

"Ready to be schooled?" Barry asked.

"Go for it," I said in my best Stallone. I looked at Pete, and gave him the nod.

Pete pushed play.

There hadn't been much to look forward to at Port Townsend High except for the dances, at least in my day. And in one of the better periods of our relationship, Mort had convinced me to join him in his love of break dancing, determined that we would be the next Boogaloo Shrimp and Shabba-Doo. But more importantly, I had my mother's love of dance in my blood.

Salt-N-Pepa's "Push It" began playing, and I let the music flow through me, move me. My head shook to the beat, my arms pumped, I began running in place, like a maniac, a maniac, exploding out of the gate.

I spun away, throwing my arms out to my sides, faintly aware of Barry doing some kind of "sexy dance" undulation as I left him behind.

I stopped, pulled into myself, then exploded outward with my arms, and went into animal clawing motions dancing side to side, as though an animal spirit had burst out from within me and wanted to get down tonight.

Yeah yeah yeah. Mock if you want, but here's the thing. I wasn't dancing in a club trying to look good for the ladies, nor applying to a prestigious dance studio. I was dancing for a bunch of brightbloods, most of whom had animal or nature spirits of some kind within them. They were driven by instinct, by feeling, much more than the average human.

I danced for *them*, like a mill-town boy in a fight for his life.

I dance-skipped around the clearing, clawing at the air to the rhythm of the music. I leap-dove forward, rolling up onto my feet and jumping, pumping my fist into the air. I fight-danced.

I howled.

And the crowd loved it. I could tell the energy was with me, the Silver brightbloods whooping and shouting, the Shadows more watching me than Barry and nodding their heads despite themselves, lost in the emotion and energy of it all.

As I passed Silene, I saw her starting to move to the music as well, but she caught herself, her hand going to her chest.

I spun, round and round, and round again. And found myself facing Barry.

We squared off.

I gave him my best pop and lock. I started with a chest pop, looking down in feigned surprise as my heart seemed to be bursting out of my chest, and then moved into some waving, moving my body through imaginary hoops. I ended with some tutting, moving my hands through a rapid series of puzzle-like formations, before giving Barry the "in your face."

Barry smiled, and went into some kind of pop and lock that seemed to defy physics.

*Dubstep,* Alynon said. *Welcome to two thousand eleven.*

The crowd soon cheered more loudly for Barry than me. And I couldn't blame them. The way he leaned and floated and locked as he moved, it was impressive. Perhaps it was his brightblood strength that allowed him such feats, but even so, what he did with that strength was pretty frakking cool, even I had to admit.

I tried to take it back, to regain the crowd. I spun away from Barry, ran around the perimeter, pumping my fist in the air, spinning, whooping, giving the occasional jump kick, but they had seen that, and now my raw emotion was being outshone by Barry's technical mastery.

And then the song ended.

I stopped, dripping sweat, breathing like a bellows, my back on fire.

Barry winked at me, looking calm as ever. The prick.

Minerva shouted, "Judges, tell us who you thought was the better dancer."

Silene shouted, "Tell us whoever you thought danced best."

Minerva growled. "That is what I said."

"No," Silene replied. "It isn't."

Kaminari hissed. "Watch your words, you little tree whore, or I'll tear out your throat and you'll talk no more!"

"Hey!" I said. "Everyone chill out. Let the judges judge. That's why we're here."

The judges looked to their left-most member. The will-o-the-wisp from the Silver said, "Finn."

Not entirely surprising, but I felt hope flicker to life in my chest.

The next Silver, a water nymph, looked like she was trying to capture a live bug with her tongue as it ran around her mouth, but finally she blurted out, "Barry!" She looked to me, and shrugged. "Sorry. He flowed like water."

Ah, crap, hold the holy. If I couldn't even win both Silver, I had no chance of winning the duel.

The first Shadows judge, a woman with the black-veined markings of a witch, smiled and said, "Barry. So tasty."

I felt my knees go a little wobbly, but managed to hide that and the sudden sick feeling from my expression. I was about to die. *Sorry Aly. Maybe when I get beheaded, you'll just be set free.*

\*Yeah, that seems likely.\*

The final Shadows judge, a man I assumed to be a waer of some kind, spat out, "Finn."

I began to turn as he spoke, to dissuade Pete and the Silvers from trying to do anything foolish, when his decision registered.

"Wait, what?" I said, turning back.

Minerva looked at the last judge. "You're a gods-damned waer-jackal. How could you not vote for Barry?"

He looked miserable, and when Kaminari also turned to look at him he looked outright terrified. He stammered, "Finn moved me. I never liked that robot crap. I didn't ask to be a judge!"

I had a second chance at life.

So did Barry. He'd pulled out some amazing moves at the end there. But I felt like I had a strong connection with the audience, and now that I knew what had persuaded the judges, I could play to that. Barry could, too, sure, but I had an edge—I wasn't hampered by a need to look cool. And ironically, that would let me show Barry how it felt to be the less popular one, no longer the crowd favorite.

"A break," I said. "If that's okay?" I asked Barry.

He shrugged. "Sure. Ten minutes?" Barry tried to sound casual, but was that uncertainty I detected?

"Ten minutes," I agreed.

I felt like I'd need ten days to recover, but ten minutes would do for now. I headed back toward Pete and the boom box, stretching my back to fight the stiffness wanting to settle in for a long visit.

I could do this. I could actually beat that bastard.

I stopped. I looked at Barry a minute, then I looked at Silene.

I could beat Barry. Maybe. But that wasn't what was at stake here. And I wasn't the one who really needed to beat him.

Pete slapped me on the shoulder. "Good moves, Brother!"

I smiled. "Thanks, Pete. Excuse me a minute." I pulled Silene away from the crowd. As I did, I heard Kaminari practically screech, "Barry, you stupid cow, I want to talk with you NOW!"

Silene and I moved beneath the swing set, and I saw Kaminari and Barry disappear behind the camp's office cabin. I didn't envy Barry. I hoped he had that sleep potion ready.

I rested against one of the cold steel support poles.

"I'm tagging you in," I said to Silene. "I'm making you my champion. Well, your own champion, really."

Silene took a step back and shook her head. "No. I cannot. I do not dance anymore."

"I know. But if I do this, it won't show them the strength of the Silver, it will just show them that I can dance. You need to do this, for your clan." And for herself.

"If you will not face him again," she replied, "then I will find another."

"We only have a couple minutes. It has to be you."

"I said I cannot. I—I've lost the grace, the music of laughter and life that once flowed through me." She looked at the tops of the evergreens swaying gently in the evening breeze. "I cannot hear it anymore. And I no longer have the confidence of beauty—" She shook her head again. "I am a creature of knots and hardened sap, I am a rosebush in winter. I am a vessel of love and light no more."

"Then dance what you feel," I said. "Don't try to be the Silene you were, playing on the passions of others. Be the Silene you are. Show them *your* passion."

Silene looked back to the crowd. Barry had returned, juggling pinecones. Kaminari was nowhere to be seen. Hopefully that meant Barry had knocked her out with that potion. I didn't want to think about her out there somewhere in the trees, plotting to attack.

The crowd parted for Barry, and he gave them his easy smile.

"He is everything I once was," Silene said softly, watching him. "Beautiful. Confident."

"Do you think you were better then than you are now?" I asked.

She looked back at me, as if surprised by the question. "I was happy then."

"And your fellow brightbloods were being addicted and used, and had nobody they trusted to lead them to a better future," I said. "Think of Challa. Aren't you happy for her, that she's safe and healing rather than being abused?"

"Of course."

"Then see, you have happiness now. Focus on that, on everything you've gained and done. If anyone can celebrate growth, it should be a tree spirit."

She looked again at the crowd, her hand going to her chest. "I am not sure that will be enough to move them."

"Everyone has their own scars," I said. "Not always physical, but we have them. Brightbloods can certainly understand the power scars hold. And what strength it takes to move past them."

"Hey, Finn," Barry called from the circle. "Time's up, brah! Not giving up, are ya?"

"Well?" I asked Silene. "Are you giving up?"

"No," she said. "No. I will dance. And I will show him how thin and barren is the foundation his charm rests upon."

## Back to Life

Silene stepped into the circle as I moved to stand between Sal and Pete.

Barry gave Silene a smug smile.

"What's this?" Minerva asked, looking past the pair to me with her bright wolf eyes. "Afraid of losing?"

"No," I said. "I had my fun. It's Silene's turn."

Barry shrugged. "Seems a shame to remove such a pretty head from such pretty shoulders, though. 'Course, from what I hear, that's about as far as the pretties go."

"Is that your best thorn, puppy?" Silene responded. "You should have stayed at home and humped your master's leg."

"Whoa, harsh," Barry said with a smile. "I'm so going to enjoy marking your tree as mine. Now, are we going to dance or waste more time?"

"Ready?" I said, and pushed play.

"Flashdance . . . What a Feeling" began playing with its soft synth and vocal intro.

Barry began moving at Silene in a sinuous, suggestive back-and-forth movement.

Silene whirled away from him, her eyes closed. And she began to dance.

It started with subtle, hesitant movements. Then, like the increased swaying of trees that heralds a growing storm, the movements became larger, more sweeping, more powerful. And every movement carried her smoothly away from Barry, dismissing him without Silene ever seeming to be aware of him.

I saw hints of the dancing I remembered from her memory in the Other Realm, the dance of a creature whose existence centered on free love and the celebration of joy, but the motions evolved as she moved, as her new self found expression. The movements hinted somehow that the love that now flowed through her was love for her tree, for her clan, for her cause.

The song's dance beat kicked in, and Silene's movements became stronger, reminding me a bit of the passionate anger dance from *Footloose,* a compelling call to never, never, never hide your heart.

Silene's thorny bodysuit broke apart and drifted away like falling leaves, and she raised her arms to the sky as if in triumph.

She no longer danced. She had become a creature of passion given physical form. She did not seduce with her movements, but rather she seduced us toward her passions. She challenged, and she raised in me a sudden desire to do more, to somehow match the passion of her dancing in some form, any form, in my own life. She celebrated the power of her limbs, the grace of a body created of magic and nature to be impossible to resist. And in her dancing, the scar no longer seemed a blemish on nature's design, it became part of her beauty, a reason to be drawn to her. It became a pink knotted rune of courage. A symbol of strength. A map of possibility. And then it simply ceased to matter.

When the music stopped, I realized I'd barely registered what Barry did for most of the dance, that I'd forgotten to watch him for comparison.

Given the way the rest of the crowd blinked and looked around, I was not the only one.

"Silene," the first judge said without being asked.

"Silene," the second said immediately after.

"Silene," the third said, her tone one of grudging respect.

Silene turned as the fourth judge made it unanimous, tears running down her cheeks, and was quickly surrounded by her cheering brightbloods. Barry, who'd begun to walk toward her with an upheld hand, frowned in frustration. He didn't seem particularly afraid or worried about what his loss meant, though.

"Please," Silene said, raising her hands. She practically glowed with her own light. "I wish to speak."

Her clothing reformed, green flowing up from the ground to wrap around her and create the bodysuit as her brightbloods moved back to give her space. She stood on tiptoes to see over their heads.

"I hereby spare the life of my opponent as a show of mercy and goodwill between the Silver and the Shadows," she said. "We have both lost cousins in these past months to the plots and plans of others who would pit us each against the other, and one more life lost will not help any but our enemies."

She held out her arm, and the thin line of brightbloods between her and Barry parted as she moved forward to shake his hand. "I hope that this marks the end of our battle with each other, and the start of a battle for the safety and rights of all—"

Barry grabbed her hand and yanked her to himself. At the same time, spider legs sprouted out of his back, and he screamed, "Attack, attack!"

Chaos erupted. Several Silver brightbloods and I rushed toward Silene, but Barry—or rather Kaminari, who'd obviously taken Barry's place—jumped away in the direction of the forest, and the river.

The movement of a few Silver brightbloods into the circle caused several on the Shadows side to rush forward in reaction. Which opened the floodgates on both sides as the Silver and Shadows brightbloods poured into the circle, charging at each other.

A wall of vines erupted out of the ground between the two clans. Several Silver brightbloods ran into it and were lifted up and flung back as the wall continued to explode upwards. I looked around for the source of the wall, and realized Silene must have created it as she was carried away. She had acted to save her clan before herself. I doubted Kaminari would give her a chance to do more.

Sal, Challa, and Dunngo ran after Kaminari and Silene. I thought I'd seen Waerjerk, Minerva, and the redcap angling in that direction, too, before the wall went up. I snatched up my backpack and began to follow.

"Retreat!" Don Faun shouted from the tree line behind us. "Back to your defensive positions! We'll cover you!"

Frak. I fumbled at my backpack, struggling with the zippers in my haste, and almost dropped the plastic Taser with my sweat-slicked hand. I snatched up the baton with my other hand.

The tangled wall before me rustled as something attempted to plow through it. At the same time, a scorpion-like form scrabbled up onto the top of the wall, and a bulldog the size of a small bull careened around the far end, almost losing its footing as it turned sharply to lope at the gathered Silver brightblood. I paused, uncertain which direction was safest.

The Silvers ran, hopped, and galloped for the tree line. Arrows and crossbow bolts whispered through the air to *shtik!* into shadow-brights and the vine wall. One bolt punched into the charging bulldog. Battle cries and screams turned the campground into a war zone.

All ways were chaos. I continued running in the direction Kaminari had taken Silene. Pete and Vee fell in on either side of me. Pete hefted the silver sword, and his eyes flashed wolf blue. Vee whipped Zeke's backup baton to full extension, while at the same time a giant squirrel tail sprang up from her lower back, pushing up the back of her shirt and rising behind her head like a samurai's Sashimono banner.

The Shadows brightbloods swarmed through, over and around Silene's wall, and chased after the retreating Silvers. A pair of ghouls angled off from the main pack to intercept us, their Mumm-Ra–looking bodies transforming into hyena as they ran.

"Keep going!" Pete shouted at me, then, like blockers guarding a runner in football, he and Vee broke off to stop the ghouls.

I hesitated, unwilling to just leave them.

Pete swung his sword at the first ghoul-hyena, who slid in the grass and scrambled to avoid the blow.

The other ghoul began to angle toward me. I raised the Taser, but Vee made a chittering sound and shook her giant, fluffy tail in a rapid quivering motion. The ghoul's steps slowed, and a confused expression settled on his hyena face as his attention fixed on her tail. Vee charged at him and swung the glowing baton in an arc that hit the beast's head with a bright flash, knocking the ghoul-hyena to the ground.

The first ghoul recovered from its slide and stalked Pete again with more caution. I swung the Taser around to target it, but Pete was in the way of a clear shot.

"Go!" Vee shouted at me. "We've got this!" She moved to back up Pete.

"Silene!" I heard Sal's voice roar in the distance.

Damn it.

I continued chasing after Kaminari.

I reached the tree line and had to focus on where I was running as I followed the narrow dirt trail. I heard shouts ahead, mixed with distant screams and vicious animal sounds behind me and somewhere off to my left. I kept jerking around at sounds real and imagined in the forest behind and beside me, expecting some Shadows creature to ambush me from behind a cedar tree or the thick cover of ferns and holly.

I was so focused on spotting large monsters that I almost missed the spriggan that stood waiting on the path as I rounded a bend. A short, gnarled-looking creature with mottled brown skin and leaves growing out of it, it was easy to miss in the dappled evening light. The creature hissed at me and began to grow rapidly in size.

I fired the Taser at it. Two darts shot out, one hitting the creature and the other plunking into the dirt, wire trailing behind them to the gun.

The spriggan yelped, then fell to the dirt, convulsing and smoking as electricity coursed through its tiny body.

I ran up and swung the baton in an underhand swing that sent the creature flying back into the undergrowth. "Out of the way, Peck!"

The Taser wires tangled in a holly tree.

"Damn it." I dropped the Taser after a couple of frustrated tugs, and continued running along the path.

I broke out onto the main service way to the Elwha Dam, a gravel road with a chain-link fence on the far side that protected against a sharp drop to the Elwha River. A large section of the fence had been torn open and bent aside, by a crazed jorōgumo I was willing to bet.

In front of the gap a battle raged.

Sal lay on the ground with Waerjerk in wolf form on top of him. Sal held the beast by the throat, keeping its snapping jaws from his face while Waerjerk's claws tried to scrape at Sal's furless and vulnerable chest and stomach. Sal already bled freely from a number of nasty-looking bites and scratches. Thankfully, already being a brightblood, he couldn't be infected with the waer curse even if Waerjerk were unfettered, but that wouldn't mean much if he bled to death.

Sal swung both arms in an arc to the side, which would have smashed Waerjerk's head against the ground. But the wolf managed to twist free, tumbling across the gravel only to spring right back up and run at Sal as the sasquatch pushed to his feet.

Challa and wolf-Minerva appeared to be in a standoff, the sandy-colored waerwolf not strong enough to get past Challa's armor, and Challa not fast enough to hit the wolf with her full strength. Minerva growled and stalked around Challa, probably trying to get to her back.

Closest to the fence's gap danced Willem the redcap and Dunngo. The dwarf punched and hurled stones at Willem, while Willem cackled and spun his staff, knocking aside most of the attacks. Willem returned blows with his staff that sent chunks of Dunngo flying off into the night, but Dunngo swept up gravel and dirt from the path to replace whatever was lost. They were evenly matched, but the actions drained both of them—Willem of the blood that fueled his strength and healing, Dunngo of the magic required to regenerate. Soon, one would run out and the other would have the advantage.

Dunngo's head spun around like an owl's to face me, and he shouted, "Save Silene!" He swept over Willem then like an

avalanche. Willem scrambled back, swinging furiously at Dunngo,
but the momentum carried them both through the gap and over
the cliff edge.

Challa, alerted by Dunngo, spotted me and shouted, "Hurry!"
then pressed her attack on Minerva, moving the wolf away from
the gap.

I ran for the gap in the fence, skidding on the gravel as I neared
it, and grabbed at a length of chain-link that hung like a lolling
tongue over the edge, barely stopping myself.

Dirt crumbled from beneath my toes to fall through the air, and
I scrambled back to press against the fence beside the gap.

The cliff edge was a deceptive layer of leaves and ferns and ivy
that hid where the actual solid ground ended. Beyond, a row of
moss-covered maple trees rose up and entwined branches as though
inspired by the chain-link fence to create an interweaving barrier
of their own, joined by the occasional cedar tree spaced out like
fence posts.

I held onto the length of chain-link and eased my way out to
the edge again, probing with my foot for the edge of the cliff. I
leaned out and looked down, flinching at each blow and shout
behind me, acutely aware that a waerwolf might leap on me at any
second.

The river bent its way back and forth through a narrow ravine
with walls gray and soft and crumbling. Dunngo had landed in the
river, and clung to a rock as his body washed away from him bit by
torturous bit. The redcap must have been swept away, along with
the blood that kept him alive.

A narrow band of coarse grass ran along the near edge of the
river. Kaminari held Silene standing on that grassy ledge, legs
bound in webbing. The pigtailed terror slapped Silene and screamed
words that were incoherent between their madness and the white
noise of the river.

I tried to see a clear path down to the pair, but the slope was too
steep and I was no spider.

Kaminari snapped Silene's arm back at the elbow so that it bent at an unnatural angle, and Silene's scream echoed down the river, sending a murder of crows flapping out of the nearby trees.

I took a deep breath.

"Prepare for ludicrous speed," I muttered.

*No, don't!* Alynon said. *It's suici—*

I went over the edge.

# (I Just) Died in Your Arms

The cliff face held just enough slant that maybe two out of ten linguists would agree the word "slide" could be acceptably used instead
of "plummet" to describe my descent toward the Elwha River. And
even then, it would only be the two linguists who got kickbacks
from the National Slides Are Awesome Council.

I aimed for rock outcroppings and tree trunks to slow my descent,
and instead seemed to find every opportunity for back scraping,
elbow knocking, and groin impaling on the way down.

I hit the ledge hard enough that my leg crumpled out from
beneath me in a sharp explosion of pain, and I tumbled to the wet
grass and moss.

"Ahh! Fuck!" My leg writhed with the pain, which some part
of my brain deeply buried beneath all the "Ow ow OW!" said was
a good thing if I could move it at all. No bones were sticking
through my skin, either, which also seemed a good thing. But it
still hurt like hell.

"Oh, look who's come to play," Kaminari said with childlike
glee, and began clapping her hands in rhythm. "Two murderers,
each to flay." She began skipping around in a circle on her little-
girl legs, her spider legs pulling in so that they poked out of her
back like the skeletal remains of wings. "One a tree whore, here to
stay. One arcana, now my prey. My sister's death I'll soon repay!"

Her skipping circle brought her close to me, and she lashed out
with a kick to my face. I made a grab for her leg, but she moved
far too quickly. I grabbed air, and her foot hit my face with the force
of, well, a kick to the face.

I fell back to the grass, my eyes instantly watering and my face feeling in desperate need of an ice pack filled with oh-my-god-I-want-to-be-anywhere-else-right-now.

As I blinked away the tears, I saw that Dunngo had been reduced to little more than a baby-sized lump of his former self, the rushing river still washing away bits of dirt and rock as it splashed over the small boulder on which he sat, trapped.

Kaminari skipped back to Silene. "Broken girl, broken girl, let's crack you open and find the pearl."

*Drop into the river!* Alynon said. *Let it carry you away. At least you might survive!*

*Unless you have real advice, shut up,* I snapped back. Alynon's voice did not help with the head pain. Yet I found myself actually looking downriver for a second where a fallen tree spanned the water. I considered the possibility that I could, in fact, survive and escape if I just jumped.

No.

I began crawling toward Kaminari, biting back a cry of pain with each movement of my leg.

Kaminari slapped Silene, whose eyes fluttered closed.

"No no no, no sleeping yet." Kaminari spread her hands apart, producing a rope of webbing like a magic trick. "Not until you pay your debt."

She began skipping rope, moving in a circle around Silene. "One, two, three, four, what flows in a tree whore? Is it blood? Is it sap? Or is it stinky sticky crap!" She lashed out with her web, snapping it like a whip and cutting a slash across Silene's cheek.

She scurried forward and leaned upward to lick the wound. She gave a little shudder of delight like a child tasting sugar for the first time, her eyes closed.

I was halfway to her. If she remained distracted—

Kaminari's hand shot out past Silene to point right at me, though she still stood with her eyes closed. "No more crawling, at least not yet, soon enough you'll be my pet."

That stopped me, and I felt a cold revulsion creep through me.

Did she intend to make me her slave, the way Brad the enforcer had become enslaved to Hiromi? Even though she could take the form of a grown woman at will, I somehow doubted she would make me her love slave. I didn't want to think what other sadistic ways she might use to "condition" me to obey her, or what being enthralled to a psychopathic demon child would be like.

The sound of crashing earth and cracking tree limbs came from the cliff, and Sal plummeted to the grass between Silene and me amid an avalanche of leaves and dirt. He fell to his knees, but pushed himself back up quickly, one of the metal fence posts gripped in his massive fist. He swayed slightly when he stood, but then steadied. His entire body was a maze of cuts that covered his gray-tan skin in dark blood. He looked terrifying.

He spat in Kaminari's direction, and I saw something glittering arc through the air to land at Silene's feet.

Waerjerk's earring. With a bit of wolf ear still attached.

"Leave, or I kill youself," Sal said. He leaned down and picked up a small log with his free hand, holding it by a branch so that it hung along his arm like a shield.

"Scary scary, when you're all hairy," Kaminari said, the fury in her tone rising as she looked at the earring. "But now I'll crush you like a berry."

Kaminari took a couple steps back from Silene, and her spider legs extended, lifting her off of the ground.

Sal raised the fence pole. "Come, badfool darkbright. Think youself tougher than Hiromi, or youself's five cousins I pulp-smashed on the way here?"

Kaminari took another step back and hissed.

I felt useless. I had a baton and my necromancy, both of which required me to get within touching distance of Kaminari. At most I might distract her by getting trampled between her and Sal.

"Help!" Dunngo shouted.

I looked over at the dwarf, now a basketball-sized collection of crystalline stones held together with a thin mortar of dirt. A couple more minutes and he would be dead.

I watched the river's flowing water for a minute with growing dread. All of my choices felt equally hopeless, equally likely to end in death.

I limped to the edge of the grassy ledge as far upstream from Dunngo as I could get before a wall of rock cut me off.

My knees felt too weak to hold me upright, and I broke out into a cold sweat as I looked at the river flowing swiftly below me. I grabbed at the rock wall with a trembling hand. I counted to three, and—shivered.

*Do not psych yourself out,* Alynon said. *Just do it!*

*I'm trying!*

I must not fear drowning. Fear is the mind killer. Fear—

*JUMP! NOW!*

I closed my eyes and jumped into the river, trying to pretend I only hopped off of a curb because otherwise I feared I would delay just long enough that Dunngo would be gone and the need to jump also gone.

The pretending ended pretty damn quick.

Jumping into a mountain river in Washington State is like brain freeze, except all over your body. As my injured leg first screamed in pain and then went numb along with the rest of my skin, I wondered how snowmelt could possibly be colder than snow. The freezing, silty water swirled over my head and carried me along with the current.

And then my brain recovered from the shock and realized that I was completely immersed in water. I could not breathe. I panicked.

I splashed, and turned in the current, as rocks knocked into my arms and legs and ribs. I somehow found my way to the surface just in time to see Dunngo's rock rushing toward me.

I swam as hard as I could using only my arms, and managed to slam into his rock. I grabbed hold of it and hung on for dear life. The act caused a wave of water to wash over the smooth boulder, carrying more of Dunngo away. I tried to adjust, to find a way to block the water with my body, but it just flowed around me.

Dunngo's eyes shifted to me, two pieces of obsidian in a pile too small for him to even form a mouth now.

"I'm sorry!" I said, wishing I'd had time to think this through. "I . . . I don't think I can save you. I could try to throw you to shore?"

His eyes shifted side to side frantically, the closest he could come to shaking his head.

"Right." He'd just scatter. And I'd probably dump half of him in the water. My teeth began to chatter, and my whole body shook from the cold.

I looked to the shore. Kaminari had tried to web Sal, but he'd used the log shield to block it and threw the log now at Kaminari. She screeched and dodged it. Sal charged and swung at her with the fence pole, but she easily skittered back out of range. From the looks of Sal, the longer the fight lasted the weaker an opponent he'd be. I just hoped Kaminari wasn't sane enough to realize that.

The metal corners of the spirit trap amulet pressed painfully into my chest as I hugged the rock.

"Wait, Dunngo," I said. "When you die, I can at least capture your spirit, and take what I can of your body. If I can get you to shore quickly enough, maybe I can find a way to bring you back." Like reviving someone who'd drowned in freezing water, an analogy that came very easily to mind for some odd reason. "If not, you'll at least get to say your good-byes, and I'll make sure you get the proper rituals."

Dirt closed over Dunngo's polished black eyes, then opened again. There probably wasn't much to say even if he could talk.

I lifted the spirit trap in a shaking hand, and laid it on the edge of what remained of Dunngo.

"M-may your spirit f-find p-peace," I stuttered. "M-may your energy b-bring light to the d-darkness."

Dunngo looked up at me as a splash of water carried away yet another piece of him. And whatever light or life had made his eyes glow, it faded and went dull.

I placed my hand on the spirit trap and reached out with my

will, with my magic, through the artifact and pulled Dunngo's spirit into it.

"You o-okay?" I asked when the summoning was done.

"Dunngo okay," his voice issued from the spirit trap, tinny and distant but there.

"Let's g-get out of here," I said. I grabbed at the rocks and crystal remains of Dunngo, and shoved them as best as I could into my pockets, a difficult task against the river current and the extreme tightness of wet jeans. When I'd saved all that I could of him, I let go of the boulder, and swam with the current for the fallen tree that bridged the river.

I slammed into the trunk like running full speed into a wall. I grasped blindly for hand holds, and managed to keep from going under. I pulled myself to the river's edge, and clawed and pulled my way up the steep bank to the far end of the grassy ledge on which Kaminari and Sal still fought.

Sal had a nasty cut across his scalp that sheathed his face in a mask of blood, giving him a demonic visage but doing nothing to improve his condition. Kaminari moved somewhat awkwardly, one of her spider legs cracked and unable to fully support her.

Gods. I wanted to just lay my head down on the grass and pass out, whatever that might mean for my future.

"Help Silene!" Dunngo said.

"I don't know how," I said. "I don't have any weapons." I could maybe use my magic to revive Silene enough to help, but it would be pointless as long as the webbing continued drugging her right back into a stupor, and I didn't have the strength or tools to remove the webbing.

Sal made several vicious swings at Kaminari, but she managed to dodge every one, and sliced a pretty nasty line across Sal's thigh.

"Let Dunngo's spirit go," the dwarf said. "Use trap on spider-bright."

"I can't," I said. "She's alive. That'd be dark necromancy."

"Bah! Arcana words," Dunngo said. "Use trap."

"I can't!" I said again. "It doesn't work that way. I'd have to destroy you, use your spirit to trap hers."

"Do it!"

"No!"

Dunngo was silent for several heartbeats as Sal and Kaminari continued their dance. "You arcana," he said finally. "Do *something*."

I moaned like a zombie on NyQuil, and pushed to my feet. My leg still ached, but the cold of the river seemed to have done it some good, or at least the lack of feeling in general was helping to mask the pain. I focused on Silene, who stood like a statue still wrapped in Kaminari's webbing.

She had defeated Hiromi. She could probably do the same to Kaminari. But I couldn't even touch the webbing around her or I'd be knocked out, too.

No. Wait. I wouldn't.

Dawn's protection amulet. I lifted it from beneath my shirt, confirming I still had it. It wouldn't give me the strength to break the webbing, but if I could get it in contact with Silene's skin it would protect her from the web's effects.

"I love it when a plan comes together," I muttered.

I limped toward Silene, practically hugging the cliff wall on my left in case I needed its support, and the ferns and vines gave me some cover.

Kaminari maneuvered behind Silene, using the dryad as a shield between herself and Sal—and blocking my way to Silene.

Frak! Seriously! Just one break would be nice.

The jorōgumo laughed at Sal. "Why so loyal to a tree whore, fool? She's not your clan, you're just her tool."

"Youself not talk about Silene like that," Sal growled. "Or I make youself badhurt before I kill you."

"Oh my! Bullseye!" Kaminari giggled, then continued in a mocking sing song, "Sasquatch in love. Sasquatch in love. Huff and puff, is he so tough when I give him a little shove?"

She raised one of her spider legs like a psycho wielding a knife and lunged not for Sal but at Silene.

BIGFOOTLOOSE AND FINN FANCY FREE     407

Sal must have anticipated such a move because he flung the fence pole like a spear in the same second that Kaminari moved. She screeched and dodged the pole, then raised her sharply serrated spider leg and plunged it at Silene's neck again.

Except the distraction gave Sal time to reach Silene. He plowed into her, knocking her out of the way and tumbling to the ground.

Kaminari spun, and covered Sal in webbing before he could recover his feet.

"Use trap!" Dunngo said. "Now!"

"But—"

"Do it!" Dunngo said. "Dunngo beg you! Now!"

"No! I . . . I'll try stopping her without it."

I just had to be strong enough to pull her spirit free. Or at least immobilize her long enough to place the protection amulet on Silene.

I lurched at Kaminari while she finished binding Sal in webbing, her back to me as she admired her work. "Now—" she said.

I grabbed her leg, and tried to pull her spirit free of her body. I poured all of my strength into it.

Her spirit bucked wildly against me, her own will powerful in its madness.

I was not strong enough. Not even close. I felt the summoning slipping out of my control.

Kaminari backhanded me, sending me sliding across the muddy grass. She twitched, and recovered faster than should have been possible. She was so full of pain, my attack had been a drop in an ocean.

She turned toward me, a terrifying fury twisting her features. "You—"

Another crashing noise, and Petey tumbled down onto the landing. Kaminari hissed.

Petey pushed to his feet. He looked as bad as Sal had, perhaps worse, his clothing shredded, his body covered in cuts and slashes, but his wounds were already crusted over and well on their way to healing. Pete took in the scene, and spotted me on the ground.

His face went red as he looked at Kaminari. "Nobody hurts my family!"

"Pete! No!" I shouted. But he was already running at the jorōgumo. He leaped, transforming into the giant gray-brown wolf mid-air.

Kaminari screamed in frustration and disappeared in a loud *Whoomp!* as air rushed in to fill the space where she'd stood. Petey flew through the empty space and landed hard, skidding on the moss and wet grass.

Kaminari reappeared with a percussive bang of displaced air, and her spear-like leg plunged through Pete's side.

Petey howled in pain, and transformed back into his normal self, naked and impaled through his abdomen, pinned to the ground.

"Petey! Oh gods!"

I jerked the spirit trap from around my neck. Damn it! "I'm sorry, Dunngo."

"No sorry," he said. "Save Silene."

I reached out with my will and with my magic, and armed the spirit trap using the spiritual energy within it instead of my own. Using Dunngo's spirit.

Kaminari tried to pull her leg free of Pete, but he grabbed it, held onto it, keeping it caught in his abdomen and screaming in pain as he was jerked up to his knees. Kaminari hissed, and tried to stab him with her other foreleg, but Pete grasped her leg and wrenched her to the side, throwing her off balance. He pushed unsteadily to his feet, causing Kaminari to shift backward. She tried to spear him again, and again he jerked her to the side, but I could see it was costing him to do so, that he grew weaker by the second. I couldn't imagine the pain he was in.

I limped toward Pete and Kaminari as they continued to dance in circles, each trying to get the advantage on the other. As I did, I pulled Dawn's amulet free with my other hand, activated it and tossed it onto Silene, aiming for her cheek. The amulet struck her face, flashed briefly, and bounced onto the grass.

Silene stirred weakly, and blinked groggily at the battle being waged.

Vines tried to climb up one of Kaminari's spider legs but too few, too slow. The jorōgumo easily ripped free and continued moving.

I gripped the trap in my hand as I drew close to the two combatants. Maybe I didn't need to use the trap, if I could just summon her soul enough to distract her, let Pete and Silene work together—

Pete stumbled, and fell to his knees. Kaminari gave a triumphant scream, and raised one of her free legs to finish him off.

"NO!" I shouted.

I lunged in and slapped the trap against Kaminari, and summoned her spirit through it.

There was a flash, and the scream that ripped from Kaminari's throat sounded like it was disappearing down a long tunnel.

I felt an expansion of spirit, the rush of being larger than myself as I consumed Dunngo's spirit energy, burned it away to create a vacuum within the trap that pulled in Kaminari's spirit.

It felt incredible. If I had enough spirit energy, I realized, I could do anything. I could control everything. Everyone.

"I am Tetsuo," I whispered, and giggled. "I am all."

Kaminari collapsed, pulling Pete down to the ground with her.

As I stood wavering, floating on the euphoric rush of the spell, Pete managed to pull himself off of Kaminari's leg and collapse to the grass with a sigh, his eyes fluttering closed.

Kaminari's spirit screamed in fury from within the spirit trap as her body curled in on itself.

Her scream dragged me back into the present. I silenced her, and blinked as I took in the scene around me.

"Pete." I limped to my brother, and checked on him first, my movements sluggish and heavy. He was breathing steadily, his waer regenerative powers already closing the ragged wound.

I went next to Silene and Sal. Using one of Kaminari's claws, I managed to cut most of the webbing away from them before collapsing onto my butt on the wet grass, utterly wiped out, my entire body shaking uncontrollably now. I felt strangely hollow.

Silene slowly pushed herself up into a sitting position, leaned back against the cliff wall, and took a deep breath as her hand dug into the thick green grass. Her bent arm snapped and straightened into a normal angle. She screamed, then shuddered.

After a second, Silene looked down at Sal, still unmoving and covered in wounds that leaked blood. She blinked slowly like she'd had way too much to drink, then she shook herself.

"No. Oh Bright, no, please no." She put a hand on Sal's chest, and closed her eyes. She opened them after a second, and said, "Please. By all the Bright, please, I have to have enough left." She closed her eyes again, and her hand dug deeper into the grass.

Sal's eyes snapped open, and he took a deep, shuddering breath, his back arching. Then he eased back down.

Silene swooned, and slumped over Sal.

"Ouch," Sal grunted.

Silene stirred, and lifted her head weakly. "Saljchuh," she said, and touched Sal's face. "I—" she stopped, and shook her head. "That was so like a sasquatch to just go charging in. But a few heartbeats more, and you would have been dead. What were you—"

Sal growled softly, and Silene stopped. Sal covered Silene's hand with one of his own. "Iself's heart beats for youself only. And always."

Silene stared at him for a second, and Sal blushed.

Then Silene kissed him.

# It's the End of the World as We Know It

Challa, Garl, and several more of the stronger Silver brightbloods lowered ropes and pulled us back up to the road. Sal was the last to be lifted. Antler Head caught us up on events as the brightbloods struggled to lift Sal's enormous weight, and Vee worried over Pete.

"The Silver drove off the Shadows," Antlers said.

"How many of our brightblood fell?" Silene asked.

"At least five. And Don Faun and several others are gravely injured. But the Shadows lost many more."

Silene turned away, grief and anger warring across her features.

"Damn," I said. "I guess Don got his fight. What about Barry?"

Vee snorted. "He was found behind the campground office, bound up in webbing. He blamed the whole fight on Kaminari, said this made things 'even Stephen,' and left."

I can't lie and say I was completely relieved that Barry had escaped unharmed and free to still haunt my life.

"And," Vee said, and hesitated before continuing, "Heather disappeared again."

I just sighed. I'd hoped she would stick around, that the plight of the brightbloods would move her to do the right thing. But it seemed she was still more concerned with herself.

Sal reached the top of the cliff, and pulled himself up over the edge. As he did, Silene turned to me. "Come to my tree, and I will do what I can for your wounds."

"No thank you," I said. "I promised Dawn I would make it to her show. I need to hurry."

"I understand," Silene said. "Love is important." She looked at

Sal as he stepped onto the path, and smiled. "I understand that in new ways."

I turned to Sal as he joined us, and held out my hand. "Looks like our business is concluded, Sal."

He pulled me into a quick hug, my damp clothes smearing the dried blood on his skin, then he pushed me back, almost knocking me off of my feet. I did my best not to shout out in pain as I put sudden weight on my injured leg, and instead gave Sal a smile through gritted teeth.

Sal grunted. "Youself true at finding love. And a good friend to the brightbloods."

"Uh, thanks," I said, feeling the weight of the spirit trap around my neck, and looked away. I didn't exactly feel like a shining knight. "I guess I can finally update my matchmaker website, anyway."

Speaking of dates—

I pulled my phone out of my pocket. It was dead. Cell phones didn't play well with water, apparently.

If Dawn had tried to call or text me to ask where I was, I had no way of checking now.

I looked at my Pac-Man watch. It, too, was dead. I stared at it a second, feeling a deep sense of loss.

Frak. "Does anyone know what time it is?"

"A quarter to eight," Vee replied.

Double frak. Dawn's show began in fifteen minutes, and I was an hour and a half's drive away. The show would be long done before I could even get there.

I made a decision before I could chicken out. "Silene, there *is* something you can do for me, actually. I need to take the fairy paths."

*Don't do it!* Alynon said. *I do not wish to be stuck within a freak. Well, more of a freak.*

His concern was valid. The stories of arcana who had dared to travel the fairy roads—or Fey Way system—sounded like urban myths: tales of emerging with additional limbs, missing organs, or lost senses, and most often of being driven mad.

The fairy roads were remnants of a time when the Other Realm and our world were closer, when spirits and energy passed more freely between them. Whether some part of the Other Realm had been merged with our world, or the fabric of our space and time had been warped in an attempt to reconcile with the chaos of the Other Realm, nobody knew for sure. Only the results were known. No protection spell had been found to guarantee safe travel for humans; but the brightbloods, being of both worlds like the Ways themselves, were able to travel them safely. Usually.

Silene frowned. "I must caution you, Finn, the ways are not safe for humans."

"I know. But I have a Fey spirit within me. Perhaps that will protect me."

Silene shook her head. "Changelings are not immune to the Ways' changes."

"I know. But I'm not a Fey spirit leasing a human body while its human spirit is away. I have spirits from both worlds in me, same as a brightblood."

Silene's eyebrows raised. "I had not considered that. You truly are a cousin to us."

*I am no diluted offspring of some Elder Spirit! I—*

Chill out! I'm no brightblood, either. But that doesn't make what I said any less true. As much as I'd wanted to deny it the past three months. "Look, if something does happen, I'm sure I can find a way to reverse it, even if it costs some time and serious mana. But one thing I'll never be able to undo is letting Dawn down if I miss her show."

Silene looked toward the woods, her brow furrowing in thought.

*There shall be other shows,* Alynon said.

Not as important. And not when she'll have to get up there and face the reality that she can't play guitar, maybe ever again—which is my fault.

*'Tis a difficulty to be sure, but you do not owe—*

She's made a real effort to meet me halfway, to support me. I must show her I will do the same.

*She also doesn't want you taking stupid risks.*

*It is a risk,* I replied, *but it is not a stupid one, not as far as I'm concerned.*

*Fa! You are not trying to punish yourself, are you? For what happened with Dunngo?*

I sighed. *No. That, I will have to atone for for the rest of my life.*

"If you are certain," Silene said at last, and from her voice I thought she might be acceding as much from exhaustion as anything. "I feel such a danger is a poor reward to offer for all you have done, but Farquhar can guide you, he knows the Ways well." She motioned Antler Head over.

"Thank you," I said.

Silene nodded. "Farquhar also may see you swiftly to a healer should your journey prove . . . damaging. I wish you luck, Gramaraye. And again, I thank you."

"I wish you and your brightbloods luck, in whatever you do from here," I said. "And, if there's anything I can do to help make sure your dead are properly cared for, let me know."

"That means a great deal," Silene said. "Farewell." With a wave of her hand, she and Sal half-walked, half-stumbled in the direction of her tree.

I walked across the gravel road to where Pete and Vee sat on the mossy hillside, waiting for me. The brightbloods had applied some kind of poultice to Pete's wounds, and between that and his waer healing ability, he appeared out of danger. Vee had a number of cuts and bruises as well, healing just as quickly. And on the ground beside her, her giant squirrel tail lay, apparently ripped from her.

"Are . . . you okay?" I asked, looking at the tail.

"Yes," Vee said. "I will grow another in time."

"Oh. Uh, Pete, how you feeling, buddy?"

"Tired," Pete said. "And hungry."

I smiled. "I'm shocked."

A faun walked up, his attention on Pete and Vee. "Pardon, cousins, but I just wanted to thank you for fighting by our side. It will be remembered."

Pete blushed. "Thanks," he said, "but I was just protecting my brother."

"All the same," the faun replied, and with a nod, strolled off.

"Seems you made some friends," I said, smiling. My smile faded. "Listen, I'm taking the fairy roads back. I want you guys to go ahead and drive home without me."

They both stood, and made all the same arguments Silene, Alynon, and my own fears had made. And when it became clear neither of them could talk me out of my plan, they exchanged a look that I felt pretty sure was them considering dragging me off by force. But in the end, we all exchanged hugs and said farewell.

As I hugged Pete, I said, "I love you, man." I hugged him tighter. "I'm glad you're my brother. Really."

"I love you, too, Brother," Petey said, and squeezed back, nearly cracking my already-bruised ribs.

We said farewell, and they headed for the car, and home.

Farquhar approached and nodded his antlered head in the direction of the forest. "Come, I will lead you to the nearest Way if you are still determined to walk it."

"Yep. Still determined."

The entrance to the fairy paths was well-concealed, even from me. Farquhar pointed out its location on a rock face between two trees. But when I tried to actually approach it on my own it was like trying to press two opposing magnets together: in whatever way reality was twisted around the paths, it bent normal perception and physics around it.

In the end, Farquhar had to put his hands on my shoulder and walk me into it.

One second we were in the forest, the next we were being squeezed like the last bit of toothpaste along a tube of warped color and sound. I might have found it hard to keep my balance if I'd been walking on a regular path, what with the world spinning around me and all, but since the path itself quickly decided to join in on the prank against my senses, there was little sense in worrying.

It reminded me of the unshaped wilds of the Other Realm, as

seen through a warped lens. I had no idea how Farquhar navigated the chaos.

And as in the Other Realm, I felt my body losing its shape, stretching and bending and changing to match the reality around it. A second head began to grow out of my shoulder, expanding like a balloon, the mouth gasping like a fish desperate for a cold refreshing Pan Galactic Gargle Blaster. I recognized the features. Alynon. Was this my unconscious fears, or his spirit finding form in this between space?

I did my best to exert my will over my perceptions and my own existence. I had spent twenty-five years in the Other Realm. More than most arcana, I had been prepared for this, trained for this. I was Finn Gramaraye, human, arcana, necromancer, and I only had one head, damn it.

Alynon's head deflated and reformed into a frog-like lump that glared up at me with bubble eyes. And I felt as though my own head spun now. If Farquhar had not pulled me along, I might have just whirled away into the void.

Had I made a mistake? Would I emerge sane and whole enough that Dawn would even recognize me, let alone appreciate that I'd made it to her show?

Dawn. I focused on her, and the memory of making love to her floated to the surface.

When I had tried to think of the "feel" and shape of my own skin, my own limbs, it had been intellectual, an attempt to enforce my self-concept. But in remembering Dawn's touch I *felt* my skin where her hand and lips had brushed. In remembering her fingers digging into my back, into my butt cheeks, I *felt* them. I remembered my body.

The frog head melted away, leaving only my shoulder, the shoulder where Dawn had lightly bit me, teasing me with her teeth.

And then Farquhar gave me a hard pull, and I tumbled out into the night air.

I was clothed again. Those clothes were still damp and filthy, but at least I wasn't naked. Which was especially good since we'd emerged from a hillside in Fort Worden, not far from the campground.

I patted myself all over, craning my neck to make sure I had all my important bits and nothing extra.

And I seemed sane, though I supposed if I weren't I'd be the last to know.

"Woo hoo!" I shouted.

Farquhar looked at me with a genuine expression of surprise. "You are well, Finn Gramaraye?"

"Yes. Wow. Now that was one major slime-related psychokinetic event!"

*You jerk!* Alynon said. *You almost got us mutated!*

And I slapped myself. Hard.

Not by choice.

"Ow!" I blinked in surprise. "What—"

*Holy Bright! That was me! I did that!*

No. Oh no—

*Let me try again!* My hand twitched, as if with a muscle spasm, but did not move. *Fa, I—oh, I feel . . . weak. I—* His voice faded out.

*Alynon?* I projected. But there was no response. "Alynon?" I asked out loud, just in case.

*Here,* he responded, though I could barely hear his voice. *I just feel . . . sleepy.* His voice faded out again.

Farquhar's eyes narrowed. "You are sure all is well?"

I sighed. "That's a good question. But I'm not crazy. Or dying." I was, however, at least a thirty-minute walk away from Dawn's show, and probably much longer given my injured leg. "Not to sound ungrateful or anything, but, uh, could you get me closer to town?"

"Not by the Ways," Farquhar responded. "But there may be another means." He tilted back his head, and made a strange, bleating sound into the night air.

I didn't question, I focused instead on trying to swipe as much of the dirt from my clothes and skin as I could. A few minutes later, a two hundred pound white-tailed buck bounded out of the forest and up to Farquhar, tilting his head in a bow. His antlers were lop-sided, all of the branches on one side, the other side a single simple tine.

I thanked Farquhar, and soon was bounding along the beach on the back of the buck.

While the ride was much appreciated, I can't say as I'd recommend it. The buck's spine was sharp, painfully so, and his gait bounding. By the time we neared the marina in town, I seriously questioned my ability to have children in the future. And I was more than a little worried about ticks.

A young couple at the marina's RV park took pictures of me arriving and dismounting. I waved. At least I wasn't riding a centaur or anything the ARC's infomancers would have to scrub from the interwebs and possibly people's memories.

I limped quick as I could to the Undertown. As I hopped down the stairs, I could hear Dawn's voice and a guitar humming from below.

I'd made it, at least for most of it.

The place was packed. I stayed near the back of the cafe/bar, but it was a small enough space that Dawn still easily spotted me.

Her smile made every risk and pain I'd endured to get there worth it.

She looked beautiful, radiant. She'd traded her normal T-shirt and hoodie for a satiny green dress with brown lacy patterns down the sides, and her violet hair sparkled in the stage lights.

Amber played the guitar well enough, but I could tell Dawn felt exposed and uncertain of what to do with her hands at times. Still, she sang as perfectly as I'd ever heard her.

After she sang her last song, and climbed down from the stage to loud applause, she thanked her way through the crowd to me.

She took in my stained, rumpled clothes, and my face that felt like it was made of one-hundred-percent real organic bruise.

"So," she said. "I'm guessing Heather's drug didn't solve everything, and more wackiness ensued? What's tomorrow's quest, steal the Spear of Destiny from the top of the Space Needle?"

"No more quests," I said, wincing as the movement made my swollen lip hurt. "It's all done. For real. You were amazing. I think this was the best show you've done, singing-wise."

"I felt it," she said, grinning. "I was really in the flow. It was . . . religious." She glanced back in the direction of the stage. "And Sheila wants to talk to me."

"Go! Talk to her! This is your big break!" I said, squeezing her hand. "I'm so happy for you. How about I go home, clean up real quick while you two are talking, and come back for the after party?"

Dawn shook her head, but with a loving smile. "No. You look like crap. And I know you don't like to hang out with my friends, anyway. I'll be fine. You go home and rest up. And I'll come by later to kiss all your boo-boos." She waggled her eyebrows at me, then leaned in and said softly into my ear, "Thank you, Finn, for being here. It made a difference. I love you." She kissed my cheek.

Then she turned without waiting for my reply and walked back into the crowd.

And in that moment, whatever residual adrenaline or sheer willpower had kept me going ran out, and I could feel every single one of my cuts and bruises.

Sleep sounded like a fine idea. Perhaps I'd take the next week off. In bed.

With Dawn.

# Epilogue

I watched the morning fog swirling and pooling in the low bowl-like areas that dotted Evergreen Cemetery. Dark, moss-covered crosses, headstones, and statues stood worn and cracked by time and weather and the occasional teenage idiot. They rose out of the mist like promises, and stood upon the grassy hilltops like judgments. I glanced back occasionally to the largest and most famous of the cemetery's crypts, a large stone-gray ziggurat called the Rucker Tomb. My family and Vee had already entered the ARC Crypt hidden beneath it for the interment of Vee's brother, Zeke. Three months the ARC had held his body as they investigated the aftermath of Grayson's plot and our actions in response, but at last he was being interred with honor. I looked again at the text from Dawn, short and to the point: *I'll meet you at Evergreen.* The only words I'd had from her since her show last night.

"Gramaraye," a munchkin voice declared. I turned to find Priapus marching toward me. He held out a folded piece of parchment. "For you."

"Perfect timing. Thank you, Priapus." I took the parchment. "Any progress on finding out who destroyed your records?"

"Got my suspicions," he said. "And I ain't liking where it's leading. But if I find out something worth something, don't worry, I'll let ya know."

"Uh huh. And I'm sure you'll also let me know how much it'll cost for you to share the info, right?"

"Ha!" Priapus said. "Seems like you're finally wising up, kid.

Watch your back." He turned, and quickly disappeared back into the mist.

"Beautiful morning," Heather said behind me.

I jumped, and turned to find her standing behind me. At least she wasn't pointing a squirt gun at me.

"What the hell are you doing here?" I asked. I doubted she'd come to turn herself in to the enforcers who were present for Zeke's interment, and that would be in bad taste anyway, given her involvement with his death.

"I came to say good-bye. At least for a while," she replied. "I tried to catch you at home, but you'd already left."

There was something different about her. She looked . . . healthy. Almost younger.

"You look better," I said. "Trade some of that mana drug of yours for a health potion?"

Heather sighed. "No. I had Garl bite me."

*Damn,* Alynon said. *She could have asked *me* to bite her.*

"What?" I was certain I'd heard her wrong.

"I've decided to join the brightbloods. I figured out the cure for the mana drug. You didn't tell me Silene had brightlilies; I thought they were extinct."

"It, uh, sorry?"

"We're spreading the word on how to make the cure, along with sharing the brightlily seeds. And I thought I might be able to help the brightbloods with their other problems, try to make up for what I did to them."

"You told them what you did?"

"No. And I'd appreciate it if you didn't, either."

I frowned. "You could have helped them without becoming a brightblood yourself, you know."

"I couldn't help anyone from exile," she replied. "It was either a life in exile, or life as a brightblood pledged to the Silver. I'll be protected from ARC retaliation—well, as much as any brightblood is. More importantly, I'll have a second chance. A new life, literally."

I shook my head. "Well, you always wanted to get out from under the ARC. But I never thought you'd go this far."

"Me either," she said, and rubbed at her arm. "But I was tired of running. I was out of options. And Silene's cause seems like one worth fighting for. Besides, and don't laugh, but I think I've always felt like I'd fit in with the brightbloods."

I laughed.

"Hey!" she said, and playfully shook a fist at me.

I waved my hand in apology. "Sorry. Well, I'm happy for you, I guess?" I said.

The truth was, I *had* hoped that she would choose to help the brightbloods if confronted with the real effects of her drug. I'd hoped that the Heather I remembered, the young woman who wanted to not just break free of the ARC's control but also to make the world a better place, that she was still there underneath all the bitterness and self-preservation.

But becoming a waerbear?

"Yeah yeah," she said. "I'm sure you're thrilled."

"What? No. I mean, I'm glad you're going to help, sure, but—"

"Uh huh. Whatever. I just wanted to say thank you. I think this is going to be a good thing."

"I hope so," I said, then remembered why I was standing there. "Look, uh, Dawn's supposed to be meeting me here, and—"

"I know. She's coming, I can smell her." Heather smiled. "Something I'm still getting used to. Like I said, I just wanted to say good-bye, and thanks. And let you know you didn't make a mistake, giving me a second chance."

"I'm glad, for both of us," I said. "I hope I'll see you around."

"Me too. Under better circumstances." Heather turned and headed for the trees that surrounded the cemetery, disappearing back into the mists.

Dawn appeared over the nearby hill a minute later, wearing black slacks and a jacket.

I immediately moved to meet her, my leg stiff in its Ace bandage wrapping, and gave her a hug.

"Hey," I said. "I'm glad you could make it."

She moaned and put one hand to her head. "I feel like I drank All the Wine," she replied.

"Wow, a rock star for one day and you're already becoming a stereotype," I said.

She punched me in the arm, gently at least this time. "Sit and spin, Ralph. Come on, let's go say good-bye to the big guy."

We held hands and strolled up to The Rucker Tomb.

*I just realized, I could slap her butt right now,* Alynon said.

*Do it, and I'll play "We Didn't Start the Fire" nonstop for the rest of the week.*

*Ha! I'll just shut it off.*

*And pass out from the effort.*

*You say pass out, I say nap and come back ready to slap more butts!*

*Fine. I'll sing it then.*

*I'll hold your jaw closed.*

This was going to get old. Real fast.

The trip through the fairy path had obviously strengthened the bond between us, somehow. But I still preferred to think it was mostly my love for Dawn that had saved me from mutation and madness, not an annoying Fey spirit in my brain. Call me sentimental.

We reached The Rucker Tomb. The gray ziggurat sat upon a raised concrete platform, and the front entrance was reached by stairs that passed between two man-sized stone pylons. I placed my persona ring against a pylon, and said, "*Aperire Ostium Per Mea Ius Ex Necromantiae.*"

There was a moment's pause, then a voice came from within the stone, "Phinaeus Gramaraye, you may enter."

The stone stairs receded from us, revealing a second set of stairs that led down into an underground passage. Dawn and I entered in silence, holding hands.

We made our way along the passages, lined with the magically preserved bodies of dead arcana dressed in their favorite outfits and

posed with items and artifacts that spoke to their magical gifts and
personal interests. We finally reached the interment room where
new bodies were displayed in a ceremony before being moved to
their permanent spots. A stone-walled room about the size of a
school gym, it had heavy oak tables spaced around the edge with
various snack foods and drink options, and a dais at the far end on
which Zeke's display stood.

Zekiel Wodenson stood smiling in his *Miami Vice* outfit of white
jacket and slacks and blue T-shirt. His thinning blond hair had
been shaved in a Mr. T–style mohawk, and his enforcer-style Fu
Manchu moustache had been braided with silver beads, showing
that the enforcers had decided to restore his enforcer status post-
humously. In one hand he held a collapsing baton, and in the other
what looked like a miniature armchair.

A small crowd of arcana had gathered before the display: Reggie
and several other enforcers; a number of men and women I didn't
recognize; and my family. Sammy, Fatima, and Mattie stood near a
snack table. Pete and Vee stood before Zeke's display, Vee accepting
condolences and hearing the stories and jokes about Zeke as his life
was celebrated. Father stood with Verna, apparently trying to explain
something to her by demonstrating the difference between how
a grape versus an olive rolled off of his nose. Only Mort was
absent, being too ill, and ill-tempered, after Brianne's exorcism.

An ancient-looking man in a black suit, who I'd have taken even
odds on whether he worked there or was simply an animated
corpse, stepped up and offered us both cloth handkerchiefs. "People
always cry at these things," he said with a smile.

"Thank you," Dawn and I both replied.

The old man nodded, and walked past us.

Dawn started in Vee's direction, pulling me along, but I let her
hand go and said, "I need just a minute."

Dawn gave me a look that said she understood, then quickly
walked away.

I grabbed a piece of celery with peanut butter in order to appear busy.

Reggie spotted me, and came over. My palms grew sweaty, but I reminded myself that if he or anyone had found out I'd performed dark necromancy, I'd already be in custody.

*You should have destroyed Kaminari's spirit,* Alynon said.

I ignored him. I'd buried the spirit trap, unable to bring myself to destroy another spirit so soon, not even one as damaged as Kaminari's.

"Finn," Reggie said, and gave a nod. "Seems things have settled down between the Silver and the Shadows."

"I guess," I replied, trying to act normal. Which made me self-conscious and certain that I was acting suspiciously. "But we, uh, still don't know who's playing them against each other."

"Yeah. Well, just watch yourself. Whoever the puppet masters are, they may decide to come looking for the necromancer who threw a monkey wrench in their plans."

I sighed. "I'm not sure I did much to upset their plans. I have a feeling the Silver and Shadows aren't exactly going to hug and be friends."

"Well, as far as I'm concerned, you did some good." He slapped me on the back. "And did Zeke's memory proud. And, let's face it, your family name needed a bit of polishing."

I gave him a weak smile. "Yeah." I nodded to Zeke. "He looks good."

Reggie looked toward Zeke, and his eyes teared up a bit as he said, "Yeah, he always did." He cleared his throat. "I got a ton of paperwork to fill out on all your shenanigans, so I'll be in touch."

He left to rejoin the other enforcers.

Vincent strolled into the room, dressed in his official enforcer suit and tie. He stopped, and pulled a folded piece of parchment from inside his jacket as if to reassure himself it was there, then put it back away.

I moved to intercept him, but not before Pete and Vee spotted him as well.

"Hello, Knight-Lieutenant," I said as Pete and Vee made their way toward us. "You didn't seriously come here to demand Pete and Vee's declaration of loyalty at her brother's interment, did you?"

Vincent gave me his best stoic enforcer stare. All he lacked was mirrored shades. "They had three days to give an answer, and they did not. They chose to push this matter, not me. I tried to warn you, Gramaraye. Now they are to be declared rogue and there's nothing you, or I, can do about it. The best I can do is wait to serve them their papers as they leave. Out of respect for Mister Wodenson."

"You mean Enforcer Wodenson."

Vincent waited just a beat before saying, "Of course."

Pete and Vee arrived.

"Well, as it so happens, I have something for you," I said, and produced my own piece of parchment. "Delivered just this morning by our friendly neighborhood gnomes."

Vincent's eyes narrowed, and he made no move to take the parchment. "What is it?"

I smiled at Pete and Vee. "This officially declares my brother and Vee to be Vice-Archons of the Silver Court."

"What?" Pete said, surprised. Vee's eyes widened.

"*Vice*-Archons?" Vincent said, and took the parchment. He read over it. "The Archons haven't used subordinates for hundreds of years."

"What does this mean?" Pete asked, frowning.

"How did you do this?" Vee asked.

"Yeah, Gramaraye," Vincent asked, looking up. "What did you have to promise the Fey for this? Or are you and that Fey in your head just working together now?"

"Nothing, and no. I'm still a loyal arcana, Knight-Lieutenant. But I did help to save the Silver Court and their brightbloods both—and helped the ARC, too, by the way—and so they saw fit to grant my request in return."

*I still cannot believe Oshun agreed to your request, whatever small favor you had done us.*

*Maybe your kin in the Silver Court are not as unreasonable as you think.*

*Wait until you've lived with them a hundred years, then say that.*

Vincent's mouth puckered to the side for a second, then he gave a slight shrug, and handed the parchment back to me. "They've declared their loyalty, and that's what is important. Congratulations. Truly." He turned to Vee. "And my condolences and respect for your brother."

"Thanks," Vee said, graciously.

"Have a cookie, they're good," Pete said, waving at the nearest food table.

"Excuse us," Vee said. "I need to speak to the crowd now."

"Please," Vincent said, waving toward the stage.

I gave Vee a hug. "Don't be nervous. You'll do fine."

"I know. I have Pete and Sarah to help me if I forget something."

I patted Pete on the back, and he and Vee made their way up onto the stage.

"Everyone, a moment please," Vee said, calling for the audience's attention. "I wanted to thank you all for coming." Her voice thickened, and Pete put a hand on her back as she continued. "And thank you for sharing your wonderful stories and thoughts about my brother. I think he'd say 'I pity the fool who didn't know me.' And he'd be right to. In a few minutes, we'll let people get up here and say any last—"

"Wait," Pete said, and blushed.

"Pete?" Vee asked with a worried expression. "What is it?"

He glanced at me, and I gave him an encouraging nod, and then began making my way toward Dawn. Pete turned back to Vee. "I just, I wanted to ask you," he said, and waved toward Zeke, "while we have both our families here, uh—"

Pete dropped to one knee, and pulled a ring box out of his pocket. Vee's eyes went wide and her hand covered her mouth as Pete opened the box, his hands trembling. Even from here I could recognize the black-and-silver pattern of Mother's engagement ring.

"I love you," Pete said. "You're the best girl—or, uh, woman— that I've ever met. Well, except my mother. And no offense, Sammy, or Mattie, or—not that you're not as good as my mother, Vee, or uh—what I mean is, there's no other woman I would want to paint with, or run on the beach with, or climb trees with, or, well, spend my life with, than you and—" He pushed the ring up toward Vee. "Will you marry me?"

Vee laughed, and tears ran down her face as she nodded vigorously. "Yes. Yes, of course, yes."

Pete beamed, stood up, and lifted Vee in a passionate kiss.

The gathered crowd cheered. I reached Dawn. She smiled at me, and I kissed her, long and with all my heart behind it.

"I love you," I said as we parted.

"I love you, too, you big dork," she replied.

Then we both grinned up at Pete and Vee as they blushed and smiled ear-to-ear at the continued applause and congratulations of the crowd.

I felt like I'd cried a river in the last few days. I wished more of those tears had been happy tears, like the ones that flowed freely now. I wiped at my face with the handily provided handkerchief.

As I lowered it, words formed on the cloth.

With an uneasy feeling, I stretched out the handkerchief between my hands so the words could be read clearly.

> *You helped the feybloods and their masters. But war is coming, boy. Get wise and start fighting for your own people, or go down with the enemy. GG*

Gavriel Gramaraye. My grandfather. Alive and still stalking me. *Ah, bat's breath.*

Turn the page for a sneak peek at
the next Familia Arcana novel

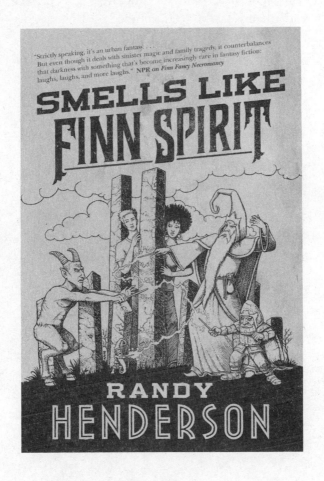

"Strictly speaking, it's an urban fantasy. . . . But even though it deals with sinister magic and family tragedy, it counterbalances that darkness with something that's become increasingly rare in fantasy fiction: laughs, laughs, and more laughs." **NPR** on *Finn Fancy Necromancy*

## SMELLS LIKE FINN SPIRIT

### RANDY HENDERSON

Available March 2017

## Constant Craving

I felt twitchy as the Bumbershoot festival crowd flowed past me in the shadow of the Space Needle. The collective hum of their spiritual energy pulled at me like the seductive whispers of a thousand sirens, strong as the compulsion to take just one more turn on *Civilization* before going to bed—compelling, but nothing that couldn't be defeated with a great act of will, or perhaps an urgent need to use the bathroom.

I leaned on a concrete ledge outside the food court, along with my girlfriend, Dawn; my sister, Sammy; and her girlfriend, Fatima, as we took a break from browsing booths and watching concerts. The light breeze offered a bit of relief from summer's stubborn September heat, though it also brought the occasional whiff of the upwind garbage cans or the body odor of an unwashed teenager. I fluffed my Space Invaders T-shirt as the throbbing beat of a distant rock-rap band provided the background for a hundred passing conversations, a dozen laughing children, and one jet flying overhead.

I took Dawn's hand and focused on it, running my thumb gently over the guitar calluses on her pointer finger, the brown curve of her palm's edge forming a kind of yin yang with the tan of mine, the warm and solid reality of her presence helping me to ground myself and shut out the call of all that energy.

I looked up to find her smiling at me. Gods, she was beautiful. And between that impish smile and the lavender cloud of finger curls, she could easily have been an animated goddess of chaos.

"You've got shiny eyes again," Dawn said. "Those for me? Or are you just hungry?"

"I'm hungry for you," I replied, and my stomach growled loudly as if to argue.

"Well, for that you'll have to wait 'til we get home, but here's something to hold you over." She leaned in, and drew me into the warm haven of a kiss.

Someone knocked against my foot as they passed—and my foot kicked out, my red Converse connecting with the folds of a yellow dress.

"Hey—" the woman said, tugging at her dress. "Jerk."

"Sorry!" I said. "I didn't men to—"

She rolled her eyes and reentered the flow of bodies.

*Damn it, Alynon,* I thought at the Fey spirit trapped in my head.

Alynon Infedriel, knight of the Silver Court and a huge pain in my spiritual butt, harrumphed, then replied in a weak voice that only I could hear, *'Tis not my fault she had no consideration.*

*What did I tell you about taking control?* I thought back.

*She interrupted a perfectly good kiss! And there hasn't been nearly enough good kissing going on lately, let alone—*

*Drop it, or I'll be staying up tonight watching* Cop Rock *instead of going to Dawn's.* It didn't help that he was right.

"Alynon being a pain again?" Dawn asked.

"Yep."

*You would not so starve your own happiness to spite mine,* Alynon said.

*Yes, well, unlike you, I have control over my lizard brain.*

*Indeed, you have more Mothra than Godzilla in your nature.*

*I'll take that as a compliment, given that Mothra was protector of the Earth.*

*Indeed? Protector of the Earth now, are you?*

I did not reply. I hadn't felt like any kind of hero since Elwha. I turned my focus back outward, but that let the energy of the crowd draw my attention again.

Three months since the battle at Elwha River, when I consumed

Dunngo the dwarf's spiritual energy—a desperate act of dark necromancy used to stop a crazy shapeshifting jorōgumo. An act that had utterly destroyed Dunngo's spirit, forever. I'd been extra sensitive to spiritual energy around me ever since, feeling something like lust at the thought of touching it, using it. The strength of the feeling had faded slowly, diminishing with lots of "me time" and some serious meditation work. But being around so many people at once made the accumulated weight of their spiritual energy hard to ignore. All of that power—

"There are just too many damned people in the world now," I said.

"Oh, people aren't so bad," Dawn replied. "It's all the Stupid, that's the problem."

I shrugged in noncommittal agreement. Maybe I was simply used to small-town life, or still adjusting to our world after twenty-five years of exile in the Fey Other Realm, but as I looked around I just saw streets clogged with cars, walkways stuffed with bodies. A great river of people in their summer clothes, buying and talking and walking and—I could feel them, their spirits, like glowing apples waiting to be plucked. All that spiritual energy, being wasted on watching reality television and eating fried nuggets of chicken sawdust. I could do so much more with—

I knocked my thoughts onto another path with the force of Bowser in a bumper car, took the irritability which desire had sparked in me and turned it toward my other source of irritation and worry: Mattie, my niece. I checked my phone, but no messages from her.

I didn't know what could be keeping her. The Seattle Center's amusement park had been torn down and removed while I was in exile. Who gets rid of awesome rides and instead offers a museum of glass sculptures? I just didn't understand this world I'd returned to, sometimes.

I leaned forward, looking past Dawn to Sammy and Fatima. Sammy typed something into her smartphone, her default state when not actually interacting with the world around here. Her red jeans, green Converse, and black sleeveless T-shirt with silver wings on the back made Sammy look more the rock star than Dawn, who just wore her simple gray T-shirt and brown pants. Fatima sat cross-legged, her green and gold dress spilling over the concrete ledge, and her black curtain of hair falling forward to shade her eyes as she sketched with rapid strokes in her ever-present sketch pad.

"Sis, any word from Mattie yet?" I asked.

Sammy didn't look up from her phone. "Yes, she texted me that she's eloping with a fire juggler and I totally forgot to mention it."

"So, no then?"

"Can't fool you, can I?" Sammy said without slowing her typing. "Chillax, brother o' mine. She's a teenager at a music fest. She's just off somewhere having fun."

Dawn squeezed my hand. "It'll be okay. You both needed to get out of that house. It's September and you look pale as an Irishman's arse in winter."

"I've been busy," I said.

"Uh-huh. You've been sitting around your room playing video games," she replied. "If I'd known you were going to go full-on basement dweller over that Genesis, I would never have bought it for you."

*Hear hear,* Alynon said.

*Sit and spin, Alf,* I thought back. "I have a lot to catch up on," I replied. "You want me to be able to talk with your friends without sounding like an idiot, right?"

I had twenty-five years of games, movies, music, and life to experience, everything that had been created or happened since my exile to the Other Realm in 1986. With Dawn's help, I was immersing myself in one year each month, so that I could really absorb it all and build up my knowledge and experience in a natural progression. This month I'd reached 1992, and was loving the music. But the past few months had blown my mind, not to mention my free time and a good deal of my regular sleeping hours, over the video games.

I mean, the RPGs alone! *Curse of the Azure Bonds, Bard's Tale, Ultima, Wasteland*—it was like I'd woken into a fantasy world myself.

But then throw in games like *Monkey Island, King's Quest, Sonic the Hedgehog, Flashback, Mortal Kombat, Dune, Super Mario Kart, Super Star Wars,* and—well, I needed three of me just to play them all as much as I wanted. And there remained nearly twenty more years of games for me to catch up on.

"Besides," I added, "I'm technically working, if you count it as research toward me learning to design my own games again."

Fatima looked over. "I thought you were running a dating service for magicals."

"I am," I said. "But it hasn't exactly been bringing in the dollars." Since helping Sal the sasquatch to find his perfect soul mate, customers had finally begun to trickle in for the magical matchmaking service I'd started. Unfortunately, most were not wealthy enough to pay much, and usually they preferred barter anyway. And despite Mort's promptings and my best intention, I never felt able to turn someone away who came searching for love. "Besides, gaming has always been my true love."

"Gee, thanks," Dawn said. "Does this mean I should dress up like a video game hottie to grab your heart?"

"You say that like you don't love the idea," I replied.

"Damn. You know me too well." Dawn grinned, and gave me a kiss. "You know I support your dreams, baby, but I just don't want you to be disappointed."

I leaned in close and said for her ears only, "I've seen you in several costumes, and haven't been disappointed yet."

"Damn straight," she said. "Though I still can't believe you look better in that Catwoman outfit than me."

I blushed, and glanced to make sure Sammy hadn't heard, but she gave no sign as she continued tapping at her phone. "Ha, ha," I said, just in case.

"Seriously though," Dawn continued, "about making video

games. I'm not sure it works the way you think anymore. They've become like big-budget movies these days, all corporate product and profit, right Sammy?"

"Not necessarily true," Sammy said without looking up from her phone, clearly able to hear us. Great. "You could probably code a mobile game by yourself. In fact, retro gaming's in right now, so you might even do well."

I blinked. Had Sammy just said something encouraging rather than sarcastic? That was only slightly less rare than Alynon being helpful. It must be Fatima's influence. That, and the number of bands that Dawn had helped Sammy meet in person this weekend.

"Well then," Dawn said, and gave me another squeeze, "we should look into some programming classes."

I didn't mention that I'd already looked into classes and been confused by all the different types of programming options—long gone were the simple days of BASIC. Dawn liked to take charge and lead the way anyway, and I'd found it easiest just to let her.

Of course, her general distrust of the Internet meant she preferred to do things by talking to real people, so we'd probably be spending a few days visiting local colleges rather than a few hours using the magic of the Google. But Dawn had her own kind of magic. Somehow she would make an adventure of it, and probably make friends with the admissions folks, and next thing I knew I'd be enrolled in an already full class for free through some kind of archaic loophole. For the same reason I'd learned not to get in her way once she had a goal in mind, I'd also learned not to question the power of Dawn, but just to sit back and appreciate it.

So all I said was, "That would be great."

The sound of a band doing a sound check echoed from the mural amphitheater stage across the way.

"Ooo, I think Starfucker's coming on," Dawn said.

I wasn't sure if that was a good thing or not. I didn't recognize most of the bands playing this music and arts fest. In fact, none of the artists I'd grown to enjoy over the past couple of months were performing. Nirvana. Boyz II Men. Sleater-Kinney. Blur.

MC Hammer. Milli Vanilli. But I'd enjoyed some of the bands that did play.

"If Mattie doesn't show up soon," I said, "maybe we should skip taking her backstage to meet the Presidents tonight." Not the actual presidents of the United States, of course, but a band.

"Nice try," Dawn said. "I know you're not excited about PotUS, but that's just 'cause you haven't heard them yet. Besides, Mattie is going to Hall and Oates with you Monday, the least you can do is see the Presidents with her."

Damn. "You know how to cut right to my heart," I said. "Like a real man-eater."

"Man-eater, huh?" Dawn said, the corner of her mouth dimpling up. "I can go for that."

A shout went up from a group of hackeysackers on the grass in front of the mural stage, and a cloud of marijuana smoke drifted over us from a passing knot of teenagers, drawing my attention back to the flows of energy.

"I just want to know she's okay, is all," I said, tearing my eyes off of the crowd and their spiritual pull again. "There's all kinds of negative energy here."

"Mattie's danger is yet to come," Fatima said as she sketched, and with the noise of the crowd and sound checks it took a second after hearing the words for their meaning to register.

"What?" I stood up, and strode quickly to Fatima. "Mattie's danger?" I looked down at her drawing. It appeared to be Dawn dancing in front of Stonehenge.

Fatima looked up at me and blinked, her eyes taking a second to focus on mine. "What?"

"You said her danger is yet to come. Did you see something happening to Mattie?" Fatima was an arcana like me and Sammy, a human magic user; but where our family gift was necromancy, hers was sorcery, and more specifically the gift of prophecy. Though if you asked me, her true gift was in making Sammy smile, a miraculous power whose strength must truly rival the gods' to break through the shield of my sister's determined cynicism.

Fatima frowned, and looked back down at her sketch pad. "I—maybe?" She lifted the page, and flipped through a series of images. I caught what looked like Donkey Kong, and Dawn playing her guitar with an expression of fury, and Mattie reaching out through a narrow window in stone, a terrified look on her face. "I don't think her danger is immediate. Though everything feels . . . unclear, distant for some reason, like the near future is encased in amber." She shook her head.

Dawn moved to stand beside me. "Something wrong?"

"I don't know," I said.

Sammy put a hand on Fatima's arm. "You okay, Fates?"

A smile quirked up the corner of Fatima's mouth. "I'm fine. Probably just tired. Two hours sleep does not a bright Fatima make."

Sammy gave Fatima a light poke in the side. "And whose fault is that?"

"Yours," Fatima replied, and finger-combed her hair back. "You know what red wine does to me."

"Uh," I said, "About Mattie—?"

Sammy sighed. "I told you, I'm sure she's fine."

"She's not fine," I said. "She may hide it well, but she's definitely hurting."

In fact, we'd come to Bumbershoot today largely for Mattie's sake. It had been a rough few months for all of us, but she was barely sixteen years old. Beyond the normal teenage challenges and changes, she'd been taken hostage by her undead grandfather, found out her mother was possessed during her conception in order to grant her the Talker gift, and then her father had almost died to keep bumping spiritual uglies with the ghost who did the possessing. Add on top of that several major shake-ups in the family, with my return, and Pete largely disappearing into his new life as a waerwolf, and her teacher and family friend Heather betraying us then becoming a waerbear—man, we were one crazy, messed-up family.

So when Dawn got the chance at some cheap festival passes through her new record label, it was decided to bring Mattie out for some normal, healthy family time at an event she might actually enjoy.

"Thanks, Captain Obvious," Sammy said. "But here's a news flash—our family has always been messed up, and we each got through it. Mattie's not a fragile egg, she's a smart young woman who's twice as together as you were at her age."

"I'm just worried—" I trailed off.

"What?" Sammy asked. "That she's going to go up in the Space Needle with a sniper rifle just because she's having a rough patch? Trust me, if you meet a teenager who never has an emotional crisis, that's when you should be worried, 'cause they're an alien or robot or something and your butt is toast."

*Indeed,* Alynon chimed in. *I would be more concerned about the enemies your family has made than what harm your niece may bring upon herself.*

*Great, thanks,* I thought. Like I needed to be reminded of that right now. "Don't forget we saw Barry here," I said.

Dawn rolled her eyes. "Barry's harmless."

Easy for her to say. Barry did nothing but flirt with her. But Barry, mister life of the party with his easy charm and perfect smile, also happened to be a waerdog pledged to the Forest of Shadows, the darkest of the Fey Demesnes. I still couldn't believe he was running around free after the battle at Elwha, but technically he hadn't participated in the battle, he'd only been there as a duly appointed representative in an official duel. And now, he was playing in a drum circle on yon grassy hill with a bunch of hippy-looking kids I suspected were a pack of his fellow waerfolk.

"Hey guys," Mattie called, appearing out of the stream of people. She wore one of Sammy's old Bikini Kill T-shirts, and had dyed her hair bright green with blue ends.

"Where were you?" I snapped, my nerves still on edge from all the spiritual temptation. "We were supposed to meet here a half hour ago."

"Sorry, Uncle Finn. I was on my way and got distracted by a breakdancing troupe. You would have loved them."

"You freaked me out," I said, but my irritation quickly faded at the sad look on her face. I sighed. "I'm glad you had fun. Just, text us or something. We were worried."

"I know," Mattie said. "Sorry. I lost track of time."

"Dawn!" another voice called, and a woman marched toward us from the direction of the mural stage, waving. A silver persona ring flashed on her hand, the ID ring of an arcana.

"Kaitlin!" Dawn waved back. Kaitlin cut across the crowd to join us. She stood a head taller than Dawn, with bleach-blonde hair and wearing all white.

Kaitlin and her partner, Wesley, formed the band BOAT, and had known Dawn for several years.

They were also arcana, a fact Dawn had been unaware of until recently. But for that reason I actually looked forward to talking to them. Of all the bands I'd met since Dawn signed to Volvur Records, they were the first I might be able to say something intelligent to instead of just feeling like a dork.

Dawn and Kaitlin embraced. A bright blue azurite gem flashed in Kaitlin's persona ID ring, identifying her as a sorceress, an illusionist.

"Grab lunch?" I asked, looking at the Casio calculator watch I'd inherited from Zeke. Sadly, my Pac-Man watch had died a watery death in the Elwha.

Just past noon.

Sammy stood, and lifted her laptop satchel. "I don't know about food, but I'd kill a damn Yeti for some air conditioning right now," she said.

Fatima gave a sad look up at the sun, but didn't protest. We all gathered our things and shuffled inside the food court. As we filed through the door, Mattie moved up beside Dawn and said, "How come *you're* not playing this weekend?"

"I only signed with Volvur a couple months ago," Dawn replied. "It was way too late to book me here."

"You'll play here next year though, for sure," Mattie said.

"We'll see," Dawn replied, but her tone was practically giddy. "They're planning to send me on tour, for sure."

Kaitlin looked over her shoulder at Dawn. "We should totally talk about doing some shows together. I think our messages mix really well."

"Shit yeah!" Dawn replied.

I wasn't sure how excited I was at the thought of Dawn getting mixed up in BOAT's brand of messaging.

BOAT had been approved by the Arcana Ruling Council to help popularize and spread disinformation about magic by creating a cultish sort of "philosophy" and mythos to go with their band. The truly weird thing was, they seemed entirely earnest about it all, and it was hard for me to tell where the line existed between them doing this as some kind of giant promotional art project, and them actually believing what they were saying, whereas Dawn's lyrics all came right from her heart. Still, sincere or not, BOAT's messages seemed positive.

It seemed the ARC had finally learned its lesson about leaving the creativity to the artists, at least. Past attempts at disinformation and creating excuses for plausible deniability had not gone over so well, and even the ones that had been somewhat successful— LSD, Orson Welles's *War of the Worlds* broadcast, Gwar—had caused some problems of their own.

A wave of cool air and food smells washed over us as we entered the Armory, Seattle Center's food court. The space looked like a gentrified warehouse, all pleasant greens and blues and grays with a high roof held up by pillars spaced widely throughout. Along the outer walls ran a series of restaurants, and there were food stands spaced throughout as well. Scaffolding for lights and speakers dangled from wires above, with a stage opposite the entrance that often held some kind of cultural performance. And in the center of the floor you could look down into a section of the Children's Museum that filled the level below, a section made to look like a mountain and bit of Pacific Northwest forest complete with running waterfall.

The spaces between were packed with people at small plastic tables.

Sammy scored seats in a table far back in one corner by an emergency exit, as isolated as we could hope to get in the crowded space, and the rest dispersed to get the food of our choice.

As I stood waiting for my order at the MOD Pizza counter, a laugh cut through the noise of the crowd, a snorting staccato beat that I would have recognized anywhere. I looked over to see Dawn laughing at something Kaitlin said a couple of counters down, and then smiling in my direction.

Damn I loved her. Granted, I didn't have the years of experience that I should have at love, but then I supposed there were plenty of people my age who hadn't had more than one true love in their life. My brother Pete and his fiancée, Vee, were getting married in a few days, and more than once as I'd listened to them talk about the traditions of a brightblood bonding ceremony, I had thought of Dawn, and—

"Whip cream?" the young lady behind the counter asked.

"What? Oh, uh, yeah! Of course."

I collected my food and shake, and turned around to find an unfamiliar older man watching me intently, with a brute of a figure lurking beside him who looked like Dolph Lundgren with a buzz cut and neck tattoo.

"Hello, Phinaeus," the older man said. "I have some rather urgent business to discuss with you."

The faint purple birthmark like an upside-down heart on his right cheek sparked recognition.

"Justin?" Justinius Gramaraye was a second cousin. I could see the Gramaraye nose now above Justin's weak chin and too-thin lips. It was definitely him. When I last saw him and his twin brother, Jared, they were barely twelve years old, a full two years younger than me at the time. But the man staring at me appeared at least sixty-five years old. And not a distinguished Sean Connery sixty-five, or a charming Beatles "will you still love me" sixty-five, but more like someone who'd spent those years earning money as a subject of medical experiments, and then blown every dime of that money at the local dive bar.

The rare "gift" of actually Talking to spirits drained the necromancer's life when used, aging the necromancer. My mother had been a Talker, which had contributed to her death. And I was a Talker, but had no desire to use the gift if I could avoid it. If Justin had manifested the gift after I went into exile, that might explain his aging, but not his otherwise sad state. I'd seen vegan albinos with more flesh and color to them. "Jesus, Justin, you okay?"

"Show respect!" Justin snapped.

My skin tightened with goosebumps as I realized my mistake. This wasn't Justin. This was—

"Grandfather."